SILENCED

Allison Brennan

St. Martin's Paperbacks

This is a work of fiction. All of the characters, organizations, and events portrayed in this novel are either products of the author's imagination or are used fictitiously.

Published in the United States by St. Martin's Paperbacks, an imprint of St. Martin's Publishing Group.

SILENCED

For information, address St. Martin's Publishing Group, 120 Broadway, New York, NY 10271.

www.stmartins.com

ISBN: 978-1-250-88997-3

Our books may be purchased in bulk for promotional, educational, or business use. Please contact your local bookseller or the Macmillan Corporate and Premium Sales Department at 1-800-221-7945, ext. 5442, or by email at MacmillanSpecialMarkets@macmillan.com.

Printed in the United States of America

St. Martin's Paperbacks edition / May 2012

10 9 8 7 6 5

Stories are created in the author's head, but many people help with the details. A very special thanks to Tossable Digits, for help in understanding virtual phone numbers; Crime Scene Writers, an amazing group of generous law enforcement professionals who always help me get things right; DC Metro's PIO who was kind enough to answer some bizarre questions; Steve Dupre with the FBI who has always answered even my most mundane questions; Brian Jones, FBI-SWAT leader who invites me to role play—I have never had so much fun! And the exercises really help with scene staging. Fellow author Dr. D. P. Lyle always helps me get the medical details right. And this time around, my husband Dan with his background working for the state and federal legislature was instrumental in helping me with the campaign and legislative details. Thank you all!

Friends and family keep me sane, especially fellow writer and conference roommate Toni McGee Causey, the gang at Murder She Writes, my mom Claudia, and of course, my kids who keep me on my toes. I also want to send a shout-out to the American Cancer Society and their patron, Cathy Hummel, who won her name in this book. We've all lost someone to cancer; they do great work. And Sara Edmonds, who also won her name at a readers convention, Readers & Ritas. Thanks, Cathy and Sara!

And of course, extra special thanks to the people behind the book: my agent Dan Conaway, my editor Kelley Ragland, and the entire team at Writers House and St. Martin's Press. Thank you for your support, and your faith.

Life is the sum of all your choices.
—Albert Camus

PROLOGUE

Thirteen Years Ago

Marie's lips moved in constant prayer as she maneuvered the rattling, twenty-year-old truck down the treacherous mountain road. Snowflakes swirled in front of the windshield and headlights, cutting visibility to only feet in front of her.

"Please, Lord, let me reach the highway safely. Please, Lord, silence the truck."

Narrow paths slithered off the main road, each leading to one of her husband's followers—serpents, all, who'd be happy to return her to their devil. One of them might hear her.

"The Lord is the Spirit and where the Spirit of the Lord is, there is freedom." Repeating the verse gave Marie needed strength. Reminded her that the Lord was her Shepherd. He would lead her and her children away from evil, down the path of righteousness, protect them all the days of their lives.

She glanced at the girls sleeping on the narrow bench seat in the back of the cab. Her sweet, beautiful daughters. The Lord blessed her, how could He have blinded her to the truth for so long?

I didn't know he was a monster. Forgive me, Lord, I did not know.

"I love you," she whispered.

"I love you too, Mommy."

Marie stifled a cry. "I thought you were sleeping, sweetheart."

"Why are you crying, Mommy?"

"I'm happy."

"You're praying. I'll pray with you."

"Thank you."

"What are we praying for?"

What could Marie say to an innocent seven-year-old? That her father was a monster? That her father was a beautiful devil, a fallen angel? That he was Lucifer incarnate?

She was nearing the gate that she'd once believed protected her from the outside world. The snow thickened, but she was too close to slow down. The truck slid on an icy patch. Her pulse quickened, but she immediately regained control.

"Sing Mommy a song. A pretty song."

Hannah's sweet voice came from the backseat. *"Jesus loves me, this I know, for the Bible tells me so . . ."*

Please, Lord, let the gate be open.

Marie passed the last road that led to the last house in the fortress. If the gate was open, they would be free.

She pressed the gas pedal. Eager. Impatient. Her heart pounded, Hannah's song faded. Marie's hands began to shake. The truck accelerated faster than she expected; she tried to brake but couldn't lift either foot.

She blinked rapidly, but her vision blurred. The headlights sparkled, twisting her perception. If she didn't slow the truck, she would crash.

She'd stopped taking the pills weeks ago, but she remembered how they felt. They distorted the truth and made her happy.

Except tonight, there was no bliss. Only anxiety. Thickness. Extreme fatigue.

The tires skidded on the slick, newly-fallen snow as the truck sped too fast around the last turn. She used every ounce of control she had to keep the truck on the road and not down the mountainside to certain death.

"Mommy! Mommy!"

"Shh, baby. Pray for me."

Her words slurred. Her head leaned to the side.

Don't let him kill my children! Protect my babies, Lord!

Her headlights illuminated faces in the snow. They lined the road in heavy jackets. Horns grew from their heads, tails from their backs.

"No, no!" She bit her tongue. She didn't want to scare her girls. The hallucination seemed so real, but she knew they were people, not demons. People who worked for the devil.

You can never escape the Pit.

A flash of metal caught her eye. The gate was closed.

Naomi had gone ahead to open the gate, taking her bike down the mountain before the snow had started. Had she been captured? Worse? Had Marie put her oldest daughter in even greater danger?

Then Marie saw her. Standing with the devil himself, united. He'd turned her daughter against her. Twisted everything that was good and made it evil.

Fear washed through Marie as the truth came clear in a flash of lucidity.

The devil had won.

My God, why have you abandoned me?

"Hannah, listen to me!"

"What's wrong, Mommy?"

"Don't believe anything they say about me. I love you, I will watch over you from Heaven. Protect Sara. You're all she has left."

"Mommy, the gate!"

With the last of her strength, Marie slid her foot from the accelerator to the brake. The truck skidded forward, sliding on the snow, and crashed into the gate.

Hannah's screams came from far, far away.

The baby cried.

Marie's head hit the windshield. She felt nothing except a heavy thud and warmth. Whatever the devil had drugged her with took away the pain.

Or maybe she was already gone, to a place beyond pain.

Where the Spirit of the Lord is, there is freedom.

CHAPTER ONE

Monday

The whore traitor lived in a secure building with live cameras and nosy neighbors. Brian had to wait for her to leave.

Waiting made him antsy. He just wanted to get this job over and done. He didn't hate the whore. In fact, he had no feelings about her at all. But she'd crossed the line from useful to problem, and problems must be solved.

Two hours of waiting—sitting on the park bench in the heat, pretending to read a book—while watching the main entrance of the condo. He'd watched her often enough in the last three weeks to know her habits. How she left every morning before ten to run in the park. How she took the Metro to visit her johns in whatever five-star hotel she'd chosen for the night. How she'd lied about what she knew and when she knew it.

Washington, DC, sex scandals were a dime a dozen: affairs with interns, sexy mistresses, even a few cougar congresswomen with stables of young studs to service them on the side. But selling sex was still taboo and could take down an elected official as fast as twittering birds would tweet.

She'd lied to protect her ass, but now she couldn't be trusted. All she had to do was keep her fucking mouth shut while they figured out who had leaked her relationship with Crowley to the press. If the truth came out, everyone would be on the hot seat. But now she was talking to the wrong people and her lies were coming full circle.

The whys didn't much interest Brian. He was a man of action and opportunity, not a man who pondered motive or psychology.

Brian stood and stretched. It was appropriate behavior, considering he was wearing running shorts and a T-shirt. The cathedral bells chimed in the distance. Soon it would be too hot for her morning run. Unexpected changes in routine were never good.

He bent over and touched his shins, stretching his hamstrings. Sweat stained his underarms. He disliked the smell of body odor, even his own. At this point, all he wanted was to kill the bitch and take a shower.

As the final bell rang the tenth hour, he stood and saw Wendy at the corner, jogging in place, waiting for the light to change. Well, shit, he'd almost missed her, even in her bright pink shorts and white T-shirt with one of those pink ribbons on the back. But her attire would make her easy to spot from a distance.

He called his brother. "I see her. You're clear."

"Don't fuck up."

"Right back at you." Brian disconnected, irritated that Ned thought he'd screw up. Ned was the crazy one, not

Brian. Ned had a record, not Brian. But just because Ned had a college degree and pretty face, everyone thought he was smarter.

The light changed and Wendy jogged across the street, into the park, and up the path that she always ran.

Good. Routine is good.

Brian kept his distance. Because it was a weekday and edging toward ninety degrees, the trails weren't crowded. There were a few people running or walking, and the rushing businessmen with those idiotic earpieces, talking as if no one else could hear them.

He'd followed her several times over the last year, important when in business with someone who lied for a living, and so far she'd run the same five-mile route nearly every day. He cut through a narrow patch of trees and trekked up a short, steep embankment so he could cut her off.

At the top, he looked at his watch. It would take her another three to four minutes to reach this spot. Brian stretched and focused on catching his breath after climbing the slope. Just another runner trying to beat the heat. He tilted his head in greeting at a male who jogged past him wearing a million-dollar running suit. The guy passed Brian without acknowledgment. *Asshole.*

Brian spotted the bright pink shorts as Wendy turned a corner. She'd be winded by now, over three miles into her run. He waited until she was thirty feet away, then ran in the same direction at a slower pace. Don't make her nervous. Don't make her think he's a threat.

A pulse of adrenaline flooded his system. For him, killing was a means to an end, and he never felt more than an initial fear and thrill. But this pulse, this vibration of danger, excited him.

That excitement made it hard to slow down, but he did, letting Wendy run past. She had one ear bud in, one out, classic style of serious runners. He pulled latex gloves from his pocket. Twenty yards ahead the path curved to the left before starting the descent back to the main park. He glanced behind him. A pair of women approached, fast-walking while they chatted. He had one chance.

As soon as Wendy rounded the curve, Brian sprinted and tackled her like a linebacker. She went down hard, opening her mouth to scream, but he'd knocked the wind out of her. She flailed for something in her pockets. He searched her, found a container of Mace on her key chain, and tossed it away.

She gasped for air, and he punched her in the face. He took no pleasure in hitting the woman, he simply needed her silent.

He jumped up and dragged her into the thick shrubs. He rolled her onto her stomach, held his hand over her mouth, and pinned her with his body until the two women were beyond earshot.

His brother had told him to fuck her, then kill her, so her murder would look random, but the fear of getting caught made his cock shrivel.

The longer this job took, the more likely he'd be seen. He didn't even have the dark of night to hide him.

She fought back, surprisingly strong for a little thing. But he had eight inches and eighty pounds on the bitch. It was almost worth taking his time, to see how long it took her to wear herself out.

But of course he didn't, because there could be any number of people coming up the path.

Brian sat on her ass and wrapped his gloved hands

around her neck. Squeezed. He didn't need to look at her, didn't particularly want to, while she died. Her being on her stomach made his job much easier. She couldn't kick him. She tried to scratch him, but couldn't reach back far enough. Her death didn't take long at all, but he kept his hold on her neck for another minute just to make sure.

He was about to get up when he heard a group of runners, pounding the trail, kicking up dirt. He waited, lying on top of dead Wendy. He'd picked a good spot for the kill—if he couldn't see any passersby, they couldn't see him. His nerves were on edge, the overwhelming fear of exposure making him want to bolt, but he forced himself to wait.

When he was certain the group was gone, he rolled off her body, disgusted by touching the dead thing. He was about to jump back onto the path when his brother's words came back to him.

It can't look like a hit.

Brian removed Wendy's fanny pack. Robbery, right? He looked inside. License, twenty-dollar bill, pen. Hardly worth killing anyone over.

He stared at Wendy's body. No fucking way he could rape it. He didn't even want to be this close to her, not anymore.

But he didn't have to rape her, right? Just make it *look* like rape.

He pulled down her shorts and panties, then spread her legs as far as they'd go. She'd hate being found dead like this. How else could he embarrass her?

He looked around, trying to come up with an idea. Then an idea struck him. He grabbed the pen and wrote on her bare ass, chuckling quietly at his own humor.

Brian was back on the trail less than two minutes later. When he was far enough away, he called his brother. "It's done."

"We have another problem," Ned said. "But I'll take care of it tonight."

Ned hung up, leaving Brian with no idea what problem Ned had uncovered.

CHAPTER TWO

Tuesday

Ivy glanced at her fourteen-year-old sister, sleeping curled onto her side, face to the wall in Ivy's bedroom. Sara's dark blond hair shimmered in the ambient glow from the streetlight creeping in through slatted blinds. Ivy had been too late to save Sara from learning the horrifying truth about their father. Too late to save her sister from the raw, unrelenting humiliation. Too late to save her from the pain.

Waves of guilt-tainted fury washed over Ivy. She bit her hand to keep from crying out. "I'll kill him before he touches you again," she whispered.

Though it was July in DC, the girl slept with the white down comforter bunched over her lanky frame, the corner tucked under her cheek. Ivy had to forget the past, keep it firmly locked behind her, if she was to keep Sara safe. It was so hard! Wasn't it Isaiah who said, "Forget the former things, dwell not on the past?"

Easily said. If she was going to create a new life for them in Canada, she had to put everything in the past. Her crimes. Her regrets. Her vengeance.

Nearly four in the morning, her head was as clear as if she'd slept eight hours instead of two. She didn't bother with the farce of trying to go back to sleep; instead, she slid from under the lone cotton sheet, the air from the ceiling fan a welcome caress on her sweating body.

Ivy couldn't remember ever sleeping peacefully through the night. Maybe as a little girl she had, before she learned that monsters came wrapped in handsome faces coated with sweet words.

But now there was no time for tears, no time for rage. Events out of her control had forced her to speed up her plans since reuniting with Sara last week. Seven years ago, when she was just fourteen, Ivy had buried her tracks—changed her name from Hannah Edmonds to Ivy Harris, worked in a cash business, and had the added benefit that her father had been so angry at her betrayal that he'd told everyone she was dead.

Being dead had its advantages.

The digital clock blinked and the numbers changed, from 3:59 to 4:00. She'd spend the hours before sunrise reviewing the plans for the final exchange. The ten thousand dollars she'd been promised for this recording would give them the resources to make it into Canada. She already had perfect false identities for her and Sara. The others were on their own.

Ivy's heart twisted with guilt. She'd been responsible for this house, for those who lived here, for so long. Could she really vanish with her sister, leaving the others to fend for themselves? They were the Lost Girls, those society didn't want to admit they'd failed. Ivy wasn't much older, but she'd been on her own for much longer.

Mina had no street smarts; Nicole would burn through her money, then fall back to hooking on the streets; no one would protect Maddie from succumbing to her pill addiction. The only thing that had stopped Maddie from killing herself—with pills or her razor blade— had been Ivy's constant pressure and support.

Kerry would always take care of her sister Bryn, but Ivy would miss her most of all. Kerry had been her rock for the last three years. Without her, Ivy wouldn't have survived. She hoped once everything settled down, Kerry would find her in Canada.

Twenty-four hours and she'd have the blackmailers on tape, and as soon as physically possible, that tape would be turned over to a man named Sergio. She honestly didn't know if Sergio was his real name, if he was an undercover cop or a criminal, but so far he hadn't hurt any of them, he acted like he cared, and he'd already helped her rescue Sara.

Twenty-four hours. Then we'll be free.

Ivy treaded silently down the hall, along the edge, avoiding the creaks in the old floorboards. The faint baseboard lights glowed enough for her to navigate to the staircase.

She stopped at the top of the landing. Something felt different.

She heard a faint snore coming from Maddie's room, closest to the top of the stairs. The ceiling fans rotated full-force in all the bedrooms, since this seventy-year-old house had never been remodeled with air conditioning. But it wasn't something Ivy heard that had her heart racing. It was a scent. Familiar, but unexpected.

Antiseptic? A cleanser? More like a hospital than cleaning day.

Alcohol.

Questions ran through her mind. Was she being paranoid? She tiptoed silently back down the hall and opened Kerry's door. Her friend awoke immediately.

"Ivy?"

"Shh, something's wrong. I think we should get out. But be quiet." Ivy didn't have to explain that there could be a threat, and Kerry didn't ask questions. "I'm checking downstairs."

Ivy ran lightly down the stairs, the pungent antiseptic smell growing stronger.

At the base of the stairs, she turned to check the alarm.

A green light blinked at her. It was off. She glanced at the front door—it was locked—but the alarm was off.

Ivy set the alarm herself every night. She'd never forgotten. *Never.*

She listened for any sounds that didn't belong—heavy steps, heavy breathing—but there was nothing.

She tiptoed quickly down the hall to the office, took the gun from her top desk drawer, and went to search the rest of the house. Six pairs of feet pounded on the ceiling and she winced. If someone was inside, now he knew they were all awake.

The front of the house was clear, but when she passed the basement door on her way to the kitchen, she stopped. She still smelled alcohol, but now she smelled smoke as well. She put her hand to the wooden door, then pulled it immediately away. Hot. Was the furnace on fire? They hadn't used it in months. The water heater?

Smoke pushed out of the cracks in the door and the floor vents had begun to belch the same black tendrils.

For one brief moment she wondered if maybe she had forgotten the alarm after all, and maybe the fire wasn't an attack, but an accident. She still needed to get everyone out, call the gas company or fire department.

Her natural suspicion prompted her to look out the window before opening the back door. On the other side of the fence that separated their yard from their elderly neighbor's, she saw a flicker of light. Just a brief flare, like a match igniting, then going out.

She blinked. Then saw it again. Flare, then gone. Had she imagined a figure in the blackness? The streetlights didn't shine into the backyard. She wanted to believe she'd seen nothing but an innocent light in the shadows.

But she knew better.

Alcohol burned.

Ivy coughed as the smoke thickened. The fire crackled in the basement, reminding Ivy that this old house would burn fast. By the time she reached the staircase, Kerry and the girls were coming down.

"Someone's in the backyard," Ivy told her. "Get everyone out the front, I'll be right there." She handed Kerry the gun and went back to her den.

Kerry ordered the girls out the front, then grabbed Ivy's arm and pulled her back.

"Ivy, you don't have time."

Ivy jerked her arm free. "I need my stuff!"

"You'll be no good to Sara if you're dead!"

But freedom was locked in the bottom of her desk. Identities and passports and money. A sudden, deep tremble under their feet told Ivy to bolt, but she closed her eyes, wishing it all away like she'd done when she was thirteen.

"Ivy!" Kerry shook her again, but before she could make a decision, a small explosion almost knocked them down.

She patted her pockets, but realized she was wearing shorts and her keys were upstairs. The key to her desk. She had no choice. She glanced behind her one last time.

She had to let it go.

"Hannah?" Sara grabbed her arm when Ivy and Kerry came out. Ivy cringed, hearing her real name. "Is it Daddy?"

Any evil was possible with Reverend Kirk Edmonds.

"I don't know," she said. "Out!"

Ivy and Kerry pushed the others from the porch into the yard. Kerry had the gun, watchful. They knew a stranger was in the back, but that didn't mean there wasn't someone else lurking in the front yard. Or that he wouldn't easily hop the fence.

Sara grabbed Ivy's hand as they ran across the yard. They'd hide out in half-deaf Mrs. Neel's detached garage while figuring out what to do. Maybe she'd call the social worker who had been practically begging to help them. Ivy hated asking for help, but right now she had nothing. Her plans, her resources, were gone.

A small explosion followed by a pulse of hot air pushed them the final feet across the narrow street. A second, louder explosion forced them to their knees on Mrs. Neel's lawn. Ivy covered her head, expecting fire or debris to rain down, but all she felt was heat searing her skin.

Sara screamed, grabbed Ivy so hard it shocked Ivy back into action.

She got up, unsteady on her feet, and took one last look at her home. The dark gray smoke couldn't hide the flames that licked at the windows.

All hope burned inside.

Ivy looked up and down the street. Lights were on, neighbors were coming out of their houses. The police, the fire department, strangers would be here soon.

Ivy motioned for them to go down Mrs. Neel's driveway, which would shield them from view. In the distance, sirens cut through the sound of ruin.

Ivy couldn't talk to the police. She'd lied to everyone in the neighborhood. She wasn't a college student. She didn't exist. She had a fake ID, not a real false identity. But worse, if her father had reported Sara as missing, her photo and prints would be in a database. She had to protect Sara.

"We have to split up," Ivy said. "Lay low until we find out who did this."

"It wasn't an accident?" Sara's face was filthy from soot and dirt, but her big blue eyes were so trusting, so innocent. Even after all she'd been through at the hands of that bastard, she was still innocent.

"No," Ivy said. "It was no accident."

Bryn silently cried. Nicole was enraged. "Everything's gone!" She held up her backpack. "Two hundred dollars and a handful of clothes, that's all I have?"

"You're alive," Kerry snapped.

"Jocelyn promised she'd help us," Ivy said. She hoped she wasn't wrong about the social worker. But she didn't trust Sergio, and though she didn't *think* he'd done this, how could she be sure? Why would the people she worked for try to kill her?

A chill ran down her back. Was one of these girls,

her friends, a Judas? She looked at their faces, one by one. Pain. Fear. Confusion.

She trusted all these girls with her life.

But did she trust them with Sara's life?

The sirens were closer, prompting Ivy to act.

"Sara, Maddie, come with me. Mina, go with Nicole."

"I want to come with you," the sixteen-year-old said, wiping away her tears, but more came tumbling down. "Please."

Ivy bit her lip. How could she manage both of them in addition to Sara? "I'll come get you as soon as we're settled. All of you."

The seven of them together would draw far too much attention.

Mina nodded, but her eyes rested on Sara. Ivy stomped on her own guilt. Mina had been like a sister to her, they all had, and yet she'd been replaced by Ivy's real sister. Ivy wished things could be different, but she'd broken untold laws rescuing Sara, and she couldn't risk unwanted attention their large group would bring.

The increasing sirens, flashing lights, shouts of neighbors from the street, added to the cacophony of panic that rose in Ivy's chest.

"It won't be long," she promised. "Forty-eight hours."

Mina didn't look at her. She took Nicole's hand.

Kerry handed Ivy her backpack and the gun. "I put some clothes and shoes in for you, and your purse."

Ivy realized everyone had had time to get dressed but her. "Thank you." She quickly put on her tennis shoes and a T-shirt over her tank top.

"Go," Ivy told them. "Be careful. Trust no one. Keep your phones charged. I'll call when I figure this out."

They left, avoiding streetlights and neighbors who

now watched with curiosity and horror as the house on Hawthorne Street burned.

Ivy glanced over her shoulder as the first fire truck rounded the corner. The red lights swirled and the siren died down as the truck *whooshed* to a stop.

Ivy not only had to keep Sara safe and hidden from their father, she had to keep her alive.

I'll never let anyone hurt you, Sara. Never again.

CHAPTER THREE

The trail closest to where the female victim had been found was blocked off with crime scene tape and guarded by DC Metro cops. The FBI rarely attended homicides, but when the victim was the mistress of a sitting congressman whose affair was recently exposed in the press, the FBI took interest.

Lucy Kincaid had spent the last two months working primarily as an analyst in the FBI office tracking online sex predators, so when her training agent, Noah Armstrong, asked her to join him in the field, she was both excited and nervous.

"Slater is heading up the squad on this one," Noah told her as he showed his identification to the cop who blocked the trail. "I'm point."

Supervisory Special Agent Matt Slater was Noah's immediate supervisor and directed the Evidence Response Teams out of the DC Regional Office. He'd made it clear to Lucy from her first day in the office that she wasn't a field agent *yet*.

"Are you sure this is okay with him?" Lucy kept up with Noah's long strides as they walked up the gently sloping trail through the middle of Rock Creek Park. She'd run in the park many times, though never on this particular trail, which was close to the condos and apartments on Massachusetts. The park could be dangerous, but most runners kept to well-traveled trails, ran in pairs or groups, and didn't get caught in the park after sunset. There were more patrols now and a steady police presence, but no law enforcement agency could cover all two thousand acres of the park all the time.

Noah stopped walking, glanced around to make sure no one was within earshot, and kept his voice low. "We're operating with reduced staff and resources, and everyone is antsy because of the victim's connection to Congress. Slater told me to bring in an analyst."

"You didn't tell him it was me." She hated the insecurity of her position. She was in limbo, neither an agent nor a civilian. Three weeks and it would be a moot point, but she didn't want to do anything that might jeopardize her admission into the FBI Academy.

"It's my call, you're qualified, plus ERT certified." He started back up the trail. "I'll handle Slater, but this isn't going to be a problem."

Lucy followed Noah, hoping he was right. She didn't know why SSA Slater made her nervous.

Trust your instincts, Luce.

She heard her boyfriend Sean's voice in her head, reminding her that her instincts were usually good, at least when it came to murder.

What that said about her, she wasn't certain, but she hoped it would help bring justice for Wendy James.

Three weeks ago, in a big front-page article, Congressman Alan Crowley had been exposed as having an affair with the much younger, beautiful Wendy James, secretary for a powerful DC lobbying firm. In typical politician fashion, Crowley had denied the affair, then claimed it was private, between him and his wife of twenty-eight years, then said he was sorry and asked for forgiveness.

Some people were calling for Crowley's head, others complaining what he did was no worse than any other politician, and still others were using the events to highlight that the media preferred sex scandals over serious policy.

In fact, Ms. James's murder wouldn't have caught the FBI's attention except for two key facts. Because of Ms. James's position with a lobbyist, she'd been interviewed by the FBI for possible influence peddling—specifically, had Congressman Crowley asked for, or suggested, contributions to him or any other campaigns? During that interview last week, Ms. James had contradicted herself and put a lawyer on retainer. The FBI had secured an appointment for a second interview this week, and now she's dead.

Was this truly a random act of violence, or was she a specific target because of her involvement with Crowley, the FBI, or both?

"Does the press know yet?" Lucy asked Noah quietly when they reached the crime scene.

"Not from us."

Matt Slater, who, like Noah, had been in the military before joining the FBI, was talking to the DC deputy coroner. He beckoned Noah. "Miles West, DC coroner's office," Slater said, in introduction. "He's ready to move the body as soon as the gurney's here."

Lucy had been an assistant pathologist at the morgue as part of a yearlong internship program, and Miles had been one of her favorite people. He was two years shy of retirement and had talked often about moving to Nashville to be close to his daughter and grandchildren.

Miles smiled at her, his teeth vividly white against dark skin. "If it ain't Ms. Lucy. Out of the Academy already?"

"I start—"

Slater cut her off. "It's not going to get any cooler. Let's take a look at the body before it's hauled to the morgue."

Lucy let Noah and Slater walk in front of her. Miles jerked his head toward the men and whispered, "You want to be one of them?"

She didn't answer. "The report said she was strangled."

"From behind."

"Behind? You're certain?"

He cleared his throat. Of course he was certain—he'd been an investigator longer than Lucy had been alive. "Possible attempted rape, no obvious sign of penetration, but the ME will confirm that when we get her on the table."

"Did he use a ligature?"

"Hands."

"Unusual." Manual strangulation was an intensely personal method of murder. Almost without exception, the killer wanted to watch the victim die. Lucy asked,

"Could he have accidentally strangled her while attempting to rape her?"

"Accidentally?" Miles snorted. "I doubt it, but again, I'll leave it to the ME. I don't think he took his hands off her neck once he started."

"You can tell that after a visual examination?"

"From the back of her neck. You'll see what I saw."

"And smell." The stench of decomposition filled the hot, unmoving air.

He put his hand on her arm. "Heat, humidity is bad enough. But animals got to her too."

Death is never pretty, Lucy thought, but when she saw what had been done to Wendy James, she realized this was particularly ugly.

It wasn't the murder itself—strangulation wasn't messy or bloody—but what had happened to her body after death was gruesome.

The moisture in the air caused the gases in her body to build and swell. Her extremities were bloated and discolored, suggesting she'd been dead for two or three days. But taking in account the summer heat, the high humidity, and the tree-sheltered area, Lucy suspected time of death was closer to twenty-four hours ago.

"Rigor has already broken, but the heat speeds that up along with decomp," Miles said. "She's been here less than thirty hours, more than twenty. We get her on the table, the ME can be more precise."

"Between three A.M. and one P.M. yesterday. I doubt she went running before five in the morning. Maybe she lives in a secure building, and we'll catch her on video." It would be too much to ask that the killer was on tape, too, but all security videos from her residence and the surrounding areas would be scrutinized.

The victim was lying on her side, moved from where she'd died—evidenced by impressions in the mulch and five feet of wide drag marks. Noah and Slater were standing beside the body, talking quietly.

She said to Miles, "The animals moved her?"

"Wild dogs. Their barking is what alerted the joggers who found the body. They scared away the dogs with noise and pepper spray."

Wendy James had been murdered and discarded without care. Lucy replaced her discomfort with anger, and her stomach settled.

"The blood—"

"Postmortem. There's bruising on her hips and thighs, but on the *outside*."

"That doesn't sound like rape."

"It looks more like he straddled her fully clothed while he strangled her." Miles shook his head. "Sometimes, this job isn't worth it."

Lucy squeezed his hand. "We'll catch him."

Miles's phone rang and he walked off to answer. Lucy slipped on latex gloves and stepped over to the body. The wild dogs had done extensive damage to the victim's left arm and leg, but her right side was virtually unmarked. She squatted down to look at the bruising on the outside of the hips and thighs, which was consistent with the deputy coroner's theory. She gently moved the blond hair away from the back of the neck. Two distinct oval bruises were visible on either side of the spine— thumb imprints. While the front of the neck was also purple, the thumbs were most distinct, indicating that once the killer took hold of the victim, he squeezed until she died.

From behind. Not looking at her face.

"What?" Slater asked. Lucy hadn't realized he'd been scrutinizing her so closely.

Lucy rose and took off the gloves. "I don't know, just thinking."

Noah raised an eyebrow, but didn't say anything.

Slater said, "West said possible attempted rape. The killer could have been unable to perform, or heard someone coming and bolted. Except—" He gestured toward the victim's buttocks. "He took the time to write that."

Lucy tilted her head. She hadn't seen the marks at first, but once Slater pointed it out, it was obvious. The bloating of the body caused the ink to spread and fade, but she could make out the words.

And this guilty whore don't cry no more

"He had no intention of raping her." Lucy didn't intend to speak out loud.

"Didn't want to or failed?" Slater asked.

"Didn't want to," she said. "Miles pointed out the bruising on the outside of her thighs, not the inside. But more important, the way she was facedown while he killed her. In manual strangulation cases the killer wants to watch his victims die. It's crucial. Part of the fantasy, his control over life and death. In the majority of cases where there is a serial murderer, the killer will release pressure, let the victim breathe for a few seconds, then start asphyxiating her again. The control makes them feel like a god."

"This," she continued, pointing specifically at the thumb marks on the back of the neck, "shows he planned to kill her, had no need to watch her die. He didn't torture her, he simply squeezed until she was dead. Of course," she added quickly, "the autopsy will provide a more definitive answer."

Slater nodded. "I thought it was unusual that she was killed facedown, but that could also indicate remorse or depersonalization. He may not have been able to go through with it if he saw her eyes."

"Have you ever seen a murder like this?" Noah asked both of them.

Both Slater and Lucy shook their heads. "The message indicates he knew who she was," Slater said. "But whether from the recent press attention, or personally, I don't know."

"A stalker? Or maybe a boyfriend—past or present?" Noah asked. "Angry that she had an affair."

Lucy didn't think this was the work of a boyfriend. The evidence indicated control, not rage.

Before she could speak, Slater said what she was thinking. "If it was a jilted lover, there'd be more anger evidenced on her body. Possible neighbor or acquaintance? Someone who knew her routine. Followed her."

"We're lucky someone found her body," Lucy said. "Chandra Levy died not far from here and it was a year before anyone discovered her remains." Though Lucy had been a teenager at the time, she'd never forgotten the tragic case of the young intern who, like Wendy James, had an affair with a congressman and ended up dead. But unlike Levy's murder, which was not connected to her personal life and the affair not discovered until after her death, Wendy James's affair had been front and center for the last three weeks, making the sex scandal a possible motive.

"Shit," Slater exclaimed, reading a message on his phone. "Damn press. Someone just tweeted the identity of our victim." His phone rang. Slater ignored it. "Noah, head over to her apartment, I already have a warrant in process. By the time you get there, you'll have it. Take whomever you need to canvass the building, talk to neighbors, find out the last person to see her, if there's anything of interest in her place. Do it fast. Josh Stein is already on his way."

Stein was with White Collar Crimes and had been lead on the Wendy James influence-peddling investigation. "Homicide trumps White Collar," Noah said.

"Doesn't matter, he was working with Wendy James and he's taking lead. He knows shit about violent crimes, spends most of his time crunching numbers and searching records. Damn good at it, too. But he's also a ladder-climber, and if he thinks a juicy case like this will get him up a rung or three, he's not going to want turn it over to us."

"I'll see what I can do," Noah said.

"Good luck. With the attorneys involved and Congress, it's going to be a PR nightmare for everyone involved." Then Slater grinned. "I don't think Crowley's PR machine is going to withstand this scandal, a definite silver lining."

"Taking sides?" Noah asked.

Slater shrugged. "Haven't met a politician I liked. Besides, he lied about the affair before admitting it. Not very trustworthy in my book."

"Par for the course."

"Hence, I haven't met a politician I liked." Slater glanced at his watch. "As soon as the body is at the morgue, while you're at James's apartment, I'm going to track down Crowley, find out where he was yesterday. Keep me informed."

Lucy looked at the body again and frowned. Her gut instinct told her Crowley hadn't killed her.

But he could have hired someone.

"We should check his financial records as well," Lucy said. "This wasn't a personal attack."

Slater stared at her so long she had to avert her eyes. Her face heated and she realized she'd just told a cop with twenty years more experience how to do his job.

He didn't comment on her observation, which somehow made her slipup worse.

"Get going," he said to Noah. "And remember what I said about Stein."

CHAPTER FOUR

Ivy's feet sank into the thick gold carpet, the luxurious hotel room oddly reminding her of the Shakespeare quote, "what's past is prologue." She didn't want to stay here, in this far-too-familiar opulence. The past was alive, ripe with sick humor, taunting her, reminding her that escape was not possible. That someday she'd be Hannah Edmonds again, standing with her older sister Naomi behind their father, two pairs of eyes glazed from self-medication. The drugs masked the pain and made the lies truth.

Ivy wasn't Hannah any more. She wasn't Naomi, willfully blind to the truth. She wouldn't send Sara back to the pretty mansion to be brainwashed into believing that teenage daughters were born to serve their father's sexual needs, that this was *normal* and *godlike*. Want proof? Look at the house! Look at the grounds! Would God give such wealth and power to an evil man? Of course not!

"Ivy?"

She heard Jocelyn speak her name, but couldn't respond. She hadn't felt so weak in spirit since the last day with her family. She almost couldn't leave the mountain. She'd almost begged her daddy to forgive her, to let her serve him as good daughters are supposed to do. The fear of the unknown had once terrified her, of what was beyond the fences of their lavish prison, the certainty that there were worse evils than her father. He had never raised his voice, never beat her, never denied her food or a warm bed.

She'd once thought he wore a halo. Now, she knew the fires of Hell burned behind him.

"Hannah?"

Ivy turned to her sister, all anger and pain directed at the young girl. "*Never* call me that name again!"

Tears spilled from Sara's round eyes and Ivy wanted to cry with her. She didn't. Instead, she whispered, "Please."

Sara nodded, but averted her eyes and turned to Maddie, who put her arm around Sara's shoulders and led her to the adjoining room. First she'd turned Mina away, now Sara. She was losing everyone she had promised to protect. She was hurting those she loved the most. What was wrong with her?

She had to get out of this place. "Is there someplace else you can take us?" Ivy asked Jocelyn.

"What's wrong?" The social worker looked around, obviously not understanding why Ivy was upset by the beautiful, well-appointed suite. "It's a little big, but Chris knows the manager and this hotel is discreet. You'll be safe here."

No place was safe.

"It's too expensive."

Jocelyn relaxed. "Don't worry about the cost, we have it covered."

Ivy walked slowly around the large room, mostly to give herself time to calm down. Jocelyn understood the path that had led Ivy into prostitution. She hadn't looked down at Ivy or the others, and though Jocelyn didn't come right out and say it, Ivy suspected she'd once walked a few streets herself. More important, Jocelyn hadn't turned her over to the cops for kidnapping. She believed that Kirk Edmonds had raped his daughters, and wanted Ivy to report him. "To bring him to justice," she'd said more than once.

How could Ivy explain to Jocelyn that no one would believe her? That if their father had five minutes alone with Sara, she'd never say a word against him? When Kirk Edmonds spoke, you wanted to believe every word he said. You wanted to believe that he was right, that he loved you and would protect you. He could make anyone believe he had the keys to the kingdom of heaven, and if you just did what he said, you, too, would be saved.

He could make you feel all that and more, right before he pulled the cornerstone from the foundation and your world crumbled.

Jocelyn sat on the love seat and said, "I have a plan."

Ivy stared out the window, but focused on nothing. Everything she'd been working toward for the last six years—gone. She had nothing left except a scared fourteen-year-old to protect.

"Ivy, please sit down."

Ivy complied, looking the woman in the eye. She already knew Jocelyn couldn't solve their problems. But right now, for the next few days, Ivy needed her. Ivy could lie better than most anyone. The key was never breaking eye contact.

Jocelyn was thirty-five, pretty, with pale, smooth skin making her appear younger. Ivy had no use for do-gooders—they rarely understood the real world—but Jocelyn was different. That she'd helped her when she most needed it heaped another layer of guilt on Ivy's soul.

It's okay, as long as Sara is safe.

"You need to report the fire," Jocelyn said.

"I think they know by now," Ivy snapped.

"I heard on the news that two firefighters were injured. You have information that will help them in their investigation!"

"That I saw a person in the shadows? Couldn't even tell if he was male or female! How tall or fat. He could have been a figment of my overactive imagination."

"You smelled alcohol. You saw an intruder. The fire spread quickly. It *was* arson. Someone tried to kill you, your sister, the other girls—don't you care?"

"Yes!" Ivy didn't want to get mad at Jocelyn, but the last eight hours had put her on edge. "You promised if I ever came to you for help, you wouldn't go to the police."

"No police. I'll talk to the fire chief, he'll—"

"Same thing!" Ivy stood and paced. "They'd have to tell the police, and I can't—" She stopped talking. This conversation was going nowhere. "I shouldn't have come to you."

"I'm glad you did. Okay, no cops, I get it."

"Do you?"

Jocelyn nodded, her expression sincere. Ivy wanted to believe her, but right now she was wound so tight she thought she'd explode. "It's only a matter of time before they find you," Jocelyn said. "You can't hide with Sara forever."

"I can hide as long as it takes to put together two new identities." Except, she had no money. She sank back into the chair and put her head in her hands. "Everything's gone, Jocelyn. My passport. Sara's passport. Money. Everything."

"We'll figure it out. For now, you're safe here."

Ivy couldn't even fake a smile. She walked to the bathroom, closed the door behind her. Locked it. She needed five minutes alone. Five minutes to *think*.

Jocelyn's problem was that she trusted the system, and Ivy knew the system was screwed up.

Still, Ivy had no money and she needed a place to regroup. Hiding in plain sight—not a bad idea. If they didn't leave the hotel room, there was no chance anyone could find them. They'd have this safe house, at least for a couple days. She'd call the rest of the girls and have them meet here as soon as possible.

But Ivy knew she couldn't count on Jocelyn indefinitely. The hotel cost nearly two hundred bucks a night, and while Jocelyn wanted to help, Ivy wasn't so sure her husband would be on board when he learned the whole truth, and Jocelyn had made it clear that she was going to tell him everything. She swore Chris Taylor could be trusted. It was one thing when his wife was doing her job getting prostitutes off the street; it was quite another being a party to kidnapping.

She dialed Kerry's number first. No answer and no messaging on the disposable phone. She disconnected and called Nicole next.

"Yeah?" Nicole answered.

"It's me. You okay? Mina?"

"In a crappy dive."

"I have a place for us, at least for a few nights."

"That's it?"

"Enough time to figure out what to do."

"Shit, Ivy, we lost everything! The only thing to do is hit the streets."

"Give me a few days to figure this out, okay?"

"Where are you?"

"Hotel Potomac."

"Holy shit, Ivy! You're liable to run into half the guys you screw."

"When you get here, let me know and I'll bring you in through the side door." She didn't give Nicole a chance to argue, but moved on. "Let me talk to Mina."

"She took one look at this dive and burst into tears. Besides, she sticks out in this neighborhood. So I took her to Marti's. You said we could trust her."

Why hadn't Ivy thought of Marti? She would have taken them all in, no questions. Except they couldn't all stay with her. Too small, too many people coming in and out. But Mina would be safe for now.

"Thanks. You're safe where you are?"

"Back in my old stomping grounds. I know this place better than anyone, all the ways in and out."

"Be careful."

Ivy tried Kerry again; still no answer.

Jocelyn knocked on the door. "Are you okay in there?"

Ivy opened the door. "I'm calling the girls. I'd feel better if we were together."

Jocelyn nodded. "I'll let you get settled. Call room service if you're hungry. I'll go shopping. Do you need anything specific?"

"Clothes, nothing fancy. Toiletries, maybe a deck of

cards so I can keep Sara from freaking out. Give her something to do." *And a passport into Canada,* she wanted to add.

"Not a problem." Jocelyn squeezed her arm. "It's going to be okay, Ivy. We'll figure this out together."

Ivy wasn't holding her breath.

She slid the security bolt into place as soon as Jocelyn left, then laid down on the king-sized bed and closed her eyes.

Five minutes to just do nothing.

Ivy had met Jocelyn over a year ago. Maddie, who'd been fighting her drug addiction for years, had a relapse when one of her clients spiked her drink. Just the little dose had her falling off the wagon, and because her tolerance had dropped, she'd OD'd. Ivy, fearing she'd die, rushed her to the hospital. She hated the paperwork, the nurses, everyone prying into their business, and the expense, but Maddie's life was at stake.

"Remember me?" Jocelyn Taylor sat next to Ivy in the waiting room. Ivy was a mess—her hair and clothes still reeked of Maddie's vomit even though she'd washed out her shirt in the bathroom sink.

Ivy didn't want to deal with the social worker. She'd been too nosy and Ivy didn't trust her. Her girls couldn't go back to their homes, and they didn't want to go to jail. She would find another way to get them off the streets, but the system had failed too many of them for too long. The lost girls. She wouldn't mind a little pixie dust right now if it would help her disappear into Neverland.

"I think we got off on the wrong foot."

"Go away."

She'd first met Jocelyn when Ivy was trying to help a

runaway. Ivy had been cornered by a pimp with a knife he was willing to use to keep his young girls working for him.

Jocelyn had been doing her own thing—Ivy knew who she was, a social worker trying to help underage prostitutes—but they'd never spoken. But when Ivy was threatened, Jocelyn came to her aid. She drove her car between Ivy and the pimp and Ivy jumped in, grabbing the girl at the same time.

They didn't talk about it afterward, but Ivy kept her eye on the social worker, and sent her a few other troubled girls—the ones with the pimps who Ivy couldn't afford to anger.

And then came Amy Carson, a runaway who Ivy had brought into the house on Hawthorne. Amy was angry, bitter, and scared, and when Ivy wasn't around to remind her where she'd been before Ivy had found her, Amy went back to hanging out with her so-called friends. It was no wonder the tenacious social worker had found her. Amy had given Jocelyn Ivy's number, and she hadn't been able to get rid of the woman ever since.

"I'm not who you think I am," Jocelyn said.

"I don't care who you are."

"I don't work for the government. I don't work for the county. I work for Missing and At-Risk Children."

"I'm not a child."

"How'd you get into this, Ivy? A boyfriend? A relative? You're smart, I can help you get out."

She didn't know how close she was to the truth. But Ivy didn't want to talk to anyone about how she started selling sex.

"I have a plan, you're not part of it. Just go."

Jocelyn didn't say anything for several minutes, but she didn't leave, either. Her presence was both comforting and annoying. Whenever Ivy pushed her away, she just stayed rooted. She couldn't make the woman angry, even though she'd tried many times.

"Amy's mother wants to talk to her."

Of course, there was always an agenda. "What are you going to do if Amy doesn't want to talk to her mother? Call the cops on me? So much for trust."

Ivy didn't want to be responsible for Amy. Ivy wanted her to go home, but the girl had been living on the streets for six months. When Ivy found her, she looked five years older and had been turning tricks for twenty bucks a pop. She wasn't a street kid. She'd been lured away by a fast-talking boyfriend during a shitty time in her life, and when he dumped her she had no money and even less self-esteem.

Ivy didn't want to go to jail. She tried to forget that Jocelyn had once bailed her out of that bad situation, no questions asked. She didn't know why the social worker, whoever she worked for, wanted to help her. In Ivy's experience, no one helped anyone for nothing. But if the cops found out she was running a prostitution ring, they'd shut her down and put her in jail. No cop would care that she'd forbade the younger girls like Amy and Mina from turning tricks. If she went to jail, she'd never be able to rescue Sara, and she wasn't going to risk her sister. Sara's fourteenth birthday was only months away. Ivy could not—would not—let her down.

"Get out of my face." She tried to stand, but Jocelyn put her hand on her arm.

"I've been where you are," Jocelyn said quietly. "I got out when I was ready. I can get Amy out. Trust me."

"You don't know me, and you don't know Amy."

Jocelyn gave Ivy her card. *"This is my cell phone. Call me when Amy's ready, and I'll take her home. That's my job—I reunite families."*

Ivy stared at the card. MARC. She glared at Jocelyn. *"And what if their family is worse? Are you going to toss them back into the lion's den like Daniel, except there's no one to protect them?"*

God forgot about some of His people. Or He never cared in the first place.

"If the family situation is unsafe, I have places for girls like Amy. But you know Amy's mother isn't a monster. If I didn't believe that with all my heart, if I didn't know in my gut that the house was safe, that her mother had forgiven all, I'd never return Amy." Jocelyn paused. *"You can come with me, check it out for yourself."*

"Just—go. Please."

Jocelyn tapped the card Ivy held tight in her fist. *"You'll do the right thing."* She started walking away, then turned around and said, *"I took care of Maddie's bill. She's going to be okay. I can even find a place for her."*

"She's twenty-one." And that was what terrified Ivy. What about when these lost girls made it to adulthood? When there were fewer chances for help? Would there be a real future for any of them, when they were constantly chased by the past?

"It doesn't matter. We'll call it a halfway house, for lack of a better name. She can go to college, find something she likes to support herself. You can too."

Ivy rolled her eyes. *"I want to be left alone."*

"No you don't."

Then she walked away.

* * *

It had taken Ivy two weeks before she called Jocelyn, and it was after Amy had sneaked out to meet up with her new "boyfriend." Ivy saw her falling into the same destructive patterns because Ivy couldn't get her into school. She had no real authority over Amy; Amy knew Ivy would never kick her out of the house or turn her in to the police, so those threats never worked. A parent had to be willing to follow through. But Ivy wasn't a parent. She was a twenty-year-old call girl who'd been on her own since she was Amy's age.

Jocelyn arranged a call with Amy's mother, no strings attached.

Her mother's tearful emotion could be felt over the phone lines. *"Amy, I love you so much. I miss you. Tyler misses you. Please come home. I'm sorry I didn't see how much pain you were in when your dad died. I was selfish, thinking only I was grieving. That only I could miss him so much. I was wrong."*

Two days later, Ivy let Jocelyn take Amy. She decided not to go with her. She didn't want to, or need to. She'd heard the truth in the mother's voice: Amy was both safe and loved.

And that is all anyone, child or teen or adult, wanted.

Ivy checked on Maddie and Sara; they both were sleeping.

She tried Kerry again, but there was still no answer. Why hadn't Kerry checked in? Where had she gone? Why wasn't she answering the phone?

Ivy wanted someone to talk to, someone she could trust. Kerry, like Ivy, would do anything necessary to protect her sister. Maybe she'd ditched the phone, fearing it could be traced somehow. But wouldn't she have let Ivy know that she'd picked up a new phone?

While she was thinking about Kerry, her phone rang, and she jumped on it. She almost answered it, but her eye caught the caller ID. She recognized the number, but it wasn't Kerry.

She silenced the phone.

For all she knew, the man she knew as Sergio had tried to kill them that morning. Or he'd want to when he found out both his money and the disks he'd paid for had been destroyed in the fire.

CHAPTER FIVE

Wendy James lived in a small but pricey condo on the edge of the park where she'd been killed.

Noah and two DC cops cleared the apartment first, then Lucy entered the immaculate one-bedroom apartment. The blinds were drawn, and Noah walked over to open them, letting in bright, morning light. The city view would be breathtaking during the sunrise, Lucy thought, though the full wall of windows made her uncomfortable. A number of office buildings had line of sight into this condo. Anyone with binoculars or a good camera lens could see inside.

A small patio off the living room was accessible by a sliding glass door. The patio had no plants—only a small iron table and two matching chairs.

A white cat with orange spots ran over to Lucy, meowing loudly as he rubbed against her legs. She squatted to pet him. "I'll bet he's hungry," she said.

"I didn't peg you for a cat person."

"Never had a cat. My dad was allergic. We should

find a neighbor to watch him until we locate Wendy's family."

"The computer tech is going through her hard drive and Stein is on his way."

Lucy said, "Do you think Slater's right? He'd take the case just because it's high-profile?"

Noah looked at her with an odd expression. "I suppose I shouldn't be surprised you've stayed out of office politics."

"I thought it best to keep my head down, considering my position here is unusual."

"Stein's a smart guy, but Slater's right. You took pictures of the body on your phone, right?"

"Yes. I know the forensic photographer will have better shots, but I wanted them for reference."

"It's not a problem. Give me your phone."

She did, not sure what he had planned. He scrolled through the dozen photos she'd taken, then his lips turned up. "This is great."

He'd brought up a close-up of the victim's arm that had been half-eaten by the dogs.

She trusted Noah had a plan, because she wasn't giving up this case.

The other agents cared about solving the murder, and both Noah and Matt Slater were good at their jobs. But Lucy cared about Wendy James. The twenty-five-year-old blonde had made some bad choices, and unfortunately, the people in this town would remember the affair more than they'd remember a young woman was dead. It would all be about Congressman Crowley—what her murder would do to his career, what his wife thought, whether he would resign, whether he would run for reelection, and if his opponent would use the affair and murder against him. And what if Crowley was guilty of more than adultery?

Lucy walked slowly through the condo while Noah talked to the computer tech. Glass was everywhere—round glass dining table with decorative flowers in the center. Glass tables in the living room. Pale gray carpet. The minimal art could have been found in a hotel room, blending in with the subdued coloring. The only brightness came from the sun and the blood-red throw pillows placed squarely on the couch.

The condo had two large rooms—the living/dining combination and the bedroom. There was a small kitchen, extra storage, and a surprisingly large bathroom for a one-bedroom condo. Even in the bedroom, there were no personal pictures. A bookshelf was lined with popular hardcover fiction, none of which appeared to have been read. Even in the bathroom, where most women left makeup and toiletries scattered on the counter, there was very little at first glance.

"Does she even live here?" Lucy wondered out loud.

Noah glanced around again. "Yes."

"It's sparse. Nothing personal."

"Minimalist. I've been in my apartment for nearly four years and it looks pretty much like this."

"That's because you work twelve-hour days."

"Or maybe because I'm orderly."

Lucy put on her gloves and opened the medicine cabinet. She found two prescriptions, one for birth control pills, one for Valium. The Valium had been refilled two weeks ago, but at sight Lucy didn't think more than one or two were missing. The birth control pills came in a six-month supply. The box was in a drawer. There were two months left.

Wendy kept her extensive makeup collection in two drawers, well-organized with separate trays for each type of product—eye shadow, lipstick, brushes, mascara. A cosmetics bag in the bottom drawer had a complete but minimal set of supplies.

Her toilet paper was stacked in neat rows under her sink. Feminine products were in separate trays. There were no extraneous boxes, each drawer was lined and clean. The shampoo, conditioner, and soap were lined up in the shower, labels facing out, perfectly symmetrical.

"She's severely OCD," Lucy said to herself. Lucy wasn't a slob like her sister Carina, but she wasn't this anal about her personal space. She lived in tidy clutter. Living like this would drive her as batty as living in a mess.

"Did you say something?" Noah asked as he stepped into the bathroom.

"I think I know the victim a bit better." She pointed out some of the personality traits. "Meticulous to the point of sociopathic."

"Sociopathic?" Noah questioned.

"A disorder. Not crazy or psychopathic, but she has some definite neuroses."

"I like it."

"Do you keep your drawer this neat?" She opened the makeup drawer.

"No, that's a little extreme, even for a military boy like me."

"Anything on the computer?" she asked, stepping into the bedroom.

"Not yet. We can't find her cell phone and she has no landline. A purse was hanging in the closet with a wallet,

but no driver's license. Her car—a late-model Camaro—
is in the garage. The keys we recovered at the crime
scene match the car and the apartment."

"There was no personal identification on the body,
correct?"

"Nothing found so far."

"I always take my ID and phone when I run."

"The only thing the canvass found was a small can
of Mace and keys. Could have fallen out of her pocket
during the attack."

"Or she tried to stop her attacker, but couldn't get to
it fast enough." Mace was a great defensive tool, but only
with proper training. Not only did the potential victim
need to know how to use the spray effectively, but she
should also have advanced self-defense training to learn
to be more aware of her surroundings and potential
threats. Lucy, who was hyperaware of what went on
around her, was sometimes guilty of complacency while
running. It was easy to get lulled by the comfortable
rhythm of a steady pace.

"The crime scene didn't feel like a robbery," Noah
said.

"Did you find anything in the drawers or closet?"

Noah averted his eyes, but Lucy picked up on the
subtle tension and looked at him, eyebrows raised.
"Clothing, personal items. There was an overnight bag
in the closet packed with marital aids."

It took Lucy a second to realize what Noah meant.
"You mean sex toys?"

He nodded.

"Why are you acting surprised?" She hoped he wasn't
walking on eggshells because of her. "Wendy James was

an attractive twenty-five-year-old woman having an affair. It's reasonable to assume she had an active sex life."

She walked out of the bedroom, realizing she wasn't comfortable talking about sex toys with Noah. Murder, sexual assault, forensics, psychology—no problem. But Lucy couldn't joke about sex like many cops did. She blamed her past, and wished she could just be normal. Or at least *act* normal. Put on a show, pretend she was just like everyone else.

But she wasn't. While she was certainly less experienced on a homicide investigation than either Noah or Slater, she looked at the crime scene far differently than most cops. And here, Noah methodically searched and assessed what he saw, but Lucy pictured Wendy living here. If she really had.

Of course she did. She has a cat. Makeup. Medication.

Something she said to Noah came back to her. When he'd said his apartment was just like this, she'd been flip that he was never there because he worked so much.

She turned around, almost ran into Noah. "Excuse me."

"What are you looking for?"

Frowning with concentration, she went through each drawer in the closet, every article of clothing. The suitcases. She went back to the bathroom, looked through the drawers again.

"How long did her affair with Crowley last?"

"According to the media, a little over a year."

"And he's never been here?"

"I have no idea," Noah said. "They could have stuck to hotels."

"More likely for him to be recognized going into a hotel in DC, don't you think?"

"What's your point?"

"She's here, but she's not. She doesn't work here, she doesn't bring men over here—there is *nothing* in her bedroom, closet, or bathroom that is masculine. No forgotten shampoo, socks, tie."

"You said she was OCD."

Lucy didn't realize that Noah had heard her talking to herself. "I suppose . . . but no pictures? No mementos? How long has she lived here?"

"The manager is pulling her records and security tapes."

They walked back to the living room and Josh Stein stood in the middle, his lips a tight line. "Slater told you I would be here, and you're already done with the search? This is my case." He glanced at Lucy, but addressed Noah. "I don't think you understand the sensitive nature of our pending investigation."

Next to her, Noah straightened his spine, the tension rolling off him, but physically she hardly noticed the difference in his stance.

He put his hands out, palms up. "It's yours, absolutely. Slater called in the tech team to access the computer, we needed to secure the apartment and do a cursory search."

Stein seemed irritated that Noah hadn't argued with him. "Find anything?"

"She's a good housekeeper, and she likes her sex toys." Noah gave Stein a wry grin. Lucy had never seen him joke, but she could see the humor wasn't in his eyes. Josh Stein, however, didn't seem to notice.

"I'd expect no less from someone like her." He chuckled and glanced around the spacious living room.

"S—" Lucy stepped forward, furious, but Noah stepped in front of her and cut her off immediately.

"Kincaid," he said sharply, "find a neighbor who will take the cat."

She bit back her anger and walked out without comment.

She stood in the hall a moment to calm down. Someone like *who*? It took two to have an affair. Two to play sex games. Why was it always the female who was ridiculed and blamed? Alan Crowley was just as responsible for the affair, and he was solely responsible for the lies he told to cover it up. Would Josh Stein be making cracks about Crowley if he'd been the victim?

And Noah had started it.

I'll handle Stein.

Lucy breathed deeply, held it, and slowly let it out. Noah had never been crude, it had to be part of his plan. If Stein cut them out, the case would be all about political corruption, not the brutal murder of a twenty-five-year-old secretary.

Lucy knocked on each door on Wendy's floor, but no one answered, not unusual for mid-morning on a weekday. She went downstairs to the security office to see if they could house the cat until next-of-kin came to pick up her belongings. She reached into her pocket to text Noah, then realized he still had her phone.

"Agent—?" The manager, a sixty-year-old woman with gray hair and sharp blue eyes, questioned Lucy.

"Lucy Kincaid," she said, extending her hand.

"Betty Dare." She handed her a tape and file. "Here's the information your partner requested."

"Thank you, Ms. Dare. Ms. James's cat—would you be able to care for it until her family arrives?"

"I'm sorry, my dog doesn't like cats. I can call some of the other residents, but most of the people who live here work during the day. A third of our apartments are only used on a part-time basis."

"This is a condominium, correct?"

"About half the units are owned. The company who manages the building doesn't allow sublets or rentals, except through the company."

"Ms. James was an owner?"

Ms. Dare nodded and gestured to the file in Lucy's hands. "She bought the unit two years ago. No complaints."

"Did you know her well?"

"She said hello, but I didn't see much of her. I don't see most of the residents unless there is a problem."

"And Ms. James didn't have any problems?"

"No, none."

"This is a secure building, correct?"

"Fairly. We have cameras in the lobby, each entrance, and the parking garage. The lobby doors are locked from nine P.M. until five A.M. Each resident has a card key to enter after hours, as well as the parking garage all day."

"Did you include a printout for Ms. James's card?"

"No, I didn't think—it'll just take a minute."

Lucy waited and five minutes later, Ms. Dare handed her a report. It was surprisingly thick. She flipped through it. Wendy didn't arrive home most nights until after two in the morning. There was no tracking of when she left the parking garage, only when she returned.

"Thank you."

"Let me know if I can do anything else. I know what the media is saying about her, poor girl. But what I knew of her, she was polite, quiet, and sweet. She baked me cookies last Christmas. Very kind. Not many young people do things like that anymore, you know."

Lucy went back upstairs. She stepped into the condo, but was immediately escorted out by Noah. "Good news and bad news," he said. "I'm running the case, but in the shadows. Stein's the lead on paper and I report to both him and Slater. But it's all on us. He's not going to get in the way, except he's coming with us to interview the victim's employer and colleagues."

"How'd you do it?"

Noah reached into his pocket and handed her back her cell phone. He winked, his eyes showing a rare sparkle. "Your pictures came in very handy." Then he returned to his usual seriousness. "Watch your step around him. He can be a jerk, but when it comes to white-collar crimes, he's one of the best. He has the same kind of instincts that you do, just in a different area."

"I understand." She handed him the files from the manager. "I couldn't find a place for the cat."

"It seemed to like you. Why don't you take it home?"

"I can't."

"Why?"

She had never thought about having a pet, she was too busy.

"I guess I could—temporarily."

"We'll come back for it after interviewing her employer."

A cat. She'd have to give her brother and sister-in-law, whom she lived with, a heads-up. Or maybe it would be better to ask for forgiveness than permission.

CHAPTER SIX

Josh Stein insisted on driving to Devon Sullivan & Associates, the lobbying company where Wendy James worked as a secretary. He wanted to exchange information about the case, but he did most of the talking. In between his off-color jokes about loose women and politics and his valuable information and insight about Wendy James's initial interview after the scandal broke, Lucy didn't know if she wanted to kill him or praise him.

Noah was right. Stein was very smart—and very much a jerk.

"I would have cut her loose then," Stein was saying, "because it seemed to be exactly what it was on the surface. A hot young chick sleeping with power. She was in no position to influence legislation, she's a fucking *secretary,* doesn't even have to register. But it came back to her knowledge of a particular bill Crowley killed in committee."

"You've lost me," Noah said.

"She went into the interview all charming, tits perky,

eyelashes fluttering, but she was no bimbo. Too smart. We were just chatting, I made a comment about one of her company's clients, an upstart company, and she immediately corrected me. The client was no longer with DSA, and the product they made wasn't a computer chip, but a specialized lens for space telescopes."

"Why's that important?"

"It was *obscure*. Some things she may know, but in that detail? Considering her employer told me she was essentially the receptionist? So I asked some other questions, confirmed that she was sharp. So I'm thinking, maybe it wasn't so much influence peddling on Crowley's part, but maybe this girl had some other boyfriends on the side. Maybe she gathers up information like we gather up evidence, sees what fits and what doesn't. Campaign secrets and whatnot."

"Is that a crime?" Lucy asked.

"Maybe, maybe not. Depending on what she does with the information. If there's money involved. If there's national security at risk. So I asked some things I knew weren't true, and one thing I knew *was* true—that she'd been involved with Congressman Randy Bristow at one point. *That* tidbit came from a contact of mine in the White House, who had seen the two up close and personal after a fundraiser. I asked her about a bunch of guys I doubted she'd screwed, then Bristow, and she denied it. No reason to, really—Bristow isn't married, he can screw anyone he wants. But she cut me off, asked why I needed to know about her past sex life, she wasn't on trial, yada yada."

"You were fishing," Lucy said.

"I'm damn good fisherman, sweetheart," he said, grinning at her in the rearview mirror.

Noah jumped in. "And then you brought in the U.S. Attorney."

"Information is power in this town, and that pretty little girl had access to a lot of information."

"There was nothing on her computer," Noah said.

"But you didn't find her phone, did you? And she could have a laptop somewhere, or save everything to a disk. Maybe she wasn't doing anything wrong. Maybe she was. Now she's dead."

Noah glanced over his shoulder as if warning Lucy to keep her mouth shut.

"Turning up dead right before a meet with the U.S. Attorney's office?" Stein continued. "That tells me she knew *something*. Maybe she wasn't the bad girl in this picture, but knew who was being naughty."

Lucy's irritation faded when the manner of death clicked into place. "The killer made her death *look* like attempted rape. Pulled down her shorts, but no penetration and no bruising on the inside of her thighs."

Stein paled. "Well, I, uh, will leave those details to you."

"Hear me out," she continued. Stein pulled into a red zone near an office building only blocks from the Capitol complex. "Her death was odd, don't you think, Noah? Strangled from *behind*. Little or no sexual gratification. And Josh said she lied about something she didn't have to, and was scheduled to talk to the U.S. Attorney. Why was she killed *now* and not three weeks ago when the scandal first broke?"

"The theory makes sense," Noah said, "but doesn't it seem unwise on the killer's part to kill her when she was an interested party in an ongoing investigation?"

"Not if the information she would have shared was criminally damaging," Stein said.

Lucy couldn't believe she and the bombastic agent were in agreement. "Desperate measures," she said. "If he felt there was no other way to silence her. Maybe she couldn't be bought off."

"Speaking of buying her off," Stein said, "I have my team going through her finances. That condo cost her far more than she'd make on a secretary's salary. Might be she comes from a wealthy family, or maybe she just has a *lot* of men keeping her in style." He laughed.

The two minutes Lucy had respected Josh Stein ended.

The three of them walked through the glass doors of a renovated corner office building. Part of the structure was reinforced marble—very likely the original structure—and part was completely new, made to blend in with the old. The result was surprisingly attractive.

Stein showed his badge to the guard and they were sent to the penthouse suite of offices where Devon Sullivan & Associates resided.

In the elevator, Stein said, "DSA is a medium-sized lobbying firm representing local governments, small unions, and private businesses, primarily in the tech industry. Their second-largest client in terms of dollars spent is a city in California—which happens to be in Alan Crowley's district. See why the affair may not be so simple after all? Definitely an affair to remember." He laughed at his own joke. Neither Lucy nor Noah joined in, but Stein didn't notice.

Devon Sullivan greeted them when they stepped out of the elevator. She was attractive in both manner and dress. Mid-fifties, tastefully dyed dark blond hair, and hazel eyes behind purple Donna Spade glasses. Her red-rimmed eyes suggested she'd already heard about Wendy James's murder.

"It's so awful. Please, come to my office."

She led them across the lobby, through glass double doors, and past her secretary. "Jeanie, please hold all calls for now." She closed the door behind them.

Devon Sullivan's office was as large as Wendy's living room and just as contemporary, with a wide expanse of windows and lots of sparkling glass. The view looked down on one of the large roundabouts, and if Lucy stood just right, she could see half of the Capitol. One wall was a bookcase with numerous political biographies and larger legal tomes. A few pictures decorated the shelves, mostly of Devon Sullivan golfing or with clients, and one of her at a shooting range, framed with a small engraving, "Virginia State Trooper Widows & Orphans Charity Shoot-Out, 2008."

Ms. Sullivan motioned for them to sit, and she took a position in front of her desk, not behind it. Lucy glanced at the desk, which was devoid of all papers except for closed file folders. A picture of two young boys sat in the corner. Children or grandchildren, Lucy couldn't tell.

"I'm still trying to understand what happened. The press, as you know, never gets things completely right. But Wendy *was* murdered?"

"Yes, ma'am," Stein said. "I appreciate you making the time for us." His tone was reserved and respectful, opposite of his earlier demeanor.

"Anything you need."

"When news of the affair between Ms. James and Congressman Crowley first broke, I spoke to your office manager about her employment. He indicated that she'd worked here as a secretary for about two years."

"Correct."

"Were you concerned when she didn't come in for work yesterday morning?"

Ms. Sullivan blinked rapidly, her eyes brimming with tears. "I fired Wendy last week."

The information surprised all of them, but Josh Stein most of all. "When?" he asked brusquely.

"Tuesday morning. I would have fired her on Monday, but she called in sick. I think she knew. I didn't have a choice—I don't think she did anything wrong, but her judgment was flawed. My business is built solely on my reputation. Her situation had gotten out of control, and I had concerned clients. I gave her a very nice severance package, and a letter of recommendation."

"What exactly did she do for you?"

"Mostly answered phones, greeted clients, made copies, and assisted with events. Wendy was very good at it."

"Why did you feel the need to fire her?"

"Reputation," she repeated.

"Did you know she was having an affair with Alan Crowley?"

"No. I would have told her to knock it off or leave. My staff knows how important image is in this business, when lobbying already has as bad a reputation as used-car salesmen and politicians. Truly, a few bad apples and we're all condemned."

"Could she have accessed sensitive information that she may have leveraged with Congressman Crowley or others?"

"Others?"

"We're keeping a broad mind."

"I suppose she could have accessed any of the files here, but most of our records are public, as required by law."

"Did you, or anyone on your staff, ask Wendy James to unduly influence Alan Crowley or any other sitting member of the House of Representatives?"

Ms. Sullivan was taken aback by the question, and Lucy was surprised as well. Stein slipped it in smoothly, in the same tone and manner as his initial softball questions.

"Absolutely not," she said firmly.

"Would you mind if I spoke to your staff?"

She hesitated, the first sign that she was nervous about something. It could be natural, stemming from the tragic situation, or it could be more calculating. Lucy wasn't certain.

"Of course you may, but if it's about my clients, I need to be present."

"Just about Wendy, who she dated, if anyone knew about the affair."

Devon Sullivan didn't relax. "I suppose. When?"

"Now would be perfect," Stein said.

"I'll make the conference room available." She left the office, closing the door behind her.

Stein grinned and said in a low voice, "I'm going to give Ms. Sullivan a rectal exam."

"Excuse me?" Lucy said.

"You think a lobbyist like her didn't know her secretary was doing the horizontal bop with a player like Crowley? Hell no."

"Murder is a long way from political corruption," Noah said.

Stein shrugged. "Maybe. Probably no connection. But

you shouldn't be surprised how fast people tell the truth when they think they're facing more serious charges. Anything going on in this company, I'll find it." He glanced at his watch. "We still have time to catch Crowley at his office. Damn, I love my job."

Lucy barely refrained from grimacing. Stein was too giddy about his work; she wondered if he cared anything about the victim—or if winning was the only thing that mattered.

They could easily have walked from DSA to the Capitol, but Stein insisted on driving even though it was close to five in the afternoon and the roads were crowded. It took him fifteen minutes to find a parking place—a white-zone reserved for Capitol Police.

He slid his official federal business placard on the dash and got out of the car, whistling.

Lucy decided that she didn't care how smart Josh Stein was, or his case clearance rate, she did not like a man who whistled while investigating murder.

They walked toward Crowley's office in the Rayburn building. "Josh," Noah said, "I let you lead with the lobbyist, let me take the lead with Crowley."

"I'm on a roll, Armstrong. Think I can't handle a homicide investigation?"

"I think you'd be great, but you've been an agent how long? Fifteen years? How many homicides?"

Stein didn't say anything.

"If you have a question, jump in, but if you don't mind . . ." he let his comment hang.

Stein jerked his thumb toward Lucy. "Why's she here again?"

"Slater wanted a forensic analyst."

"Is she going to be asking questions? Slater told you we are under the gun. Every step watched by everyone, including press."

"I understand exactly what we face."

"Noah," she began.

He shot her a look that told her to remain quiet. She was going to suggest she wait outside, knowing that Stein didn't want her involved, and not wanting her presence to jeopardize the case—even though she didn't know how that would happen.

She wished Noah had given her a better understanding of their role working with the White Collar division, as well as how he intended to question Congressman Crowley. She disliked the power plays between the two divisions, with the uncertainty of who was really in charge. And she didn't like this side of Noah.

Lucy followed Noah and Stein through security, then upstairs where they were ushered immediately into Congressman Crowley's private office.

Crowley had been in Congress for more than twenty-two years, withstanding several partisan shifts of power. His office was decorated with furniture that was a little too big for the space, including a tall glass cabinet packed with awards and trinkets. His desk was cluttered with three pen sets, paperweights, and a variety of odd items, many with gold plates identifying a place or event. Most of the photographs had Crowley in golf gear with people more famous than he.

Noah introduced the three of them.

Crowley said, "I spoke with your superior earlier today."

"We have some follow-up questions. I'm sure you understand."

"Why isn't Agent Slater handling this? He told me he was in charge." Crowley's tone was offensive, but his posture was defensive—his body was turned a few degrees away from them, his hands bounced a pen off the desk blotter, his eyes went from agent to agent, then glanced at the door.

He was nervous.

"He's the Supervisory Special Agent for the Violent Crimes and Major Offenders squad," Stein said. "I'm his counterpart, the SSA for White Collar Crime and Political Corruption."

Crowley's face reddened. He dropped the pen. "I will answer questions about my relationship with Wendy, but you're stretching to imply there was anything but a consenting adult relationship."

"Your relationship with Ms. James is public record at this point," Stein said. "We need to determine if there was anything inappropriate or illegal. It's odd that she ends up dead three days before her scheduled meeting with the U.S. Attorney. What information might she have been wanting to share?"

So much for letting Noah take the lead, Lucy thought. She wanted to pull Stein aside and explain to him that anyone with basic understanding of psychology could see that Crowley considered himself a leader and wouldn't be a pushover, just on the basis of what his office showed. His overabundance of awards and pictures was "name-dropping." The best way to get him to cooperate would be to stroke his ego and let him think he was the one solving the case, all the while answering their very specific questions. Going on the attack right out of the gate was a big mistake.

Crowley leaned forward, both hands palm down on

his desk. "I will tell you exactly what I told Agent Slater, since it's obvious that your office doesn't share information. I was in a committee meeting yesterday morning. The last time I saw Wendy was a week after the newspaper reported our affair. She called and wanted to meet at her apartment. I agreed to meet in public, at Dupont Circle. I brought my chief of staff with me, so no one could take pictures and accuse me of continuing the affair. We talked about nothing important because she was mad I brought Denise. We haven't spoken since."

He looked from Stein to Noah, then said, "I'm upset that she was killed, but her murder has nothing to do with me."

"Sir," Noah said, trying to settle him down, "we are simply trying to put together Ms. James's movements over the last few days. If she ever indicated that someone was following her, maybe an ex-boyfriend she told you about, or—"

"If you have any specific questions, I will answer them through my lawyer."

Stein said, "You understand that your refusal to cooperate makes you suspect."

"You can leave now."

They stood up and started toward the door. Lucy caught Noah's eye. "Apartment?" she mouthed. He either ignored her or didn't understand.

She turned around and faced Crowley. "Sir," she said in her most diplomatic voice, "did you usually meet with Ms. James at her apartment?"

"My attorney," he repeated without looking at her. He pretended to read a document on his desk, but his hands were shaking and he had to put the paper down. For a split second, she thought he was scared. Not that he might get caught at something, but maybe . . . was he scared someone was after him?

"Please, this is important. You must have cared about Wendy at one point."

He looked at her, sorrow crossing his face for a split second, before his arrogance buried it. She implored him with her eyes, even though how he had handled the affair made her want to slap him.

"I truly did. We usually met at her apartment on Park Way."

"Which apartment number?" she pretended to forget and flipped through blank pages in a notebook.

"Seven-ten. How does that help?" he asked, curious.

"Just fact-gathering, sir. Thank you."

As soon as they were in the hall, Stein turned to Lucy and said, "What the hell were you doing? He cried uncle and you bat your eyes at him?"

"I did not," she defended. "I needed to know where they met for sex. It was obvious to me it wasn't in the apartment we walked this morning—and apartment seven-ten is not hers. It's not even on the same floor."

"Like you can tell after ten minutes in her apartment whether she brought men there? Why does it matter where they screwed?" Stein was livid. "I had Crowley panicked and asking for his lawyer, and you act like the good cop? You don't even have a badge!"

Noah said, "Let's take this outside."

"I had this under control. If this case is blown, it's on *you*, Armstrong. You brought Nancy Drew into this investigation."

They stepped into the elevator. Noah gave a staff member a look that had the young man waiting for the next ride.

When the door closed, Noah said, "You pushed him too hard, too fast."

"That's how you have to deal with these people. They're all guilty of something."

"You don't believe that."

"I've worked in political corruption for more than a decade, and I don't care who it is, they're all corruptible. Some easier than others."

"But he's not under investigation for political corruption, Josh! He's a person of interest in a *homicide*. Once I clear him, you can do whatever you want, but for now, we focus on the murder of Wendy James."

"And if they're connected?"

"When we solve the murder, we'll know."

The elevator opened. Lucy followed behind the two men. Stein was on his phone and walked ahead. Noah still looked irritated.

"Noah," Lucy said cautiously. "We need to check out apartment seven-ten. Remember how I said it didn't look like she lived there? Maybe she doesn't, not full-time."

"You should have talked to me before questioning Crowley."

"I tried—"

"We could get the information in other ways. It was already a tense situation."

"That wasn't my fault." Why was Noah angry with her? She hadn't gone into Crowley's office on a rant. "Crowley is a classic power narcissist. He responds negatively to attacks, he needs to be praised and made to feel important, then you can get him to talk about anything."

She hadn't realized Stein overheard her comment.

He snapped his phone off and said, "I understand politicians better than you, Kincaid. I'm not going to coddle them when I know in my gut they're crooked, and I'm not going to play pop psychology games."

Noah said, "Josh, I understand where you're coming from, but right now you're fishing on influence peddling. You have no evidence. On the other hand, we have a dead body and interviewing Crowley is part of the process. I need his statement."

Stein shook his head. "I get it, Armstrong, but I stand by my approach. Now we wait and watch. He'll do something to tip his hand, I guarantee it. And then maybe we'll both get what we want—I'll nail him for corruption, you get him for murder."

"If he's guilty," Lucy said. She wanted to say, *he's not guilty,* but didn't want another argument, with Stein or Noah.

"He's guilty of something." Stein glanced at his watch. "Can you get a taxi back to your car? I have to get back to headquarters." He left without waiting for an answer.

Lucy followed Noah, who was walking quickly and ignoring her. "Noah, wait," she finally said. The heat made her hot and irritable.

He stopped under a tree near the sidewalk. "I know what you're going to say. Josh Stein is an asshole. He's impulsive and arrogant. But he's also my superior, and yours." He added under his breath, "It's my fault." He started walking again, but Lucy stopped him.

"Noah, what did I do?" Her heart was racing and she began to panic that she'd overstepped. "I'm sorry I said anything to the congressman, but I was only thinking about what we'd been talking about earlier, that maybe Wendy James has another place. And we confirmed it!"

"I planned on coming back to talk to Crowley without Stein."

"I didn't know." She felt foolish, but wished Noah had given her a clue to his plans.

"I've given you a lot of slack these last two months, but that can't continue. This case is far too complicated and high-profile."

"I haven't jeopardized anything, have I?" She couldn't imagine what she'd said or done that would put a conviction at risk.

"Not yet." Noah flagged down a taxi and opened the door for Lucy.

She slid into the cab.

Not yet.

Which meant he expected her to screw up.

It was after six by the time Noah and Lucy arrived back at Wendy James's apartment. Noah was on the phone the entire drive, talking to an analyst about property records. Apartment 710 was owned by the corporation that managed the condo and two floors down from Wendy's official residence, 910.

The manager let them in. "I don't think Wendy ever used this place," Betty Dare said. "It's leased for short-term stays—less than a month."

"Do you have the printout of who's leased it in the past year?" Noah asked.

She handed him a folder.

Noah glanced through it. "These are businesses."

"Yes—they will lease the place for staff who are coming into the city to testify, sometimes staying a week, sometimes longer."

Lucy held her hand out. "I can go through them tonight."

Noah didn't give her the file. "We have a well-staffed office, Lucy. You don't have to volunteer for everything."

Ms. Dare hesitated, then handed Noah the key. "If you can lock up and return the key on your way out?"

"Of course."

After the manager left, Lucy looked around.

The place was lavishly decorated with expensive, durable furniture befitting a high-end lease. Leather couch, plush carpet, granite in the kitchen, and a fifty-inch television on the wall. A plethora of plants made the place appear homey, but upon closer inspection, Lucy realized they were silk. The refrigerator had two unopened bottles of white wine and long-shelf-life barrel cheese. The kitchen cabinets included unopened packages of crackers and a wide array of alcohol. There were plates, glasses, utensils, all clean.

"Looks standard," Noah said.

"With food and drink?"

"For executives who come in after hours—hotels do it."

"Something seems—off."

"Maybe Wendy didn't want to bring Crowley into her apartment. Nosy neighbor, maybe she had a boyfriend." Noah added, "We got nothing from the neighbors earlier, but we should follow up now that it's after six."

Lucy was only half-listening to Noah. She stared at a discolored strip of molding along the ceiling. There was a dark mark near the edge that caught her attention.

She pulled over a chair from the dining area and put it against the wall. As soon as she got closer to the molding, she saw that it was loose. The smudge appeared to be grease. She wiggled the piece and realized it was on a hinge.

"What are you doing?" Noah asked.

"There's a hidey-hole here."

"Hidey-hole?" Noah sounded amused.

Lucy pushed up and the little door snapped off. "Sorry," she said.

"Lucy, I'll bring a team in—"

"It's wires. Lots of them. The space is only four inches wide. A building like this would have a separate room for its wiring." Lucy handed Noah the broken door. "This molding is different than the rest. It's PVC, not wood."

She stepped off the chair and led the way into the bedroom. She saw the same slightly off-color strip of molding.

Her instincts buzzed that she'd discovered something important. "Look—same thing here."

"Let me do it this time," Noah said. He brought over a chair and used it as a step stool to stand on the dresser. "There's definitely a door here." He tapped in several locations and suddenly a door sprang up. "And I didn't break it," he said, grinning.

He shined a flashlight into the hole. "Empty. But something was definitely here. There're outlets."

"Outlets *inside* the wall?"

"What's on the backside of this wall?"

Lucy walked around and opened the door. "A linen closet. There are sheets, towels, toiletries."

"Eight feet deep?"

She eyeballed it. "It's about three feet wide and four feet deep."

"This section of wall is over eight feet."

Noah jumped down.

Lucy knew exactly what he was thinking. Her heart pounded as she took the linens and two loose shelves from the closet. Behind the sheets was an obvious "hidden" panel.

Wires in the walls and ceiling, in the bedroom and living room, an apartment with no owner, where a congressman met with his mistress—sex tapes. Lucy's face flushed as she fumbled with the panel.

Don't panic! Dammit, this is your job.

She took a deep breath. Forced the memories back. Hot and cold flashes washed over her skin as snippets of her past assaulted her. The video camera with its mocking red light, reminding her that everyone who paid could watch her, tied naked to the floor. The pain and humiliation and the despair.

She had wanted to die.

Don't look. Don't look.

She repeated the mantra. If she didn't look at the past, she could forget it, at least for now.

She didn't want to break down. Not ever, but especially not in front of Noah.

"Do you need help?" Noah stood right behind her.

"I got it."

His voice reminded Lucy that no one was videotaping *her.* She was with a friend, a colleague, a mentor. She was safe.

But deep down she felt a nightmare coming on, and wished with all her heart that Sean was back from Sacramento. Sean kept the nightmares away; he made her feel safe when nothing else could.

His unconditional love healed her.

She didn't dare let on that this case disturbed her. Not to Noah, and especially not to Sean. Sean would quit his assignment in California and fly back to DC, jeopardizing his reputation and career, just because this case was stirring up memories that might lead to bad dreams.

You're a big girl, Lucy. You have to deal with life on your own.

"Lucy."

It was Noah. How long had she been standing there, bent over the shelf, fumbling with the panel?

"Sorry, mind wandering."

She swallowed, breathed deeply again, and pushed on the corner of the panel.

It swung open, much bigger than she thought, and hit her on the head.

"Ow, shit!" She jumped back, bumping up against Noah. She rubbed her forehead, came away with a small drop of blood.

"Are you okay?" he turned her around and inspected her forehead. "You're bleeding."

"It's just a bump." She pulled off her right glove. "I don't have another pair of gloves."

"Don't touch anything." He eyed her closely. "You'll live."

"Thanks." But she smiled. He could have made the situation even more awkward than it was, but Noah was a professional, and she needed that more than ever.

They traded places. "There's a light switch back here." He flipped it on.

A tiny, narrow room—carpeted along the walls—had been built behind the linen closet. It was three feet wide and about five feet long—two people *might* have been able to stand side by side, but it would have been a tight fit. Outlets, plugs, evidence of a full-tech operation was here, but no equipment.

"She was recording Crowley," Lucy said, almost in disbelief.

"Recording him without his knowledge? That sounds like blackmail."

"No wonder he was defensive."

"She was involved publicly with other congressmen as well," Noah said. "That's what got Stein's panties in a wad—and he might have been right." He pulled out his phone. "I have to call in cyber crime for this one."

"Wireless," Lucy said. "It would have been easy to set up. But then, why would she need this room? Why not use her own apartment?"

"We're going to find out. I wonder if the manager knows? Call her up, Lucy."

Ten minutes later, Noah showed Betty Dare the hidden room. She stared, a stunned expression on her face. "I had no idea," she said repeatedly.

"I need to seal off this room, it's a potential crime scene, and we'll contact the owners."

"I—yes—of course."

Lucy felt bad for the flustered manager. "This isn't your fault," she said. "There are over one hundred units in this building? Sixty-seven owned, thirty long-term leases, a dozen executive leases?"

Betty looked surprised. "You have a good memory."

She shrugged. "That's a lot of people for one person to manage. Thank you so much for your help."

"Lucy," Noah said, "go home. I have to wait for the team to arrive."

"I can wait with you."

"Sean still in Sacramento?"

She nodded.

"Weren't you going to give Ms. James's cat temporary housing?"

"Yes, but—"

"Go. Tomorrow's going to be a long day."

CHAPTER SEVEN

Brian loved his brother, but resented the fact that people called *him* stupid and *Ned* smart.

Brian had handled his part of the plan perfectly. Wendy James was dead.

After Ned found out that Wendy was still chummy with her hookers, Ned was supposed to poison them with carbon monoxide and make it look like an accident. But instead, he wanted a bang.

Well, he got it—along with six living problems.

And who did they call to solve problems?

Brian. Because he did exactly what he was supposed to. He took orders. He was a good soldier and all that crap.

Brian watched the news in his basement apartment. Ned wouldn't be happy that Wendy's body had been found so soon, but who the fuck cared? Nothing tied her to him, nothing tied him to her murder, and he wore gloves.

"The victim has been identified as Wendy James, the young secretary who admitted to having a longtime affair with Congressman Alan Crowley, the powerful chair of the Judiciary Committee.

"Police have no leads at this time, but our sources report that the FBI has taken over the case, and they have yet to issue a public statement. Sources report that Ms. James had been jogging through Rock Creek Park Monday morning when she was attacked by a possible rapist. In the last three months, seven rapes and thirteen attempted rapes or muggings have been reported from the park. Public safety officials urge joggers to run in pairs or groups and be aware of their surroundings."

Brian grinned. Attempted rape. Exactly what he'd wanted. All was right, he'd done his job, he should be the one sitting in the mansion, not in this pit of an apartment waiting for his next job.

Ned called him. "Did you see the news?" Brian asked.

"Good job," Ned said, "except that she was found. The feds are everywhere asking questions. They have no clue, but too many questions make people nervous. Once you take care of the rest of the problems, we're in the clear."

"You should have done it right the first time."

"Fuck off. I have an address for you, to start." He read off the address of a hotel in the shittiest section of DC Brian could imagine.

"That's a pit. What about the others?"

"I'm getting there. It takes time when I have to cover my tracks. But I'm close."

"When this is done, we should go on vacation. Maybe a cruise. That'd be fun, wouldn't it?"

Ned laughed. "Remember when we went to Miami for spring break? I want some more of those wild girls. I had more girls sucking me off that week than the whole previous year." He cleared his throat, then said, "You know what to do?"

"Yes." Brian hated when his brother treated him like a child.

"Wait until nighttime activity settles down, then—"

"Don't tell me how to do it. I didn't fuck up *my* assignment."

"It's not a competition, Bri."

"Good thing for you, 'cause I'd win." He hung up.

It was already midnight. Late enough.

Brian dressed in dark jeans and a black, long-sleeved shirt. He pocketed his favorite knife and left.

The cheap motel was in an all-black neighborhood two miles from his place. He'd stick out if anyone saw him. So he stayed in his car across the street from the motel and watched.

The area was unusually quiet. A gas station on one corner was still open. On the opposite corner were two fast-food joints sharing a wall and small parking lot. A group of gangbangers sat on the tables outside, even though the places were closed. Across from the motel was a section of crummy walk-ups. Half the businesses on the ground floor were boarded up; the other half had bars on their windows and doors. A dive bar next to the motel was open until two, but the parking lot was empty.

Brian had thought that the cooler night would have brought people out of their cramped, stuffy apartments.

He breathed in deeply, then grimaced at the thick, dirty air.

Nearly every light in the motel was off. He watched as a street hooker knocked on an upstairs door, almost directly above the room he wanted. A pasty white guy let her in, the door closed, and Brian wrinkled his nose at what filthy diseases they shared. At least Wendy and the others were clean. Condoms and all that. And they didn't prowl the streets looking to make a quick buck. They were paid a couple hundred dollars for an all-night screw.

Not really fair. All they had to do was lie down and spread their legs and they got two, three, even *five hundred* dollars? He'd heard some of the horny bastards liked kinky shit, but still, a thousand bucks for two nights' work? How'd they get so lucky to land such a cushy job?

He laughed, then put his hand to his mouth to keep from being heard. They'd have no job when they were dead. One of those retribution things, he thought. Like the hand of God or some such thing. Be a whore, be dead. Be a whore no more—that sounded better. It rhymed.

After Brian had seen no one else come or go for several minutes, he got out of his car and strode across the street with purpose. By the time he reached room 119, he had his tools in hand. He'd been worried about making too much noise, but the rumbling AC units masked any sound he made picking the flimsy lock. Slowly, he pushed open the door. Security chain was on. He took out a small, handheld bolt cutter and snipped the thin metal in two.

Brian crept into the motel room and grimaced at the

stink. Dirt and sweat and sex. The air-conditioning unit in the window ran full power, but only moved the stale air around the room. He doubted it had ever been recharged.

He closed the door quickly, quietly, his eyes already adjusted to the night.

One black girl—Nicole—slept in the queen-sized bed, on sheets he doubted had been washed after the last people slept—or screwed—in this room. The motel was a haven for whores. Maybe the black bitch thought she'd blend in, disappear into the streets. But she was mistaken. Ned knew everyone. Ned found people. No one could hide from his brother.

Though Brian was still mad at Ned for screwing up the fire, he was proud, too. Ned would track all of them down before the end of the week. Then Brian would follow up and bam, bam, bam, take them out one at a time. Maybe two at a time. That would be a challenge. Each one would be different, there were lots of ways to kill. Throw the stupid police off, right?

See, he *was* as smart as Ned. Maybe smarter.

The bed upstairs creaked and groaned in the rhythm of the whore and her john. Shit, the walls were thin. He'd have to be extra quiet.

He didn't remember sleeping beauty's last name, and it didn't really matter because she'd be dead and buried soon enough. He didn't go for black chicks, but if he did it would be someone like Nicole. She had those tight braids and beads that made her look exotic, big tits, and a wide mouth. She wasn't girl-next-door pretty—those were the girls Brian preferred—but she was hot.

Nicole moved in her sleep. Did she sense him watching?

He grabbed her long braids. Half-asleep, she jumped up and lurched toward him. Her hands came at him in fists, her face twisted in terror.

Before Nicole was fully awake, he slit her throat.

He immediately dropped her back on the bed. In the sickly yellow light coming through the thin curtains, he saw the blood pour out of her wide, open neck. Wow, it almost looked like it did in the movies, but it smelled awful. Not just blood, but she'd also peed down her leg. The stink made him gag.

"That's disgusting," he said.

He didn't want to see or smell it. He grabbed the corner of the sheet and pulled it over her. He jerked it too hard, and her body fell to the floor with a heavy thud.

He paused, listened. Had the rabbits fucking in the room above him heard anything? He couldn't hear the bed bouncing anymore. Then he heard the guy groan in a weird, animal-like voice, then the bouncing started again, louder and faster than before.

Brian took the time to rinse his knife in the bathroom sink. Even the water in this place was putrid, a pale yellow stream. And warm, like piss. He needed a long, hot shower after being in this hellhole.

He wiped the blade on a towel and picked up Nicole's backpack. Maybe she had a map where all the girls were hiding. He grinned. If she did, he'd be going on a treasure hunt! She probably wasn't that dumb, but she had come back here, so she wasn't too smart, either.

He searched the pockets quickly. A slip of paper had been hastily folded and stuffed in the front of the bulging bag. He unfolded it.

Hotel Potomac

He knew the place well. Could it really be this easy? Did he have time to get over there now?

That wouldn't be smart, and he was the *smart* brother. He needed to confirm the others were there, and if so, what room. How long would they stay? What kind of security did the hotel have?

Those were the *smart* questions that needed to be addressed. He'd head over there at dawn and check it out. Maybe get himself a room for the night.

Something ran across his foot. He jumped, almost yelped. A rat. It scurried to the dead body. Was it going to eat her? Kinda cool, in a gross way.

Then he got an idea.

He was *so* much smarter than Ned.

He grabbed the rat with surprising agility and slammed it against the dresser to stun it.

He was going to have some fun.

CHAPTER EIGHT

Wednesday

To call the Red Light motel seedy may have been cli-chéd, but Lucy Kincaid couldn't think of a better adjective. The motel boasted hourly rates, weekly specials, and was at least a decade overdue for a paint job. Under the sweltering July sun, the exterior appeared a molted shade of green, but up close Lucy realized it was sun-bleached wood.

"What a dump." Noah flashed his badge to the DC cop standing in front of the crime scene tape that blocked off room 119. Six people crowded the room that couldn't be more than three hundred square feet, four wearing bright Windbreakers identifying them as CSU.

"Wait here," the cop said, his husky voice matching his hefty frame. Into his radio he said, "Detective Reid? The feds are here."

A female responded. "Dammit, Taback, keep them

outside, too many people. I'll be there when I get there. Shit, Greg, didn't you—" The radio cut off.

Though the body had been removed, flies buzzed in and out of the doorway, attracted to the smell of dried blood and the lingering scent of decomposing flesh. At noon, the temperature topped ninety-nine degrees with humidity to match, just like yesterday's crime scene. It was on days like this that Lucy missed her hometown of San Diego.

Lucy and Noah stepped away from the door to let two CSU technicians exit with large evidence bags already sealed and labeled, though Lucy couldn't make out the wording.

"We shouldn't even be here." Noah stood straight, hands behind his back, legs slightly apart, looking more like former military than she'd seen him. He watched everything through narrowed eyes, his irritation increasing with the temperature.

When the call came in from DC asking for an assist, Slater assigned Noah. They'd been behind closed doors for ten minutes before Noah walked out, the apparent loser in the argument. He'd hardly spoken on the drive over.

"I thought Josh was fine about you taking the Wendy James murder."

"We're still on it. We're *here*," he jerked his head toward room 119, "because of budget cuts and lack of manpower, both for DC and us. There was no one else Slater could send this morning, unless he called in one of the resident agencies."

All they'd been told was the homicide had special circumstances. A serial murderer, maybe, or perhaps the victim was a federal official, or there was another federal crime component to the case.

Noah continued, "I wanted to be at Stein's meeting with the U.S. attorney this morning. He wouldn't postpone it."

"It's his way of reminding you he's in charge."

A dozen cops filled the parking lot, keeping nosy bystanders behind the crime scene tape. Human curiosity to stop and observe death, pain, and suffering had always saddened and angered Lucy. Did any of them care enough to help someone in trouble? Or was their compassion limited to being horrified only after tragedy?

The creepy sensation of being watched made Lucy shiver, even in this heat. Second-floor guests peered over the railing above her, many shirtless, some smoking, all watching the investigation with unveiled animosity. Watching her. One young punk made a crude gesture when she accidentally caught his eye. She averted her eyes, cheeks flaming, embarrassed and disgusted.

"This crime scene is a mess," Noah muttered.

A sharp, feminine voice snapped, "Sorry to be such an incompetent local."

They turned to face the lead detective who'd been on the other end of Taback's radio. Detective Reid had dark skin with equally dark hair cut close to the scalp. Only the wrinkles around her eyes suggested she was closer to fifty than forty.

She jerked off blue latex gloves and dumped them in a plastic bag, which she handed to another cop. Lucy noticed a long, jagged scar that started midway up her left tricep and disappeared under her sweat-dampened short-sleeved white blouse. Lucy wondered at the circumstances of the nasty injury. Had she gotten it on the job?

"Detective Genie Reid, senior detective. And you're the feds."

"Special Agent Noah Armstrong, analyst Lucy Kincaid. And the crime scene *is* a mess."

"Don't I know fucking know it. Shit!" She pulled out a coin purse from her pocket. "Whenever I get a case like this, I owe my grandson big."

She took two quarters from one side of the coin purse and put them on the other, bulkier, side.

"Your grandson?" Lucy asked, curious.

"I promised Isaiah—he's nine—that I'd stop swearing. On the honor system, I give him a quarter every time I say anything worse than 'damn.' " She looked down at her coin purse. "I started with five dollars in quarters today. He's already earned three-seventy-five and it's not even noon."

Lucy grinned. "You'll be paying his way through college."

"I already have, honey," Genie said. "I told the CSU to clear out." She hollered into the room. "I meant clear out *now,* people!"

"We're nearly done, Detective," one of the men said.

"Has the coroner been here?" Noah asked.

"Come and gone," Genie said. "Good thing because it still reeks of death and the vic was hauled away thirty minutes ago."

They stepped into the room, just the three of them, as the last of the crime scene unit left. Torn wallpaper, the dresser missing one leg, water stains on the sagging ceiling—the room was uninhabitable even before the murder. Lucy couldn't picture anyone willingly staying here.

Desperate people.

What had led the victim to this room last night? How desperate was she? Did she know her killer? Invite him in?

Noah raised his voice over an ineffective, but loud, air-conditioning unit. "What are we looking at here?"

Genie kicked the dented wall appliance. "It doesn't do anything to cool this place down, but every time I turn it off someone turns it back on." She turned the old, chipped black knob from *hi* to *off.* The unit rumbled and clanked as it shut down.

She continued in a normal voice. "Victim was a twenty-year-old hooker named Nicole Bellows. One of the uniforms recognized her, she'd been busted over a year ago. I ran her sheet, she's been clean since. Looked healthy—other than having her throat slit so deep it severed her vocal chords—no obvious drug use, no needle marks. Maybe she had a sugar daddy who got tired of her, or a pimp who thought she wasn't pulling her weight. Or, maybe, a john who can only get his rocks off when he kills."

Lucy's chest tightened at the image.

A john who can only get off when he kills.

All the people who'd stared at her outside fueled her panic. The bystanders. The cops. Watching, waiting for her to crack.

Did they know?

They don't know anything about you. They can't see you anymore. They're outside, you're inside. They aren't watching.

A flash of memory wiped out everything in her vision.

She didn't see the bed, the blood, the filth, the flies. She heard Genie and Noah talking from far away. Her blood rushed to her ears, swirling, pounding. Her knees buckled, but she willed them to work.

Focus, Lucy, get it under control.

She leaned against the wall when her knees refused her command. The memories hit her, one right after the other, in a rapid series of snapshots.

The mattress. The knife. The ropes. The camera's evil eye, watching. Always watching.

focus focus focus

Lucy shifted her body, the urge to run so great she leaned out the door. The sharp edge of splintered wood jolted her back to reality. The colors around her turned vibrant and she closed her eyes.

You are in control. Breathe in. Breathe out.

The mantra was working. Voices brought her back to the present.

Genie was explaining what they'd found in the room, how the body had been positioned. Lucy focused on the detective's crisp cadence.

Noah was looking at her, his face expressionless, but she saw his eyes questioning her. Or was he questioning his own judgment in bringing her here? God, what must he think? It was only a few seconds, had her panic been that obvious?

She forced an I'm-just-fine smile on her face and waved away flies. She didn't know if Noah bought her act.

It's not an act. You're fine. You're in control.

"Except," Genie was saying, "the coroner said no external sign of sexual assault. But that really doesn't matter, because there's something bigger here than a prostitute getting whacked."

"What do you mean?" Noah asked.

Lucy bit her lip to keep from adding a comment about how the detective denigrated the victim. That physical pain helped assuage her panic. She took a deep breath, let it out slowly. She knew, from being raised in a household full of cops and working at the morgue, that cops often needed to compartmentalize. They couldn't look at the victim as a person, lest rage and defeat cloud their judgment. But she still looked at victims as people, and while she didn't condone the prostitution lifestyle, she empathized with the circumstances that put many of these young girls on the streets.

"You need to see it for yourself. Don't think we're going to get much here—too many guests, too little cleaning—but I have my best cops canvassing. Called in the night manager, because the day manager swears he never saw the girl."

"You believe him?"

Genie shrugged. "Eh. We'll see. Don't know that anyone here is going to tell the truth, they don't like cops, don't want to get involved, don't want to squeal." She glanced out the door at the crowd, bitterness sharpening her crisp tone. "Don't matter the crime, they clam up."

Genie handed them sterile gloves from a box on the dresser. Lucy put hers on, the routine familiar and calming. She looked around more carefully now, focusing on what Noah had probably already taken in while she quietly panicked in the doorway, which had nothing to do with the crime scene itself.

The blood-soaked mattress had been grimy even before the murder. "She died here?" Noah asked.

"Found on the floor." Genie indicated a numbered card on the floor next to the bed. "Partly wrapped in a sheet."

Lucy said, "With this much blood, she bled out on the bed."

"Like I said, he cut her so deep he nearly decapitated her."

Genie gestured to the blood spatter on the wall behind the bed, the castoff to the left. "The killer was left-handed, our CSU said. From the trajectory, we deduced they were both standing. He probably killed her, dropped her to the bed, she bled out. The manager who came in and found her swears she was on the floor when he got here and that he didn't touch anything, but who the fuck knows?"

Without comment, she pulled out her coin purse and moved another quarter.

"Why?" Lucy asked rhetorically. She surveyed the room. There were no suitcases or anything personal. "Was there luggage? Toiletries?"

"No suitcase, no purse. Several travel-sized bottles of shampoo, lotion, soap, toothpaste, things like that were in the bathroom. We bagged and tagged them. But no clothing. Just the T-shirt she wore and sandals next to the bed."

"That's odd," Noah said. "She didn't walk in here wearing a T-shirt and nothing else."

"I've seen stranger things," Genie said.

"The killer may have walked off with her belongings." Noah made a note. "But why? Did she have something valuable? Why take her clothes?"

"I've been a cop for twenty-nine years and all I can say is that most killers are stupid," Genie said. "Who knows why they do what they do?"

The motive of the killer and victimology were equally important psychological clues to solve crimes. "If it were rage, I'd expect to see more brutality," Lucy said. "Multiple stab wounds. Blood everywhere. Evidence of struggle. This scene looks too . . ." she scrambled for the right word.

"Efficient," Noah said.

"Exactly."

"When the victim was arrested last year, did she have a pimp?" Noah asked. "Do you have the file on her?"

"Never admitted to having a pimp, but she was probably lying. She wasn't a regular—said she came from Jersey. Cops there have nothing on her, either. Probably lied about that, too."

"Do you have a current address?"

"I'll shoot the file over to you as soon as we're done here, if you want the case."

"You *want* to give the FBI this case?" Noah asked, unable to hide the surprise from his voice.

"Well, not hand it over lock, stock, and barrel, but I'll give you lead if you keep me on board. I have twenty-three active cases I'm working right now, and Lord knows how many inactive files. While I don't like you feds swooping in and taking over whenever you want, I know when I can use help."

"We have a heavy workload, too," Noah said. "I don't know what you think we can do that your more-than-capable department can't accomplish."

"Maybe," Genie said. Lucy watched Genie's eyes drift from Noah to the bloody bed. She could practically hear Genie's thought process.

No one's going to care about one more dead hooker.

Lucy couldn't bear the thought of Nicole Bellows's murder going to the bottom of anyone's workload. A black hooker in a bad area wasn't going to get much attention. Genie was a good cop, but if she didn't get any leads in the next seventy-two hours, the case would be cold, replaced by three others.

"But we *can* handle this," Lucy interjected.

Noah jerked his head toward her, eyes wide, surprised and angry in a way she had never seen him. She realized she'd contradicted him, and she wanted to apologize, but couldn't bring herself to back down. If she didn't fight to prioritize Nicole Bellows's death, who would?

"Genie said the killer left a message, shouldn't we look at it before we just cut loose?" Lucy said, almost tripping over her words to get them out. "This isn't a simple robbery. What if it matches with a cold case? What if the killer is targeting other prostitutes? How many of these young women have to die before people pay attention? Wendy James has the media all over the place, but a black prostitute in the slums isn't going to get an inch of column space, let alone featured on the five o'clock news."

She'd overstepped big-time. Noah's fists tightened just once, but for a man who rarely showed his temper, she noticed.

"I'm sorry," she said, and meant it. "I don't know where that came from."

But she did know exactly where her outrage came from: fear. Fear that victims like Nicole Bellows would be forgotten. Panic that more victims would follow and no one would care. That if they couldn't solve this murder and put the killer in prison, Nicole Bellows would haunt her. Worse, that she couldn't stop the violence.

Noah didn't say anything to Lucy. He turned to Genie. "Where's the message?"

Genie's expression showed her curiosity over the exchange, but she simply replied, "The bathroom. You can't miss it."

Noah walked into the small bathroom first. There wasn't room for both of them, so Lucy waited. When he came out, he said, "I'll call my boss."

He walked out of the motel room without looking at Lucy.

Lucy stepped inside. The stained and bloody pedestal sink had no counter. Inside the cracked basin lay a good-sized rat, dead and gutted. The poor creature's internal organs had been pulled half out of its body, a bloody mess Lucy could barely identify.

The butchered rat was bad enough. But a message had been written in blood on the aged, cracked mirror.

Six blind mice
See how they run

Then Lucy noticed the rat's tail had been cut off.

CHAPTER NINE

Lucy ignored the people hanging around outside the motel, though their numbers seemed to have increased during the fifteen minutes they'd inspected room 119.

Noah had stepped away to talk to Slater, and Lucy hoped he wasn't irrevocably angry.

You shouldn't have jumped down his throat.

Noah had always been supportive of her career, had stood up for her even when her ideas went against protocol. He cared about victims, but didn't wear his compassion on his sleeve like she did.

Six blind mice.

Were there six victims? Was Nicole the first? The last? Would there be more to come?

See how they run.

Lucy had studied killers of all stripes in both criminal psychology coursework and on her own. Her life had brought her face-to-face with evil many times: her cousin's murder when they were seven, her brothers and sister in law enforcement talking bluntly about their jobs, when she was raped at eighteen. Then years of schooling and internships studying crimes and criminals. She had a gift—or a curse—for getting into the heads of both killers and victims.

This killer was taunting someone, but the message didn't seem to be directed at police. It was almost an internal thought on his part, a private joke.

Six blind mice.

The children's rhyme only had three mice, so *six* seemed especially important, a signal to law enforcement or a threat. A rat could mean the victim had said something to police. Children's rhymes were singsong, and in this context seemed taunting. Why cut off the tail?

Lucy played the song in her head.

Three blind mice, three blind mice
See how they run, see how they run
They all ran after the farmer's wife
Who cut off their tails with a carving knife
Did you ever see such a sight in your life
As three blind mice.

Did the tail have any significance to the killer? Or did he cut off the tail just because of the song? Had he planned to kill the rat, did he bring it with him, or was the act an afterthought? Did he intend to mislead the cops, to cloud the motive?

The scene didn't feel like a serial killer to Lucy, but she couldn't articulate why. No rape. No rage. Clean kill, a message. Uncovering *why* Nicole Bellows was killed would lead them directly to the killer, Lucy was certain about that.

The killer didn't rape his victim. They may have had

consensual sex, and Lucy wanted to go to the morgue to get a jump on any potential evidence. Time was always a critical factor in a homicide investigation.

Noah approached Lucy. "Don't contradict me in public."

Lucy's stomach flipped. He was still angry with her. She needed to make this right. "I'm really sorry. I shouldn't have said any of that. I know you care, I didn't mean to imply you didn't."

"It stung," he said simply, then moved on. "You told Detective Reid that we can handle the case. It's not your call." Noah was stern. "Just remember, I'm the FBI agent, you're the analyst."

His words were true, but he'd never been so harsh. He'd always treated her like a partner, not a novice.

"I understand," she said, hoping she kept the hurt from her tone.

He continued. "You're going to be liaison between Genie Reid and me. You want this, you got it. If there's anything that points to a serial murderer, any verified leads, we'll reassess whether we officially step in. But right now, this is a DC metro case and we're observing."

"Thank you."

"Don't thank me. Josh Stein wants you off Wendy James, and this is the only way you're not going to be chained to your desk for the next three weeks. I'm going to talk to Detective Reid and make sure she's satisfied with this arrangement."

He strode away and spoke quietly to Genie.

She wished she could take it all back. She didn't want to work with the DC police, she wanted to work with Noah. She'd already learned so much from him, every day she felt she was better prepared not only to start the

Academy, but to be an agent. When they had downtime, he told her what to expect in classes, some of the tricks, how to maneuver through the bureaucracy. Though her sister-in-law was an instructor at Quantico and also helpful, Kate had been a recruit fifteen years ago. A different time, a different program. Noah graduated less than four years ago.

Their friendship had just taken a big hit, and it was her fault. She had to find some way to repair the damage.

Genie and Noah approached. "Welcome aboard," Genie said. "Agent Armstrong says you're with me, and I'm glad for the help, even temporary—you're still deputized, right? He said you'd come from the Arlington Sheriff's Department?"

She nodded, wishing she knew what Noah had said to Genie about her. "I worked there a year ago, yes."

"And you worked at the morgue, too? Then you get to head down there and talk to the coroner when we're done here, because I hate that place and I'm glad to have someone to pass it off on."

Genie continued. "My guys found a backpack with blood in the trash. We're comparing it to the vic. Also, the CSU says the door wasn't forced. The lock was easy to break, and the killer used bolt cutters on the chain. The doors are so weak he could have kicked it in."

"But that would have made noise," Lucy said. "If he had to break in, that means he wasn't a john. He goes in quietly, so as not to wake his victim, closes the door, turns on lights?" She glanced back at room 119's window, noted that she could almost see through the flimsy curtains. "Probably enough light from outside."

"Good guess. And the switch by the door is broken. Only the lamp on the nightstand works."

"So he comes in, grabs the victim off the bed, and kills her."

"Or she hears something and gets up—" Noah suggested.

"But he's already inside, grabs her and kills her before she can scream."

"Either way," Genie said, "it was fast. He went in with a purpose."

"He had to have known her." Lucy frowned, looking over at the room, but not focusing on any detail. "I don't know."

"Explain."

"It's not random. She was a target."

"Target?" Noah said. "Interesting choice of words."

"He meant to kill Nicole Bellows, not just any prostitute."

"Possible," Noah said, "but that's for you to run down." He glanced at his watch. "Are the managers here? I need to get to a briefing."

"In the office." Genie waved her hand in the general direction.

"Any cooler inside?" Lucy asked, pulling her sticky blouse from her skin.

"No."

Genie was right. The motel lobby's air-conditioning was no more effective than the motel room's.

The manager had a small office behind glass. Posted inside the glass was a sign with their rates: $25/hour; $69/night; $249/week. Maid service was an additional $20/day.

Genie motioned for the two managers to come out of the room. "I swear, these two are idiots," she muttered.

The night manager, Ray, was dark, wiry, and disheveled, with a cigarette hanging out of the corner of his mouth. The day manager, Buddy, was twice the size, but deferred to Ray.

"Buddy says room one-nineteen got whacked?" Ray said. He stared at Lucy through half-lidded eyes. She resisted the overwhelming urge to look down and make sure her blouse was buttoned.

Genie stepped forward before Noah could say a word. "Who you trying to impress, Ray? *Whacked*. Shit, you're pissing me off. Took you fucking long enough to get in. Buddy called you *three hours* ago. Probably called you before he called us. Makes me think you have something to hide."

"Hey, Genie babe, we go way back, no need to get all hostile."

"You 'babe' me again, I'm taking you to jail and losing the paperwork."

"*Shee*-it, Detective, you got no sense of humor."

"What I have is a dead girl, I want to know who did it. Do I need to ask for security tapes?"

"Ask, but I don't have any. You know that."

"Nice fucking place you run." Genie said. "When did Nicole Bellows check in?"

"Nicole? She didn't give me that name. Gave me N. Smith." He chortled. "But I recognized her."

"Recently?"

"Naw, last year. I say, 'Babe, you haven't been around lately.' She says, 'Just give me a room.' I should have kicked her to the curb, but she had cash, paid for a week, and was willing to wait an hour for me to flip the room."

"Did she say anything else?"

"I asked how she been, how she doin', what can she do for me, you know—" He grinned.

Noah cleared his throat. "When did she come in?"

"Yesterday. Early, like six A.M. It had been a busy night, most of the rooms were still occupied. So they had to wait."

"They?" Noah said.

"N. Smith and her sister." He snorted. "Hardly. Nicole is a foxy black bitch with—" He cut himself off when Noah's jaw tightened. The tension was hotter than the temperature.

"Her sister was white as a ghost. Pretty, I guess, if you like your girls young and scrawny."

"How young?" Lucy asked. Two girls but only one victim. She feared what might have happened to the younger girl.

"Teen. Maybe eighteen."

"Really?" Genie said.

Ray shrugged.

"Don't fuck around, tell me how old you think she was. I'm not going to arrest you for screwing her, but I will arrest you for obstruction of justice and being an asshole."

"*Maybe* sixteen. I didn't screw her. Didn't say a word. She followed Nicole around like a puppy."

"Describe her," Noah said.

"White. Dark brown hair down to her shoulders. About yea high." He put his hand to his chin. He wasn't five and a half feet, which put the girl at just about five feet. "And like I said, scrawny. I don't think she was ninety pounds wet."

"Did you get a name?" Genie asked.

"Barely saw her."

Noah asked, "Did you see them after they checked in yesterday?"

"Not the white chick. The babe—um, Nicole—came and went a couple times. Brought in food."

Buddy interrupted for the first time. "I—I—I saw the girl. Yesterday, when I was flipping a room. She was waiting outside room one-nineteen, then the black girl came out and they left."

"On foot?"

"Yeah. They didn't have a car. Not that I saw."

"What time was that?" Noah asked.

"Um, four maybe?"

"Four in the afternoon?"

"Yeah. Maybe a little earlier."

"Did you see anyone going in or out of their room? Anyone lurking in the parking lot?"

"Nope," Ray said. "It's been quiet until now."

They walked outside. Genie said, "I got my team canvassing the businesses on the street to see who has security cams that actually work. Plus, the gas station on the corner—the owner of the chain is a good guy, he has decent security. Might not know what we're looking at, but if we get a suspect, maybe we can put him in the vicinity."

Genie continued. "What do you think about the second girl?"

"There were no signs of a second person. Maybe she was gone when the killer came in. Maybe she returned and bolted when she saw her friend."

"Maybe she set her up," Genie said.

"A sixteen-year-old ninety-pound kid?" Lucy said.

"I've seen stranger things."

"Or the killer could have taken her," Lucy added.

"We don't have any evidence that he did."

"And we don't have evidence that he didn't." The whole scene felt unreal to Lucy. They couldn't discount the fact that there had been two young women in the room, but only evidence that one had been killed. "Either way, we have an unknown minor in danger. We need to find her."

"Either she wasn't there, she was an accomplice, or she's been kidnapped," Noah said. "You'll have access to our lab and database, Lucy can expedite the paperwork. I need to go. You good here?"

Lucy nodded. "Thank you."

He didn't say anything, only gave her an odd look, then left.

"Ouch," Genie said.

"I'm so sorry you had to witness that."

"I admire your drive. He'll get over it, he respects you."

"Not anymore." And that is what really hurt. Lucy didn't want to lose Noah's friendship.

"He does. He thought he had to do a hard sell to get me to work with you, but you had me sold before we walked out of the motel room. It's not like you're an untrained crime writer on a perpetual ride-along." She laughed. "Damn, I love that television show, even if they get procedure all wrong."

Lucy smiled. She had no idea what Genie was talking about because she didn't watch television.

"Seriously," Genie said, "you have more creds than most of our rookies. Let's go hit up the vic's last known address and see what we learn, then I'll drop you at the morgue. That's not far from FBI headquarters, right?"

"A few blocks."

"I'll work the hookers," Genie said. "They're not going to talk to a white fed, but they'll shoot straight with me."

They walked toward Genie's unmarked police sedan. "Don't forget to give your grandson another dollar-twenty-five."

"You counted?"

"You were too angry with those two jerks to do it yourself."

Genie sighed and took out her coin purse. "He'll be going to Harvard at this rate."

CHAPTER TEN

Nicole's last known address was only six blocks from where she'd been murdered.

The neighborhood was what Lucy would classify as a slum. One of the worst in DC, heavily segregated. While most neighborhoods were mixed, this one was one hundred percent black. Lucy definitely stood out, and not in a good way.

It seemed areas like this were worse in the summer, when the humidity made the overflowing Dumpsters smell ten times worse; when the heat shimmered off the sidewalks and streets; when the people slumped shirtless in any shade they could find from the sweltering sun.

Maybe because of the heat, no one bothered them as they walked from Genie's unmarked but obvious police sedan to the doorway of a four-story apartment building that dominated the short block. The window AC units made the entire building groan.

Genie buzzed the manager first, but the buzzer was broken and there was meager security on the main door.

Genie opened it with a shove and they knocked on the first door, 1A, with

AN G R

in broken letters underneath. "Hope that's not foreshadowing his mood," Lucy said, gesturing toward the door. Behind the door a television roared with canned laughter.

"I really hate this neighborhood," Genie muttered. "I pull a case here at least twice a week."

The manager was a rotund black woman in her sixties. She was dressed in a blinding bright pink muumuu with green flowers.

"What do the cops want with who today?" she asked.

Genie showed the manager Nicole's driver's license photo. "Nicole Bellows, four-B."

"Don't live here."

She started to close the door.

"But she used to," Genie said.

The woman stepped heavily into the hall and shut the door behind her, though Lucy could still hear the laugh track of a mindless sitcom. "Let's see her."

Genie showed the manager the photo. The woman put on her glasses and stared. "She's one of the hookers. Moved out back before Thanksgiving. Found herself a sugar daddy, I suppose."

"Do you know who?"

"Don't ask, don't tell, right?" She laughed at her own joke. "All I know is she caught up on her back rent and gave me two weeks. That covered her room through Halloween, I think. I haven't seen her since."

"How long did she live here?"

She shrugged. "Maybe a year. Little longer." She

glared at them. "She wasn't a bad girl, you know. Never brought trouble here. No drugs. I catch one of my tenants with drugs, they don't get no second chance. Drugs are killing my people, I don't tolerate that garbage."

"Nicole wasn't a problem, then," Genie said.

"Nope. Didn't think she'd stay as long as she did."

"Did she have any friends in the building?"

"Dunno. But I remember one friend, came by a couple times. I told her once, don't come here at night, it wasn't safe for a rich white girl like her."

Lucy's interest was piqued. "Do you remember her name?"

"Never introduced. She didn't belong here. I think she was in Nicole's line of work, if you know what I mean."

"Are any of Nicole's friends still in the building?"

"Four-C. Cora Fox. Been here for years. Nosy bitch, too."

"Is she here now, or are we wasting our time walking up four flights?"

"She's here, but you won't find her upstairs. Coolest place in the building is the basement. I put in some fans, bring in some blocks of ice."

Lucy's surprise must have showed on her face.

The manager said, "You wouldn't understand, *chica*."

Genie grinned. "Nice meeting you—?"

"Meggie. Meggie Prince."

"Thank you, ma'am," Lucy said, not understanding what Genie found humorous. She was still stunned at being called *chica*. Being half Cuban, she could pass for Hispanic or Caucasion, but growing up in San Diego, she blended in and rarely thought about skin color. That sounded trite, but it was the way she'd been raised.

Lucy and Genie took the stairs down to the basement. Support beams six feet apart seemed to hold up the building, and the ceiling was so low Lucy could reach up and touch it without stretching. But it was definitely twenty degrees cooler down here. In each corner of the long, narrow space was a big metal tub with a block of melting ice. A fan blew on the ice, cooling the air.

There were about two dozen people lounging about talking or watching one of three televisions, all of which had the same sitcom that the manager had been watching. Half got up and left when Genie and Lucy walked in. Genie stopped each woman and asked if she was Cora.

Finally, from the far corner, a skinny middle-aged woman who'd been watching them from the minute they entered said, "I'm Cora." She narrowed her eyes. "I don't like cops."

Genie said, "And I don't like attitude, but here we are."

"I don't rat on friends."

"I'm not asking you to. I'm here about Nicole Bellows."

"Well, seeing that Nicole ain't my friend, whaddya want to know?"

"She's your neighbor?" Lucy asked.

"*Former* neighbor. That stuck-up whore moved out last year. October, maybe. Didn't the super tell you that?"

"Yes. She also said you knew her."

Cora shrugged. "As much as anyone could. She thought she was better than us, like her shit don't stink."

"It doesn't anymore," Genie said. "She's dead."

Cora put her hands up and leaned back. "Hey, I didn't know."

"We're trying to retrace her steps. This is the last address we have on her."

"There's been a lot of steps between then and now."

"So send us in the right direction. Do you know where she moved? Did she give you an address?"

"Nope. All I knew was what she told me, that she was moving to a house with a yard. Thought she was all that, you know? I said to her, found a sucker? A pimp? You know, trying to get the truth 'cuz I knew she was still hooking. And she says, no, she was making more money working less hours. I told her she was full of shit." She shrugged.

"You didn't believe her?" Lucy asked.

"I did," Cora admitted. "But I thought she was into something. She aspired to be a high-paid call girl. I said to her, no one's going to be paying top dollar for a two-bit whore. But she cleaned up, quit snorting—all her profits used to go up her nose."

Maybe Meggie Prince didn't know everything that went on in her building, or she lied a good game.

"I remember when she was in withdrawal," Cora continued. "Her white bitch friend stayed here to keep Nicole straight. Never thought I'd see that goody-two-shoes stay overnight in this slum, but I guess people surprise you sometimes."

Lucy asked, "Her friend? Does her friend have a name?"

"No idea. She was brave, I tell you, 'cause white girls don't do well this side of town, know what I mean? But she stuck with Nicole for three days."

"You remember what she looked like?"

"Blonde. Shorter than Nicole. Skinny. Dressed like a rich bitch slumming—new jeans, worn T-shirt, but it was designer shit all the way, and clean. She was sparkly clean." She rolled her eyes and stuck gum in her mouth, cracking it loudly.

"And after this slumber party?" Genie pressed.

"They left. Both of them. Nicole gave her notice, but I don't think she came back. Put all her stuff in a couple of boxes and disappeared."

"And you have no idea where they went."

"I said, a house with a yard. That's all I know."

"And you haven't seen her since?"

There was something in Cora's eyes that made Lucy think she had seen her. "Maybe not here," she added, "but in the area." When Cora didn't immediately answer, she pushed. "She was murdered a few blocks from here."

"Cora, this is important," Genie said. "Have you seen Nicole Bellows anytime in the nine months since she moved out?"

Cora rubbed the sweat off her nose. "Yeah, I did. I saw her at the Big Boy two blocks over. Last night, ten or so. I work there part-time. I thought she was walking the streets again, but she wasn't dressed for it. She was wearing a hoodie and it was a hundred fucking degrees. I cook in the back, wouldn't have even looked twice except for the way she was dressed. Went up to her and said, Nic, long time, and she said, just passing through. That's it. No how's you been, nothing. She looked scared when I said her name, that was my first thought. Maybe some guy was hassling her or something."

"Was she alone?"

Cora shrugged. "Far as I know."

Genie said, "If you see the blonde, let us know."

They thanked Cora for her time, gave her their cards, and left.

"Hiding out," Genie said. "Going back to her old neighborhood where she'd blend in."

"Her description couldn't have been more vague," Lucy mumbled.

"People here keep their heads low. The law-abiding citizens don't want any trouble, so they don't make waves. Nine months ago? I'd say that's a pretty good memory. Nicole hanging with a young, rich blond girl. I'd say drugs, except knowing what business Nicole was in I'm leaning toward call girl."

"As opposed to prostitute?"

"Nicole walked the streets, but if she was smart and clean, she might have found an underground escort service. You know how many girls for hire there are in a town like this?"

"Unfortunately, I have some idea."

"Sex clubs, escort services, streetwalkers. Doesn't matter the means, there's a lot of men willing to pay for sex." They got back into Genie's car. "I'll put out some feelers, but I think we'll come back with some pictures for Ms. Cora Fox and see what she remembers. I'm going to drop you off at the morgue. Call me if you learn anything important."

Miles West was the deputy coroner assigned to the Nicole Bellows death investigation.

"Twice in two days after no word from you in months," Miles teased her.

"I'm just lucky." With cutbacks, there were fewer investigators with the coroner's office, and senior staff like Miles West took more cases because their experience helped them close faster.

"This is an FBI case, too?" Miles asked.

"We're working with DC on this one. It's a bit unusual." She didn't feel the need to explain her odd position on this case. Instead, she showed Miles a photo of the dead rat and written message.

Miles closed his eyes, slowly shaking his head. "Retirement is looking better and better. Want my job?"

"Have one."

"Well, there's a job here if you want it. We miss you."

"I kind of miss the place too." Working at the morgue had been oddly comforting for Lucy. The atmosphere was calm, the people professional, and though every day was different, every process had an established routine. Every corpse was a mystery to be solved, whether the person died naturally, accidentally, or by violence.

Miles pulled the paperwork on Nicole Bellows. "Sheila's team is prepping the body now. Prostitute, right?"

"We don't know that she was still working," Lucy said.

"Not saying it to be judgmental, Kincaid. No one deserves to die like that."

"But it's important that we find out definitively. I was hoping you could put in a good word and let me observe the autopsy."

He laughed again. "I don't need to put in a good word. Let's get you suited up. Like every morgue in the country, we're shorthanded. Your pathology certification is still valid. You worked with Sheila before."

Lucy remembered Sheila. The morgue had high turnover among assistant pathologists because of low pay, budget cuts, and internships, but the senior pathologists tended to stay once they carved out a niche. As if to prove her point, when Sheila walked into the scrub room, the two assistants—one male, one female, both young—were unfamiliar to Lucy.

Miles said, "Sheila, you have an extra set of eyes. Your slit throat is a federal case now."

"How've you been?" Sheila asked. She introduced Ann and Ben, two interns from the biology department at GWU. Lucy had been in their position not long ago.

They chatted while they scrubbed, and Lucy immediately felt comfortable in the familiar surroundings.

The ritual of an autopsy was almost soothing. The victim's body had already been weighed, photographed, and cleaned—in a homicide, they scraped under the fingernails, processed the clothing, combed the hair, did everything to extract possible trace evidence, all of which was sealed and stored in an airtight chamber. Evidence with blood or wet biological matter was first dried to prevent mold and other contaminations.

The victim had been found in panties and a tank top, standard sleep attire for many women in a heat wave. Both were soaked in blood and now hung in the drying unit.

There was no doubt that Nicole Bellows had bled out from a severed artery in her neck when her killer slit her throat, but in a homicide, they needed to be thorough and determine if she'd been raped or beaten or drugged first. Biological trace evidence could lead to her killer; the coroner and forensic labs were an essential part of the investigative team, and working at the morgue last year had given Lucy a new, deeper appreciation for this vital part of homicide investigation.

Lucy stood aside and let Sheila do her job. The process was standard and they used a checklist to ensure they covered all their bases—if the case went to trial, everything they did now mattered that much more.

While Sheila and her team handled the body, Lucy inspected the sealed evidence on the far table. Nothing jumped out at her as significant.

She took out her phone and scrolled through the pictures she'd taken at the crime scene.

Wendy James's killer had also left a message.

There was no obvious connection between Wendy James and Nicole Bellows, but that the killer of each had left a message was definitely odd.

There was a singsong quality to the first one.

And this guilty whore don't cry no more

And the second was definitely the killer's version of a nursery rhyme.

Six blind mice, see how they run

"From the angle of the wound," Sheila said, jolting Lucy from her thoughts, "I can say fairly confidently that the killer was taller than the victim." She tapped the chart. "She measured at five foot six. I can't tell you how tall the killer was, but definitely several inches taller."

"What if she was on her knees?" Lucy asked.

Sheila considered. "No, because the cut would most likely have an upward angle, especially at the end. This was straight across. Non-serrated blade. He tilted her head back with such force that he broke several capillaries in her throat. Put the knife on the soft area just below her chin and sliced deeply, without hesitation, severed her trachea and her carotid artery. She died immediately from massive blood loss."

"There was no obvious sexual assault at the scene," Lucy said.

"No evidence of recent intercourse, vaginal, anal, or oral. But I found something else you might find interesting."

Lucy looked at the table. Nicole's chest and abdomen were exposed. Lucy stared at a perfectly formed fetus.

"She was pregnant."

"I'm guessing fourteen weeks. I'm going to run standard tests and DNA. You get a suspect, I can tell you if he's the father."

"That's a solid motive," Miles said, making note.

Motive maybe—but why leave the rat in the sink? Nicole being pregnant didn't play into the message on the mirror.

Lucy stepped out of the room to text Noah about Nicole's pregnancy, then remembered she was working with DC police on this case. She sent Genie the text message instead, then made a note to herself to write up a report for Noah at the end of the day.

When she returned to the autopsy station, Sheila had just finished closing the body.

"We're done here," she said. "You know what I know, but I'll write up the official report, pending labs."

Sheila stripped off her gloves and tossed them in a bio-bag. Her assistant started the process of cleaning the body so it could be placed in cold storage pending release.

Who wanted you dead? Who were you running from? The baby's father?

Maybe Noah had been right and this case was a common homicide. But while she had the case, she would unearth the truth. The dead may not be able to speak, but their life and death told a story.

Ben motioned for Sheila to come over. "Do you know what this is?" He lifted Nicole's left hand. Her skin was dark brown, but her palm was several shades lighter. In the center were three numbers, very faint.

"She wrote something on her hand," Sheila said. "A locker combination? Date?"

Lucy tilted her head. *565.*

She looked more closely. "I think there's more here. Can you bring out the ink so we can tell?" There was just a hint of the other numbers, so faint and incomplete she couldn't make out anything but the 565.

"Maybe—but it'll take some time."

"I have an idea," Lucy said. She opened a supply drawer and retrieved a flashlight. "Cut the lights, please," she said.

She put the flashlight on the backside of the victim's hand. The high-wattage bulb illuminated the area.

"It's a phone number." She tried to contain her excitement. The phone number was faint, but Lucy read it out loud.

555-6598

She left to call Genie. They might have their first break and the case wasn't even a day old.

CHAPTER ELEVEN

Lucy finished typing her report for Noah on the Nicole Bellows homicide. She could have done it from home, but she liked being at FBI headquarters in the evening when the office ran on minimal staff.

She'd heard there was a debriefing in the conference room about the Wendy James investigation, and she wanted to be there, but Noah hadn't invited her to attend. She didn't know what had happened when the cyber crimes unit came in to inspect the wiring and hidden room. She wanted to know what they'd found, if they had uncovered evidence of blackmail.

Her relationship with Noah was strained, and she still didn't understand why Josh Stein was so opposed to her involvement. She'd even e-mailed an apology, but he hadn't responded.

If she hadn't questioned Crowley, they may never have known about the executive apartment or the hidden room. At least not this early in the investigation.

She had to put it aside. Hard as it was, it wasn't her

case. She had an equally compelling assignment with Detective Genie Reid. She liked the detective, and was learning a lot watching how she observed a scene and questioned witnesses.

With that in mind, Lucy proofread her report to make sure she hadn't forgotten anything, then she e-mailed it to Noah. She gathered her things and walked to the front of the building, where the guard buzzed her out.

"Hold up," Matt Slater called from behind her.

She waited, a bit nervous, and glanced around looking for Noah. He wasn't with Slater.

"I wanted to talk to you if you have a minute."

"Of course. Your office?"

"I'll walk you out."

Lucy caught herself biting her lip. She stopped, but her stomach tightened. What did Slater want? To reprimand her?

"I'll cut to the chase," Slater said as soon as they stepped outside, out of earshot from the guard and any lingering staff. "I didn't like the idea of letting you work in the field. You should have been cooling your heels at home or working another job when there was the delay getting you into the Academy. Don't think I don't know you have friends in high places."

Her heart pounded in her chest. She almost couldn't hear herself speak, her voice sounding like she was at the far side of a long tunnel. "I didn't ask for any special privileges."

"I don't know whether you did or didn't. You're smart, and you'll make a good agent once you get more training under your belt, but I wanted to make sure you understood something that I doubt Noah has made clear."

Though terrified by what he might say, Lucy didn't break eye contact.

Slater said, "If you screw up, it's on Noah. He's given you a lot more leeway than I would have. I wouldn't have let you out of the office."

"You're the SSA. If you wanted me at a desk, I would have stayed at a desk." She was nervous, but at the same time, she wanted him to know that she was happy just to have a position.

"I don't know that you would have." He sounded serious.

"I'm good at following orders. I'm sorry about what happened with Agent Stein after the Crowley interview, but—"

"Forget that. Josh has his own way of investigating, he gets the job done. He doesn't make a lot of friends, but again, he gets results. The problem is that you aren't even an agent, but you act like one. It's making some people in the office uncomfortable.

"You're very good at getting your way," Slater continued. He stepped forward. "Lucy, I'm not upset with you or your performance. You've been an asset. Noah explained it was your diligence that landed us the biggest break in this case, the hidden room at the Park Way building. But the situation with Josh illustrates the primary problem with having you in the field, which I explained to Noah months ago."

"I don't see wh—"

"Stein is your superior," Slater interrupted. "I'm your superior. Noah is your superior. Why were you even raising a question during the interview? Noah tried to smooth it over, then when that failed, he gave you a case with DC Metro. Do you understand the limbs Noah is bouncing off for you? You're not going to get another chance. You screw up again, you're not only out of the field, you're out of the office.

"Remember, you're an analyst, and that analyst title is thin, at best. Which means Noah will take the heat if the case goes south and you're involved. So think twice before you do *anything*. There is a chain of command for a reason. Use it."

"I understand," she said quietly. She didn't want Noah to get into any professional trouble because of her, either.

He rested his hand on her shoulder. "Like I said, you have a good head and good sense. You'll make a fine agent someday."

Lucy forced a smile while she waited for Slater to go back inside. Her chest felt like it was going to split in half.

Do not cry. Do not cry.

Matt Slater was right. It didn't matter how much experience she had, she wasn't an agent.

She practically ran to the Metro station, wishing for the first time she had a car so she could sit behind the wheel and cry in private.

"Sorry I'm late," Matt Slater said as he walked into the conference room.

Noah caught his eye, but couldn't read Matt's expression. He knew his boss was angry with what had transpired yesterday, but Noah thought he'd fixed the problem. He wished he hadn't had to pull Lucy off the Wendy James case, especially now. Her insight would be invaluable.

Yet, she had frozen yesterday in the linen closet. Noah didn't think she'd even noticed she didn't move for more than a minute. Just stood there, hunched over, staring at the back wall, not doing *anything*.

Noah knew she still battled panic attacks on occasion, but until now he'd never seen it while she was working. But last night, the brief hesitation, and then this morning at the Red Light Motel it was obvious.

Frankly, he was concerned. If she panicked at the wrong time, it could put the lives of fellow agents in jeopardy.

He adjusted his seat. He was also worried about Lucy, personally. Working with her he realized she put the weight of every case, no matter how big or small, on her shoulders. She internalized it, rather than compartmentalizing.

He had asked Slater to bring Dr. Hans Vigo, a forensic psychologist and assistant director from national headquarters, in for a preliminary psych analysis on Wendy James's killer, but he also had an ulterior motive. Hans Vigo had been the one to clear Lucy for the Academy, after she failed her first psych profile. Noah needed to know that she wasn't going to have a breakdown on the job. Not just for his safety, or her future partner, but for *her*.

Miriam Douglas and Henry Archer from cyber crimes were in the room along with Josh Stein, Slater, and Hans. Noah pushed aside his thoughts about Lucy.

Slater asked, "What's the word on apartment seven-ten?"

Henry said, "The cables and wires are consistent with audio and video recording equipment, but we found no equipment anywhere in either seven-ten or Wendy

James's apartment. We sent her laptop to the lab as a priority, hoping they can rebuild deleted files, but our examination indicates they were deleted by a high-end erase program. It's doubtful we can get anything from it."

"What about other apartments in the building?" Slater asked.

Noah was about to respond when Stein said, "I'm working with the U.S. Attorney's office on warrants for all executive apartments, but the management company is balking. We asked, they refused, we got the warrant for number seven-ten"—he shot Noah a dirty look— "*after* we nearly blew the case searching without one."

Noah wasn't going to let that comment stand. "We had the express *written* permission of the manager to search that apartment, and the general warrant for James's residence covered our subsequent searches."

"As soon as you found the first hidden compartment you should have sealed the room and contacted me."

Stein wasn't budging, but neither was Noah. "We didn't know what was in there until we found it."

"If this case gets blown because of an illegal search, I'll have your badge."

Slater put up his hands. "No one is stripping badges. Precedent allows management to give access, and we got the warrant before a full and complete search. There was no fishing on this one, it's a gray area, but the law is on our side."

"I want Crowley. We have to do this right," Stein said.

"If Wendy James was making sex tapes, that opens up a whole array of possible suspects," Noah said.

"Who? We have no evidence of other affairs, other than Congressman Bristow who, by the way, has also lawyered up." Stein was turning red in frustration.

Hans spoke up. "I think we're all missing an important component here. Did Ms. James clear out the apartment? Was she the only one who used it?"

Slater asked, "Where are we with the rentals?"

Miriam spoke up. "The last lease was for one week, the governor of Oregon. That was over a month ago. Before that was ten days for an environmental protection organization that was lobbying Congress, before that a one-month stay, the wife of an alternative energy executive, then a long dry period. In February, a union representative stayed for two weeks. I'm digging deeper, seeing if any of them had meetings with Congressman Crowley or Congressman Bristow. We should send agents to interview each of them, none are local."

"Miriam," Slater said, "contact each local agency and brief them. We need the interviews stat."

Hans said, "Tell them to go in easy, no hint that we think they were recorded. I suspect if they were being blackmailed, as soon as the Park Way apartment is mentioned they'll show signs of distress. Tell them to be on the lookout for not only the standard signs, but subtle clues. Anyone who acts suspicious or nervous, we'll look at harder."

"But Crowley's the one who's sitting in Congress and admitted to having an affair with her!" Stein exclaimed. "It all comes back to him."

"Who tipped off the media?" Hans asked. "Maybe Wendy tried to blackmail him and he didn't bite, so she released the photographs."

"The pictures weren't taken in seven-ten," Miriam said. "We believe they were taken at a local hotel, and we're working on finding the exact location."

"Let me know," Slater said.

"None of that means Crowley didn't kill her—or have her killed," Stein said.

Noah had had it with Stein. "Why do you want him so badly? What if he's just an asshole who cheated on his wife?"

"Get off my case," Stein said.

Hans intervened. "Crowley is arrogant and didn't want to be caught in the affair—or, if it was blackmail, he didn't want anyone to know, but he had no reason to kill Wendy James."

"Except for what she was going to tell the U.S. Attorney this week," Stein said.

"But you don't know what she was going to say," Hans said. "She could have been nervous about being interviewed. Her personal life had just been exposed by the media and she lost her job because of it. She was under a great deal of stress, and no grand jury is going to take that one interview where she lied about an affair with another congressman as evidence that she had some damning information against Crowley."

"It's too much of a coincidence," Stein said.

"It seems that way, and I'm not saying that her murder *isn't* connected in some way to Crowley, but his alibi cleared and so far his finances have held up and there's no evidence he hired someone to kill her. It could be if she *did* blackmail him that *he* released the pictures so as not to be under her thumb."

Noah hadn't thought of that angle, but it made sense. "And all the lies about the affair, the subsequent apology—?"

"To make it seem like a common affair, when it was anything but."

"What about the murder itself?" Noah asked Hans.

"It doesn't look like a professional hit to me."

"What do you think it is, Dr. Vigo?" Slater asked.

Hans flipped through the crime scene photos. "I've only given a cursory glance at the report. The killer may not have known her, but he knew *of* her. He may have spoken to her on occasion, but he wasn't close to her. I don't think this was a random crime, it was definitely premeditated. There's something odd about it, but I can't put my finger on it."

"What about the way she was strangled?" Noah asked. He glanced at Stein. He couldn't mention Lucy's name without getting Stein's panties in a twist, so he kept his comment vague. "The coroner said she was strangled from behind."

Hans stared at the photo of the victim's throat. "That is odd. I don't think I've seen this before. And she wasn't raped?"

Before Noah could speak, Stein said, "Attempted."

"There's no evidence of an attempted rape," Noah said.

"Her pants were pulled down and he wrote on her ass," Stein snapped.

"Respect for the dead, Agent Stein," Hans snapped.

Stein mumbled an apology, then continued. "My guess is that Crowley hired a lowlife to kill her. If she attempted to blackmail him, that gives him motive. The killer got his hands on her and got horny, wanted to rape her, but lost his nerve."

"If someone like Crowley hired a professional hit man, James would either never be found, or her death would be made to look like an accident," Hans said.

"Or," Stein pushed, "a random crime."

Hans conceded that point. "Possibly."

"We have no other directions to go in."

Slater leaned back in his chair. "Nothing on the security cams, nothing useful on her computer—yet. Several potential suspects to interview based on room seven-ten. She may have been juggling more than one guy."

"Multiple affairs," Hans said. "Have you identified any of the other men, other than Bristow?"

"Bristow is single, no big scandal for him to be sleeping around," Slater said. "No one has come forward, and she didn't keep records."

"That's another odd thing," Noah said. "We couldn't find a calendar in her apartment or on her computer."

"Hmm." Hans looked again at the photo. "We definitely need more information. If there was blackmail involved. If there were other men. If there was a financial or other motive."

"Financial is easy to track," Stein said.

"If not financial, then what? If not for money, why blackmail a congressman?"

"Votes!" Stein slapped his palm on the table. "I'm on it."

"It's right up your alley," Slater said.

"Can I go?"

"I think we're done here."

"Agreed," Hans said. "But I can tell you two things about the killer. First, this isn't the first time he's killed. And second, this is not a sexual crime."

"You're sure?" Stein asked as he stood at the door, rolling on the balls of his feet. Noah cringed. Hans Vigo was one of the sharpest, most experienced forensic profilers in the FBI. While Hans appreciated thoughtful analysis and disagreement, Stein's flip comment was inappropriate and disrespectful.

"Yes, Agent Stein, I'm certain," Hans said.

Stein was properly repentant. "Thank you, Dr. Vigo." He quickly walked out.

Miriam and Henry followed, both seeming eager to put in another couple of hours even though it was already past dinnertime.

Hans said to Slater, "Why was Lucy Kincaid pulled from the James homicide? She probably could have told you exactly what I just did."

Noah was about to speak when Slater said, "She doesn't have the experience to work this case. We can't have internal bickering over how we deal with witnesses, or worse, having the press call into question anything we do. It's better that she steers clear. I know she's a friend of yours, Hans, and I'm sorry, but right or wrong, Josh nixed her and this is his case."

"I'm not questioning your decisions. I came here to provide a psychological profile of the killer, which I did. I'd also suggest something you already know—if this is blackmail, there's more than one person involved. There's nothing in Wendy James's background that suggests she had the technical skills necessary to create an elaborate system as what you suspect was in apartment seven-ten."

"We're already on that angle, Hans. Thank you."

"Anytime. I'll let you get back to work."

"Actually," Noah said, "if you have a minute, I'll give you a rundown on the prostitute Nicole Bellows. It's the case Lucy is working on. She sent me a report."

"You assigned her to DC?"

"It's the best way to keep her involved without crossing paths with Stein," Noah said. He walked over to the printer and pulled the report.

While Hans read it, Slater rose from his chair and stretched. "I'm outta here. I'm already late for the Nationals game, but I should get there by the fourth inning."

"Good to see you, as always, Matt," Hans said, shaking his hand, then going back to the report.

"There was a number written on the victim's hand?" Hans asked. "To where?"

"It was a virtual number. You buy a virtual number from a company to give to people who you don't want to have your real number. Like an answering service, only when the person dials the number, it gets transferred to whatever phone you want. Popular with doctors, lawyers, CEOs, and not surprisingly, criminals."

"It would make sense for a prostitute to use such a service," Hans concurred. "A way for her regular clients to contact her."

"But the number was written on the victim's hand, so likely someone gave her the number. DC is working on getting warrants for the phone records to find out who bought the number and where it's forwarded, but Detective Reid doesn't expect to have anything until tomorrow afternoon."

"Do you have a picture of the message the killer left?"

Noah slid a printout over to the psychologist.

Hans studied the message for a long minute. The silence in the room would have been unnerving to most, but Noah found peace in this process. Like his years in the Air Force, his success was based on gathering information, analyzing, and acting.

"Do you know if he brought the rat with him?" Hans asked.

"We have no evidence either way, but DC sent the rat to our lab for dissection. Our people think they can analyze the stomach and tissue samples and determine what area of the city it came from."

Hans nodded. "I think we can assume the rat was found in the motel room or on the premises. It was certainly killed there, and unless the killer was carrying the rodent in a cage—which would have brought undue attention—he probably acted spontaneously. The question to me is did he intend to leave a message before he saw the rat? Or was the message a last-minute idea?"

Hans continued with his theory. "I suspect the message was spontaneous, but accurate. He is planning on killing six women. He certainly has killed before. You don't slit someone's throat that deep, with no hesitation, without some experience in murder. He went in with purpose." Hans frowned as he flipped through the pages of the report.

"See something?" Noah asked.

"Lucy wrote that the victim had lived in the neighborhood until nine months ago. Where has she lived since? Why did she come back?"

Noah said, "Detective Reid is following up on the prostitution angle. It's a violent business. Not just the sex trade, but drug use and distribution, money laundering, you name it."

"Don't be surprised if another prostitute ends up dead in the near term. The killer is a sociopath—cold, calculating, remorseless, no empathy with his victims—but he's not a psychopath. He has a purpose and isn't killing for emotional release. This, however," Hans tapped on the photo of the rat, "is his own personal game. He doesn't care if the cops see it. He's of above-average intelligence, but thinks he's smarter than he is, and smarter than everyone else. Truly, one of the most dangerous types of killers I've encountered. He'll kill again before anyone catches him, but it'll be his own arrogance that will bring him down."

Noah thanked Hans for his analysis and walked him to the front of the building. He'd always admired the assistant director for his ability to see things no one else saw. Noah preferred facts and physical evidence, while Hans—a lot like Lucy—saw what was just beneath the surface.

"How is Lucy?" Hans asked when they were alone.

"The same."

"Is something wrong?"

Noah wasn't surprised that Hans had picked up on the tension. Noah had no intention of formally reprimanding Lucy for her insubordination, but it had deeply bothered him that she had been so brazen completely ignoring protocol. He worried he had been wrong in his recommendation to approve her for the Academy. He saw for the first time what the original interview panel had seen—her tunnel vision when it came to victims. He didn't know how she could remain so deeply involved with the dead. How could she survive day after day, year after year, working cases like the one they were at today? She hadn't had the same reaction to the Wendy James murder.

"Noah?"

"I've been working with Lucy for two months now, and she's been an asset as an analyst. Diligent. Methodical. Very smart. But today—I saw a side of her I haven't seen before, and I'm not sure I like it."

"I don't understand."

"I read all the transcripts from her two FBI interviews."

"Those aren't public."

"She's working under me, I had a right to access them. I know you've read them."

Hans nodded his head once, but didn't comment.

"Are you at all worried that she might snap?"

"What happened that has you concerned?"

Lucy's insubordination wasn't the issue. Noah preferred working with people who had strong opinions and weren't afraid to share them, as long as when decisions were made and orders given that those decisions and orders were followed to the letter. But Noah kept replaying the morning. Not focusing solely on Lucy's words, but also on her behavior. It wasn't just when she jumped in about taking the case. It was before that, when she stepped into the room and looked like she was about to collapse.

He didn't answer Hans's question directly. "You signed off on her psych profile after her second interview," he said.

"I did."

"I don't have access to that report."

"No, you do not."

"Is she prone to panic attacks?"

"Has she done anything that gives you reason to believe that she's a danger to herself or others?"

"She hasn't been in the position to."

"I'm not giving you the report, but I would not have

signed off on her admittance to the Bureau if I didn't think she was emotionally capable of fulfilling her duties."

"At what cost?"

"Excuse me?"

"She doesn't know how to compartmentalize. She is prone to empathy with victims, over and above what is required."

"According to who?"

"No one can survive internalizing victimization."

"Are you telling me that Lucy considers herself a victim?"

"No, I'm saying she personalizes the crime scenes. I don't do that. Do you?"

Again, Hans didn't answer his question directly, and his obfuscation was frustrating.

"We all bring different backgrounds, different experiences, to our jobs. Lucy is not a victim, but she has a deep understanding of victimology, far deeper than most of us. Because of what she endured, she sees victims differently. It's not something that can be taught. Like playing an instrument. Most people can learn to read music and play the piano where the tune is recognizable. But some people become the music. Not only can they play, but they have a natural talent."

"You're saying her obsession is a gift?"

"Obsession?"

"For a moment this morning, Lucy would have said or done anything to get this case. It's like she feels personally responsible."

"Empathy, Noah." Hans looked out at the near-empty parking lot. "We need people like Lucy in the Bureau. Too many of us are jaded, are focused on the job and

not the people. She sees everything through a lens that
I can't even see. It's not easy for her, or for you, or for
her future partner. None of this is going to be easy.
Look what happened with Stein. You know why he
wanted her off the case, right?"

"Because she didn't get with his program?" Noah
honestly didn't know what Stein's problem was, other
than he didn't like sharing authority.

"She sees through him. And he knows it."

Noah shook his head. "I don't see any good coming
to Lucy with this curse."

"Curse? Is it a curse if it saves lives?"

"For her? Maybe."

"She has a strong family unit, her foundation. And,
she has Sean Rogan. I know you don't like him, but he's
exactly what she needs to keep her focused on her tal-
ents without succumbing to the pressure."

"You give him too much credit."

"You don't give him enough."

CHAPTER TWELVE

By the time Lucy got home, it was after eight and she had a miserable headache from suppressing tears during the Metro ride. Her body felt like it had cried for hours, but she hadn't shed a tear.

Part of her problem, she knew, was the long day—brutal crime scene in the morning, followed by the afternoon at the morgue and an evening full of paperwork, coffee, and energy bars. It was no wonder she was emotionally off-kilter.

But the dressing-down by Matt Slater had been the bitter icing on the cake.

She unlocked the door and was surprised when the alarm didn't beep, warning her she had sixty seconds to disarm it before it went off. The rich scent of spaghetti sauce filled the house. Her stomach growled, reminding her she hadn't eaten anything of substance since her breakfast bagel.

Dillon and Kate must have canceled their dinner plans. She suspected her sister-in-law, who claimed to hate cats, was secretly attached to their temporary pet. Lucy had caught Kate giving the cat milk this morning.

Good thing, it saved her from eating another peanut butter and honey sandwich, her favorite when her brother wasn't home to cook and she was too tired to stand. Food, sleep, that's all she wanted. She hoped they didn't want to talk.

"It's me," she called, putting her purse and keys on the small table and walking down the hall to the kitchen. "I was at a homicide half the day, then the morgue. I'm going to get some aspirin and shower before dinner if that's okay."

She stopped, stunned to see her boyfriend, private investigator Sean Rogan, standing at the stove stirring a steaming pot. He smiled at her, revealing his solitary dimple, his dark hair falling over one eye, making him look both innocent and devilish at the same time. God, he was nice to look at.

"You're back!" She ran to greet him, throwing her arms around his neck and hugging him tightly. She was grinning like an idiot, but she hadn't ever been so happy to see anyone. Especially now. Especially after this evening.

He lifted her up off the floor and squeezed tightly, then put her down and kissed her. "Surprise," he said.

She felt like a lovesick teenager. "I missed you." She kissed him back, feeling light on her toes and ridiculously happy. "A lot."

Her tension disappeared. Sean was just what she needed.

"I know," he teased. Suddenly, she was off her feet again and in his arms.

"Sean!"

"You said something about a shower before dinner. And I know better ways to relieve a tension headache than aspirin."

"My brother—"

"Dillon and Kate won't be home for hours. It's just you and me, Princess." He maneuvered to turn off the stove without putting her down. "And apparently a cat."

"Just temporary."

"Tell me about it. Later."

"I don't think—" she began, not sure what she was objecting to because right now being in Sean's arms was exactly what she needed after her difficult day.

He kissed her as he walked down the hall and up the stairs. "That's right. Don't think."

At the landing, he continued to the end of the hall, then up half a flight of steps to her room. The attic above the garage had been converted long before the Kincaids moved in, giving her some privacy. Sean pushed open her door with his shoulder.

"You can put me down now."

"I could." But he didn't. Instead he kissed her as he carried her to the bathroom. Only then did he put her down. He turned on the water in the shower, grinning impishly as he pulled off his shirt.

"What—" But she stopped mid-question and stared at the baseball-size bruise on his upper shoulder. "What happened?"

"I was stupid. Breaking into the warehouse the last time Duke modified the alarm, I didn't expect him to put in a physical obstacle. A security guard."

Sean's brother Duke, one of the founders of Rogan-Caruso-Kincaid Protective Services, specialized in creating solid security systems. Sean specialized in cracking them. They made a great team, except Duke had yet to create a system Sean couldn't hack.

"You broke all his codes?"

Sean shrugged, but Lucy could see he was pleased with himself. "He was being lazy. Or preoccupied. I suspect I complained one too many times that his incompetence was keeping me away from you far too long."

"Preoccupied? About what?"

"Nora's pregnant."

"That's great." Lucy was happy for Sean's brother and sister-in-law. Nora was over forty and didn't think she'd have children. They'd been trying since their marriage three years ago. "That means you'll be Uncle Sean pretty soon. The kid's going to be spoiled."

Suddenly, a flash of the unborn baby, dead in Nicole's womb, crossed her vision. She shook her head, not wanting to think of death when there was life to celebrate. Hers, Sean's, a future Rogan niece or nephew.

"Hey—Luce—what's wrong?"

Steam from the shower began to fill the room. "Nothing—just this case. I'll tell you about it over dinner."

"Put it out of your mind." His kissed her as he unbuttoned her blouse. "Far, far out of your mind."

She savored his kisses. With Sean, it was easy to put work aside for an hour or two of play. "What mind?" she whispered.

"Better." His hands skimmed her legs as he slid her slacks down to the floor. He knelt in front of her, lifted one foot out of the tangle of clothing, and kissed her toes. Then he picked up her other foot and kissed it. As his hands moved back up her body, his lips followed, and her body turned liquid. She would have fallen if he didn't support her.

He rose, nearly a full head taller than her, and kissed her forehead, then her nose, then her lips. He held her face while she unbuttoned his jeans. She pushed them down to the floor, along with his boxers, and they both stood naked in the steam-filled room, their hands roaming, touching, remembering where they'd left off last week, before Sean's business trip.

Before she met Sean, she would never have been this brazen, would never have participated in sexual banter. He had been both determined and patient, giving her space to learn her own desires while pushing her to seek them. She put her arms around his neck and kissed him warmly, whispering, "I'm really, *really* glad you're home."

He didn't smile, but walked her backward into the shower.

She jumped. "Too hot!" She turned the faucet much colder.

"You like hot showers."

"Not when it's a thousand degrees outside."

"Enough talking." He grinned as he pushed her under the stream of lukewarm water, his body pressed firmly against hers. Everything that had happened that day, all that she had seen and heard, rolled from her thoughts as the refreshing water cascaded over them, cleansing her, emptying her memories of all but how much she loved Sean.

The moment was pure bliss.

Sean had been thrilled with Lucy's spontaneous joy when she saw him unexpected in the kitchen. The last two months, since they'd returned from their non-vacation in the Adirondacks, had been an exercise in managing schedules. Between her job with the FBI and his partnership in RCK, they were lucky to see each other more than one night a week. It didn't help that he shared a house with her brother Patrick—his partner—and that she wouldn't let him stay over if Dillon and Kate were home. He would have taken her to Sacramento with him, but he didn't even want to ask her, considering she was just now building her career, a career that was extremely important to her.

But seeing her raw happiness tonight, and her obvious pleasure at being naked in the shower with him, any worry that she might not have missed him as much as he missed her disappeared with the grime of the day.

He grabbed the soap and lathered up her body, their slick skin sliding together erotically, making him even more horny. He wanted the shower over *now*. He licked Lucy's neck and she laughed, then he bit her earlobe and she grabbed his shoulders.

He didn't want to wait. He'd thought of her each night he slept alone in his old bedroom. Wondered what she was doing, if she was working too hard, if she was eating right. If she was having fun. Because Lucy didn't know how to have fun, not unless he was with her. For Lucy, it was all work, all the time, and while Sean believed in working hard, he also believed in playing hard. He'd realized months ago that he was Lucy's anchor, the one thing she needed to keep her focused on her own needs, her own desires, her own fun.

He reached down and grabbed her leg at the knee, pulling it up until it was around his waist. He held it and braced her against the wall.

"I want you right now, Princess," he said. "Trust me."

Her dark eyes locked onto his as he pushed himself into her, slowly at first. Her breath hitched and her eyes fluttered closed. He kissed her open mouth, and she responded in full, her arms locked around his neck, trusting him. That trust coupled with the sounds coming from her chest as he made love to her against the shower tile had him peaking far too soon to satisfy either of them. He hadn't tried to control himself, didn't want to. He would make love to her again, properly. In bed. Where he could take his time and show her how much he'd missed her.

"Let me wash your hair."

She smiled languidly. "I can do it."

"I want to."

He found her shampoo and lathered a good amount into her thick, black hair. He spread the lather across her breasts, her stomach, between her legs. He could get used to this. He used her shampoo to soap himself, then had her stand under the shower head to rinse off. He watched her, the way she enjoyed the water cascading over her. Fully relaxed. Happy.

"Enough," he said and turned off the water. He grabbed a towel, wrapped it around his waist, then another and started drying Lucy off. "Let's go to bed." He wanted her again, right now, but he would take his time.

She raised an eyebrow and feigned surprise as she let him pick her up. "What about dinner?"

"It's not going anywhere." He kissed her breasts, first one, then the other. Her eyes closed and her mouth parted. "And neither are you."

CHAPTER THIRTEEN

Sean watched Lucy sleep.

They were on the couch in the family room. Lucy had put her head in his lap, telling him about the two homicides she was working, why the feds were involved in the first place, and why she was focusing on the black prostitute. Of course Sean had heard about the sex scandal with Crowley and the pretty blond secretary. No one who lived in DC and listened to the news for more than five minutes could have missed the affair. But Lucy seemed more concerned about the brutal murder of a hooker from the bad side of town. The killer was a sick bastard to leave a gutted rat for a calling card. And dangerous. But Lucy felt that Nicole Bellows wasn't the last victim, and because Lucy was who Lucy was, she put the weight of the case on her shoulders.

Sean loved her for her commitment to her job, but also worried that sometimes she cared too much, and sacrificed too much of herself for others.

What he was more concerned about was the hidden

room Lucy had uncovered yesterday. The dark circles under her eyes, visible now that she'd showered and all traces of makeup had been removed from her face, told him she hadn't slept well last night.

He should have been here for her. She should have told him. But when he was going to ask why she hadn't talked to him about the case when he called last night, she was already asleep.

He stared at her, his heart in his throat, wanting so much to take away the pain she harbored inside. He combed her hair with his fingers, lightly, not wanting to wake her. She needed sleep, and he was pleased she could relax with him. He felt her weight shift on his legs when she slipped deeper into sleep, trusting him.

He would never betray her trust.

Lucy was a classically beautiful woman, but the beauty was secondary in his intense attraction.

Going back to his hometown of Sacramento for a week had been difficult on many levels. Not just working for his brother and being treated like the irresponsible black sheep of the family, something he'd been striving to shake for years, but seeing old friends—and old girlfriends. Word got around fast that he was back, and the calls came in. He went to one party and left early—it wasn't his thing anymore.

Sean had always been attracted to girls who knew they were beautiful and enjoyed the attention their good looks and hot bodies elicited. He also liked smart girls, because talking to an airhead got old real quick. But the girls he'd dated before Lucy were short-term girlfriends—smart and beautiful, but also shallow, conceited, and demanding. Still, for years, he had preferred the no-strings-attached lifestyle.

And then came Lucy.

More important than looks and brains was Lucy's lack of selfishness. She had so much hope and compassion, even after the shit life had handed her, and every day dedicated herself to helping others. To seeking justice.

Sean was the first to admit that he was selfish. He liked having toys, he liked being smarter than other people, and he wanted Lucy all to himself. Sharing her with her career and her family grated on him occasionally, because he wanted to come first.

But he couldn't imagine his life without Lucy in it. Six months they'd been together, and he didn't miss his carefree past. Going home had proven it, if he needed proof.

He'd hated being away from her for so long—eight days this time—especially since she would be leaving for Quantico soon, and he'd only get to see her one night a week for nearly six months.

Stupid rule, he thought. He wondered how difficult the security would be to crack. Did they have security cameras on campus? Or just on the perimeter? He'd have to get Lucy to take him on a tour one day. He'd figure it out. No way was he going six days a week without seeing her.

He kissed her forehead and she smiled in her sleep. Maybe she wasn't sleeping. He leaned down and kissed her lips. She kissed him back.

The doorbell rang.

She sighed and opened her eyes. They had a sleepy, content look. "Dillon never forgets his keys," she said. "What time is it?" She rose and stretched.

"Ten thirty."

She walked down the hall to the front door and peered through the peephole. Sean watched from behind.

"It's Noah," she said.

What the hell was Mr. Law & Order doing here so late at night? Sean didn't know he'd be home today until he got on the plane. He'd surprised Lucy. Had Noah tried to weasel in on Lucy while Sean had been gone?

Lucy opened the door. "Come on in."

Sean stared at the Fed. "Noah."

"Sean. I didn't know you were back."

"Surprise."

They'd agreed to a truce after their adventures in upstate New York—Sean had a grudging respect for the guy. But he still couldn't shake the jealousy whenever Noah was around Lucy. Lucy had done nothing to make Sean think she was at all interested in Noah—they were just colleagues. And friends. But Sean couldn't explain why he felt the way he did—except that a lot of people Lucy cared about had been critical of her decision to get involved with him. That normally wouldn't bother him, but with Lucy it did. It annoyed him.

He trusted Lucy.

He didn't trust Noah. Not when it came to Lucy's heart.

"Would you like some spaghetti?" Lucy offered.

"I just stopped by to brief you on a couple things."

"Did you eat?"

"No, but I'll get a sandwich—"

Lucy shook her head. "Sit. Sean made plenty."

Lucy went to the kitchen and dished Noah a plate. Sean came up behind her and kissed her behind the ear. "So much for our quiet night."

She glanced at him, and he saw she was worried

about something. She was still concerned about their relationship, so he winked. The last thing he wanted to do was upset Lucy. He'd work through this jealousy thing on his own.

"Beer?" Sean called out to Noah.

"Sounds good."

Sean opened a couple bottles of imported beer, put one in front of Noah, and sat across from him.

Noah nodded his thanks and drank, then dug into the spaghetti.

"So, do you always stop by Lucy's house in the middle of the night?" Sean said.

"If it's important," Noah said between bites. He glanced at Sean. "And it's only ten thirty."

Lucy wished the sniping between Noah and Sean would stop. It had gotten better since New York, but Sean liked their time alone, and she had to admit they didn't have enough of it.

"It's fine," Lucy said to Noah. "Any big break? Did the killer walk into the police station and turn himself in?"

"No," he said, "but since I was on my way home, I thought I'd swing by and fill you in on the Wendy James homicide."

Lucy was secretly pleased. "Thank you."

"Thank you?" Sean asked. "For keeping you informed about your own case?"

Lucy had fallen asleep before she told Sean about Josh Stein. "I got pulled from the case."

"Pulled?"

Noah put up his hand. "The SSA has his own way of doing things, and considering the high-profile nature of the case, having Lucy publicly involved was problematic."

"That sounds like a load of bureaucratic bullshit."

"It's fine, Sean," Lucy intervened.

"Like hell."

"I overstepped. I've been doing that a lot lately." She caught Noah's eye, but couldn't tell whether he'd truly forgiven her or not. He had too stoic a poker face.

"Crowley's alibi checked out—he was in committee during the window Wendy James was murdered."

"And his finances?"

"Still being reviewed, but on the surface, nothing odd. Our techs confirmed there had been video and audio equipment in the hidden room, but they can't tell when it was removed or by whom. We're going over both apartments meticulously for trace evidence, but the consensus is someone tried to blackmail Crowley, and either he didn't play and the affair was exposed, or he exposed the affair himself to take the pressure off."

"What do you think?"

"I don't—not enough information. It could be random, or a stalker—she drew a lot of attention when the affair broke. But in light of the hidden room, I think that's the reason she was killed."

"It also opens a whole new roomful of suspects," Lucy said.

"And no way of knowing who was there."

"What about security cams?"

"The management only keeps them for thirty days. We've already got a warrant for the last thirty days, and Cyber Crimes is going over them."

"No archive?" Sean said. "Where are the tapes stored? Digital or analog? Wireless or hardwired? Stored on-site or off-site? Virtual or physical? Even if they only officially keep thirty days, they may have months of data that hasn't been overwritten. And, depending on the system, even overwritten data might be recoverable."

Noah stared at Sean. "I'm sure Cyber Crimes is covering all avenues, but I'll pass on your questions."

Sean shook his head. "This is my *job*. It's what I do. I can consult for you, help out—"

"No," Noah said. Then, grudgingly, "Thanks for the offer, but we're keeping the case in-house. It's one of the reasons Lucy was pulled. Media is an issue, we can't give the killer anything to use to get the case thrown out of court when and if we find him."

"I have clearance," Sean said.

Lucy took Sean's hand under the table. She really didn't want him to push this. He was good, but so was the FBI Cyber Crimes unit.

"On the Nicole Bellows murder," Lucy said, changing the subject, "Genie sent me a message that they got the warrant for the virtual phone company. It might take a couple of days, but we should have the registered owner, a record of numbers, and where they are forwarded."

"Virtual numbers? There are a half dozen ways to get around that," Sean said. "Buy a prepaid credit card with cash, use that credit card to get the number."

"Why am I not surprised you know this?" Noah said.

"It's a no-brainer," Sean said. "But not everyone uses virtual numbers for illegal activity. There are legitimate and important business uses."

"It'll definitely take a few days," Noah said. "I've dealt with these companies before, and the warrant has to be airtight. Privacy laws and all that."

"And you're against privacy laws?" Sean snapped.

"When they protect criminals."

Lucy intervened. "It's a lead, and the system works in this case. Protecting privacy *and* getting us the information we need to find Nicole's killer. We don't know that the number will lead to her killer, but it may give us another piece of the puzzle."

Noah put his fork down; he'd cleaned his plate. "More?" she offered.

"No, thanks. I have an early morning tomorrow. Keep me in the loop on your case."

Lucy walked him to the door. "Of course."

Noah hesitated in the doorway. He said, "Hans Vigo came to our briefing tonight. I talked to him about the Bellows homicide. He agrees that the killer is going to strike again. He also said the killer isn't a psychopath. Honestly, I don't know how he can tell."

"I know what he means."

"You do?"

"Because he's violent and shows no remorse, some may categorize him as a psychopath, but a true psychopath has a mental disorder that compels him to commit his crimes. Violent psychopaths *may* show remorse for their crimes, they *may* have human empathy but their need to kill or hurt others overshadows that empathy. A sociopath may not be violent, but they have complete lack of remorse. Take a con artist who steals the life savings of an eighty-year-old woman. No guilt at destroying that life, even if that woman dies destitute on the streets. But that same con artist wouldn't, for example, shoot the woman in cold blood. Sociopaths aren't always violent.

"But when you have a violent sociopath, he's more unpredictable than a psychopath whose disorder makes him easier to identify once the MO is established. I think Hans realizes that the killer wanted Nicole Bellows dead, so he killed her. The reason wasn't because killing her was satisfying to him in any deep or meaningful way. A psychopath would likely wait a few days, possibly weeks or months before killing again. This killer doesn't need a cooling-off period. He's going to complete whatever plan he has, then he may never kill again."

Noah said, "If there's another homicide, call me immediately."

"Of course." Lucy wanted to ask Noah what he'd said to Hans, if anything, about their conversation this morning. She wanted to know if Noah had put anything in her record. But he didn't say anything, and she didn't ask.

"Night."

He left without resolving this odd tension between them. But he did come by and he didn't have to—maybe that was his way of letting her know everything was okay.

She turned around and walked back to the family room. Sean was standing there, the vein in his jaw throbbing.

"What was with him tonight?"

"You always ask that."

"But there was something else."

"I told you what I said to him this morning. I was out of line."

"Hardly. He's not perfect."

"Sean—" She hesitated.

"What?"

"Matt Slater, the SSA, talked to me earlier. What I did yesterday really made waves, and Noah took the heat for me. Any mistakes I make are his responsibility. I don't want to sit around the house for the next three weeks, but I don't want Noah to get into trouble if I screw something up. Slater said I have special privileges, and people know it."

"That's ridiculous," Sean said. "You've earned your spot."

"Maybe," Lucy said.

"No maybe. The FBI isn't a charity; they wouldn't have put you in as an analyst unless you were qualified and they knew you'd be an asset."

Lucy sat down on the couch. "I don't want special privileges, Sean."

He sat next to her and pulled her head to his chest. "You can't stop people thinking what they want, right or wrong. But you *earned* everything you have."

She hoped Sean was right. The last seven years of her life had been such a roller coaster sometimes she didn't know what to think about her dreams and goals. Were they really hers? Who might she have been had she not been raped, live on the Internet, seven years ago?

"Luce?" Sean turned her head so he could look her in the eyes. She squeezed back tears. She wanted no pity from Sean. From anyone. Especially herself. "Talk to me."

She shook her head.

"I'm sorry I wasn't here for you last night," he said.

"I'm okay." Saying it almost made it true.

"If you ever need to talk, about anything, you know you can talk to me. Right?"

"Yes." Her voice cracked. "Most of the time, my mind convinces me that it all happened to someone else. That I was an observer, like the camera that recorded those god-awful days. And then I see something and I'm right back there again. My head *knows* I'm not, but my body reacts and I can't stop the panic."

Sean's grip tightened around her, and she leaned her head back on his shoulder. "Having you here makes all the difference," she whispered.

"I'm not going anywhere, you know that."

"When Matt Slater said I had special privileges, I think I knew it had to be true. What if I shouldn't be in the FBI? What if I lose control over these panic attacks? I was turned down from the Academy once, what if I should have just let that dream die? There are other dreams out there." As she said it, she believed it—except she didn't want any other career. Seven years, obsessed with joining the FBI and fighting crime, had changed her. Irrevocably.

"You listen to me."

She tilted her head to look at Sean. His blue eyes were so intense she couldn't turn away.

"The FBI is damn lucky to have you, Lucy Kincaid. This Matt Slater is an ass to think that anyone is just handing you the career you want. You *earned* it. You are a damn good cop now, even without a badge. You're going to be a *great* agent. I know it, you know it. No more doubts, Princess. Okay?"

She smiled. "Thank you for having so much faith in me."

"It's easy." He leaned over and kissed her. "Besides, I could have helped, too."

Lucy realized he *wanted* to help. He liked puzzles and needed something to keep his intellect challenged.

"You could have gotten the information faster," Lucy said, playing up to his ego. "But Cyber Crimes is good. The FBI hires the best computer people."

Sean cocked his head to the side. "The best? I'm hurt."

She grinned and shook her head. She loved Sean so much. He could release the tension with one well-placed comment.

She kissed him. "The second best."

"You're going to have to make up that insult. My ego needs stroking. Maybe a massage, too."

"Oh really?"

"There's nothing I want more than to spend the next three weeks basking under your undivided attention," Sean said. "But you're not a quitter."

"I know, but—"

"There is no but. You love this work. You need it. You'd go crazy being around the house all day, and I'd want to entertain you twenty-four–seven and then I'd get no work done. My brother and your brother would be livid at me for slacking off and not bringing in the big bucks."

"I just—" She stopped. What did she want? Sometimes she didn't know.

Sean tapped her chin and looked directly in her eyes.

"Stop doubting yourself. I don't care how much experience the other cops have, your instincts are as good as theirs."

"Thank you."

"I don't think I would like this Stein jerk."

She had to bite the inside of her cheek to keep from smiling. "You wouldn't. But he's good at what he does. And he has more experience than me."

"He took you off your case."

"It's his case, and Noah's. I'm an analyst."

"A damn good analyst."

She pursed her lips. "You're good for my ego."

He pulled her into his arms and kissed her. "I'm good for a lot of things."

The cat wound around their feet.

"You should name this cat," Sean said. "So when he annoys me, I know what to call him."

"I can't keep it."

"Why not? You like him."

"Yes, but I'm going to the Academy in three weeks. I can't ask Kate and Dillon to take care of my pet."

"I'll keep him for you."

"I didn't know you liked cats."

"I like this one."

"Then you name it."

"All right." He picked up the cat and stared into his face. The cat meowed.

She grinned. "Did he just tell you his name?"

He gave her a crooked smile. "I need to get to know him first. It'll come to me."

They sat down on the couch and Sean wrapped one arm around Lucy and petted the cat with the other.

"Thank you for listening."

"Anytime, Princess." He kissed the top of her head. "I love you. And I think you'll crack this case wide open and Noah had better rub it in this Josh Stein's face, otherwise I'll do it. I, for one, can hardly wait."

CHAPTER FOURTEEN

Ivy watched the news with growing horror.

This is not happening.

She glanced over to the door of the adjoining room where Sara and Maddie were sleeping. They'd been sleeping too much, but Ivy didn't have the heart to wake them up. She definitely didn't want them hearing the news yet.

The jogger found strangled in Rock Creek Park has been positively identified as the mistress of powerful Judiciary Chair, Congressman Alan Crowley.

Wendy James, a receptionist for lobbying firm Devon Sullivan and Associates, was found dead Tuesday morning. DC police had no comment, but sources indicate that the FBI has taken over the investigation.

Last month, Ms. James was exposed as the mistress of Congressman Crowley. At first the congressman from Los Angeles denied the accusation that he was having an affair, but after compromising pictures surfaced on the Internet, he admitted to the accusations.

Repeated calls to the congressman's office have not been returned. His chief of staff issued a statement that said Congressman Crowley is fully cooperating with the authorities. The FBI is not commenting, but sources indicate that agents don't believe the crime was random. A source in the Capitol said Congressman Crowley canceled a scheduled trip to California last Friday.

We'll keep you informed of any new developments in this stunning case.

Ivy stared at the television screen. She flipped through all the stations, trying to learn more about Wendy's murder, but the reporters had nothing new.

Wendy was dead.

She paced the hotel room, trying to convince herself that Wendy's murder wasn't connected to her or the fire, but she was only lying to herself. Of *course* it was connected.

Someone had found out that she'd taped Wendy with that congressman, and others. Now Wendy was dead and someone had tried to kill Ivy and the other girls. Except the tapes had been destroyed in the fire.

Sergio? Was it the guy who bought the tapes? But why? He could easily have killed Ivy after she turned them over, but she hadn't had a chance, unless he stole them then set the fire. But why?

He rescued your sister. He gave you ten thousand dollars. He was going to give you ten thousand more before your house burned down. What's his motive for killing you?

Wendy was smart, but eventually the police would find out that Wendy and Ivy had been in business together.

She tried calling Kerry again; no answer. Dammit, why hadn't she checked in? She dialed Nicole, panic making her misdial twice. Nicole was supposed to have been here this morning. Ivy hadn't thought about her absence. She dry-heaved, realizing that she'd put Nicole out of her mind while trying to plan how to keep Sara safe.

Someone picked up the phone, but didn't say anything.

Ivy listened. Breathing. Was it Nicole?

She didn't speak, but she didn't hang up.

"Are you looking for Nicole?"

The voice was male, mocking. At first Ivy thought Nicole had picked up a john, but even as the thought entered her mind, she knew Nicole was dead.

Just like Wendy.

"Where is she?" Ivy said. Her voice too weak to talk to a killer. She was scared and it showed.

He chuckled. "The morgue. You're next. I'm closer than you think."

She hung up. Her phone rang and she ran to the bathroom and dropped it in the sink, running water over it. She bent over the toilet and threw up violently, until acid burned her throat. She collapsed on the floor, her head on her arm, her stomach full of sharp knives.

"Ivy?" Maddie stood in the doorway. "Are you okay."

Does it look like I'm okay?

"Get your stuff. We're leaving."

"I don't wanna go."

She sat up, shaking. In a voice much harsher than she intended, she said, "We have to. Nicole is dead!"

She might as well have slapped Maddie. Her lip quivered and tears dampened her eyes. Ivy pulled herself up off the bathroom floor and rinsed her mouth out with water. "Give me your phone."

Maddie reached into her pocket. Ivy added Maddie's phone to the water in the sink. When the basin was full, she shut the water off.

She walked past Maddie and back into the hotel room. She hadn't unpacked. She pulled her backpack from the closet and zipped it up.

Maddie followed her, but made no attempt to pick up her things. "Why can't we stay here? It's safe here."

No place was safe. The only way they'd be safe was if Ivy disappeared. But she had no money, no place to go.

Wendy's dead.

There was one other option, but Ivy had no idea if Wendy had changed her hiding place after their falling out. Wendy must have known Ivy turned over the pictures of her and Crowley that ended up all over the news. Except Wendy hadn't confronted her, and she wouldn't have kept her mouth shut about it, even though they hadn't spoken in months.

"We have to go," Ivy said, weary and emotionally drained.

"No!"

Maddie never defied her. Ivy didn't know what to say, but stared at her friend.

"Jocelyn is trying to help," Maddie pleaded. "You said so yourself. Why would you run away now? Why do you have to do everything yourself?"

Because there's no one else.

"I have to get Mina," Ivy said. "Nicole left her with Marti. They might be in danger, too. Don't you get it?

Wendy and Nicole are *dead*. I don't want anything to happen to you or anyone else." *Or Sara. God, what have I gotten her into?*

"Wendy's dead, too?" Maddie shook her head, her hands covering her face.

Dammit, Ivy, you are full of tact!

She spoke softly. "I just saw it on the news. I'm sorry, Maddie." Ivy had to be strong for all of them. She had to remember that they'd been through hell, but she'd been the one to get them out.

She just didn't know if she could save them all this time. Her conscience weighed so heavy, she wished she could click her heels together and go anywhere else.

Anywhere but home.

A card key slid into the slot, a computerized *whoosh* releasing the latch. The door opened into the hotel room. Heart racing, Ivy reached into her backpack for her gun.

"It's me," Jocelyn said. She put a large bag of takeout on the table next to the door. "I brought my husband, Chris."

A man stepped in behind Jocelyn. He was of average build with a baby face and kind eyes.

Ivy stared at Jocelyn. She'd promised to protect Sara, but Ivy couldn't expect Chris Taylor to keep the secret.

"Let's sit down and discuss the situation," Jocelyn said. "You're in danger. Your sister is in danger."

"Don't do that. It's complex."

Chris said, "I can arrange—"

Ivy cut him off. "Nicole is dead!"

Jocelyn looked stricken, she walked over to her and took her hands. Ivy shook her off and felt bad about it, but she was in no mood to be coddled. Jocelyn wasn't wanted for felony kidnapping. Jocelyn didn't have a killer after her.

Ivy had been responsible for herself since she was fourteen, she didn't even know how to accept help. She'd tried, and look where she was? Her makeshift family separated. Two friends dead. Kerry not returning her calls. What if she was dead, too?

"Ivy, are you sure? I didn't hear anything about it on the news—"

"I'm very sure."

"Then we really do need to call the police."

"No, no, no!" Ivy rubbed her temples. She didn't know what to do.

"They're not going to send Sara back to a man who raped her."

"You don't know my father," Ivy said through clenched teeth.

Everyone was looking at her, looking at *her* to make the decision. Looking at *her* for answers. She had none. What had she and Wendy started? What had seemed like a brilliant idea to earn money to buy her and Sara new identities and a home in Canada had blown up. Wendy was dead. The money was gone. Ivy was responsible for three needy teenagers and no way to keep them from harm.

Sara stepped out of the adjoining room and said, "Ha—Ivy? What's wrong?"

Jocelyn said quietly, "Let's talk about this tonight. Chris knows people who can fix this. We can protect you all."

Except they'd call her father. Sara, the one person who needed protection the most, would be sent back into the lion's den.

Ivy had only one idea, and she prayed to the Lord to give her this one request. For Sara.

"On one condition," Ivy said. "I have a place where Sara will be safe. I'll take her there. We keep her completely out of this, pretend she doesn't exist, then I'll talk to the police."

Jocelyn glanced at her husband and they shared something unspoken.

"Please," Ivy begged. "They can't protect Sara."

"If Sara testifies against him—"

"Those are my terms. I want this all to stop. I'm so tired, Jocelyn." Her voice cracked.

Sara started to cry. Ivy took a deep breath. She couldn't be weak now. "It's not just Nicole," she said. "Wendy is dead, too."

"Wendy?" Jocelyn questioned. "Who's that?"

"Wendy James. It's all over the news."

Chris's eyes widened. "Congressman Crowley's *mistress*?"

"Mistress? Hardly. You asked a long time ago how I got into this business," Ivy said to Jocelyn. "It was through Wendy. We used to be partners."

Chris frowned and sat on the couch. Ivy ignored him and turned to Jocelyn. "I'm going to take Sara to the only person I can trust, then I'll talk to the police. I need a couple of hours."

Jocelyn handed Ivy her car keys. "Call me for anything. We'll wait here."

"I destroyed my phone—I was afraid whoever killed Nicole might have some way of finding me."

Chris asked, "How do you know Nicole is dead?"

"A man answered her phone when I called. He told me she was dead."

Maddie stifled a cry and ran from the room. Ivy wished she could talk to her, but she had no time.

"Take mine." Jocelyn handed her the cell phone. "I'll call you from Chris's phone."

"Thank you." She hugged her. Suddenly, she didn't want to go. She wanted Jocelyn and Chris Taylor to make all the decisions. For once, she wanted someone else to tell her the right thing to do.

For once, she wanted someone else to protect her.

Over Jocelyn's shoulder Ivy saw her sister, so sheltered and vulnerable and not deserving any of this.

She stepped away from Jocelyn and cleared her throat. "I won't be long."

Maddie didn't like hearing Jocelyn and Chris arguing. Chris didn't want to wait to call the police; Jocelyn wanted to give Ivy until morning.

She interrupted, "I'm going to take a bath, is that okay?"

Jocelyn nodded. "Of course, Maddie. Are you hungry?" She gestured toward the bags of food.

She shook her head and tried to smile, but it felt like a crooked frown.

She picked up her backpack and took it into the bathroom and closed the door. The suite had a large, oval-shaped bathtub that she could easily sink into. She turned on the water and stripped. Steam rose and began to fog the mirror. Good. She didn't want to look at herself, knowing what she was going to do.

From the very bottom of her backpack, with her tampons and birth control bills and condoms, she pulled out a small tin. Ivy had searched her room many times for drugs, and Maddie had gotten better about hiding them.

It wasn't like she was taking them all the time. She really wanted to make Ivy proud of her, to stay off the stuff, to help.

But what could she do? Ivy was the strong one. She kept them in the pretty house, made sure they had clients who didn't hurt them, had found ways to make more money than Maddie could have imagined when she first started hooking to support her drug habit.

She didn't want to be that desperate girl again, selling her body for drugs. But Ivy's priority was her sister. Maddie wouldn't be surprised if Ivy never came back. If she just disappeared with Sara.

Tears rolled down her cheeks.

She opened the tin. Six little blue pills left. She took two, swallowed them with water from the sink. The phones sat dead at the bottom, reminding her that Nicole was also dead.

The tub filled quickly, and Maddie turned off the water. It was too hot; she waited a minute for the water to cool and the happy pills to work.

She leaned against the bathroom door.

Jocelyn and Chris were still talking.

"You can't trust her," Chris said.

"She's just like me."

"No she's not!" Chris said something else, quietly, that Maddie couldn't hear. Then she caught, ". . . never have done that."

"I would have done anything to survive," Jocelyn said. "If Cathy hadn't found me when she did—I understand Ivy. I'm not giving up on her."

"If she doesn't go to the police first thing in the morning and tell them everything she knows, you have to walk away. You're hurting, I see it every night. I can't stand to see you suffer like this."

"You've been my rock, Chris. But—don't tell Ivy you knew from the beginning. I told her once that we didn't have secrets, but I don't think she processed that I shared everything with you."

"She doesn't have to know when I knew."

Jocelyn mumbled something, then Chris said, "If Sara makes a statement about her father, no court would place her with him. I don't want you getting in trouble for being an accessory after the fact."

"Stop sounding like a lawyer. Kirk Edmonds is a powerful, wealthy man with people who will support him. Powerful people get away with unspeakable crimes. You know that, Chris."

"And you don't think that Ivy has been lying about him?"

"No, I don't."

"You have more faith in that girl than I do."

Maddie bit her hand to keep from crying. Men with pretty faces were just as mean as ugly men.

Her head felt light, but she was so sad. She took one more pill, wanting to bury the sorrow.

She slid into the water. It was still hot, but tolerable. She didn't want to listen to any more talk, she didn't want to hear any doubts.

Ivy had saved her over and over again. Without her, Maddie would have been dead long ago.

She put her earbuds in and listened to Evanescence, the soulful, heart-wrenching sounds soothing and comforting.

Slowly, she relaxed, forgot the Taylors, forgot her pain, forgot that someone wanted her dead.

* * *

When Ivy walked Sara into the church, peace touched her heart and she knew immediately she'd done the right thing. Why hadn't she come to Father Paul right after the fire?

She found it ironic that the only person she truly trusted with Sara was a man of God. Father Paul had given her hope when she had none, and for that, she owed him her life.

Sara walked through the small, old church with a sense of awe. Ivy watched her sister relax, comfortable and safe.

Father Paul stood next to Ivy. He was a diminutive man of seventy whose presence belied his stature. The first time she saw him, six years ago, she thought she'd seen a halo over his head. She'd dismissed that as a hallucination from anger and fear, but an she looked at him now, his serene expression gave her a rare glimpse of true peace.

"I'll watch over her," he said.

"Thank you," she whispered, her voice cracking. "I don't—"

"Shh, child."

Ivy walked down the empty aisle to where Sara stood in front of a statue of a saint. "Listen to Father Paul," she told Sara.

Sara hugged her tightly. "It's going to be okay, Ivy. God's going to protect us. He answered my prayers and brought me to you, and I'm going to pray every minute that you're safe."

Ivy didn't have the heart to tell Sara that God didn't care about them. If he did, he would have thrown a lightning bolt through the heart of Kirk Edmonds the first time he raped his oldest daughter. But if her beliefs calmed Sara, that gave Ivy some relief.

Father Paul caught her eye. He didn't say anything else; he didn't need to. She left without looking back.

St. Anne's wasn't far from where Ivy had lived, but the two neighborhoods were vastly different. Father Paul's church was in a depressed area northwest of the Capitol center while Ivy's house on Hawthorne was in a pocket of well-kept homes surrounded by businesses that still managed to keep their doors open.

Marti North was the pastor of His Grace Church, a small church and preschool wedged between two larger buildings. Growing up, Ivy had never known there were female ministers, and maybe that's why she was drawn to the small, struggling church. His Grace was the opposite in every way to her father's opulent worship center, from the gender of the pastor to the size and quality of the structure to the color of the parishioners.

Ivy didn't like to dwell on the fact that the people she trusted the most were in the same profession as her father. As Marti would say, *it is what it is.* That simple, clichéd sentence had helped Ivy many times when she wanted to scream that life wasn't fair.

Ivy stared at the dark building and realized she didn't know where Marti lived. It was in the area, but it wasn't at the church. It was after midnight, she didn't want to wake her up. Nicole had trusted Marti with Mina, and so did Ivy. Maybe it was better this way, to let her sleep and Ivy would handle the police on her own.

Ivy turned the car around and drove the four blocks to the burned remains of her house on Hawthorne Street.

She parked down the street and walked half a block. Even though the fire had been extinguished forty-eight hours ago, the scent of charred wood hung in the still, hot air. As she neared, she thought the house looked particularly dark because of the shadows; when she stood across the street she realized that the house was simply gone.

It had burned almost completely to the ground, only the shell remaining.

Everything she owned, everything she'd saved, thousands of dollars in cash, passports, identification, and the video that would have yielded her another ten thousand to give them a jumpstart in Canada . . . gone.

By the time she returned to Jocelyn's car, the tears were falling.

Ivy smelled death the moment she stepped into the hotel room.

Bile rose in her throat, the sickening scent of blood mixed making her gag.

Blood sprayed everywhere. Jocelyn's husband was on the floor closest to the door, his throat slit. Arcs of blood slashed the puke green walls and sickly gold carpets. His eyes didn't look real anymore, clouded and lifeless. How long had he been dead?

It's my fault.

Jocelyn's body was curled into a ball at the foot of the bed. Ivy went over to her, squatted, tears burning her eyes when she saw what the killer had done to the person who'd tried to help her.

She was unrecognizable.

"Joce—" Ivy closed her eyes, breathed through her mouth so she wouldn't throw up.

How had the killer gotten in? The hotel was supposed to be secure! Wouldn't he be on tape? Why didn't they scream? Why didn't anyone stop this insanity?

She should never have brought Jocelyn into this mess. *You're next. He's going to find you and kill you.*

Who, dammit? Who was killing everyone who helped her?

Ivy rose to her feet and realized that she was standing in blood. Her plastic flip-flops made the damp blood pool around the edges. Her hand went to her stomach and she turned and ran to the bathroom, but didn't make it. She threw up in the garbage can next to the desk and realized at the same time that she didn't see Maddie.

Ivy spun around the room, didn't see Maddie.

The bathroom door was closed.

Ivy pulled her gun from her backpack. With shaking hands, she reached for the doorknob. Slowly turned the knob and pushed the door in with one movement. She jumped back, both hands on her gun, ready to fire at the first threat.

No one hid in the bathroom. But it wasn't empty.

Maddie lay in the tub, filled close to the top with water so red it looked fake. But it wasn't fake, it was Maddie's blood, leached from her arms that floated just beneath the surface. Her eyes were closed, thank God her eyes were closed. Ivy didn't know if she could handle the accusation had Maddie stared at her. Her head was slumped to the side, as if she'd fallen asleep.

Ivy turned around and saw the mirror.

In blood, someone had painstakingly written

Run, run, as fast as you can

Ivy ran.

CHAPTER FIFTEEN

Thursday

What disturbed Lucy the most about the ornate suite in the historic Hotel Potomac wasn't the blood soaking into the plush gold carpet; it wasn't the familiar, coppery scent of blood, decomposing flesh, and fresh latex; it wasn't even the bodies that had yet to be removed.

What caught Lucy's eye and would continue to haunt her was the blood spatter arcing over the avocado green walls, dried drops sprinkled over a painting of a famous American Revolutionary battle, giving a vivid depth to the tragic scene. The spatter covered the heavy, patterned damask drapery, and sliced across the window. Except for one overturned chair and a two-liter bottle of soda spilled on the carpet—adding a stale, sweet scent to the closed room—nothing else appeared disturbed, at least on the surface. Odd and disconcerting, considering the violence that had been done inside.

Two bodies lay dead in the main hotel room and one

in the bathroom. The suite was an oversized hotel room, with the "living" area consisting of a couch, chairs, desk, and meeting table for six. The sleeping area was up a step and included a dresser and king-sized bed. Jane Doe had bled out in the adjoining bathroom. The difference between yesterday's crime scene and this was stark: the cheapest hotel in DC versus one of the most expensive.

Lucy stood aside while Detective Genie Reid issued orders laced with profanity. Mentally, Lucy added up how much Genie owed her grandson. She was at two-fifty now and no sign of slowing down. The task soothed Lucy's frayed nerves.

Though the crime scene was disturbing, it wasn't the source of her angst. What bothered her was that this was the work of the same killer.

Genie hadn't spoken of the connection, but when Lucy walked into the hotel room she saw a similar blood pattern as had been in the Red Light Motel. How many left-handed throat-slashers were there in one city?

"Well fuck me from here to Jersey," Genie said from the bathroom.

Two dollars, seventy-five cents.

Lucy had already put on gloves and booties. She carefully walked through the room and looked over Genie's shoulder.

The floor was covered with pink water from the naked female victim who had bled out in the tub. One stab wound to her chest, plus her left wrist cut so deeply her hand had nearly separated from her arm.

The victim's body disappeared into water darkened by her blood.

Lucy had to close her eyes, just for a moment. The

violence in the main hotel room was disturbing, but Lucy had seen crime scenes like that before.

The body in the bathroom was a whole new level of gruesome.

"What the fuck does that mean?" Genie demanded, her voice cracking.

Lucy opened her eyes and looked at the mirror. The killer had written another message on the mirror.

Run, run as fast as you can

"You can't catch me, I'm the gingerbread man," Lucy whispered.

"What?" Genie spun around, pushing Lucy away from the door.

"I was finishing the rhyme."

"He's taunting us. He thinks I won't catch him? Watch me. I'm going to nail the bastard."

"It could be a taunt, or it could be a message to the others."

"What others?"

"One of the six," Lucy said.

"You're talking Greek. Six?"

"From his message yesterday."

"So we have three more victims today, he's going to kill two more?"

"I don't know."

"But you just said—fuck it. I don't want to know. Taback! Where's the security? The manager? Has someone gotten me the damn ID on our vics? Anything?"

Three dollars.

Genie stormed out of the room. Lucy stayed while DC

forensics photographed the scene. The coroner hadn't arrived, so no one had touched the bodies.

Lucy walked the scene, starting at the door.

Without more information, she couldn't figure out what exactly had happened—if the male victim had been followed into the room, or if someone was waiting inside. Or if he had known his attacker and let him in.

The male victim had his back to the door. He was of average size and build, approximately five foot ten, lean, dressed in beige slacks and a button-down shirt that had once been white. His shoes were leather loafers, the soles worn but the tops polished. A man who walked outdoors frequently as part of his job, common in the Beltway.

A hotel card key was next to his body, a small overnight suitcase next to the door. She closed her eyes, pictured what she would do if she had an overnight bag. Unlock the door—push the key in, wait for the beep, open. Put the bag down, particularly if it was heavy. Close the door. Bolt it.

The door hadn't been bolted. The maid had come in and found the bodies.

The male vic had been killed quickly—his throat deeply slashed just like Nicole Bellows's. Grab, slash, drop. The blood spatter indicated the attacker grabbed him from behind, used his left hand, slit his throat hard and fast, showing the killer was not only as tall or taller than the victim, but also physically strong.

It took both strength and a good knife to slice the neck so deeply.

No sign of hesitation, no sign of struggle.

Why hadn't anyone screamed?

The woman was fully clothed and near the bed, her body huddled in a protective fetal position. Castoff left the ceiling dotted with arcs of blood. Lucy couldn't even count the multitude of wounds on the victim, and she was only looking at her back. Her head was buried in her arms and Lucy was relieved she couldn't see her face.

Man—quick death. Woman—brutally murdered. Young woman in the bathroom—possibly quick. Lucy hadn't been able to tell what came first, the chest wound or the wrist.

Except . . .

She went back to the bathroom doorway and pulled the door closed. Opened it. The door swung toward the bathtub, but the killer would have been visible in the mirror—unless the mirror was foggy with steam.

The girl in the bathtub may have jumped up—which would account for the water on the floor sloshing over. He had to stab her to keep her from screaming. To pull her up out of the tub to slit her throat would have caused a mess, an opportunity for the girl to scratch him or scream for help.

Lucy looked at the angle of the wound. She pretended to hold a knife. Adjusted her hand to throw the knife. The doorway was approximately six feet from the entry wound. He stepped, threw the knife into her chest— that's why the wound was more horizontal than vertical. It was the angle at which he threw it, because he was left-handed, standing, while she was reclining in the tub— possibly trying to get up.

The killer threw the knife without hesitation. He then either had a second knife, or he pulled the knife from her chest—

Lucy looked around, saw faint marks that could have been blood spatter, but the moisture from the bath had caused the trail to nearly disappear.

He then slit her wrist deeply, dropping her hand in the water to facilitate bleeding out.

She wasn't dead from the wound to the chest. If she were, there wouldn't have been so much blood in the bathtub.

She had convulsed or tried to get up, causing more water to slosh out, leaving the tub only half-full.

Had he watched her die?

No. He didn't get his thrills from watching death. Nicole Bellows at the Red Light, the male victim here, fast kills, a job, get it done and get out.

No, he didn't need to get out *immediately.* He wanted to leave the message.

She turned to the mirror. He'd wiped steam from the mirror, the quick strokes of his hand or arm visible, along with blood smeared across the mirror.

Did he reach over to the girl for her blood or take it from his knife?

The knife, Lucy guessed. The message faded near the end. He'd gone back to the knife—or body if Lucy's hypothesis was inaccurate—three times, the blood thicker on the first *Run,* then on *as,* and finally on the last word *can.*

Each letter dripped down the slick surface, drying in long streaks.

Who are you talking to? Why this message? Are you engaging the police? Think you're uncatchable? Or are you writing to someone else?

He'd changed the first rhyme slightly, but not the second rhyme.

Wendy James's killer also left a message.

Not every killer left a deliberate message.

She'd thought about the similarities when she was at the morgue, but dismissed them.

Now, she couldn't.

And this guilty whore don't cry no more.

Not a children's rhyme, but Lucy had an ear for languages and there was a very familiar rhythm to the message, it had the exact same beats as other common rhymes, but Lucy couldn't pinpoint which one he'd used, if he'd done it on purpose.

"Kincaid!"

Genie stepped back into the room.

"Yes?" Whatever was in her head disappeared. She would go home and analyze the line structurally against popular children's rhymes. But she was 90 percent certain that the man who killed Wendy James had killed Nicole Bellows and these three victims.

"I just spoke to the manager and security chief. We have an ID on two of the victims. Christopher Taylor and his wife Jocelyn."

"And the girl in the bathroom?" She appeared too old to be their daughter.

"Unknown."

"I want you to see something," Lucy said.

Genie grimaced, but followed Lucy to the bathroom.

"There are two cell phones submersed in the sink."

"I already made note of that. CSU will bag them, see if we can get anything off them."

"Look at the victim's arms," Lucy said.

"Just tell me, Kincaid."

Genie avoided looking at the girl. Lucy hadn't pegged Genie as being squeamish, but yesterday the body had been removed by the time Lucy and Noah had arrived. Today's crime scene was far more grisly.

"The girl was a cutter, though not recently." Her arms, which floated on the surface of the bloody water, showed the telltale scars of a longtime cutter. Her hair was long and dyed bright red, the roots showing her to be a natural blonde. "But what's more interesting are their belongings. Backpack, stuffed like an overnight bag. Toiletries—all for women. I don't think the male victim was staying here."

"Or he kept everything in a razor kit."

Lucy looked around. "And put it back in his suitcase? I don't know. But look at this backpack—it's old, ratty, hardly worth keeping. Do you bring a backpack like that to a hotel like this?"

She pointed to a small, open tin that held three blue pills.

"These are unmarked. Look at the edge of the capsule—illegal lab, I think."

Genie concurred. "Barbiturate?"

"Probably a benzodiazepine." Lucy and Genie walked back to the main room. "Jocelyn Taylor was overkill, this victim was quickly killed. If she was drugged first—self or forced—it might explain the lack of fight."

"Whatever it is, we have a bigger issue," Genie said. "Taylor is the chief of staff to a newly elected congressman, Dale Hartline. His wife is a social worker for a nonprofit group. They live in Chevy Chase. Checked in here Tuesday before eight in the morning—paid extra for that privilege. But get this—security cams have *five people* in this room and next door."

"Adjoining room?"

Genie jerked her finger toward a door on the far side.

"Two double beds. The Taylors didn't register any other guests and only asked for two room keys, but we definitely have five in here. Unfortunately, the security cameras only monitor the lobby and garage. But they're having a shitload of problems with the feed—damn! I must be over five bucks by now."

She continued. "If there was no message on the damn mirror, I would never have thought the Nicole Bellows case was connected to this, but now? It makes no sense. Cheap-ass motel, five-star hotel. Black street hooker, white congressional staffer. Maybe he was into kink? Maybe the dead girl in the bath is a hooker? Wife watches? Pimp gets pissed? Fuck if I can figure it out."

Three dollars, seventy-five cents.

Lucy understood Genie's frustration.

"Detective?" One of the CSU officer's came from the adjoining room with a large plastic bag full of clothing.

"Tell me the killer left his clothes and his name is sewn on the label."

He cracked a smile. "A couple T-shirts, tank tops, pajama bottoms. Found them in a drawer. They reek of smoke, and I'm not talking tobacco. Whoever wore these were in or near a fire."

Genie ordered the cop monitoring the door, "Taback, find out if the Taylors had a fire at their house."

The crime scene investigator interrupted. "Already checked. Negative."

Genie threw her arms up. "Guess that would have been too easy. Check all structural fires in the city in the last seventy-two hours. See if there's any reason that the Taylors or the girl in the bathroom could have been in any of those locations. Did we get the girl's face into the database?"

"They're running her through now—we can't get prints because her body's waterlogged, maybe the morgue can."

Genie looked at Lucy. She shook her head. "Doubtful, but there are some computer programs that may be able to extrapolate. It really depends on what they have to start with."

The investigator continued. "There's evidence that the killer showered in the other bathroom. A towel with blood, a smear on the tile. We're processing the room carefully hoping to get hair or fiber samples."

"The killer showered?" Genie said.

Lucy said, "He had to. He stabbed three people to death. He'd have had a lot of blood on him, and even if he managed to elude the security cams, he wouldn't want to be seen in bloody clothes."

"So he showered, brought a change of clothes with him? That takes a lot of planning."

"He didn't shower at the Red Light Motel, maybe he realized he had more blood on him than he expected," Lucy offered. "So he came better prepared this time."

"Well shit."

Four dollars.

"Coroner's here," announced the uniformed officer standing at the door.

"Send 'em in."

To Lucy, Genie said, "Let's go see if security fixed their technology screwup." She paused. " 'Screwup' isn't a swear word."

CHAPTER SIXTEEN

Lucy crowded into the small security office with Genie, two cops, the manager, and security chief. She stood near the back, barely able to see the laptop monitor on which the head of security had downloaded the tapes from the last twenty-four hours.

Genie gave a quick rundown on the timeline.

"Jocelyn Taylor checked in alone at eight A.M. Tuesday morning, but the reservation was made an hour earlier over the phone by her husband, Chris."

Officer Taback added, "You said three girls were with her, correct?"

"Yes. After she checked in, she went back to the front, where we presume she got into her car and drove into the secured garage. Free parking if you're a guest, just slide your room key into the kiosk. That was at eight ten in the morning."

The security chief, Tom Wright, flipped the screen to a wide-angle garage shot. "The garage is hardwired into the system—it's older than the hotel's security system, more secure, but takes more people and space to maintain," he said. "Mrs. Taylor parked near the elevator and three girls got out."

Lucy recognized the victim, who was the tallest of the three, but not the other two girls. One was in her early twenties, but the other was definitely younger, with the awkward movements of a young teen who had recently grown. Thirteen? Fourteen?

Genie said, "We'll take the best head shots of the girls and distribute them widely so we can ID them quickly. We'll send them to your cell phones to show witnesses. We need to know who these girls are, so we're doing a complete canvass of the hotel and nearby restaurants."

Wright flipped to the hotel system. The feed was much clearer than in the garage, and in color instead of black-and-white.

"The girls went to the room with Mrs. Taylor, and until last night, none of them left."

"Do you notice that each of the girls has a backpack," Lucy said, "but Jocelyn Taylor has no luggage?"

"She left Tuesday afternoon and returned a few hours later with shopping bags. Then she left and didn't return until Wednesday afternoon."

"So she wasn't staying here," Genie said.

"Doesn't appear that she was," Wright said. "On Wednesday evening she left the room, met her husband in the lobby. They walked out—didn't take their vehicles—and came back nearly two hours later with carryout from a nearby restaurant."

Taback said, "CSU found a receipt in the room for

two meals eaten at the restaurant, and a large carryout order charged separately. We didn't find any food bags, only one half-eaten container."

"At ten thirty P.M., approximately thirty minutes after the Taylors returned, the brunette and the blonde left," Wright continued. "You can see they're each carrying a backpack and the younger teen has the food. They went to the garage, and footage shows them leaving in Jocelyn's car."

"Do we know that the Taylors were alive at that point?" Lucy asked.

"Chris Taylor made two phone calls between ten thirty and eleven P.M., and we're tracing them now," Genie said. He also called down to the desk asking for a six A.M. wake-up call. The hotel rang three times, ten minutes apart, and there was no answer."

"Did they find the bodies then?"

"No," Wright said. "Housekeeping found the bodies just after eight this morning. Last night, Taylor left the room at eleven fifteen and went to the garage, removed a suitcase from his car, and shortly after that, the main hotel security went down until twelve-oh-three A.M."

"Jammed," Lucy said when she saw the fuzz on the screen. "It was jammed—very easy to do with wireless. The hotel is on wireless, correct?"

The security chief nodded. "The garage is hardwired, but the hotel security cameras were upgraded to a secure wireless network."

"Not very secure," Taback muttered.

Lucy glanced around and wished Noah had arrived. She'd called him right when she got the call from Genie. He was in the middle of a meeting, but said he'd be over as soon as he could.

"We called our IT department and they were working on the problem when it resolved itself," Wright said. "We've had some glitches with the system, but it had never been down for this long before, hotel-wide."

"We need copies of film from all security cameras in the immediate area," Genie said. "Two-block radius."

Taback nodded. "We'll get it."

Lucy said, "Downed network, master pass key, killer who showers after killing three people? I think we're dealing with a professional. Premeditated, planned attack."

"There's more," Wright said. He fast-forwarded the tape. "We get visual shortly after midnight. At one forty-five A.M., one of the two girls returns."

Lucy watched as the brunette parked in the garage. "Is the other girl in the car?"

"Negative," Wright said. "We have a camera at the entrance and unless she was lying down in the back-seat, she wasn't there."

The brunette had a backpack and went in the elevator. "After hours, all floors are locked unless you have a room key," Wright said. "She used the room key to access the sixth floor. Seven minutes later, she's back in the garage." While he spoke, he fast-forwarded through the film until they could see the brunette exiting. Though the film wasn't sharp, it was obvious the young woman was in distress. She left the garage in Jocelyn Taylor's car.

"She's not a suspect," Genie said, "but she's definitely a person of interest. Why didn't she report the crime? What happened to the teenager? Who are these girls? How are these murders connected to Nicole Bellows at the Red Light?"

"They're connected?" Taback asked.

"I see a lot of homicides each week, but rarely does the killer leave a message. Two messages in two days?"

Three messages. But Lucy didn't say anything. She had to run her theory by Noah first. She wasn't going to overstep her place again.

But it all made sense. The hidden room. The prostitutes. *Whore* implied prostitute. *Slut* would have been more appropriate for a promiscuous young woman as Wendy appeared to be on the surface.

What if the three murders were connected because the girls all knew each other?

There was one easy way to find out. Go back to Nicole's previous residence and show pictures of the other victims and find out from Cora Fox who had gotten Nicole out of the slums.

"Kincaid, ready for a road trip? Let's talk to the people who knew the Taylors best, starting with their employers."

"Detective." One of the CSU investigators stepped into the cramped room.

Genie said to Lucy, "Meet me in the lobby." To everyone else, she ordered, "Get to work, people. You know what to do."

Lucy took the opportunity to call Noah.

"Armstrong," he answered brusquely.

"It's Lucy. I'm still at the Hotel Potomac. Genie and I are going to interview the victims' employers."

"Good. I don't need a blow-by-blow, you're in good hands with Detective Reid."

"The male victim is chief of staff to Congressman Hartline."

"Call me if anything comes of it, or e-mail a status

report. You wanted to work this case, work it. You don't need me to babysit you."

"No, but—"

"Lucy, do you have a question?"

"No." She bit her lip. She was trying to be diligent. She wasn't an agent—as she'd been reminded countless times in the last three days—and she didn't want to screw this up.

"I have to brief Assistant Director Stockton in ten minutes. Since Wendy James's identity has been plastered all over the news, the media has been doing our case more damage than good with their speculation. Stockton is going to give a statement and hopefully stop some of the leaks and misinformation."

"I know you're busy. I'm sorry. I'll e-mail a report tonight."

"Lucy—" Noah hesitated. He must have put his hand over the phone because she only heard muffled voices, then he came back on. "Sorry. Lucy, you don't need me to hold your hand, okay? I wouldn't have let you work with Genie if I didn't think you were more than capable of handling this investigation."

You don't need me to babysit you.

You don't need me to hold your hand.

He must think she was the neediest agent-in-training the Bureau had ever hired.

Lucy decided to take the compliment at face value and not read anything into it, otherwise she would be paralyzed into inaction.

"Thank you." She hung up.

Genie crossed the lobby, her skin shiny with perspiration. She grabbed a tourist pamphlet off a rack near the registration desk and began fanning herself. "I swear, menopause in summer is God's way of punishing me for the sins of my youth."

Lucy smiled. "I'm sure you were an angel."

Genie laughed deeply. "Honey, I was a little devil. Where'd you think I learned my colorful language? Not just because I started as a beat cop." They walked out.

"Are you going to Mrs. Taylor's place of employment first?"

"No, we have a much bigger fish to talk to first. I have Chris Taylor's phone records. He made two calls last night—one to his office where he left a message on voice mail that he wasn't coming in today, and one four-minute conversation to Senator Jonathon Paxton."

Lucy nearly stumbled off the curb.

Genie didn't miss the recognition. "Know him?"

"Yes."

"Conflict?"

She shook her head. "No."

"Are you sure?"

Was her face that expressive?

"Yes."

She got into the passenger seat and waited until Genie pulled into traffic before she spoke. How could she explain her relationship with Jonathon Paxton in a way that didn't make it sound bizarre?

You can't.

She hadn't seen the senator in nearly six months, and she didn't want to see him today. But her curiosity would keep her on this case, because she needed to know why Taylor called Paxton.

"Taylor worked for Hartline, right?" Lucy confirmed.

"For the last six months. Before that, he was a legislative aide to Senator Paxton. I need information, Lucy, before we walk in there. I'll admit, I don't like dealing with these guys, and if there's any chance that the senator is guilty of a crime, I gotta turn it over to the feds, and I won't be heartbroken about it. But as far as I know, Taylor is a former employee."

Lucy didn't want Genie to know about her past, but she couldn't avoid it now. If she found out later, the detective would think Lucy had lied or intentionally withheld information.

"I've known Senator Paxton for seven years," Lucy said.

"You must have been a kid."

"Eighteen. I met him when I moved to DC for college. Both his daughter and I were attacked by the same man. Monique wasn't as lucky as I was."

"You knew his daughter?"

"No. She was killed years ago, but her killer was never caught until he kidnapped me." Lucy hesitated, considering telling Genie the whole story, but now wasn't the time or place to explain that Jonathon Paxton considered her some sort of hero for killing the man who'd killed his daughter and raped Lucy.

"Senator Paxton took me under his wing, so to speak. He gave me a recommendation for the FBI Academy, and I interned for the Senate Judiciary Committee for a semester when I was in college. I haven't seen him in six months."

"It sounds like a conflict. Shit."

"It's not. He won't lie to me."

"How can you be so sure?"

"He thinks of me as a daughter. But believe me, I don't consider him a father figure."

"Is he capable of murder? Do you think he killed the Taylors?"

Two different questions. Lucy answered the latter. "He didn't kill the Taylors, or that poor girl. If Chris called him for anything, it was for help. Senator Paxton is very loyal to the people who work for him."

"So our vic calls an old senator instead of the police for help?" Genie made a ticking sound with her tongue. "That sure sounds fishy to me." She glanced at Lucy. "All right, I'm going to trust you on this. Let's find out what they talked about during those four minutes."

CHAPTER SEVENTEEN

Lucy straightened her stance and put an impassive expression on her face, steeling herself against any emotional reaction. Jonathon Paxton read people well, and he would see through her if she gave him even one small crack in her composure.

She walked into his office behind Genie.

"Senator Paxton," Genie said extending her hand. "Thank you for agreeing to meet with us so quickly."

"Of course." He looked at Lucy, his eyes lit with surprise and unspoken questions.

"Senator," Lucy said formally.

"Lucy. It is so good to see you." He took her hand. He held on long enough to have Genie change her posture. The detective was now hyperalert, and Lucy would have to be doubly diligent not to say or do anything that would make Genie think there was a conflict. Because there wasn't. If Lucy could prove the senator was guilty of any felony, she would make sure justice was done.

"I'm sorry the circumstances are so tragic," Lucy said carefully.

He motioned for them to sit on the couch in his sitting area. He sat in a leather chair and said, "Do you know what happened to Chris? If you knew him, you'd know he's a good man. He doesn't get into trouble."

Genie said, "Mr. Taylor and his wife were found dead in their hotel room along with an unidentified woman. We confirmed that he left a message with Congressman Hartline's office that he would not be coming in to the office today, and then he called you. You were the last person Mr. Taylor spoke to, and near as we can tell based on the evidence, he was killed less than an hour later. What did you discuss?"

Paxton was processing the information, but Lucy couldn't help but think he was calculating his response at the same time.

"Chris wanted to meet with me. I told him come by anytime today, I'd leave whatever meeting I was in."

"Would you do that for any of your former staff members?"

"Most of them. Chris? Absolutely."

"Did he say why?"

"He didn't share a lot of details, but told me that Jocelyn—his wife—was helping a couple girls who were in trouble and he wanted my advice. You know what his wife does, right?" He looked at Lucy.

"She works for Missing and At-Risk Children," Lucy said.

"It's a vocation for her. She reminds me of you, how dedicated she is to the people she's trying to help."

Genie said, "You didn't find that odd? That he would

call you and not someone else? If they were in trouble, why not call the police?"

Lucy knew the answer before Paxton said it. "Detective, the girls were scared of the police. Jocelyn worked primarily with teenage prostitutes. I've given a substantial sum of money to MARC, and Chris knows I'm always willing to help. I suspected he was going to ask for money, as well as advice."

"You normally hand over money to prostitutes?" Genie asked.

Paxton didn't miss the double entendre, and Lucy held her breath.

"These are troubled girls who are often dragged into this business by people they trust. If they show the desire to get out, and if they need help to do it, yes, I'll give them money. Usually, I'll give it through MARC and they direct it where it's most needed. But sometimes, if the need is immediate, the director will call me."

"Chris isn't the director," Lucy said.

"But he knows I'll help. I didn't know about the organization until he started working for me. That was nearly four years ago."

Genie said, "Let me make sure I have this straight. Chris called you last night and asked for a meeting to seek advice to help teenage prostitutes."

"Chris would do anything for his wife, and his wife would do anything to help these girls." Paxton leaned forward, his compassion tinged with anger. "These girls are unwanted by everyone. Many were turned out of their homes. Abusive fathers. Molestation. Fast-talking boyfriends who uprooted them, then forced them to sell their bodies. The system failed them, over and over. Most don't survive. If they have enough hope left to try and create a new life, why wouldn't I help?"

In one conversation, Lucy was reminded about why she had liked and admired the senator for so long.

Everything he said was true. Chris had called him for help, and the senator planned to help him. But Lucy suspected he knew more than he was saying. For Jonathon Paxton, "help" meant a lot of different things.

Some of them illegal.

Genie said, "There are two missing girls that were seen with Jocelyn Taylor yesterday. Can you identify them?"

Genie showed the senator the photos of the brunette, then the dark blonde. Lucy watched his expression for any reaction.

There was none.

And that's when Lucy knew that *he* knew who they were.

The Jonathon Paxton she knew would have shown compassion and tenderness toward the girls, suspecting what they had suffered that led them to this point in their lives.

Then he would have been enraged toward those who had made them suffer.

"I'm sorry, I don't," he said. "Are you going to go wide with this in the press? I can help, whatever you need."

"Thank you, I'll get back to you on that. We'll see ourselves out."

Jonathon followed them to the door anyway. "You have no suspects? You don't know who did this? Or why?"

Lucy turned and looked into his eyes. "Do you?"

She couldn't read his expression. "I wish I did," he said evenly. "I would make sure justice was served."

Senator Jonathon Paxton sat at his desk and considered his options.

Chris is dead.

Jonathon put his head in his hands and breathed deeply, sorrow flooding his heart. Chris was a good man, loyal, trustworthy. Jonathon had recommended him for the chief of staff slot when Dale won the special election in their home state of New York. Chris was smart, but not jaded like so many young staffers.

Maybe if he had been more jaded and less trusting, he would still be alive.

Jonathon needed more information about the murders, about what the FBI knew. He wasn't going to volunteer information that they didn't know, but he didn't want to withhold information they might need.

He recognized with profound regret that he had some culpability in Chris's death.

After all, he had set this chain of events in motion.

Jonathon glanced at his closet door. "You can come out," he said.

His security consultant stepped into the room. "You should put a chair in there."

"Find Ivy and her sister."

"She's spooked and not answering her phone. But I'll do everything I can to find them."

"Spare no expense, but be discreet. They have a photograph of Sara, it's only a matter of time—"

"I understand."

Jonathon always had a contigency plan. Now that Ivy wouldn't be able to record the blackmailers, he had to find another way to get back what they stole.

"I'm going to bring in Sean Rogan." He didn't want to, because Rogan was a wild card. Jonathon wasn't certain where his loyalties were. It all rested on how much he loved Lucy—and what he was willing to do to protect her future.

"Are you sure you can trust him?"

"I need the locket back," Jonathon said, his voice rising. "It's all I have of Monique."

"He's not going to buy that."

He might not. But Jonathon didn't trust Sean Rogan enough to tell him that what was inside the locket was more valuable than the locket itself.

"I have an idea. But make sure Ivy and Sara are safe. I made a promise; I'm going to honor it."

"I'll take them to the safe house."

Jonathon breathed easier. "Thank you, Sergio. As soon as the police make the connection to Wendy James's murder, I'll confess my part. But if I say anything now, I won't be in a position to help them."

CHAPTER EIGHTEEN

Jocelyn Taylor had worked for Missing and At-Risk Children, a nonprofit social welfare organization that focused on finding and reuniting runaways with their families, or finding homes for abused children. Many runaways left because of abuse or neglect, and MARC worked to place these difficult cases with homes outside of the foster care system.

MARC's small suite of offices were on the third floor of a squat office building wedged between two skyscrapers on K Street. Genie and Lucy were ushered immediately into the director's office.

Cathy Hummel was a tiny Asian woman, barely five feet tall, with an impossibly narrow waist. She wore fashionable red-framed glasses and a pale gray suit, crisp even in this sweltering heat. Hummel's office was small but extremely tidy—no paper could be seen anywhere. Two locked oak file cabinets filled one short wall; the desk and two guest chairs crowded the remaining space.

After getting over the initial shock of the triple homicide, she asked, "Who did such a thing?"

"We're pursuing all leads," Genie said. "What did Jocelyn do for you?"

"She's a social worker." As if that explained everything.

"Can you be more specific?" Lucy asked. She held up the brochure she'd taken from the small lobby. "It says here that you also work with law enforcement to rehabilitate underaged prostitutes. Senator Paxton said that was Jocelyn's specialty."

"You spoke with Jonathon Paxton?"

"Chris used to work for him."

"I know, but—why is that important?"

"We're trying to retrace the Taylors' steps," Genie said. "How long has Jocelyn worked here?"

Cathy took a deep breath. "Fifteen years, started right out of college. Jocelyn had been raised in foster care, she knew how bad the system could be, and she also knew how good the system could be when it worked. She wanted to help teenage girls make better choices, and the only way they could make good choices was if they had options. So many of these girls feel hopeless. They think no one cares what happens to them." She stared at a picture on her desk. From her angle, Lucy couldn't see who was in the photograph.

Cathy shook her head, then continued. "Jocelyn worked mostly with teenage runaways and prostitutes. She cared."

Unspoken was *"She cared too much."*

"And recently? This past week?"

"Jocelyn hasn't been in the office much this week, but that's not unusual," Cathy quickly added. It almost sounded as if she was protecting her, and while that wasn't strange, here she sounded defensive.

Genie said, "So you don't know what she was doing?"

"No, of course not, it's just that—" She stopped. "You said there was a third victim?"

Genie said, "Unidentified. The photograph is disturbing, but it's important we identify her."

Hummel took a deep breath, braced herself, then nodded.

Genie had a Polaroid picture of the Jane Doe in the bathtub, face only, but there was no mistaking that she was dead.

Her face fell. "Maddie."

"Maddie who?"

She shook her head. "I don't know. Just . . . Maddie. She, oh my God, excuse me." She ran from the room, her hands to her mouth.

Lucy wanted to go after her, but Genie put a hand on her arm. "She's okay. Just give her a minute."

"She knows what Jocelyn was doing and she's not sharing. It's dangerous."

"She will. It's natural to want to protect those you care about, but Cathy will do what's right. We crossed paths before, she's a class act."

Lucy hoped so. She had far too much experience with people who, thinking they were doing the right thing, ended up hurting far more people than they helped.

Cathy was extremely protective of Jocelyn—not just MARC, her organization, but *Jocelyn,* her employee. Her friend.

The day before Lucy was supposed to graduate from high school, she'd never thought much about privacy. She wanted to do something special with her life, have fun doing it, and share it with the world if she had the chance. She was friendly, talkative, almost carefree—at least as carefree as possible with her military and law enforcement family. She'd wanted to study languages, which came naturally to her, to swim competitively and maybe earn a place on the Olympic team. She wanted to someday raise a family and travel around the world. She thought the world was her oyster, the cliché so appropriate to growing up as the youngest in a large family of seven who doted on her.

She'd been sheltered and protected, knew it and didn't care.

Then every dream she'd ever had was stolen from her the day she should have walked down the aisle in her gown and cap to accept her diploma.

She'd never go to the Olympics; though she swam in college, her heart wasn't in it. Instead, she became certified in water search and rescue where her strength as a swimmer helped her find and retrieve people both dead and alive.

She'd never study language, because how could she help people and appease her need for justice if she was a diplomat or a translator? But her language skills helped her understand people from different backgrounds and lifestyles, both spoken and unspoken.

And she'd never have children of her own because she no longer had a womb to carry a baby.

Worse, her pain and suffering, all of the evil that had been done to her, was part of the public record. She had no privacy and never would. Though she'd accepted it, there were days she wanted to scream at the unfairness of life.

But she didn't. She went on. Because there were no other options.

Her family protected her, and she loved them for it, but sometimes it was too much.

Her eye caught the simple silver picture frame on Cathy's desk, the one Cathy had glanced at several times during their conversation. She leaned forward and tilted her head so she could see who was in the photo.

Cathy Hummel, much younger, with a man Lucy presumed was her husband, and Jocelyn.

Except Jocelyn was much younger as well. Eighteen? Nineteen? Long before she was working here.

Cathy Hummel stepped back into the room. Her eyes were rimmed red, but dry, and her hands grasped several pieces of crumbled tissues. "I'm so sorry," she mumbled. She sat back down. "I don't know what else I can do for you."

"How long have you known Jocelyn?" Lucy asked.

"I told you, she came to work for me when she was twenty-four, out of college—"

"Did you know her before she worked for you?"

"Why?"

"I saw the picture on your desk."

Cathy stared at the picture. "That was taken the day Jocelyn got her GED," she said quietly. "She was nineteen, but she hadn't been in school since she was sixteen." She shook her head. "This is all sealed, and I'm not going to share it with you. I'm sorry."

"It may have something to do with her death."

"It doesn't." Cathy's voice took on an edge of hostility.

Genie spoke up. "Was Jocelyn working with Maddie? Was Maddie in trouble?"

"I told you, Jocelyn wasn't in the office this week."

"But you would know why," Genie said. She leaned forward. "I understand you want to protect Jocelyn. I'm not going to drag her reputation through the slime. I'll do my best to keep anything not directly related to the case off the books."

Genie continued. "We haven't released this information to the press, but we believe that the Taylors and Maddie were killed by the same person or people who killed a known prostitute, Nicole Bellows. Do you know her?"

Cathy's shocked expression revealed the truth.

"Nicole was the murdered prostitute I read about in the paper this morning?" she asked weakly.

"Yes." Lucy watched the director closely. "Anything you know, anything that could send us in the right direction, we'd appreciate."

Tears streamed down Cathy's face. "I told Jocelyn not to get involved. Not with those girls."

That surprised Lucy. An organization like MARC *always* got involved. To them, no one was beyond help.

Cathy continued. "Six months ago, we were hired by the mother of a fourteen-year-old girl who had run away with her boyfriend, a nineteen-year-old high school dropout. She filed a missing persons report and went through proper channels, but the police couldn't find her.

"Jocelyn tracked down the boyfriend and he was more forthcoming, because she wasn't a cop. He dumped Amy, left her in Baltimore, and didn't think twice about her. She wouldn't 'pull her weight,' he said.

"Jocelyn has cultivated a lot of contacts in the tristate area. She traced Amy from Baltimore to DC, and finally to this group of girls who lived in a house on Hawthorne."

"That's a nice area," Genie remarked. "Not where I'd expect prostitutes to live."

"Jocelyn had met Ivy, the woman who ran the group of call girls, a year ago. She didn't talk about her much, but they had an understanding, I suppose. Jocelyn claimed Ivy wasn't like other *madams,* but in my experience, anyone running prostitutes is a criminal."

"Ivy?" Lucy asked. "Do you have a last name?"

Cathy shook her head. "I never met her. I told Jocelyn I wanted to, to assess her sincerity, but Ivy wanted no help whatsoever."

Lucy started to see what the problem was. "And that's why you and Jocelyn started having problems."

"No," Cathy said, without conviction. She shredded the tissue clasped in her hands. "I told her to go to the authorities. The girl, Amy, was fourteen; if we knew where she was, we had a responsibility." She bit her lip. "I should have done it myself. Jocelyn convinced me to do it her way."

"What happened to Amy?" Lucy asked, fearing the worst.

"Jocelyn reunited Amy with her mother. A happy ending. I've talked to Amy's mom—she's doing great. She's going back to school in the fall, getting her life back. Because Jocelyn didn't give up.

"Jocelyn had it in her head that she had to save all the girls in Ivy's house, but some of these girls—like Nicole—had been on the streets for years," Cathy said. "They were nineteen, twenty, maybe older. There's a point where you have to focus on your best hope for success. Jocelyn wanted to help those whom no one else would. The hardest cases."

That's why Senator Paxton was involved. He was helping those hard cases, the lost causes. Because that's what he did.

Lucy's stomach twisted with her conflicted feelings about her former mentor.

"We had an argument about Ivy," Cathy said. "Jocelyn stopped talking to me, spent more time with that girl, and then on Tuesday morning she called me on my cell phone, early—five A.M. Said Ivy's house had burned down and she was helping the girls find a place to stay. Nothing else. I came into the office yesterday, and she'd cleaned out her desk. I've been trying to call her—" Her voice caught. "How long? How long has she been dead?"

"She was killed late last night."

"Why didn't she call me back? She knows I would have done anything for her! I loved her like a daughter."

Lucy didn't have the answer to that question. This situation was far more complex than she'd originally thought. But finally, they had a solid direction. It should be easy to find the house on Hawthorne Street that had burned down in the early hours of Friday morning.

"Was Maddie one of the girls in Ivy's house?" she asked Cathy.

The director nodded. "I don't know the others, or how many—six, eight, ten." She put her hands up, then they fell limply to her desk. "Jocelyn was very protective of them. She was driven. And now she's dead!"

Lucy suspected she knew how many girls had been in the house.

Six blind mice. See how they run.

Cathy unlocked her bottom drawer. She hesitated a moment, then pulled out a file and handed it to Lucy. "I shouldn't be giving you this. It's all I have on Ivy. I'm sure Jocelyn has more; I don't know where, if it's not at her house."

The file was thin. Lucy opened it. Inside were two pages of handwritten notes apparently taken by Cathy Hummel. Time Jocelyn was spending with Ivy, observations. The third page was a photograph. It wasn't a sharp picture, but it showed a young brunette with an aristocratic bone structure and attractive face.

It was the same girl who had taken Jocelyn's car from the hotel the night the Taylors had been murdered. The same girl who'd returned, presumably found the bodies, but ran instead of calling the police.

"This is Ivy?"

"Jocelyn gave me that a few months back, wanting to know if she'd been reported missing. I ran her picture through our database; she didn't come up."

What secrets are you hiding, Ivy?

Cathy continued, "Trust me when I tell you this: Ivy is bad news. Why else would Jocelyn keep things from me?"

CHAPTER NINETEEN

"It looks like these murders are connected to Jocelyn's work," Genie said as she drove across town to Hawthorne Street. "I want to talk to the neighbors, check the house." She got on the phone with her team to get the details about the fire.

Lucy sent Noah an e-mail through her phone about what they had learned, growing increasingly frustrated with the small keyboard. She wanted to talk to him about Wendy James and the message left on her body, along with the idea to show both Wendy and Maddie's pictures to Cora Fox, but she didn't want to do it over messaging.

And she especially wanted to talk to him about Senator Paxton. She wanted to talk to Jonathon one-on-one, but she wouldn't do it behind Noah's back. He wasn't involved in killing Chris and Jocelyn Taylor, but she had no doubt that if he knew who had killed them, he would seek his own vengeance.

He'd done it before.

But she could put none of that in e-mail. And she couldn't tell Noah that, because he would ask her why she hadn't come forward with the information she had on the senator. And she would have to say she didn't have proof, she had no evidence, she just had her intuition and a theory and her masters degree in criminal psychology.

Plus the fact that she understood Jonathon Paxton better than anyone else.

She closed her note with a request to talk to him as soon as possible about a theory. She hoped he'd call her immediately, and waited for her phone to vibrate the entire drive over to Hawthorne. It didn't.

Genie pulled up in front of the burned remains of what appeared to have been a large, Craftsman-style home—though it was hard to tell as every wall was black from soot and smoke.

Caution tape surrounded the crumbling structure.

What was left of the house was on a quiet, tree-lined street with well-maintained, stately, older homes. It was only blocks from a main thoroughfare, but the blocks surrounding it were equally attractive. It wasn't what most people think of when they think "Washington, DC," but Lucy had lived here long enough to know there were many pockets like this in the city.

"I talked to the lead fire investigator," Genie said. "They believe it started in the basement. The house was on an old furnace system, but the owners"—she looked at her notes—"George and Karen Schwartz, currently of Satellite Beach, Florida, said they have maintenance records that the furnace had a clean bill of health as of March."

"Any fatalities?"

"No, though two firefighters were injured fighting the blaze. The renters haven't come forward."

"And the house was rented to Ivy? Do we have a last name yet?"

"The owners don't know—they use a property management company."

"And?"

"And no one has talked to them yet. The fire started before dawn Tuesday morning, the owners were contacted later that day. By this morning, it got buried under eight more investigations. They're sending me a copy of the file."

They walked around the property, but found nothing of interest. Everything inside the house had been destroyed by fire or water from the fire suppression. There seemed to be little left. Lucy wasn't an expert on fires, but this one must have burned hot and fast.

"Was there any accelerant?" she asked.

"That's inconclusive as well—they're awaiting lab results."

"It's highly suspicious that the house where two of our victims lived was burned down this week," Lucy said.

"You're thinking that the killer tried to take care of all of them at once."

"But they got out—or maybe they weren't here."

"Then why burn it down?" Genie asked. "As a warning?"

"We should talk to the neighbors."

"I'll take left and right, you go across the street," Genie said.

The first house Lucy approached was a white, two-story, clapboard-style home with an inviting covered porch. She knocked and an elderly woman answered the door. After identifying herself, she learned that Mrs. Patricia Neel was a retired federal employee. She was shriveled with age, but had all her faculties.

Lucy said, "I'm looking for the young women who lived in the house." She gestured toward the remains across the street.

"A tragedy," Mrs. Neel said. "What happened?"

"The arson investigator is looking into it, but we think they may be in danger. They haven't come forward since the fire."

"Of course they're in danger, their house burned down. That was no accident."

"You know for a fact it wasn't an accident?"

"I didn't see anyone toss a match on the place, if that's what you mean. But houses just don't burn down like that. There was an explosion, everyone on the street heard it, and my hearing isn't what it used to be."

"What time was that?"

"Just after four in the morning, it woke me up and I looked at my clock. It wasn't a big explosion, and I think there were two, and I heard the second. You know how that is, where you think you hear something, but aren't quite sure. I thought they all died in the house."

"The fire department said there were no fatalities."

"I know, but it burned so fast, and when I went out on the street I didn't see any of the girls. I told the fire chief the same thing, and they inspected the building, didn't find anyone inside."

The girls had to have been at the fire—the CSU had found clothing that reeked of smoke. Maybe they had some kind of a warning and got out quickly. Or they had been involved. But why would Ivy or any of the other girls burn down a rental house?

Unless they wanted someone to *think* they were dead.

"Do you know the girls?"

"Some of them. They're very quiet, keep to themselves. But I went over there a couple of times—kept my eye on the place, you know. Karen Schwartz—she and her husband moved to Florida when they retired—asked me to let her know if there were any problems. They were good girls. All in college. Except for Mina."

College? "Who's Mina?"

"Sweetest girl. Very sad, though. Her sister was upset she kept coming over here to talk to me, but Mina was lonely, and with her sister and the other girls taking night classes, she was scared being alone in the house. She'd come over for tea after dinner and we'd chat or watch television. Nothing important—she was very quiet, just liked company."

"Do you know her sister?"

"Ivy."

"Does Ivy have a last name?"

"Hmm, Harris, I think." Lucy made a note, and Mrs. Neel continued. "After the second or third time Ivy found Mina here, she told me that their parents were killed in an accident, and she was taking care of Mina, but that she worried that social services would separate them because Ivy was only eighteen. At least she was eighteen then. It's been nearly two years. I told her as long as Ivy was as responsible as she seemed, there didn't seem to be any reason to notify anyone. Mina loved her sister. I think they had a very rough childhood."

"Do you know how old she was?"

"Oh, I don't know—she's been here for nearly two

years, I think she was thirteen when they moved in. Beautiful young woman. Ivy agreed to let Mina visit me when she wanted, but I haven't seen them much the last few weeks."

"How many girls were living there?"

"They came and went, no more than eight, I don't think. I didn't keep tabs on them. They probably had changes in roommates with each semester."

Lucy wondered whether that was true or not, or if Mrs. Neel didn't want to seem to be a busybody.

"They probably liked that someone in the neighborhood was looking out for them, especially if they were from out of the area and not familiar with DC."

Mrs. Neel smiled. "I try. I love this little street."

"Do you know how many girls lived in the house right before the fire?"

"Six or seven." She thought. "Ivy, Mina, I didn't know the others. There was a new girl—young, I couldn't imagine she was in college, but my eyes aren't what they used to be."

"New girl? How new?"

Mrs. Neel closed her eyes, counted silently, her lips moving. "About a week before the fire. It was a Wednesday, garbage day, and I had forgotten to take mine out. I got up early, and couldn't go back to sleep. Saw a car drive up, a girl and a man get out. I assume her father. They went in, and a while later the man drove off."

Mrs. Neel sat down on the porch swing. "Please excuse me, I'm getting old." She sighed as she relaxed. "They really kept to themselves, and I don't think Ivy would have spoken to me if her sister hadn't wanted to visit. It must have been hard on them, but I'll admit, I liked seeing how they looked out for each other. Families get torn apart these days, living everywhere around the world. I have three children, all of them more than a day's drive!" She shook her head.

Lucy took a chance. She pulled Jocelyn's driver's license photo on her phone and said, "Have you seen this woman around lately?"

Mrs. Neel put on her glasses and looked closely. "Yes, yes I have. She's been over several times. I haven't met her."

"Do you recall the last time?"

Mrs. Neel thought. "I can't say, really. But it's been awhile. More than a month, maybe two."

That surprised Lucy. "Thank you." She handed Mrs. Neel Noah's card, but wrote her cell phone number on the back. "If Ivy or Mina or any of the girls contact you, please let me or Agent Armstrong know."

"Is something wrong?"

"We're worried about them. Since the fire, no one has spoken to any of them."

"But they weren't hurt, right? The firemen said no one was inside. I told you that, right?"

"No one was hurt in the fire, but we need to talk to them." Then Lucy had another idea. She pulled up the unidentified girl from the Hotel Potomac. "Is this one of the girls?"

She squinted, put on her glasses again, and smiled. "Yes, yes, the new girl. Doesn't she look young to be in college?"

Lucy didn't respond to the rhetorical question, thanked Mrs. Neel for her time, and made sure she remembered she'd put Noah's card—with Lucy's cell phone written on the back—in her pocket.

* * *

Ivy didn't want anything bad to happen to Pastor Marti North, but she didn't know what else to do.

"If you can just keep Mina awhile longer," Ivy said.

"As long as necessary," Marti said.

Marti was pastor of His Grace Church. She was a forty-five-year-old former Army chaplain who ran the church and preschool for lost souls. At least, that's how Ivy viewed it. She'd been coming to services ever since moving to the house on Hawthorne. She listened to the message of forgiveness, redemption, and love, but didn't truly believe she deserved it.

Not when she harbored dark feelings of murder.

"Please be careful," Ivy begged. "I'll come for her as soon as I can."

"Ivy."

She turned to the pastor. "Once I get my sister safe, I'll be back."

"There are people who can help."

"Like Jocelyn?" Ivy paced, her voice rising. "She's dead. So is her husband. I'm worried about what could happen to you if you help me."

"No one knows Mina is here. She hasn't been outside. I'll do everything I can to protect her."

"I hate asking—"

Marti showed a rare irritation. "Ask, and you shall receive," she quoted.

"Don't—if God cared, Jocelyn would be alive. She never hurt anyone, she was only trying to help *me*. As soon as I get Sara settled, I'm coming for Mina. No later than tomorrow."

She turned and started to leave the small, simple church.

Mina stood in the back.

"You don't have to come back for me," she said. "I'm okay."

Tears threatened, but Ivy wasn't going to cry. "I promised to take care of you, even after I rescued Sara. I promise I'll come back."

She shook her head. "You only had two passports."

"I was working on getting yours."

"It's okay, Ivy."

"You have to believe I care about you!"

"Sara's your sister."

Ivy strode over and hugged Mina. "So are you. In my heart. I'm not leaving you in DC. You're coming to Canada with me. I just need to get the money, I already have three passports lined up."

Marti said, "I have some money."

"I can't take your money."

"It's not enough, but it will help."

Ivy squeezed her eyes shut, nodded her head once. "We'll talk tonight." She hugged Mina again and left.

Hawthorne Street was six blocks over. Ivy went the long way, through alleys, staying off the main streets. Truly, she didn't know who was trying to kill her, and that made everyone a potential killer.

Ivy knew Mrs. Neel kept cash in a wall safe in her house. She also knew, because of Mina, that Mrs. Neel never remembered her password, so had written it in her address book, which was in her top desk drawer.

It was probably not enough, but it was something, and she would make it work.

She didn't want to steal from the old woman, but she'd leave a note, promise to pay her back. Mrs. Neel had been so kind to them. Ivy already missed the house, the neighborhood, the small sense of peace.

No time for regrets.

If she had to, she'd sell her body to ten guys tonight, give blow jobs to a hundred, if that was what it took to raise the money to go to Canada.

Ivy came at Mrs. Neel's house from the narrow alley that backed up to the rear yard. She kept hidden as best she could along the side of the garage, but she'd have to cross the driveway to reach the house.

Voices came from the front porch, and Ivy feared she'd have to wait. She didn't have time. She peered around the corner and saw the back of a woman with long, dark hair pulled back, dressed professionally in slacks and a thin blouse. Cop? Arson investigator? Ivy didn't see any law enforcement vehicles on the street, but she only had a partial view of the road.

Mrs. Neel seemed occupied, and the desk was in the back of the house, far from the front door. She had to take the risk.

Without giving herself time to change her mind, Ivy slipped in through the back door, using the key that Mrs. Neel had given Mina for emergencies. Guilt made her head ache, but she had no other choice.

She heard the voices, but not what was being said. Without hesitating, she flipped the address book over, memorized the passcode, and carefully took off the picture frame from the wall. She typed in the numbers, heard a click, and the light turned from red to green.

Her heart started beating again.

There were a lot of papers—insurance, bank statements, tax records, and for a moment Ivy feared Mrs. Neel had no cash.

Then she found the white, business-sized envelope.

She had no idea how much was inside, but she put it

down her shorts, closed the safe, put the picture back, and slipped out of the house.

She'd been inside for less than four minutes.

The woman was still on the front porch, and down the long driveway, a black woman was talking to her next-door neighbor.

They had to be cops.

Almost at the same time, a dark blue van turned down the street. The driver wore a ball cap, but there was something familiar about him.

She'd seen him with Wendy many times.

What did Wendy call him? Dumb and Dumber. He had a brother. She called the two of them Dumb and Dumber, said they were her partners, but she ridiculed them.

But that was so long ago. Why was he here?

Did he have a hand in Wendy's death? He shouldn't even know where Ivy lived! Did Wendy tell him? Did Wendy hate her so much that she sent a killer after her?

Ivy didn't believe it. They had a major disagreement, but Wendy wasn't violent. And Wendy was dead.

Had the killer tortured the information out of her?

Ivy had to keep her wits about her. She'd run—but not to Marti's church or St. Anne's. She had to go far away, turn the attention away from her sister and Mina.

She wished Kerry had gotten in contact with her—she needed to be warned. But it had been three days and total silence.

What if she and Bryn were already dead?

A cry escaped Ivy's chest and she swallowed it, the lump sticking like unchewed steak in her throat.

She squatted behind the shed, hoping he was gone.

Waited. But she was nervous and antsy and couldn't just sit here waiting for Dumb or Dumber to find her.

Wendy was obviously wrong about their intellect if they could kill so many people and not get caught.

She started across the backyard, but moved too fast. Or too slow.

The woman at the door caught her eye.

Ivy sprinted to the fence sealed it quickly. Then she and saw Dumb's van again. He grinned at her, pointed his finger like a gun.

Ivy ran faster.

CHAPTER TWENTY

Lucy ran across the street to Genie's car. "Genie! I think I saw Ivy!"

Genie ran down the sidewalk and jumped into the driver's seat while Lucy ran around to the passenger side. Genie called in the pursuit of a subject on foot, and Lucy directed her around the corner.

"She jumped over the back fence."

Genie squealed around the corner and turned down the alley. It was much harder to pursue a suspect on foot while driving.

"Do you see her?" Genie asked. Lucy was scouring the area, looking around the Dumpsters and garbage cans and through cracks in the fence.

"Dammit!"

"I'll go down the next alley, then go around wide, backup is on its way."

Genie crossed a two-lane street and drove into the adjoining alley. She slammed on her brakes when a woman darted out in front of her car.

It was definitely Ivy. She looked over her shoulder, terror etched in her face, then back at Lucy.

Lucy shouted, "Get in!" and manually unlocked the back door.

Ivy was obviously torn, but another glance behind her had her running around the car. She grabbed the door handle, pulled it open, and jumped into the backseat, keeping her head low. Before she'd even closed the door, she shouted, "Go, go, go!"

Genie sped down the narrow space, looking in her rearview mirror.

"Is someone chasing you?"

"Yes."

"Who? I don't see anyone."

"I don't know!"

The bumper clipped a garbage can and the crash of metal made Lucy jump.

"Don't slow down!" Ivy cried.

Lucy turned in her seat and looked through the back window of Genie's sedan.

"I don't see anyone," she said. "Genie, slow down."

"I got it under control." She glanced at Lucy and grinned. "You look green."

"I don't like car chases."

"Let's just get to the station."

"No!" Ivy screamed. "Please, no!"

Lucy looked back again and saw a van turn down the alley from a side street.

"Genie! Van, dark blue, behind you."

"Can you see the driver?"

"White male. Baseball cap."

"Tags?"

"There's no front plate. He's gaining."

Genie turned out of the alley, but the street was also narrow, parallel to but higher than the main road. A low guard railing separated them from a steep drop. She called in the pursuit.

Lucy said to Ivy, "I'm sorry we have to meet like this. I'm Lucy Kincaid—I'm an analyst for the FBI, and I can help."

"You did—you got me away from that guy. Now let me out."

"You're in danger. This is Detective Genie Reid with DC police; she'll put you in protective custody. She's investigating the murder of your friends."

"You don't understand. Just let me out!" Ivy hit the seat.

"Who else is in danger? We can protect them as well."

The unmarked car wasn't designed for carrying prisoners, had no shield separating the back from the front. Lucy watched Ivy's hands, realizing she had been impulsive, that Ivy could have a gun, she could be dangerous.

"Ivy, please trust me."

Ivy snorted. "I can't trust anybody."

"Do you know who killed Nicole and Maddie?"

"How—" She stopped talking.

"I know about your sister."

Silence.

"Mina, right? Where is she?"

A screech behind them caught Lucy's attention. The van had gained on them.

"Shit!" Genie exclaimed.

The van was on their bumper. The driver hit them hard. Genie barely kept the car on the road.

"That's him!" Ivy said. "Can't you drive any faster?"

"Officer in trouble!" Genie said into her mic. "Cleveland near Thirty-first. Dark blue van—shit!"

The van hit them again. A red light was ahead, cross traffic in front of them. Genie had her grille lights flashing. She flipped a switch on the dashboard and a siren whirled then died, whirled then died.

The cars ahead of them slowed, blocking the intersection.

The van rear-ended them and Lucy let out a startled yelp. Ivy had a grip on the door, as if debating whether to jump out.

Genie veered to the wrong side of the street and turned the wrong way down a one-way street. It bought them only a few seconds. The van squealed, sideswiped a parked car, and followed.

He stuck his hand out the window. Metal flashed in the sunlight.

"Gun!" Lucy cried out.

The gunman fired at the tires and missed. He fired his gun again and her back window cracked.

"Stay down!" Genie ordered.

A crossing guard guiding small children was right in front of their car. Genie turned the wheel sharply right, down an embankment, losing control of the vehicle. It was going too fast, and then it hit the bottom and almost went end over end. The airbags exploded, sounding too much like a gunshot. Lucy's head banged hard against the airbag. Her body was jerked sharply back and suddenly the car fell on all four tires.

Lucy coughed from the powder released with the airbags. "Genie?"

The steering column was wedged tight against the detective and blood was dripping down her face. She was unconscious, but breathing.

"Ivy, are you okay?"

Ivy had a cut on her head and was coughing as well. "I'm so sorry. I'm so sorry." She tried her door but it wouldn't open.

Lucy's vision was blurred, but she located her handbag on the floor by her feet and retrieved her gun.

"Don't," Lucy told Ivy. She spit blood out of her mouth. Her head was spinning. She tried to unbuckle the seat belt, but it was jammed.

Their attacker had started down the embankment. He had a gun. There were onlookers at the railing looking down. Any of them could be a hostage or get caught in the line of fire. Lucy didn't trust her aim because of double vision; she would have to wait until he got closer to fire.

She heard sirens at the same time as the gunman. He hesitated. She fired her gun at his feet—both pairs of them—then ducked. Screams from the road above cut through the ringing in her ears. He fired once into the side of her car, then a much closer siren and bullhorn sounded from the road below the embankment.

The attacker ran back up and jumped in his van.

Lucy leaned back.

"He's gone," she told Ivy. "You're safe." She had to convince Ivy to trust her, but how? All she had was a theory. "I know about Wendy," she said. It sounded like she was talking in a tunnel.

Ivy stared at her. "What?"

"The room. The recordings. Let me help you." Lucy reached up and touched her head, came away with blood.

"I have to go!" The door was still stuck. Ivy climbed out the shattered window in the back.

"Ivy. Stay—"

She stumbled through the thick shrubs along the embankment and disappeared.

Lucy tried to unbuckle her belt, not knowing if it was really stuck or she was more seriously injured than she thought.

Genie moaned, but didn't open her eyes. The radio played static, but Lucy fumbled with the channels. "Officer down," she said. "Need ambulance."

Two uniformed officers approached from the road below. Lucy closed her eyes. She needed a minute to catch her breath. Just. One. Minute.

CHAPTER TWENTY-ONE

Sean bypassed the nurse's station and went straight to Lucy's room. No one tried to stop him. As long as he looked like he knew where he was going, and didn't make eye contact, he'd bet his Mustang no one would intervene.

And if anyone tried, they would fail.

Lucy was in the emergency room, a nurse changing her bandages. He stood outside the door, the privacy curtain partly obscuring her view so she couldn't see him at first.

Sean pushed down on the fear, burying it under layers of false confidence and bravado. He'd seen Lucy in far worse shape than a few scrapes and bruises. She'd seen him worse as well. In fact, looking at her, other than her unusually pale complexion and the fact that she was wearing a hospital gown, she looked just fine.

She's fine. Lucy's just fine.

He had to repeat the mantra before the pendulum in his stomach stopped swinging. When he knew he could speak without his voice cracking, he shook off the remaining anxiety like a dog shakes off water. Took a deep breath. Only then did Sean push the curtain aside and step into the cubicle.

"You picked a lovely day to relax in the hospital." He smiled broadly to mask his lingering fear. He walked to the opposite side of the bed from the nurse and took Lucy's hand. He leaned over and kissed her forehead. "If you needed a vacation, you should have called me. I'd fly you up to Maine. Beautiful in July."

"Isn't your plane still being repaired?"

"I'll borrow one."

"You're not supposed to be in here." The nurse glanced at him over the tops of her thick glasses. She was younger than Lucy, but the glasses made her look twenty years older.

He winked at the trim, efficient RN. "I won't stay long. Cross my heart." He made the gesture.

"She should rest. She'll be going for X-rays in a minute."

"Nothing is broken," Lucy said. "I told the doctor that."

"You're probably right, but we'll X-ray just the same." The nurse walked to the foot of the bed and picked up the medical chart.

"And you say *I'm* a bad patient," he whispered, his voice cracking once as he fought to control the building rage.

"You're worse than me," Lucy grumbled. "I am *fine*."

Sean touched Lucy's bruised face. When he found the bastard who had shot at her, he'd kill him. There was no doubt in Sean's mind that if he could get away with it, he'd do it.

But was it the *shooter* he was truly angry at? Lucy was training to be a cop. She would be facing an untold number of bad guys, and Sean wasn't planning on turning vigilante and whacking every criminal she faced.

It was partly the shooter, and partly the woman who had run from the scene—a prostitute, according to Noah—who left Lucy and a detective unconscious in the car.

But mostly, Noah was the focus of Sean's still bubbling anger.

When Noah had called him thirty minutes ago and told him Lucy had been in an accident, Sean had wanted to throttle the agent. Sean always had something to say, but this time when Noah called, Sean listened, then hung up.

What he *wanted* to say would have caused Lucy untold future problems with the agent. And while Sean didn't care if they remained friends—and would prefer if they didn't—he wasn't going to incite the battle.

As long as Noah stayed away from him for the next hour. Or year.

Lucy frowned, her dark, soulful eyes seeking something in his. "Sean?"

He smiled, trying to mask his simmering anger. He'd worried her, and that was the last thing he wanted.

"Were you wearing your seat belt?"

"Of course."

"Bet your chest hurts."

"Yes, but—"

He slipped the gown off her right shoulder, since she hadn't been driving. A nasty bruise was already forming where the seat belt restrained her. "I'll have a lot of fun playing nurse tonight," he said with a grin. His vision blurred, but he averted his eyes. The nurse looked at him a moment too long. He faked a smile. It didn't work.

"This really sucks," Lucy said. She squeezed his hand.

Sean forced himself to relax. Lucy was alive. Nothing broken. Just bruises. "I've never heard you say that word before."

She rolled her eyes. "Genie's foul mouth is rubbing off on me." She said to the nurse, "Monica, right?"

"Yes." The young nurse seemed pleased Lucy had remembered her first name.

"Would you mind checking on Detective Genie Reid for me? She didn't regain consciousness in the car, and I'd feel a lot better if I knew she was okay."

"I'll see what I can find out. Stay put, the orderly should be here in about ten minutes to take you to X-ray."

"And then I can go."

"And then the doctor will look at the film and let you know."

The nurse left and Lucy said to Sean, "I'm not staying tonight. I didn't even want to come, but Noah made me."

"Where is he now?"

"He met me at the scene, I briefed him, he said he'd stop by later. They're looking for Ivy. It's all jumbled in my head, but I told him they're all connected."

Ivy . . . the name was familiar to Sean, but he didn't know why. When Noah called him earlier, he'd been worried about Lucy, but now he wanted to remember why *Ivy* was important. "What's connected?"

Lucy whispered, "Wendy James and the two prostitutes. Their murders are connected. I think Jocelyn Taylor was trying to help them all."

"I'm three steps behind you. Noah didn't tell me anything." Lucy's brow dipped in concentration, and Sean tried to stop her from thinking too hard. "You can catch me up later. You need to rest. You could have a concussion."

"If you make me tell you that I'm fine one more time, I'll call Dillon for a ride home. I just need to get my thoughts together. Everything was falling into place right before the crash."

Sean sat on the edge of the bed and kissed her, trying to ignore the cuts and scrapes on her arms and face. He kissed her again because it felt good. To remind him that she was here, whole, healthy.

"You keep scaring me like this, I'll have to hire myself to be your bodyguard—and I don't do personal security. For you, Princess, I'll make an exception."

"*Me?* You're the one who fell two stories down a mine shaft not two months ago."

"You crashed my plane."

"Did not. It was shot down."

Sean raised his eyebrow.

"You," she added, "were kidnapped by a lunatic."

"So were you."

"I'd say we're even then."

"Maybe we should move to an uninhabited island where neither of us can get in trouble."

"We'd probably run into a poisonous snake." Lucy brought Sean's hand to her lips and kissed it. "Now, where was I?"

"You weren't going to tell me you were fine."

"Right."

Sean breathed much easier. In their banter, Lucy's tension eased, making him calmer as well. Unlike him, she wasn't a good actress. If she was stressed or worried, she wouldn't tease him.

He kissed her again. "So you put these murders together?"

Again, Lucy made sure no one could overhear, and she kept her voice low. "Some of this is just theory—"

"Lucy, no qualifications, okay?"

"I told you about the crime scene this morning?"

"Briefly. A triple murder at the Hotel Potomac?"

"Yes. The woman was a social worker for a nonprofit. She specialized in working with teenage prostitutes. The other woman was a girl named Maddie, a known prostitute and drug addict who was on and off the wagon. And the third victim, the husband, a congressional staffer."

"Congress? Don't tell me he worked for Crowley."

"Dale Hartline."

"I know next to nothing about who's who in the Capitol." That wasn't completely true. He knew enough. RCK was often hired to provide personal security for high-ranking officials when they traveled overseas, but Sean rarely, if ever, took those assignments. He did, on occasion, run background checks for campaigns or high-security checks that weren't covered by the FBI or another agency.

And it was clear that Lucy didn't buy his disclaimer. She said, "And he used to work for Senator Paxton. In fact, the last call Chris Taylor made before he was killed was to Senator Paxton."

"Paxton," Sean said flatly. He had mixed feelings about the senator, from the time he'd first met him in January, but he didn't share this with Lucy. Paxton had been her mentor for years, though after Women and Children First was shut down six months ago, they had a strained relationship. Lucy didn't talk about it, and Sean suspected she had grown tired of trying to fill the shoes of Paxton's dead daughter. Sean had seen pictures of Monique Paxton. The resemblance to Lucy was uncanny.

"He said Chris called to meet with him for advice, then admitted that Chris likely wanted money to help Jocelyn and the girls, but he was vague on details, claimed Chris didn't give him any. I think he was more or less telling the truth about the call. What tipped me off that he knows something more was that he recognized the prostitutes we showed him."

"He said that?"

"No. He kept his face completely blank, showed no recognition whatsoever."

"Does he have a tell? Did his eye twitch or something?"

Lucy rolled her eyes. "*No*. It was his total lack of empathy. You know him—he's hired you and RCK, right?"

"Yes, but—"

"He has this way of being quietly enraged when women are in danger. It's subtle, but it's always there. And he buried it. I think because he didn't want to show that he recognized the girls."

"You're not stretching on this? Reading something into it?"

"No! Dammit, Noah said the same thing. But I swear, Ivy Harris is the type of girl he feels compelled to save. Same basic physical features as his daughter."

"And you."

She closed her eyes.

"Luce, talk to me."

"Today was the first time I saw Jonathon in nearly six months."

"Why is that strange? WCF was disbanded. Would you have a reason to see him?"

"Maybe not."

But something was on her mind, and he pushed. "Did something happen when you last talked to him?"

"I haven't talked to him since the last WCF fundraiser, the week I learned my boss was a killer."

"But I took you to the Capitol to see him. Remember? A few weeks after that fiasco."

Lucy didn't say anything, and Sean had the uneasy sensation that she was trying to come up with a lie. Lucy was one of those rare people who couldn't lie convincingly.

"Lucy?"

"It's nothing."

"It's not nothing. Something is bothering you, what is it?"

"I didn't actually talk to him."

"What do you mean, you didn't talk to him?"

She looked at him, her eyes uncertain. "Did you ever know in your heart that something was true, but couldn't prove it?"

"Tell me what you're thinking."

"I think Jonathon was an active participant in the vigilante group that destroyed WCF."

Sean absorbed that stunning accusation.

"How active?"

"I suspect that he knew about it."

"Do you think he's a killer?"

"Maybe." She glanced away. She was hedging.

"Who do you think he killed?"

"Shh," Lucy admonished, glancing around the semi-private room. She whispered, "Roger Morton."

Sean looked at her for a long minute. "Why?"

"Something Mick Mallory said."

"Mallory confessed to killing dozens of sexual predators."

"Yes, but when I spoke to him, *before* his formal confession, he said something that had me thinking the senator actually pulled the trigger."

"I can't hate him for that," he said simply. He brought her hand to his lips. Lucy was aching about this, and he wanted to remove her conflict. Roger Morton didn't deserve to live, but saying that out loud wasn't going to help Lucy. "Why didn't you tell me?"

"I don't know! What was I supposed to say? A powerful U.S. Senator killed a scumbag rapist and I'm actually kind of happy about it?" She shook her head. "I don't have any proof. It's just a bunch of little intangible things that have been bothering me. You kill once, it makes it easier to do it again."

"Don't go there, Lucy." She'd killed two men. They were evil bastards who'd hurt and murdered numerous innocent people. Why did she keep torturing herself over it?

"I don't know how deep he was involved," she said. "I don't want to know. Like I said, I have no evidence— and I want to keep it that way."

That, Sean understood. "Don't let it hurt you like this."

"I've made peace with it." Again, her eyes darted away. She was so easy to read.

"Have you?"

"Yes—"

"I think you're torn. He *may* have killed a rapist. A

killer who was let out of prison far too early. Someone who hurt you—and who hurt his daughter. Deep down, you can't condone it. But I'm not going to lose sleep over this, and neither should you."

"I'm not."

"Yes you are. It's all clear to me now. If the senator is guilty, you think not saying something is wrong. But the truth is you have no proof, and saying anything about it would be the mistake. But I can find out."

"How?"

"Talk to Mallory."

"No!"

"You deserve the truth, and I know you don't want to face that bastard."

"I don't *want* to know the truth. If I know for a *fact* that Jonathon killed Roger Morton, I'd have to tell Noah and the FBI. I don't want to."

"Okay."

"Okay?" She was obviously surprised he'd given up so easily.

Sean kissed her forehead. "You think the senator is capable of not quite legal activities," he began.

Lucy raised an eyebrow. "Murder is illegal."

"Not justifiable homicide."

"Sean." She shook her head at him.

"Okay, sorry. I'm proud of you." He kissed her again. He'd crawl into the hospital bed with her if he thought he could get away with it.

"What is really bothering me was talking to Jonathon today, what he said and what he *didn't* say, I think Chris called him to help Ivy specifically. I can't figure out *why* or *how*. But Jonathon is involved with MARC, maybe not to the extent he was with WCF, but it's a pattern with him. Getting involved with victims' rights groups and taking it too far."

"This makes a lot of sense," Sean said. "Except the why."

"Because Jonathon is like you. He cannot stand bullies. He has always stood up for victims of violent crime. And teenage prostitutes—many of them were victims before they turned to selling sex. According to Jocelyn's boss, Ivy was involved in this business for a long time, but helped other girls get out. She helped Jocelyn get girls off the streets.

"And somehow, Ivy is connected to Wendy James. I mentioned her name and it was written all over Ivy's face. Three crime scenes, three messages, all a variation of a children's rhyme."

Lucy frowned, lost in thought, her lips moving, but he only heard an unintelligible murmur.

Sean didn't like the expression on her face. She was internalizing the crime. He hadn't seen her this intense in a long time, not since they had tracked an obsessive psychopathic killer in New York City five months ago.

"Luce—"

Ivy Harris.

Sean remembered why he knew the name. Talking about Senator Paxton was the connection.

Paxton had hired him to do a background check on Ivy Harris. Said she'd applied for a job on his campaign.

Sean had learned that Ivy Harris didn't exist, but her Social Security number belonged to a dead girl, Hannah Edmonds. He offered to dig deeper, but Paxton said it wasn't necessary. That was right before Sean and

Lucy went to the Adirondacks, and Sean had put it out of his mind.

Lucy suddenly sat up. "I got it!" She winced at the sudden movement. "I needed to say it out loud, and then I heard the rhythm. Listen:

"And this guilty whore don't cry no more; And this little pig goes wee, wee, wee."

Sean heard it, but didn't know how Lucy extrapolated it.

She said, "It's the exact same rhythm, the exact same beats. He was having fun; it means absolutely nothing. Remember, he didn't intend to rape her. He only wanted to make it look like a failed rape. He strangled her from behind—there was no sexual component. He wanted the police to think she was killed by a random stranger. But it *wasn't* random. And in his effort to make it *appear* random he pulled ideas from thin air. Maybe he wanted to embarrass her, something he couldn't do except in death.

"And," she continued quickly, "when he killed the others he realized he'd had fun with the message. He saw the rat at the Red Light, spontaneously came up with the poem. Six targets. Witnesses say that at least six girls lived in the house on Hawthorne. Except—"

"Slow down," Sean said, helping Lucy lean back onto the pillows. "Really, slow down." His heart was racing, needing to keep her from overworking herself. What was he thinking? If the roles were reversed, he wouldn't want to lie down in bed while a major investigation was happening. He could, however, keep her calm.

"I need to explain this all to Noah," Lucy said, excited about her theory. "It wasn't clear earlier but now I see it."

Monica the nurse came in with an orderly pushing a wheelchair. "You can talk to whomever you want after your X-rays."

Sean kissed Lucy on the forehead, then helped her sit up. "Listen to the nice nurse and do as you're told and you can have ice cream in bed when you get home."

Lucy gave him a reprimanding look, but she couldn't hold it and started laughing. "No, no, don't make me laugh, it hurts."

Her laugh was the best thing for Sean's nerves.

Sean watched Lucy being wheeled away and heard her ask the nurse, "Did you find out anything about Genie Reid?"

"She's in surgery, but the doctor said she's healthy and he expects her to fully recover."

When everyone was gone, Sean sat heavily on the bed and rested his head in his hands.

Lucy is fine.

He'd find a way to keep her from working too hard tonight, but tomorrow morning she'd be back on this case.

By then, he'd have the answers from Paxton. Why the senator hadn't gone to the FBI already, Sean didn't know, but he'd damn well find out.

Sean sat up and called Lucy's brother Dillon.

"Is Lucy all right?" Dillon asked.

"She's fine. She's in X-ray." Sean smiled, remembering how irritated Lucy had been, repeating herself.

"I'll let Kate know, she's on her way to the hospital."

"I have an errand, and I'm afraid I won't be back before she's done. I wouldn't go if it wasn't urgent."

"No explanations necessary. Kate will bring her home."

CHAPTER TWENTY-TWO

Noah walked into FBI headquarters and was instantly bombarded with questions from his boss.

"What the hell happened?" Slater demanded. "Where's Kincaid? I have the DC Metro police chief yelling at me, and it was his damn detective driving the car!"

Noah said with forced calm, "Genie Reid was shot in the arm. She's in surgery. She was unconscious for twenty minutes and has a serious concussion, but is expected to recover. I made Lucy go to the hospital for X-rays, she insists she's fine. She probably is, except for bruises, but she needs a full checkup."

"This is why I didn't want that girl in the field!"

Noah raised his eyebrow, biting back a more volatile retort. " 'That girl'? That girl just cracked our case wide open."

"My office, Armstrong."

Noah followed Slater and shut the door behind them. He stood at attention. He'd been a soldier for too long to blatantly disobey orders, but right now he wanted to be either working the case or checking on Lucy. He took responsibility for what happened. Lucy should never have been injured on the job. Not like this.

"Do you think she's right?"

"About what?"

"That Wendy James was a prostitute."

"There's no hard evidence, but it fits with the information we have. The multiple affairs. The video recording room—"

Slater interrupted. "Which we have no confirmation was ever used by Wendy James or anyone else—it's clean."

"Which is another reason we need to find Ivy Harris and talk to her."

Slater flipped through his e-mail, then opened Noah's report. "You said Kincaid and Reid picked Harris up near Hawthorne Street and they were pursued by an unknown male in an unmarked dark blue van, wearing a Yankees cap."

"Correct."

"And how did Harris get out of the car?"

"She climbed out the shattered rear window and fled on foot. Lucy didn't see an accomplice."

"Doesn't mean there wasn't one."

"Lucy thinks she was scared, that she didn't know who was chasing her, and she was only concerned about her sister."

"Sister?"

"Lucy said her name was 'Mina.' That's from a neighbor on Hawthorne Street."

"Stockton's coming in any minute, you and Josh need to brief him on every detail. Curb your animosity toward Josh—"

"I've shown no animosity."

"I was afraid that now—"

"He didn't run Lucy off the road. Our divisions approach crimes differently. I hope that you'll now give me the reins on this case. With Reid out of commission, we can't afford to have DC turn this case over to someone else."

"DC wants it. Their detective was shot. Shit, Noah, can you relax?"

Noah adjusted his stance, but didn't sit down. "You need to make this happen, Matt. They can give me anyone they want, but it's our case. Three similar crime scenes with a brief cooling-off period is textbook serial murderer."

"Dr. Vigo said he wasn't a psychopath."

"I didn't know one had to be a psychopath to be a serial killer."

"Semantics."

"We don't know what Wendy James was doing in the apartment with the secret room, but we can make the case that she was killed because of her involvement in a federal crime, either as a witness or a perpetrator. It's a working theory. We don't have time to play inter-jurisdictional politics, sir."

"Don't call me 'sir.' How long have we been friends?"

"Since I was assigned here. Four years this October."

"Exactly. It's yours. I'll make up something to appease the DC chief. Brief Stockton, I'll talk to Josh. But he's your partner on this, keep him in the loop. He's already deep in all the finances."

"That's exactly what he should be doing. In fact, I want him focused on every individual and organization that leased an executive suite in the Park Way building.

And the manager, Betty Dare. She's been there for years, I can't imagine that she didn't suspect *something* with Wendy using the executive apartments. Maybe Wendy bribed her."

"Talk to her—push her. See if she cracks. If she doesn't, as soon as Stein gets even a hint of financial shenanigans, we can get a warrant for her finances as well. Right now, we only have a warrant for apartment seven-ten."

"I have Miriam going through the records from Haw-thorne Street and doing a complete background on Ivy Harris." His phone vibrated. It was an unfamiliar local number.

"Agent Armstrong."

"Hello?" The voice belonged to an elderly woman. "Hello, Agent Kincaid?"

"This is Agent Noah Armstrong. Who is this?"

"Hello, Agent Armstrong. My name is Patricia Neel," the woman said slowly. "How are you?"

"We're kind of busy here. Did you get this number from Ms. Kincaid?"

"The pretty dark-haired girl? Yes, she gave me this card. She wrote her number on the back, but I've been calling it and there's no answer."

"Can I help you with something?"

"I've been robbed."

"That's really a matter for the DC police."

"Well," Mrs. Neel said, "Agent Kincaid told me if I heard from any of the girls in the pictures, to call her."

Noah straightened. "And have you?"

"Well, that's why I'm calling. I went into my family room and the back door was open. It was when I heard all the sirens and I was worried. We get some of those gang kids running in the alley, so I locked the door. Then I noticed my picture was askew. My safe is behind the picture. I opened it and discovered my emergency fund is gone."

"How much was in it?"

"Five thousand dollars in cash."

"And who do you think took it?"

"She left me a note saying she'd pay it back when she was able. I don't want to get her in trouble, but Agent Kincaid thinks she's in danger."

Noah squeezed his temples and forced his voice to remain polite. "Who?"

"Well, she didn't sign it, but I recognized the writing. I'll read you the note.

"'Mrs. Neel, I'm so sorry to take your money, but we're in serious trouble. I promise I will pay you back every dime as soon as I can. Thank you for your kindness. God bless you.'"

"And who wrote it?" he asked for the third time.

"Ivy Harris. Poor girl lost her house and everything in it Tuesday morning. I would have given her the money if she'd asked."

Now he knew why Ivy Harris had been in the neighborhood earlier that day. "I'm sending an agent over to check your house and retrieve the note. Lock your doors, please."

"Thank you for your concern, Agent Armstrong. Have a good day."

Noah hung up. "Ivy Harris stole five thousand in cash from her neighbor. She could be anywhere by now."

Slater slammed his desk drawer shut. "Shit. I'll put pressure on that BOLO."

"Make sure DC knows she's a witness, not a suspect."

"You don't know that she's not deep in this shit."

"Lucy said she was terrified and worried about her sister. She might be reckless, but Lucy didn't think she was dangerous."

"Let's get her in custody and decide then if she needs to be in jail or in a safe house."

Noah left Slater's office and was heading back to his desk in order to prepare for his meeting with Assistant Director Rick Stockton when he ran into the man himself in the hall.

They shook hands. "How are you, sir?" Noah asked.

"Could be better. We have an ID on the girl from the garage. Her name is Sara Edmonds, and she was reported missing ten days ago by her father. Reverend Kirk Edmonds."

"The televangelist?"

"The one and the same. The Baltimore office showed him the picture and he positively identified her. He also identified the brunette."

"Ivy Harris."

"Wrong. Hannah Edmonds. His middle daughter, who he thought was dead." Rick said. "Tell me you have her in custody."

"No, sir."

"He'll be here in the morning. This is going to be a media nightmare."

"Because his daughter ran away?"

"He says Hannah kidnapped Sara. He says she's mentally unbalanced. When she was fourteen, she stopped taking doctor-prescribed antidepressants and threatened suicide. He thought she'd killed herself when he found her clothes and blood in a car she stole."

"What did the police say?"

"Same thing. The car was found near the lake, she was known to be suicidal, and her older sister found Hannah's prescription bottle empty. Ten days ago, Sara disappeared in the middle of the night. Our people treated it as a kidnapping, but there were no clues—no trace evidence, no witnesses, no ransom note, nothing."

Slater stepped out of his office. "I heard about that case. There was some speculation that she might have had a boyfriend?"

"Nothing confirmed," Stockton said. "I have the local agent assigned to the case coming in with Reverend Edmonds. She'll have more insight about the Edmonds family."

"This changes everything," Slater said.

Noah said, "We can't assume anything in this case. We assumed there was no connection between the three murders, and now we know there is."

"It's a theory, Noah," Slater said. "We have no hard evidence that links Wendy James to Ivy Harris or the other crime scene."

Stockton said, "I'm very interested in these new developments, but we have a recent sighting of a missing minor, fourteen, who may be in danger, and that takes precedence over all else."

"Understood," Noah said.

"How's Lucy?"

"She'll be fine."

"Good. Debrief her as soon as possible. She's the only one who's talked to Hannah Edmonds." He glanced at his watch. "Let's get this done, I have ten minutes until the press conference."

CHAPTER TWENTY-THREE

Sean walked into Senator Jonathon Paxton's office in the Dirksen Building without an invitation or an appointment.

"Mr. Rogan," the receptionist followed him. "Mr. Rogan, Senator Paxton's in a meeting."

Sean opened the door. Paxton was on the phone. "I'll see you then, Agent Armstrong," Paxton said and hung up.

"Tell me the truth," Sean said.

The senator said to the receptionist, "It's fine, Ann. Sean is working on a project for me. Let me know when Agent Armstrong arrives."

Ann left, closing the door behind her, though the concern didn't leave her face.

Paxton said, "Hello, Sean. I suppose I shouldn't be surprised to see you here."

"Tell me about Ivy Harris."

The senator narrowed his gaze. "Do I detect an implication in your tone that I have been less than truthful?"

"You'll detect a hell of a lot more, and you'll see it on the five o'clock news, if you don't tell me the truth *now*."

"Noah Armstrong informed me that Lucy was in a car accident. How is she?"

"Alive."

"I don't understand your hostility, Sean."

"Stay away from Lucy."

"What happened?" Paxton lost his fake politeness. "You come into my office with an accusatory tone and tell me to stay away from a friend?"

Sean barely resisted the urge to push Paxton up against the wall and pound the phony indignation off his face. His restraint came more from the fact that Paxton was twice his age than because he was a senator.

Sean glanced behind Paxton's desk. There was a picture of Paxton and a young, dark-haired woman. Lucy? He stepped closer. No, it wasn't Lucy. It was his daughter, Monique.

Sean walked around the large office, at the array of pictures on the walls and tables. He stopped in front of a framed photograph of Paxton and a much younger Lucy. She was about twenty, twenty-one—probably during her internship with the Judiciary Committee. Again, Sean was reminded that Paxton's feelings about Lucy were complex. And, he considered, quite unhealthy.

"You realize your obsession with Lucy is sick."

"I'm not obsessed, Rogan. I care about her. Yes, like a daughter. But I recognize that she's *not* my daughter."

"Three months ago you hired me to track down a woman named Ivy Harris, and now she's in the middle of a murder investigation. She's the reason Lucy was in the car crash today!"

Paxton seemed stunned. "I didn't know—"

"Bull-fucking-shit!" Sean backed away from the wall of photos. Paxton had weaseled his way into Lucy's life for years, and Sean had tried to understand, but now Paxton was using *him*. Something was off about the senator, and Sean wasn't going to be party to whatever chess game he was playing.

"Don't try to con me," he said. "I've done a lot of work for you these last few months, and I learn you had me track down a girl who someone is trying to kill. Is it you? Did you put a hit on her?"

"That's ludicrous!"

"Don't lie to me, Paxton. I'm telling Lucy everything. She needs to find this girl."

"I don't know where she is. If you would listen—"

Sean was too angry to listen to anything Paxton had to say, though the security-trained portion of his brain told him to shut up and pay attention. He said, "You're waiting for Noah Armstrong? I'll wait with you. I'm sure he'd love to know that you're withholding information in a federal investigation. Do you want Ivy Harris dead?"

"Of course not. Are you going to listen to me or just accuse me?"

"I like the accusing part." Sean had to get his temper under control, but he couldn't resist jabbing the senator.

"I cannot discuss this here. I will come by your house tonight, when you've calmed down."

"Tell me now, or as soon as Noah shows up, I'm turning over my files on Ivy to him."

"You can't do that."

"Read the fine print. If I find out that a client has used me to commit a felony or to cover up a felony, all investigative material can and will be turned over to the proper authorities. The FBI wants Ivy Harris, I have information that may help them find her."

"They already know she's Hannah Edmonds."

That information threw Sean off-balance. He had the police file on Hannah Edmonds's suicide. There was no reason to think she was alive, but there had been no pictures of the real Hannah Edmonds to run facial recognition. "She *is* Hannah Edmonds or she's pretending to *be* Hannah Edmonds?"

"She *is* Hannah. The FBI is in the process of confirming the information, but I've been in communication with her. I know she's Hannah."

"How?"

"That's not important."

"Like hell it isn't."

"Noah's coming here to talk about my former legislative staffer, Chris Taylor, who was murdered this morning, and specifically why Chris called me at eleven o'clock last night."

"You already talked to the police—and Lucy. Or does Noah have evidence that you're a lying prick?"

"You don't know when to stop, do you?" Paxton was furious, but Sean detected his confidence was waning. He didn't respond, just stared Paxton in the eye. Sean sat down on the couch and put his feet up on the coffee table.

I'm not going anywhere, buddy.

"I'm being blackmailed," the senator said in a low voice. "And if it gets out, not only will Lucy lose her job, the media will destroy her."

Sean laughed, certain Paxton was bluffing, trying to scare him into leaving so he could lie to Noah and not be caught.

"You think I believe that?"

Paxton straightened and tilted his chin up defiantly. In a low, even, prideful tone, he said, "I killed Roger Morton."

Sean kept his poker face on, and posture casual. He didn't move from the couch. He could hardly move without wanting to hit something.

Lucy was right. Paxton had killed Morton.

Carefully, he said, "True or not, it doesn't hurt Lucy."

"She knew."

Was he trying to pin it on her? Destroy her reputation? "Like hell she did. If you say a word, I'll destroy you. You won't know when or where or how, but if you hurt Lucy, you're through."

But she'd known. Maybe not with hard evidence, but her instincts had told her Paxton was a killer. She was right.

Paxton sat across from Sean.

"She didn't know at the time," Paxton admitted, "but she knows now. She's an accessory after the fact. Lucy can't lie. It's why she's avoided me all these months. When she figured out what I had done, she left me a note. That note is missing."

Sean didn't know how to respond. He couldn't imagine that Lucy would put anything incriminating in writing, or that she would keep Paxton's guilt a secret from not only the FBI but also from Sean. Not if she had proof.

"You're lying," he said. But in his gut, he knew something was wrong. He remembered how Lucy had avoided eye contact at the hospital. What had he asked her? What had made her hedge?

What had Lucy not told him?

"When Adam Scott killed my daughter, he kept her locket as a sick reminder of his perversion. The reason Roger Morton came to Washington, DC, was to bring my contact a box of jewelry that he was led to believe was worth a small fortune. But the box was recovered by the FBI.

"Lucy recognized the items for what they were—the sick souvenirs of a cowardly bastard. Monetarily, they were worth next to nothing. Emotionally, they are priceless. She gave me Monique's locket with a note. It read, 'I know the truth. This belongs to you.'"

"That doesn't incriminate you or her." Sean couldn't help but think he was missing something, but on the surface, those two sentences meant nothing.

"In context, it means everything. I need to find out who stole my locket. I need to know what the blackmailers know. If they're jerking me around, or if they have inside information. The FBI already knows about Ivy, and I'm going to give them another important clue."

Sean put his hands behind his neck to give them something to do other than strangle Paxton. "You're playing a fucking game when *five people are dead*?"

"That had nothing to do with me." Paxton pounded his fist on the desk. Sean had never seen him lose his temper so abruptly. "I couldn't have stopped those murders! As soon as I found out that Chris and Jocelyn Taylor were murdered, I called Noah Armstrong. He'll know everything I do—"

"Except that you hired me to do the background on Ivy Harris."

"I had to verify her story."

Sean didn't know what to think or believe. Paxton was a manipulative bastard whose penchant for playing God now affected the woman he loved.

"No one is going to believe Lucy knew you killed that bastard rapist. Mallory already confessed."

"I'm trying to explain!" Paxton slowly rose from his chair and leaned over Sean.

"You think she got into the Academy because of the second interview?" Paxton grinned snidely and shook his head. "*I* made it happen."

Before he could say any more, Paxton's phone buzzed. He answered it. "Thank you, Ann. I'll let you know when I'm ready for him." He hung up. "Noah's here."

"Bring him in. See what he thinks."

"Dammit, Rogan, you're too stubborn for your own good." He ran a hand through his thick gray hair. Paxton pointed to a door. "Go in there."

"Why?"

"Can you trust me on this?"

"No."

But now Sean was curious. He opened the door. It was a deep closet with plenty of room for someone to stand comfortably. He wondered how many people had eavesdropped from this small room.

He stared at the senator, torn.

Then he stepped inside and closed the door behind him.

CHAPTER TWENTY-FOUR

Noah spoke to Lucy on his cell while he waited for Senator Paxton. He didn't like waiting, especially since Paxton had called him, but was glad he had the opportunity to verify that Lucy had no serious injuries.

Lucy was emphatic that the murder of Wendy James was connected to the other crime scenes, and she made a compelling case, but what Slater said earlier was still true: They had no hard evidence.

"You're taking the rest of the day off," Noah told Lucy over the phone.

"Is that an order?"

"Yes. I'll stop by later. Where will you be?"

"Home, where else?"

"I assumed Sean would take you to his place."

"Oh. Maybe. Kate's here now."

Noah was surprised Sean wasn't glued to her side. He hoped the hotheaded Rogan didn't do something unwise, like try and find the driver of the van. Noah wouldn't put it past him.

"Don't work too hard," he told Lucy.

"You just ordered me to take the day off."

"Were you going to obey me?"

She laughed. "No. But I will stay at home. I don't think Kate is going to take me anywhere else."

"Good. If you're compelled to do anything, write up a report on the accident. I need to debrief you anyway, and putting it on paper will help you remember the details. And I'll have a courier bring over a copy of the James file for you to review. I have two analysts going over everything we've uncovered, but you have a different perspective."

"I can't wait."

She sounded excited about paperwork. She'd be the first, Noah thought. "I also want to get your assessment on the suspect."

"I already told you I didn't get a good look at him, but his van will be damaged."

"I meant Hannah Edmonds, aka Ivy Harris."

"Ivy isn't her name?"

"No. She's the daughter of televangelist Kirk Edmonds."

"I've never heard of him. Why did you call her a suspect?"

"She is a person of interest in the kidnapping of Sara Edmonds."

"Sara? Mrs. Neel said her sister was named Mina."

"I'm going to talk to Mrs. Neel shortly, but I think Mina and Sara are two different girls. One a prostitute, the other the missing daughter of Reverend Edmonds. I'll send everything I know so you can get up to speed."

"You don't know that she kidnapped her sister. Sara could have run away."

"But we won't know until we talk to her. She's a fourteen-year-old girl who was living for the last ten days in a house with known prostitutes, two of whom are dead."

"Ivy was extremely protective of her sister. If you find her, she's going to be difficult to talk to. Get someone like Hans to work with her."

"You were with her for less than ten minutes. I don't think that's enough to judge."

"It's more than enough."

Paxton opened his door and waved at Noah. He said to Lucy, "I have to go. Just read the file and then we'll talk." He hung up and walked over to shake Paxton's hand.

"Senator."

"Sorry to keep you waiting, Agent Armstrong, it was one of those calls that's hard to get off. Please come in."

Paxton closed the door and sat down behind his antique desk. He motioned for Noah to take a seat across from him.

Noah glanced around the room before he sat, getting a snapshot assessment of Paxton. He'd been here before, months ago. Standard Senate office—large, ornate, stately.

"I've debated with myself whether to call ever since I heard that Alan's mistress was murdered."

Noah was certainly curious, but he couldn't imagine what Paxton had to say. "I can't discuss the investigation with you. I thought you wanted to talk about Chris Taylor."

"I did want to inquire about the status of your investigation, but when Detective Reid came by this morning with Lucy, I was under the impression that it was a Metro Police investigation, not federal."

"We're working with them." Stockton hadn't officially released the information that the FBI had taken over the case. That situation was still being smoothed over with DC Metro, as best as could be done under the circumstances.

"I'm not proud of my actions, but I don't regret them. Unless what I did led to that poor girl's death."

The hair on Noah's skin vibrated with energy. It was the same feeling he'd had in the Air Force when he sensed something was amiss. Noah homed in on Paxton's carefully chosen words.

What I did led to the poor girl's death.

"Explain."

"It's no secret Alan and I don't get along. Frankly, I think he's a pig. Everyone in the building knows he's cheated on his wife. And most everyone looks the other way. It's like infidelity is a misdemeanor. But if someone can't respect his marital vows, how can he respect promises to his constituents? If he can lie to his wife, it must be that much easier to lie to the American people."

"Senator, I'm not interested in a campaign speech."

Paxton's cheek twitched with irritation.

"I was the anonymous source who gave the pictures of Alan and Ms. James to the tabloid."

The confession surprised Noah. He had to pause before he could ask a question without stammering.

"You told the press about the affair?"

Paxton waved his hand in the air as if swatting a fly.

"The press already knew. But they didn't have proof. It's sad that to run with the story, they wanted sordid photographs."

"Which you provided."

"I did."

"I have a hard time believing you followed Congressman Crowley."

"I didn't. I hired a professional. Don't be so skeptical, Agent Armstrong. Husbands and wives do it to each other all the time. If Janet Crowley had hired a private investigator to get photos of her husband's infidelity in order to divorce that bastard, no one would think twice."

"Why did you do it?"

"Why do you think?"

Noah didn't answer the question. He stared at Paxton until he answered.

"Alan's a prick."

"He's in your political party."

Paxton laughed heartily, then cleared his throat. "After California went through their redistricting, Alan was gerrymandered into a much different seat, one that would be far more outraged about his infidelity. I have a protégé who can defeat him in the primary, but it would be costly. I would much rather have him resign over the affair."

"You did this as a campaign stunt?"

"Stunt? Hardly the right word. I did it because he's a jerk. He's talking about running for U.S. Senate and I don't want him on my side of the building."

"And you don't feel an ounce of remorse for what happened to Wendy James?"

"If she was killed because I exposed the truth, I

sincerely regret it. But however much I despise Alan Crowley, however much I *want* him to be guilty, he's not a killer, or a rapist."

"She wasn't raped."

Paxton said, "The press reported there was an attempted rape."

"The press isn't always right."

Paxton visibly relaxed. "Good."

"Good?"

"It's tragic she was killed. She was a young, beautiful woman with her whole life ahead of her, regardless of the mistakes she made. But to be raped and then murdered is the most vile crime that can be committed on a woman. There's a special place in Hell for men like that."

Noah hoped there was a special place in Hell for puppeteers like Paxton. He wished there was some way he could officially bring Paxton in for questioning. He could probably think of something—withholding information from the FBI for one, because he suspected there was more to this story than Paxton had told—but his actions would be out of spite.

The truth was hard to argue against.

CHAPTER TWENTY-FIVE

Sean stepped out of the closet. He didn't know how he felt about what he had just heard. He understood Paxton's motives—he'd done similar things, exposing people who deserved it while keeping his own hands clean. He'd learned the hard way that gloating could get him in trouble.

He didn't want to like Paxton. He *didn't* like Paxton. But he understood him.

What he didn't understand was how Paxton could hurt Lucy. She would be devastated if she found out that Paxton had pulled strings to get her into the FBI Academy. And if he was determined to be corrupt, her career would be tainted. If that note she allegedly wrote came out, the media, or the FBI, could make it sound like anything they wanted. Even if it *was* innocuous, they could make it appear like she was keeping Paxton's secret—accessory after the fact—so that she could get his help. She had made it very well known that all she wanted was to be an FBI agent. The people in charge could even make it look like Paxton got her in so he could have his own bought-and-paid-for agent.

"Now do you understand?"

Sean had been trying to put together the information Paxton had given him earlier with what he said to Noah. "What do the note and locket have to do with exposing Crowley?"

"It has everything to do with it. The locket disappeared *after* I turned over the photographs to the press."

"Coincidence?"

"No. I was threatened. If I didn't back off, the caller would expose the secrets of the locket. The thing is, there are no secrets. It belonged to my daughter. It's all I have left of her. I want it back. But if they know about Morton—if that's what they meant about 'secret,' then I can't risk exposure."

"But you killed him," Sean said matter-of-factly.

"Lucy will be irreparably damaged as well. I'm not willing to take the risk. Are you?"

"You bastard. You've dirtied her entire career."

"Don't be so melodramatic, Rogan. I'm going to set things right. I always do." He almost sounded pained, but Paxton was a politician and a liar. He didn't care about what happened to Lucy.

"Who else knows about the note?"

"No one. At least, no one knows Lucy wrote the message. But several people know she had the locket. Noah Armstrong gave her Adam Scott's box and told her to make the decision about whether his victims' families would want the items back. She worked with the FBI to locate the families and wrote them letters."

Sean hadn't known. Six months ago, he and Lucy had just started seeing each other. He shouldn't be hurt she hadn't included him, but he was. The experience must have been extremely painful and difficult for her, in light of the fact Adam Scott had kidnapped, raped, and nearly killed her. Yet she worked with Noah on it.

Sean didn't want to help Senator Paxton, but did he really have a choice? Even if the note could never be linked to her, Paxton's unspoken threat to reveal that he'd pulled strings to get Lucy into the Academy hit home.

"Whoever took the locket has access to your office," Sean said.

"I've already had you run background checks on everyone I thought might have done it—"

"I'll run background checks on *everyone* who's come in and out of your office."

Paxton reluctantly agreed. "Very well. I have a window as to when it went missing. I'll get you my appointment books. But Sergio Russo already went through—"

"Sergio Russo isn't me."

"I'll get you everything you need first thing in the morning."

"Tonight."

Sean was about to leave when he remembered what Lucy had said about the three murders. Paxton didn't know that Wendy James was connected to the two prostitutes. But if the photos started this chain of events, that made Paxton indirectly responsible for all five deaths.

He couldn't help but rub that in.

"Noah didn't say anything to you, but the FBI is taking over the investigation into the murders at the Hotel Potomac. They're connected to Wendy James. The same person who killed her also killed four other people.

Think about that, Senator, since you don't seem to regret what you did. If it were me—and it has been in the past—my fingerprints would never be on it. I've destroyed pricks like Alan Crowley. And no one will know who, because I don't need to brag about my successes."

Sean grinned, gloating. "Hope you get a good night's sleep."

Before he could walk out, Paxton said sharply, "Rogan!"

Sean turned around.

"Watch yourself. The statute of limitations isn't quite up on one of your *successes,* as you call it, up in Massachusetts. And I don't think you would do well in prison."

CHAPTER TWENTY-SIX

After leaving the senator's office, Noah called Rick Stockton directly and told him about Paxton's confession.

Unfortunately, it wasn't a crime to expose an extramarital affair. The motive didn't matter: Truth was almost always a defense.

Paxton seemed contrite that his clandestine release of the compromising photographs might have led to the murder of Wendy James. If he had known that his acts would result in a death, he could be culpable. It was a stretch, and proving it would be next to impossible. Noah didn't know how many affairs were publicly exposed, but rarely did they end like that of Wendy James.

But Paxton was a politician, and Noah wasn't sure how much of his sincerity was an act.

Noah needed to find the woman who called herself Ivy Harris, so he drove back to where she was last seen. He had reviewed what little they had on her—under both her alias and her real name.

Hannah Edmonds was one of three daughters of televangelist Kirk Edmonds. A widower, Reverend Edmonds had a successful ministry in Allegheny County in the northwest of Maryland. The closest city to his base was Cumberland, but the small unincorporated town he lived in had less than three hundred people, almost all of whom worked for Hope Ministries.

Noah could imagine that growing up in a small, sheltered religious community was the breeding ground for teenage rebellion, but faking a suicide seemed awfully sophisticated for a fourteen-year-old.

According to the records the local FBI office had on Hannah Edmonds, she'd been diagnosed bipolar manic-depressive when she was thirteen, after she first tried to kill herself. Eighteen months on a variety of medications seemed to be working, then her father learned she'd tricked the household staff and hadn't been taking her medication at all.

There was a history of mental illness in the family. Hannah's mother had killed herself and tried to kill her two youngest children. Hannah had been seven at the time. She and the baby, Sara, had miraculously survived when Marie Edmonds intentionally drove her vehicle into a security fence.

Noah didn't have a lot of experience with mental illnesses like manic depression, but he knew enough to know that Hannah was dangerous to herself and others. If she felt trapped, scared, hopeless, what might she do to her sister? Could they believe anything she said?

He needed to get her into custody and have her evaluated. She seemed to be the one connection between everything that had happened since Monday—what if she was behind the deaths? What if she was working with an accomplice?

It seemed a stretch, considering that she'd been shot at after Lucy and Genie picked her up, but maybe that wasn't what it appeared to be on the surface. Maybe her partner thought he was breaking her out of custody.

It didn't feel right to him, but he had to focus on the facts, and right now, he didn't know why Hannah Edmonds had changed her name, how or why her sister was in DC and whether she was truly kidnapped or ran away, or what Hannah's relationship was with Wendy James or the other victims. All he had were statements, some which conflicted, from a sitting U.S. senator, a social worker, and a retired neighbor. There were a lot of facts, but few connections.

Noah retraced Lucy's steps from the Hawthorne house to the crash site.

Genie's car had already been pulled from the embankment and sat on the back of a flatbed tow truck. It would be transported to the FBI garage for forensic analysis and trace evidence, which had meant Noah had used a lot of fast-talking and arm-twisting to take custody of it from Metro. But someone had shot at a federal employee, and even though Genie was a DC cop, the federal government still had more resources to process the evidence.

It would be easy to match up the damage on the car with the van. But first they had to find it, and so far, nothing. He had the tech squad looking at traffic cams, but in this neighborhood, they were few and far between. He had them focusing on the major streets out of the area, but it was a labor-intensive project that often failed to yield results.

Where had Ivy gone? She disappeared as law enforcement arrived. She knew the area well. They still hadn't found Jocelyn Taylor's car which had last been seen when Ivy drove from the Hotel Potomac the night of the murders.

Or maybe she knew someone who lived in the area, someone who was willing to help her.

He went back to Hawthorne Street and knocked on Patricia Neel's door. The elderly woman answered and smiled broadly, her reading glasses falling off her nose and hanging on a chain around her neck.

Noah held up his badge. "Mrs. Neel, I'm Agent Noah Armstrong with the Federal Bureau of Investigation." He pocketed his identification. "We spoke earlier today on the phone."

"Yes, about the theft."

"Did my agent come by and take your statement?"

"Oh, yes, they just left. Would you like some lemonade? I made it for them, I have plenty."

"No, thank you. I need to follow up on your statement earlier today to my colleague, Ms. Kincaid."

"What a sweet young woman," Mrs. Neel smiled broadly. "So polite."

"Yes, ma'am. I have a few follow-up questions."

"Would you like to come in? It's really warm out here."

"This won't take long." Noah suspected if he went inside it would be difficult to leave quickly. It was no surprise that Mrs. Neel had taken an interest in her young neighbors—she wanted someone to talk to.

"Do you know where Ivy might go to if she were in trouble and needed a place to stay?"

"She knew she could come to me." She frowned. "I wish she'd just asked for the money. I would have given it to her."

"Yes, ma'am."

"She left a note. She's not a bad person."

The woman was repeating herself, and Noah feared he'd get nothing useful from her. This excursion was becoming a waste of time.

"Any other neighbors? Friends? A business she frequented? A church? School? A nearby library?"

"She liked to walk to that little church on Thirty-first. I can't remember the name. Very small. But she walked there nearly every Sunday morning. Sometimes she took Mina with her, or one of the other girls, but I don't think they were proper churchgoers. You know how kids are these days."

"Yes, ma'am." He handed her his card. "You have this, but I wrote my cell phone number on the back. If you see Ivy or any of the other girls, call my cell phone immediately, okay?"

"Of course. I promised Agent Kincaid I would do the same. I hope Ivy and Mina are going to be okay. They are sweet girls."

Noah didn't know if *sweet* was the right word for the prostitutes, but he didn't comment. He thanked Mrs. Neel and went back to his car.

Thirty-first was two blocks over. He drove slowly down the street, looking for a small church. He didn't see anything, turned around and went back up the road toward Hawthorne. He did a double take and realized he'd missed it—the church wasn't so much a *church* as he was used to seeing, but a small converted business partly hidden between two larger buildings. In addition, it was set back from the road and had a small sign half-obscured by an old tree.

His Grace Church & Preschool
Sunday service 9 A.M.

Noah parked down the street and walked to the church. It was late afternoon, the hottest time of the day. A small, covered playground behind a security fence was empty of children.

A door around the side led to the school; it was behind a locked gate. The front door that led into the church was unlocked. He walked in, a brass bell overhead announcing his entrance.

The church had ten rows of mismatched pews down the middle, with aisles on either side. If people sat shoulder-to-shoulder, the room *might* be able to seat a hundred people.

The altar was simple, with an empty cross, a pulpit, and a few chairs, maybe for a choir or speakers. High, narrow windows let in natural light, what little could come through with the taller buildings on three sides. A room opened to the right, set with more chairs and two tables of different heights.

Noah didn't notice the door behind the altar until it opened. An older man who would have looked like Santa Claus had he a beard, stepped out. He wore slacks and a button-down short-sleeved shirt that puckered at the midriff. "May I help you?"

Noah identified himself, and said, "Are you the pastor?"

"No, sir. I'm the custodian, Remus. Are you looking for Marti?"

"Yes, is he around?"

Remus's thick eyebrows furrowed in suspicion. "You don't know Marti."

"No, Remus, I'm investigating the crash that happened a few blocks away."

"The FBI investigates car crashes?"

"When they involve a federal employee and a fugitive, yes."

A gazelle-like black woman emerged from a hallway off the right. "Thank you, Remus, I'll talk to the agent." She waited until Remus shuffled down the hall muttering to himself.

"I apologize. I'm Marti North. Let's sit." She gestured to a pew in the front. Noah sat and she sat a few feet away, bending her left leg under her, and turned to face him with a bright smile that didn't quite match her suspicious eyes.

"Special Agent Noah Armstrong. Correct?"

"Yes, ma'am. I'm looking for a young woman who goes by the name of Ivy." He showed her the current picture she had of Ivy. "Do you know her?"

Marti North didn't look at the picture. "What did this young woman do to draw the attention of the FBI?"

"We believe she's in danger."

"A lot of young women are in danger in this town. The FBI doesn't seem to pay them no mind. Why this girl?"

"Do you remember a fire last week, a few blocks over, on Hawthorne?"

"Yes, I do. I live upstairs."

"Ivy lived in the house with five other young women."

As Noah spoke, he had the distinct feeling that he wasn't telling Reverend North anything she didn't already know.

Marti smiled at him, as if waiting for a question that she already knew she wouldn't answer.

Noah asked, "Did Ivy attend church here?"

"I don't keep a roster. Everyone is welcome."

"But you recognize her."

"That photo is unclear."

Noah was growing frustrated. He changed tactics. "Do you also run the preschool?"

"Yes. When I left the Army I got my degree in Early Childhood Education."

"You served?"

"Yes, sir. Corporal, Fort Hood. Spent a year in Iraq as a Chaplain."

"Air Force," Noah said. "Captain, Raven Force."

"The Ravens. Elite."

He shrugged it off. Ninety percent of his job had been guarding aircraft and transporting international prisoners. Not very exciting. "How many students do you have?"

"The numbers fluctuate. We average ten to twelve, but can have more. We're licensed with the city."

"There was a car crash down the street earlier this morning, followed by gunfire."

"I heard about it after the fact. I didn't hear any gunshots, but Remus told me about the crash. He'd taken the children to the park before it got too hot, and the crash meant they had to take the long way back."

"Ivy was in the car. I think she came here after the crash. Did you see her? Anyone who had been in a wreck?"

Now Noah realized he had the pastor. Marti had been

trying her best to obfuscate and not tell a lie—either
because she was devout, or because she didn't want to
be caught lying to a federal agent, which was a crime.

"A young woman did come in here," she said momen-
tarily, "with a cut on her arm. She didn't say she'd been
in an accident. I offered to take her to the hospital, she
declined. I gave her a small first-aid kit, and she left."

Noah was getting tired of twenty questions. "Had you
seen her before?"

"Yes, she had been here for services in the past."

"Did she leave on foot or in a vehicle?"

"She walked out."

Noah handed Marti his card. "You may think you're
protecting Ivy, but you're putting her in more danger.
Someone is trying to kill her, and nearly killed my partner in that crash. I can help her, but only if she comes to
me. Two of the girls who lived in that house are dead,
and it's my opinion that whoever killed the two girls
intends to kill Ivy and the others. If he finds Ivy before
I do, she will die. I'm sure you don't want that on your
conscience." He started to walk out, then stopped and
turned to face her. "If she contacts you in any way, give
her my number. If you find out where she is, let me
know immediately. She has a diagnosed medical condition that could make her a danger to herself or others. I
want to help her, but she has to come forward. If she
comes in on her own, it will help her."

Marti rose from the pew. She was taller than Noah,
at least six foot two. "Agent Armstrong? *A lying tongue
hates those it hurts.*"

She tilted her chin up, making the stately woman appear even taller. "Don't take everything you hear as
Gospel. You may leave."

* * *

Ivy waited until the FBI agent had left before she came downstairs.

"He's still outside. I see him watching."

"You're safe here. I locked the front door."

"The Reverend is coming. He's going to take Sara. He's already lied and they believe him."

Only one person would have told the FBI that she had been diagnosed mentally ill. Her father.

Her entire body shook so hard she thought she'd crack right down the middle. She had to get it together or she'd never make it out of town.

Marti came over and put her large, narrow hands on Ivy's shoulders. "You are no longer safe here. The FBI will be back."

"I know." She breathed deeply. "You'll find Mina a home?"

"I have an old friend in Fort Hood. We went to theology school together. She'll love Mina like we do. I'm already getting the papers in order. As far as the rest of the world is concerned, Mina is her niece from upstate New York. No one will question it. You've done the best you can, Ivy. You saved Mina, protected her all this time. Now let me. Let me help."

Ivy nodded. "Thank you."

"Your identities will be here in the morning. Take Sara, do not tell me where. I am not a good liar."

"And I'm too good."

"God has forgiven you. Now forgive yourself."

Ivy chest heaved in silent sobs. Marti pulled her into a tight, bony hug, and Ivy had never felt so loved since the night her mother tried to save her from the monster.

CHAPTER TWENTY-SEVEN

Sean did not take well to being threatened.

He considered calling his brother Duke about Paxton's bombshell, but decided to keep it to himself for now. He didn't want to tell Duke what he'd done. Not because he regretted it, but because he'd learned the hard way to keep his not-quite-legal activities a secret.

It was nearly eleven years ago while at Stanford University that Sean hacked into a tenured professor's computer and exposed him as a child pornographer. It was a brilliant plan. When the FBI got involved over the illegal hacking, he came forward, admitted what he'd done, expecting a medal for getting the pervert thrown off campus and under indictment.

Instead, he'd been arrested.

Duke had fixed it, but Sean had never trusted the FBI after that. Duke got him into MIT, even though Sean wanted nothing to do with any educational or government institution. But of course he went. He'd always done what Duke wanted, at least on the surface.

Sean knew exactly what Paxton was referring to, because there was only one felony Sean had committed that had a statute of limitation of ten years. The ten years was up next March. Eight months, one week from yesterday.

He had to put the situation on hold because right now, there were far more important things to worry about than his freedom. As soon as he solved Paxton's blackmail problem, he'd find the answer he needed.

He pushed the thoughts aside and got to work. Paxton had e-mailed Sean his appointment schedule from the week he said the note Lucy wrote had been stolen.

He hated being put in the position of keeping something this important from Lucy. His stomach ached, a sure sign that he was torn. And there was no one he could talk to about it. Patrick was out of town, and Sean didn't know how he would react if he knew Lucy had kept such an important piece of information secret. Her sister-in-law Kate would understand, and Sean trusted her more than any other fed, but Kate was *still* a fed and Sean would be putting her in a compromising position.

Sean wasn't as conflicted about keeping the information about Lucy's acceptance into the FBI a secret. It would destroy her, and Sean wasn't going to be party to that. If she quit because he told her, it would taint their relationship forever. Worse, she'd give up on her dream. She would say she understood, but he remembered how upset she'd been when she failed her first personal interview.

She not only deserved this assignment, she would make an amazing cop. Better than most cops out there. Sean would much rather she work for RCK. Her instincts were sharp and she certainly had the brains for private security work, but that's not what *Lucy* wanted.

Paxton's schedule had been full the last week of June. He had meetings with locally elected officials, lobbyists, nonprofit groups, other congressmen—more than a dozen meetings on Monday alone. How could someone work like that? Sean kept meetings to a minimum. Sitting around doing nothing, in Sean's mind. He knew part of it was his kinetic personality—he had to be doing *something*, physically or mentally.

Normally, Sean would forward the list to RCK West and have their support staff do the grunt work, but he didn't trust anyone else with this job, and he didn't want to explain it to his brother. This kind of work, though simple, needed to be thorough. At least it kept his mind going, and he ran multiple searches simultaneously.

He put the out-of-town visitors at the bottom of his list. It wasn't that they *couldn't* be guilty, but the chances were minimal. He wrote a quick program to run basic background checks on those people, as well as Paxton's staff, and forced it to work on another server, to keep his at peak performance. When it was done, the program would e-mail him a report.

There was a national law enforcement group, a national victims' rights group, multiple congressmen and staff, and several lobbyists representing a variety of clients.

If he were going to steal something, he would prefer to be alone in the room. He made a list of all meetings where there were only one or two other people. That eliminated half the meetings. Two people would work— either a conspiracy, or one of them stepped out.

Paxton wouldn't have been in the room.

What made Paxton think that someone hadn't accessed his office after hours? Capitol security was extensive, and Sean bet the first thing Paxton had done was look at the security feeds outside his office for any intruders. But there were no security cameras in the individual legislative offices. So he'd deduced that someone who had access to his inner office had taken the note. Paxton had dismissed his staff as viable suspects, and Sean supposed a man as wily as Paxton would be able to assess his employees accurately.

Then there was his pet PI, Sergio Russo.

Sean knew very little about the PI. How had Paxton found him? Was he from DC or the New York district that Paxton represented?

Running a background on Russo would be a little more difficult. A good PI would have alerts when certain databases were accessed. Sean would have to go into each database through a back door. It wasn't legal, but at this point, if Russo was not who he appeared to be, Sean didn't want him knowing that he was digging.

Paxton said that the note and locket had been kept in a box in his bottom right-hand drawer. Close to him, where he could look at it anytime he wanted, but hidden from public view.

There had to be something more than the theft of the locket and note. There was no evidence at all that Paxton had killed Roger Morton. Someone else confessed, the gun had been recovered, no one was even *looking* at Paxton as a coconspirator, let alone the man who pulled the trigger.

Why not call their bluff?

Because Paxton's lying to you.

He wasn't lying about killing Roger Morton—why would he confess that to Sean when someone else was in prison for the crime? But he was lying about something else.

Mick Mallory had pleaded guilty to avoid the death penalty and gave a detailed rundown on every predator he'd killed.

What's one more in the big picture?

But if Paxton killed Morton, Mallory knew. Which meant Mallory might know why the locket was so important to Paxton.

Why would someone take the fall for Paxton's crimes?

Someone like Mick Mallory, the bastard, was so broken he'd take the truth to his grave. But there were others. Lucy's former boss, Fran Buckley, had made a plea agreement. Did she know about Paxton's involvement? Sean couldn't see how she *didn't*. She took his money, he had headlined a fundraiser for her, they had been friends.

Except . . . that didn't fit the rest of the scenario. It didn't fit why two call girls were dead, a congressional mistress, or a social worker and her husband who were helping them. There was a big gaping hole of information, and in that missing information was motive.

His phone vibrated. It was a text message from Lucy.

I'm finally home. Clean bill of health.

Sean wanted to see Lucy, but he needed to talk to Paxton again. Fill in some of these blanks.

He called to arrange a meeting, and Paxton tried to postpone until tomorrow. Sean wouldn't let him, and

Paxton agreed to meet him at nine, at Paxton's residence in Alexandria.

He never wanted Lucy to know what had happened in Massachusetts. He would destroy Paxton if it got out.

Sean might take the senator down anyway, just for threatening him.

He responded to Lucy's message.

Up for a visitor? I have chocolate ice cream for you.

He had enough time to check on Lucy and get to Alexandria early. He planned to do a little investigation on the senator himself.

He grabbed his laptop and bag of tools, locked up, and tossed everything in his trunk.

Noah watched His Grace Church for thirty minutes.

Reverend Marti North knew exactly who Ivy Harris was. He had already called to get a warrant, but it was late and he had not one teeny piece of evidence that Marti had lied to him, that Hannah/Ivy was there, or that she would return. And whenever they were dealing with registered churches, legitimate or not, they had to be extremely careful in how they approached the situation. No one in the Bureau would forget Waco.

Still, Rick Stockton thought Noah was on to something, and was working with his people and the U.S. Attorney to see what they could do. It might mean simply sending in another agent. Or authorizing a stakeout. Or digging deep into Marti North's past and finding something they could leverage. Not Noah's favorite approach, but when a fourteen-year-old girl was missing and the people she had been with were all dead, he would do whatever it took.

Cyber crimes had called him with the information obtained from the virtual phone company. The number was registered to a pay-as-you-go phone and the account purchased with a prepaid credit card.

Noah didn't find it humorous that Sean Rogan had predicted that method to hide the identity of the phone number holder.

The credit card yielded nothing—it was in the dollar amount for the yearlong subscription to several virtual numbers, all of which went to the same disposable phone number. The account had been opened three months ago, and changed disposable numbers four times. The current disposable phone, however, had been reloaded at a nearby location three weeks ago.

When he got the call that the surveillance team had finally arrived to relieve him from the impromptu stakeout, he left to check out the business.

Noah drove to a small convenience store only six blocks from the church, on the corner. Like other businesses in the area, bars covered the windows. When he pulled up, several loiterers left the area.

He walked in and the tall, young black kid behind the counter gave him the once-over. "You a fibbie?"

"Special Agent Noah Armstrong." He showed his ID. "I'm looking for the owner."

"That's my dad. He's not here."

"I'm looking for this girl. She lives not far from here, and may have come in to refill a disposable phone." He showed Ivy's picture.

He shrugged. "I don't know."

Noah wasn't certain the number belonged to Ivy, but

since it was only a mile from her house, he was taking a chance thinking it was her. With the multiple virtual numbers all going to the same phone, it suggested she was giving different numbers to different people. According to the company, the caller ID was set up to show which virtual number was being used. That would help Ivy keep track of who was calling her.

Noah had also asked about tracing the numbers calling in to the virtual numbers, but the company didn't keep that data.

This was his closest lead. "The last time the phone was filled was three weeks ago, two hundred dollars cash."

The kid lit up. "She-et, why didn't you say so? Two bills, crisp and clean."

"Was it her?"

"Naw, it was some older dude. Forties."

"Do you remember what he looked like?"

The kid shrugged. "White. Maybe Mexican, Italian, something like that—but not a spic, if you know what I mean."

Noah let the racial slur slide. "How was he dressed?"

"How'em I supposed to remember that? Not like a scumbag. No suit, but I thought he might have been an undercover cop. 'Cept the narcs I know try to look like addicts, you know what I mean?"

"You have a good memory."

"Two bills? Don't see those here. Counting pennies for a bottle of beer, sure, got that going down."

"Anything else you can remember?"

"No, and I'd tell you, honest. You just killed my business for the next two hours, buddy. Everyone on the block pegged you for a cop. My dad is going to shoot me."

Noah handed him his card. "Thanks for your help." He glanced up and saw the security camera. "Any chance you have that guy on surveillance?"

The kid shook his head. "No chance. We copy over the tapes every twenty-four hours. My dad's cheap, and tapes cost a lot, and do you know how much it costs to go digital?"

CHAPTER TWENTY-EIGHT

Lucy closed her eyes as she savored the dark chocolate Häagen-Dazs ice cream Sean brought her.

"Umm."

"Good?"

"Umm-hmm."

Kate hit Sean in the shoulder. "You didn't bring me any?"

"I'm sure Lucy will share."

"No I won't," Lucy said between bites. "I'm the invalid here."

Kate snorted and waved her hand around the family room. Lucy had taken over the coffee table with all the files and notes Noah had sent over. Her laptop was open and Noah had given her access to the complete Wendy James file. Because she'd been out of the loop on the James case for the last two days, she wanted to go through those documents first, with an eye for any connection to Ivy Harris or the murder victims.

"I need the chocolate to keep me focused on the task at hand," Lucy said.

Kate sat on one of the chairs, tucked her shoulder-length blond hair behind her ears, and picked up a file.

"Wait," Lucy said, "if you want to help, first read the Cyber Crime Unit report." She leaned over and handed Kate the appropriate file, then took another big scoop of ice cream and put the lid on the carton. She started to get up to put it in the freezer, when Sean grabbed it from her.

"Sit." He walked into the kitchen to put it away. Lucy glanced up when he came in a few minutes later, holding the cat. He sat down and adjusted the cat in his lap to pet him. The cat purred happily.

"Did you pick a name for him?" Lucy asked.

"Why does Sean get to name the cat?" Kate said.

"Because he's taking him when I'm at the Academy."

"No he's not." Kate looked from Lucy to Sean, narrowing her gaze to a glare. "You travel too much, Rogan."

"Patrick and I are rarely gone at the same time."

"I'm here every night. The cat needs consistency."

"Admit it," Sean said, "you like the cat."

"I never said I didn't."

Lucy laughed. "You told me you didn't want a pet."

"Cats are easy."

The cat suddenly meowed loudly and jumped off Sean's lap.

"See, he doesn't like you," Kate said, picking the cat up. "Good kitty. I knew you wanted to stay with me." She stuck her tongue out at Sean, an odd and hilarious gesture for a woman who was nearly forty.

"There's a bump on his neck that's probably sore, that's why he jumped down. You should take him to the vet."

"If I'm taking him to the vet, I'm keeping him while Lucy's gone," Kate said.

"I guess that's final." Sean winked at Lucy and she suspected the conversation wasn't over on the cat.

Lucy finished going over the Wendy James reports while Sean worked on his laptop.

Next, she picked up the arson report on the Hawthorne Street house and reviewed it again.

"What I don't understand," Lucy said, "is how Ivy Harris was able to rent that house on Hawthorne when she was using a false name. Did she have a complete fake identity? Social Security number and everything?"

"Where's the rental agreement?" Kate asked.

"I haven't seen it."

Sean said, "Maybe someone cosigned the agreement, or she took an ID. Often, the companies do only a cursory background check. Or, if someone has a good record as a tenant, a reference from a previous landlord is sufficient."

"It's not here," Lucy said. "At least, it's not in the arson reports. I don't know that we requested it."

"Tell Noah to request it tomorrow," Kate said.

Lucy didn't want to wait that long. "The agreement may give us an emergency contact, someone who knows Ivy—maybe even knew she was using a fake name."

Kate pulled out a paper. "Here's the contact information for the owner. Give them a call."

The doorbell rang as Lucy was on the phone with the owners. Kate jumped up to answer it.

By the time Kate came back to the family room with Noah, Lucy had the answers she needed. "The owner is going to fax me a copy of the rental agreement."

"For what?" Noah asked.

"The Hawthorne Street house. Check if Ivy Harris has any references or a previous address. Someone knows where she is."

"Good plan." He sat down. "I can't stay long, but I need to follow up on your accident."

"I sent you a report. That's everything I remember."

"And it was detailed. I went back to talk to Patricia Neel, the neighbor, and she identified a church that Hannah Edmonds had attended."

"You mean Ivy?" Kate asked.

"Ivy Harris is a false identity," Noah explained. "We have confirmation that the girl known as Ivy is in fact Hannah Edmonds, who's bipolar and suicidal."

Lucy shook her head. "She wasn't acting suicidal. She was definitely in preservation mode, believing that she's the only one who can protect her sister."

"Which is asinine," Noah said. "She must not be thinking straight if she thinks she can protect a fourteen-year-old better than the authorities."

"She may have some reason for distrusting law enforcement. She got in the car because she was terrified of the guy chasing her—she said she didn't know him, and that may be true, but she'd seen him before, I'm certain of it. If we can get her to work with a forensic artist, we can get a good rendering."

"That's a big if, because she ran from the crash site."

"You're treating her like a criminal, not a victim," Lucy said.

"You don't know that she's a victim. She is accused

of kidnapping her sister, a fourteen-year-old minor. She is using a fake identity after making her family believe she committed suicide. She's a known prostitute who fled a murder scene. Yes, she is most certainly a person of interest."

Lucy felt chastised, and Noah wasn't wrong about the situation, but at the same time they didn't have all the facts. Pieces were missing that would make the picture clear.

"I understand," she said, "but she's a classic victim, particularly if someone in authority let her down. Distrustful of the police—"

"So are criminals," Noah interrupted.

Lucy continued, "Protective of her family, scared, hiding."

"I know a lot of bad guys who fit that bill, too," Noah said. "You know nothing about her. She's considered dangerous."

"Her house was burned down in the middle of the night. She went to someone she trusted—Jocelyn Taylor—who wasn't under duress. We know that Chris Taylor contacted Senator Paxton for advice, but was killed before he could meet with him."

"Maybe Ms. Edmonds didn't want him talking to anyone."

"You think she's party to the murders of her friends?"

Noah hedged. "No, but I think she knows more than we do about who is responsible."

"Have you talked to the runaway that Jocelyn relocated?" Kate asked, trying to break the tension in the room. "She might have some insight."

"An agent from the Richmond office had an interview this afternoon with the girl and her mother." He looked at his watch. "She said she'd have the report to me this evening."

He said to Lucy, "We're going off the theory that the three crime scenes are interconnected, but we have no suspects and the one witness who can help ran. We need her in custody."

"I agree, to protect her. Her house is gone, her friends are dead, she's terrified, and she's trying to protect her sister." Lucy didn't like how Noah was putting Ivy in the role of suspect.

"All signs of desperation—and that's what I'm worried about. She's going to do something desperate and get someone killed. Genie Reid is damn lucky that bullet didn't kill her. If it was a higher caliber, or she was turned only a few degrees, it would have hit her chest, not her arm." Lucy had rarely seen Noah angry until this week. Now, every time they talked about the case, he seemed to be angry.

But Lucy was confident Ivy was as much a victim— and target—as those who had already been murdered. "I agree, we need to get her into protective custody, but someone is targeting all the girls in the Hawthorne house. There were at least six, and we know about five of them. Maddie and Nicole were murdered; Ivy, Mina, and Ivy's sister are in hiding."

"The pastor of His Grace Church near their house knows more, and I have a team outside the church watching for any sign of Hannah Edmonds or her sister. I also have a lead on the virtual phone number you ID'd on Nicole Bellows's body."

Noah glanced at Sean, who had been oddly silent during the entire conversation. "You were right, Rogan. Someone bought a prepaid credit card to use for the virtual phone service. We have a vague description of a forty-year-old white male of Italian or Spanish descent who last reloaded the card. Now that we have that number, we're going back to the virtual phone company to run a reverse program, to trace that credit card to any other virtual numbers it purchased, under any name."

Sean nodded and said with mock surprise, "Smart."

Noah snapped back, "The FBI has a good cyber crimes team."

"They're adequate," Sean said.

"Hey," Kate said, "I'll take you on head-to-head with a computer anytime, Rogan."

"You're not on cyber crimes, you teach them," Sean grinned. "You're head and shoulders above anyone else there."

Noah sighed and rubbed his eyes. "I don't have time for this, Rogan."

Noah was showing signs of strain and fatigue, and Lucy realized there was a lot of pressure on him from all angles—Congress, Matt Slater, AD Stockton, DC Metro, Reverend Edmonds.

She forced herself to stay calm and not take his anger personally. "Let's put the Ivy-Harris-as-suspect theory aside for a moment. Consider her as a target. Wendy was killed the day before the fire. Ivy and the others at Hawthorne Street were in the house when the fire was set—which is still ruled as inconclusive and a possible arson. We know this because of the clothes found in the hotel room. Ivy calls Jocelyn and asks for help. The girls split up for some reason—"

Kate interrupted. "That has me perplexed. Wouldn't there be safety in numbers?"

"Maybe not everyone was home during the fire,"

Lucy said. "Or they felt hiding individually was safer. Or maybe they had a falling-out."

"And we won't know until we talk to Hannah Edmonds, but," Noah said with rare sarcasm, "she ran from the authorities."

Everyone turned to Noah, equally surprised by his tone.

He didn't notice, and said, "Just get to the point, Lucy."

Out of the corner of her eye, she saw Sean tense and lean forward, just a bit. Couldn't he tell Noah was on edge? Did he want to push him even more?

"My point," she said crisply, hoping to defuse the tension for everyone, "is that when we know why these girls were targets, we'll know who the killer is."

"That's a big revelation?"

Again, Lucy tried not to take the slight personally, because Noah was under strain, but it hurt. Was she stating the obvious? Except everyone was focused on finding Ivy Harris, and no one was looking now at *why* she was on the run.

"I think the focus has changed from finding the killer to finding Ivy. We need to do both," Lucy said.

"We are."

"Okay, then we have no problem."

She swallowed her frustration and embarrassment. Her voice cracked just a bit when she said, "I've been thinking about the killer's strategy. He started by trying to cover up his motive. First the attempted rape, then a fire that he tried to make look like an accident. But when that fire didn't give him the results he wanted, he grew bolder. Killing Nicole and leaving the rat. Jamming security at a hotel, killing three people and then *showering* in the same room. He's arrogant, thinks he's smarter than most everyone and definitely smarter than the police. He will not hesitate to kill again. While he has above-average intelligence, he's not wholly focused on self-preservation. Coming after Ivy in daylight was dangerous for him."

"Especially," Kate said, "because she jumped into a cop car."

Lucy shook her head. "He might not have known. Genie's car is unmarked—not even a government plate. But if you get closer—like he did—he might have been able to see the radio panel, or maybe he knew what Detective Reid looked like."

"You think he went back to his crime scenes?" Noah made a note. "We photographed bystanders."

"No, he's not the type of killer who would go back. He's not killing because of a thrill. I can't say whether he gets any personal rush from murder, but that's not the reason he kills. He *does* like to play games, however. That's why the messages are important. He's taunting his victims, but there's no guarantee his targets will even see the messages. He *is* the type who would monitor the investigation. Listen to the media. Read the newspapers. Follow online media for any rumors or theories. He doesn't want to be caught, but he definitely wants to finish his mission. And his mission is to kill the six girls who lived at the Hawthorne Street house.

"And the only thing that makes sense," Lucy continued, "knowing what we know about Ivy Harris and Wendy James's secret room, is that together they knew something that was dangerous to one of their clients. That maybe they worked together to record men like Alan Crowley to blackmail or threaten them."

"So far, finances on Crowley and the other men we

know Wendy was involved with are clean. No unusual payments. But," Noah added, "Stein's team is going through them again at different angles, as well as those zindividuals who rented apartment seven-ten. Maybe there's something there, but it's buried. And Stein's team is going through all the public filings of DSA, to see if something matches up to the other records."

"DSA?" Kate asked.

"Devon Sullivan and Associates, James's former employer. They're lobbyists."

"They fired Wendy after the affair with Crowley was exposed," Lucy said.

Kate rolled her eyes. "So a single female secretary gets fired for having an affair with a married guy, but the said married guy is still a sitting congressman pulling in over a hundred thou annually, with perks? That sucks."

"Things haven't changed much over the centuries," Sean interjected. "Look at Hester Prynne."

Noah cleared his throat. "Psychologically speaking, do you think we can bluff the killer into making a move?"

"Yes," Lucy said. "Without a doubt. But it can't be heavy-handed. He has sharp instincts."

"I'll talk to Stockton and Hans and see what they want to do with that. In the meantime, Kate—I'm pulling you in for the next day or two. Slater said I can use anyone I need, and considering that you're the top cyber crimes guru that the FBI has . . ." He shot a glance at Sean with a hint of a smile, almost daring him to contradict him. Lucy was relieved. The tension began to dissipate.

"You've got me," Kate said.

Noah asked, "Where's Dillon? I'd like him to run a forensic psych profile." Dillon often served as a civilian consultant to the FBI and other law enforcement agencies. His specialty, forensic psychiatry, was in great demand.

Sean said, "Lucy just gave you one."

"I can dig deeper, write up an official report, get validation from Behavioral Sciences," Lucy said. She wanted to do it—and she was good at it. Her background in criminal psychology was enhanced by her experience— the good and the bad.

"I'm not talking about the killer," Noah said. "You're not unbiased, Lucy, and I need someone I can trust to give me an honest assessment on Hannah Edmonds."

The tension skyrocketed as fast as Sean jumped up. "Is that a requirement to be a cop? That you have to be unbiased? Because none of you guys fit the bill."

"And I know a lot more about this case than you do, Rogan, so back off."

"What haven't you told me?" Lucy asked.

"It's all here," Noah said. "Get yourself up to speed because Rick Stockton wants you in the office first thing in the morning."

"I have an appointment," Sean said. He kissed Lucy, hard and fast, and said, "I'll stop by on my way home."

He walked out, slamming the door.

Noah pinched the bridge of his nose. "It's been a long day. I apologize if you think I don't trust your judgment. But this is my case, and I have to live with every decision I make. And right now, I need experience over eagerness."

Kate said, "Dillon is out of town at least until Monday night. He was called up to Philadelphia today to assess a guy who went on a two-day killing spree and says he can't remember anything."

"I'll talk to Hans," Noah said. He looked at his phone.

"DC police found Jocelyn Taylor's car parked in a Metro station lot. I have to go."

"I'll walk you out," Kate said.

Lucy didn't relax until she heard the door shut. Then she leaned back and closed her eyes.

She was so embarrassed. Maybe she had hit her head harder than she thought, because she didn't know why that conversation had gotten so out of hand, or what she'd said to make Noah think she was so biased that she couldn't work up an accurate psychological assessment of Ivy Harris. She didn't know that anyone could, based solely on what they knew.

Kate walked back into the room. "Don't let it get to you."

"I'm not."

"Yes you are. Here."

Lucy opened her eyes. "The rental agreement?"

"I found it on the fax. Anything interesting?"

Lucy scanned the document. "It's all standard—but she does have a Social Security number here; we should find out if that's false as well as her name. There's also a reference." She frowned.

"What?"

"Under personal references it lists Paul Harris, her father."

Kate blanched. "Could she have assumed the identity of a real person?"

"Identity theft? Anything's possible. No address, but a phone number."

"I'll call it in and get the address, run a background on the guy. Good catch, Lucy."

But it didn't make her feel any better.

CHAPTER TWENTY-NINE

Brian loved his younger brother, but he wanted to pummel him for his stupidity.

"You shot at a fucking *cop*?"

Ned glared at him. "I didn't know she was a cop— why would that bitch get in a car with a cop?"

"Maybe because we're trying to kill her?"

Shooting at cops escalated police involvement. If it was just a couple of dead hookers, no one would care after a while and the crimes would disappear from the radar, but a cop?

"It's not like she's *dead*," Ned said. He pulled a matchbook from his pocket and took out a match. "The news said she was stable. That means she's fine. Probably a scratch."

Ned lit the match, watched the flame flare, the smell of phosphorous hanging in the still air. The matchstick burned down, he pinched out the flame, and lit another.

Brian ignored his brother and flipped through news stations trying to get more information. If anyone saw his brother or found any damn fingerprints, Brian'd shoot him. Ned was in the system. That would be just fucking *awesome* for the feds to match his prints and find out Theodore Adam "Ned" Abernathy had spent three years in prison for extortion and fraud.

"I took the plates off the van," Ned explained. He lit another match, watched, pinched it out.

"You think they can't trace the van off the paint you left all over the city? You rammed their *car.* They have paint samples, glass, who knows what else. You are such an idiot!"

Brian couldn't find anything that said there was a composite sketch. According to the news, the police were "investigating." Good. But a witness *could* come forward, the police *might* trace the van to Ned's next-door neighbor. And while they had paid off the lowlife drug addict, he would squeal if he was put under any pressure.

Brian didn't enjoy killing people, and he especially didn't enjoy killing people because his brother screwed up. He'd been looking after Ned ever since they were kids. Ned was the baby of the family, the one who could do no wrong, the one who could charm the habit off a nun, as their dad said before he croaked. For years, Brian had been cleaning up after him. The extortion gig happened when Brian had done his own thing for a while, in Hawaii, where girls wore bikinis under a hot sun and no one was stressed, everyone relaxed all the time.

He should never have left.

But you can't pick your family, right?

His mother had flown to Hawaii after Ned was arrested, begging Brian to come back to DC and help her fix it. But Ned had been arrested before, and they'd always fixed it. Now he was stuck. "Maybe a few years in prison will toughen him up," Brian had told her. "Make him less stupid."

That infuriated his mother. She'd always thought Ned, who got straight As in school and was voted Most Popular and was the quarterback of the damn football team was *smart*. Smarter than Brian, who barely graduated high school and never went to college.

Brian would take common sense over book smart any day. Not that people like his mother valued the ability to stay out of trouble.

Twice she came to Hawaii, begging him to come home. The second time was when Ned was up for parole, and his lawyer said he'd be getting out. Brian wanted to know how he knew. It wasn't just conjecture, his mother came to him and said, "Ned is getting out of prison next week and I need you to watch over him. You're his big brother. It's your responsibility."

"Ned got five to ten, why do you think he's getting out in three?"

"Good behavior," she'd told him.

Now Brian knew the truth. Information is power. He wondered how different his life would have been today if his mother hadn't married the lawyer. He wondered if Ned would be back in prison because he was an idiot, and if he, Brian, would still be in Hawaii enjoying the scenery and the sun.

Brian turned off the news when he was satisfied that the police had nothing on Ned being the shooter. Ned turned the TV back on and flipped to a baseball game.

"What the *hell* are you doing?" Brian pulled the plug out of the wall.

"The Yankees are playing—come on, Bri, you told me to lay low, this is how I lay low. I can't just sit here and do nothing."

"You'll do what I say if you want to stay out of prison." Why did Brian even care if Ned went back?

Because he loved his brother, warts and all. And he didn't want to see his mother cry. Even though deep down he knew his mother had manipulated him most of his adult life, he still had a deep need to please her.

Protect Ned at all costs. Even if he was so stupid he'd get them all tossed in prison.

Ned pouted and lit another match. Brian watched it burn out. The heat didn't bother Ned—his fingerprints had been burned off his thumb and index finger. But the police had all five fingers, plus a palm, and probably DNA for all Brian knew.

Brian was no saint, he'd done his fair share of bad things, but Brian had never been caught. Because he knew how to be careful.

"Let's think this through," Brian said. "The good news is she went back to her neighborhood. That means she's staying local, at least for now."

"She's probably long gone."

When Brian first learned that Poison Ivy—his pet name for the wily bitch—was with the cops, he panicked. If Wendy told her everything, the girl was an immediate threat. That's why he planned on getting out of town *now*. He had a train ticket for New York that he could use anytime, and from New York he could go anywhere in the world.

He needed to leave before the cops got smart and flagged his name. Let someone else clean up Ned's messes. Mom loved him so much, let *her* track down the bitch. Or get her pretty-boy husband to do it. Why did it always have to be *him*? It wasn't like it was *his* idea to use Wendy to gather information. He'd never trusted her. Like Ned, she thought she was better, smarter than everyone else.

Neither of them were as smart as he was. Which was why he was alive without a criminal record, and Wendy was dead and Ned had been to prison.

But when he was in the middle of packing, he had the radio tuned to his favorite twenty-four-hour news station. As soon as the report came on about the crash, he turned it up. Two cops transported to the hospital. One civilian may have fled the scene. May have? Damn straight Poison Ivy ran away. That meant the game was still on. And though Brian didn't want to go to prison, the thought of losing to that little whore made his head hurt.

He just wanted to kill her so he could disappear.

What he didn't understand is why she was still in town. If it were *him,* he'd be halfway to the islands by now.

Which meant she had something here, or no way of getting out of town. No money? No car?

He considered *why* she'd come back, exposed herself.

She was desperate.

She was hiding locally. Why?

What was keeping her here when she knew he wanted her dead?

"Ned, why did you think she'd go back to her house?"

"I dunno. Maybe because I'd go home if I were in trouble."

But the house was gone. She must know someone in the area, someone she could trust.

"You followed her for a few blocks before she saw you."

"Yep. I was so close to grabbing her. But there were people around, I didn't want her screaming and causing a scene." Ned lit another match. Brian extinguished it himself and grabbed the matchbook.

Then he closed his eyes and counted to ten. Slowly.

Your chasing and shooting a cop caused far more problems than some bitch being grabbed off the street could ever cause.

Brian pulled a map out of his desk and spread it out. He circled Hawthorne Street. "You show me where she went. What streets she walked, if she made any sudden turns, if she stopped for more than two seconds. Then we'll go back. Smoke her out, so to speak. We'll find her, or we'll find the other girl, but we're going to find *somebody* and Poison Ivy will regret fucking with the Abernathys."

When this was over, he'd fly to Hawaii, or better yet, an island that didn't have an extradition agreement with the U.S. He hoped that this time, six thousand miles was far enough.

CHAPTER THIRTY

Sean drove too fast to Alexandria, but he needed to calm down before he met with Paxton. His custom Mustang GT gave him the power necessary to purge his anger.

Noah was a prick, he decided. For the last six months he'd been worried that Noah had a thing for Lucy, and Sean didn't like them spending so much time working together. Stupid jealousy. Lucy sensed it, but not the cause, certainly not that Sean was jealous of Noah. She thought it was all about Noah being a rigid cop. But after they returned from the Adirondacks, his jealousy had lost its edge. After all, Lucy told Sean she loved *him*, not the damn fed.

If Noah *did* have feelings for Lucy over and beyond a professional friendship, Sean hoped he continued acting like the jerk he was tonight.

Except Sean couldn't stand to watch Lucy struggle with the harsh, unwarranted criticism. And Sean couldn't do anything for fear of messing with Lucy's career goals. Once she went through the Academy and had her badge, he'd be relieved. Her confidence in her abilities would be validated.

Sean's left hand gripped the steering wheel tightly as he downshifted to avoid rear-ending a jerk who thought he needed to stop twenty feet behind the red light. He breathed deeply, forcing himself to relax, and prayed Lucy never learned the truth about how she got into the Academy. *If* Paxton was telling the truth. Sean was fifty-fifty on believing him, and he planned to do his own digging on that angle. But he had to tread carefully. Two of Lucy's sisters-in-law were Feds and Noah had ins with people Sean didn't know. He couldn't afford to let anyone learn he was snooping.

A pleasant breeze had come in with the night, a harbinger that the heat wave might break. As the natural light dimmed and the horizon's glow darkened, the old, tree-lined street full of narrow, three-story brick homes on which the senator lived became a sepia-toned nostalgic snapshot.

Sean parked around the corner from Paxton's house. Paxton said he'd be there by nine; it was already eight thirty. Sean didn't care if Paxton caught him inside—he just wanted the time to find what he was looking for.

Unfortunately, he wasn't sure *what* he was looking for.

He'd come early for two purposes. The first, to find out what the senator knew about his crime in Massachusetts and, more important, how. The second was proof, one way or the other, that Paxton had pulled strings to get Lucy into the Academy. Sean wanted to know who was in Paxton's pocket.

Paxton's security was decent enough to thwart would-be burglars, but Sean wasn't a thief. After a quick assessment, it only took him ten seconds to bypass the alert system, then another ten seconds to crack the alarm code. He was inside in less than a minute.

Sean's eyes adjusted to the dark and he kept his penlight low to the floor. He was familiar with the general layout of these older homes. The bottom floor was usually storage, an office, utilities. Sometimes the area was a large open space, sometimes an in-home office, sometimes an added bedroom suite.

On the middle level was a large living room overlooking the street, a dining area and kitchen overlooking a small postage-stamp-sized yard, and the alley beyond. The detached single-car garage was accessible only through the alley or backyard. The middle level also had a den and small utility room.

Sean went upstairs mostly to ensure he was in fact alone. Two large bedrooms, each with their own bath, completed the home. One bedroom was sparse with a bed, dresser, and small, empty desk. The closet was full of winter suits and coats—Paxton was a clothing hog. The master bedroom was crowded with more furniture and obviously lived-in. The closet was also packed with suits, pressed shirts, casual clothing, and at least a dozen shoes.

Sean decided to search the bedroom first because if there was something personal that Paxton wanted to hide, it would be in here.

He opened the nightstand and hesitated. Why had Paxton kept the locket at his office and not at his home? His office had visitors, staff, janitors coming and going. But he lived alone.

Sean went through the nightstand. There was little of any personal interest—a few books, mostly military history, and catalogues. There was also a .38 special handgun—simple and effective. As a senator, he could easily obtain a permit to carry, but he kept his gun at home. That didn't mean he didn't have a second weapon. Sean started through the closet, looking in the obvious places to store secrets—shoe boxes being common—but he didn't find anything except shoes.

It was nearly nine when Sean decided to forgo the bedroom for the den. He wished he'd had more time.

He went back downstairs and turned the den knob. Locked.

That was interesting. Security system on the house *and* a locked door inside?

Sean pulled out his lock-pick kit and popped the lock easily. He slipped in and closed the door behind him. Then he locked it. It would give him a moment's warning in case Paxton was early.

Sean skipped most of the desk drawers, focusing on the sole locked drawer.

A locked drawer in a locked room in a locked house. Paxton might as well have painted a giant red X on the desk, but this lock was the easiest to pick.

Hanging files held tax forms and other financial documents that didn't seem to be questionable.

There was an article about a killer named Boylan, who went to prison. Sean almost skipped it, but a name caught his attention: Sergio Russo.

He skimmed the article, his stomach queasy. More than a decade ago, Russo's twelve-year-old daughter had been raped and killed by a known predator, Barnaby Edward Boylan. Boylan was sentenced to multiple life terms for the rape and murder of six young girls. There was no death penalty in Massachusetts.

Russo was from Massachusetts. Coincidence?

Doubtful. If there was a connection, Sean would find it now that he had a nugget of evidence.

According to the article, at the trial Russo broke down and charged at Boylan screaming, "Why?" He was removed from the courthouse, charged with contempt of court, but it was later dropped by the judge.

Three weeks after Boylan went to prison, he was killed. He'd been erroneously placed with the general population instead of a special cellblock for child molesters. It seemed that violent criminals hated child predators, and when it got out that Boylan had a fondness for little girls, the inmates literally gutted him with a knife made from empty toothpaste tubes.

Sean could see why a man like Sergio would be drawn to a charismatic crime fighter like Senator Paxton. He could see that a man like Sergio, a widower who had lost his daughter to a vile predator like Boylan, would have a skewed sense of justice.

Sean saw Sergio Russo in a different, more tragic light. What he despised was how Paxton obviously manipulated the grieving father's emotions to pull him into this vigilante justice game.

Another folder had numerous clippings, transcripts, and official records. Sean was about to bypass them when he saw the majority were dated seven years ago.

His vision sharpened and the room blackened around him as he skimmed the articles. They were from a variety of newspapers across the country, all related to Adam Scott and his eighteen-year-long career as a violent sexual predator.

Lucy's name was never mentioned since she'd been a surviving rape victim, but Hans Vigo was quoted, as

well as others Sean knew had been involved in the hunt
for Adam Scott.

There were articles about Roger Morton, the man
Paxton claimed to have killed, who provided detailed
information about the women Scott had killed and what
happened to their bodies. FBI documents were mixed
with the newspapers, including Morton's confession to
helping Adam Scott cover up the murder of Monique
Paxton.

PETERSON: Were you present when Adam Scott
  killed Monique Paxton?
MORTON: No.
PETERSON: When did you find out Adam killed
  Monique?
MORTON: He called me and said he needed help
  with something. I got to his house and she was
  dead. We got help from Trevor and that whiny
  snot Ullman and got rid of the body.
PETERSON: How?

Sean didn't want to read anymore. He flipped through
more files and saw a document marked "confidential"
that made his skin crawl.

It was Lucy's debriefing interview after her kidnapping and rape seven years ago.

Too late, Sean heard the key in the lock. He'd been
so focused on the papers in front of him, he hadn't
heard Paxton enter the house or come up the stairs. He
remained sitting at the desk, made no move to turn off
the desk lamp, and waited until Paxton stepped into the
room.

"You broke into my house?" Paxton said through clenched teeth.

Sean had to remain sitting or he would have attacked Paxton. His vision was sharp, focused, his hands steady. His heart beat fast, but steady. He was ready to fight. But if he touched Paxton, the senator would be dead.

"You have no right to these files," Sean said quietly.

"You read them?" Paxton raised an eyebrow. He didn't come closer.

"Not all. And I'm not going to."

"You need to. You should know what that bastard did to my daughter. To all those other women. To Lucy."

"I don't want to know."

"You think ignorance is the answer? Our minds sanitize the truth so we can cope. I don't want the sanitized version of events. I wanted to know what he did to my daughter. That he strangled her while they had sex, then literally destroyed her body with acid he stole from the high school laboratory. Monique suffered at his hands. She shouldn't suffer alone."

"It helps you to know? You're sick."

"You want to know. I see it. You want to know what Lucy endured. My God, Sean, she suffered and then she fought back and killed him. I want to give her a medal. I had to know how he died, what he said, why he targeted my daughter. You know he picked Lucy because she looks like Monique. He said—"

"Shut the fuck up!" Sean's arm shot out and all the papers went flying across the den.

Paxton pushed. "You want to know what drives me? You want to know why I can keep fighting when all I want to do is put a bullet in my head and join Monique?

It's because of Lucy. If she can endure, I can endure. If she can fight back, I can fight back."

"It's over. I'm not helping you. I'm done."

He walked over and picked up all the FBI transcripts he could find, tearing the pages.

"Stop!" Paxton shouted.

"You don't get to keep these. No one does."

"You're no saint, stop acting self-righteous."

"Let the chips fall, Senator."

"All I have to do is make one call to the FBI Special Agent-in-Charge in Boston and you will be arrested. You know that."

"I don't care anymore." He did care. He didn't want to leave the country to avoid arrest and he didn't want to go to prison. Not for what he'd done—something that shouldn't have been a crime to begin with. But he wasn't working with this twisted bastard.

"You do care. You'll lose her."

Sean's jaw tightened.

"I love Lucy like a daughter, but I will tell her the truth about how she got into Quantico. I lied to you."

Sean had suspected as much, but he didn't know if he could believe Paxton now.

"I tried to pull strings to get her in, but I didn't have to. One of the panelists, the one I knew would vote for Lucy because he's a close friend, gave me the heads-up that she was being declined—again, based on a psych profile. I called Hans Vigo and asked him what I could do to get her in. I was willing to pull any string. You know what he said? 'It's already taken care of.'"

Paxton sneered and shook his head. Sean was standing in the middle of the office, half-torn papers scrunched in his fists. "Lucy has a lot of friends. But she also has enemies. It would benefit you to find out who they are."

"I'm not interfering with Lucy's career."

"You already have!" Paxton walked around to the back of the desk. "If you don't want Lucy to know that her friend and mentor Hans Vigo rewrote the psych report so that she could get into the Academy, I'd suggest you sit down and we get to work to find out who has my locket. Because Lucy won't be the only one to suffer. I would hate to see Dr. Vigo's stellar career destroyed because of one act of clandestine kindness."

How could he betray Hans? Did Dillon and Kate, Hans's closest friends, know? Sean couldn't be party to damaging their careers, but he wished he didn't know. He didn't want to keep this secret from Lucy, but he didn't have much choice.

In the corner of the office Paxton had a shredder. Sean walked over and shredded the file on Lucy. He wasn't going to read it, and Paxton would never read it again.

CHAPTER THIRTY-ONE

Kate made grilled ham-and-cheese sandwiches at nine that night. "Since I cooked—and I hate cooking," Kate said, "do I get some of your ice cream?"

Lucy pretended to think about it, then smiled. "Don't eat it all."

Kate made a beeline for the freezer. "Before dinner?" Lucy called.

"You might change your mind." She grabbed a spoon, and like Lucy, ate right out of the container. "Oh, God, this is orgasmic." Her eyes flew open and she stared at Lucy. "Sorry."

Lucy rolled her eyes. "Why apologize? It *is* orgasmic." She was twenty-five, and yet sometimes her family still treated her like a child. Kate wasn't the worst, though, and Lucy loved her sister-in-law as if she were her flesh-and-blood sister.

Kate's phone rang while she was eating the second bite. She glanced at the caller ID. "I swear, when I get *two minutes* someone needs me."

"Donovan," she snapped when she answered.

Lucy stood and stretched. Her muscles ached from not only the crash, but from sitting on the couch for so long.

"Rachel," Kate said, "I'm going to put you on speaker, okay? I don't want to have to repeat all this to Lucy." She put her cell phone on speaker and put the phone on top of the piles of papers on the coffee table.

By way of introduction, Kate said, "Special Agent Rachel Burrows, meet analyst Lucy Kincaid. Rachel is in Richmond and just finished interviewing Amy Carson, the girl Jocelyn Taylor reunited with her mother."

"Hi, Lucy," Rachel said. "What Agent Donovan didn't say was that she was my cyber crimes instructor at Quantico *and* my advisor."

"That was my first year teaching at the Academy," Kate said. "You know what's scary? How many agents I meet now who I taught at some point over the last seven years. It makes me feel old."

"You are forty," Lucy teased.

"You are a cruel, cruel woman." To Rachel, Kate said, "What do you have?"

"I tried Agent Armstrong and he was in a meeting, so he told me to call you. I spoke with Amy and her mother, but there was something odd going on."

"Odd?"

"They wanted to get rid of me. Their answers were short and clipped. I have all the details—how Ivy Harris pulled Amy off the streets and got her off drugs, how she wouldn't let Amy turn tricks anymore as a condition of living in the house. You'd think this girl was a saint the way Amy and even the mother talked about her."

"Did they deny she was a prostitute?" Kate asked.

"No, they were very upfront about that. And I pushed a bit, and Amy admitted that Ivy was volatile. She had no tolerance for drugs, and when she caught one of the other girls using she tossed the house completely until she found every hidden pill, every hidden bottle of alcohol, and tossed everything down the sink. But in the process, she broke a few things, and Amy said the rampage had scared her. Part of that, I think, was that some of the hidden drugs were hers, though she didn't explicitly say."

"Did she have any specific information about the other girls in the house?"

"That's when she clammed up. She was upset about the murders—very upset—but didn't want to talk about the other girls. I have names—first names, anyway—Mina, Kerry, and Bryn."

Lucy wrote them down. She said, "Did she have any idea where they might have gone after the fire? Has she been in contact with them since she left DC?"

"You jumped to the end of my story!" Rachel said. "Yes, she was in contact with Kerry, and get this—Kerry showed up at Amy's house late Tuesday night."

"You didn't leave her there, did you?" Lucy asked. "She could bolt."

"That's why I'm sitting in my car outside of the house calling you guys. When I was talking to Amy, I asked about Hannah or Sara Edmonds, and Kerry came out of the kitchen, where she had apparently overheard everything I had said. She was freaked. Wanted to know how we found out. At first I thought it was a big scam—she wasn't at all concerned about her culpability in leaving the arson fire, but was very concerned about

Ivy's safety. She has no identification and refuses to tell me her last name or where she's from. Says she's nineteen and met Ivy three years ago, before they moved into the house on Hawthorne. They were both working the streets. I asked her about Wendy James, she said that Wendy and Ivy knew each other and had a big falling-out. She definitely knows more, but she's hedging. I think she's going to bolt, not from us, but to go back to DC and help her friend."

"Does she know that someone is killing her friends?" Kate said. "That she could be in deeper trouble here?"

"Yes. Amy's mother doesn't want her to go. When I asked how Kerry ended up in Richmond, the mom said she called, told Amy what happened, and Amy invited her to come down. The mom says Ivy saved Amy's life, she wanted to help. But Kerry hasn't been able to reach Ivy, and she's been on edge."

"I need to talk to her," Lucy said. Then she glanced at Kate, realizing she'd probably overstepped again.

"We need to bring her back to DC," Kate said. "Protective custody. If she doesn't come voluntarily, arrest her."

"On what grounds?"

"Obstruction of justice."

"Can I talk to her first?" Lucy asked Kate. "She has info we need *now*, not tomorrow morning after she's processed and debriefed. The killer isn't going to stop until he's done."

Kate didn't say anything for a minute.

Rachel said, "You still there?"

"Yes," Kate said. "I'm thinking. Okay, go back to the door and ask if she's willing to talk to us. I'll assess the conversation and decide if we should bring her up. Call us back as soon as she agrees."

"Got it."

Rachel hung up. Lucy said, "If she knows Wendy and Ivy, and has lived with Ivy for three years, what do you bet she knows exactly what they were up to?"

"I'm sure you're right, but we're in no position to offer immunity."

"She wants to help Ivy—she'll talk to us."

"I hope you're right."

Lucy grabbed her own cell phone, then before dialing realized she should run her idea by Kate first. "I want to call Hans and ask him to listen in. He'll be able to assess the situation impartially."

"Is what Noah said about you being biased still bothering you?"

"It doesn't bother me," she lied.

"You are a shitty liar, Lucy."

"I don't want anything tainting this case. Hans is the best."

"Call him. I'll fill Noah in."

CHAPTER THIRTY-TWO

The attic room above the rectory was cool when Ivy climbed in through the window Father Paul had left unlatched for her. The heat wave might not have broken, but it had cracked enough that the evening was pleasant.

Sara was sleeping in the twin bed, curled into a ball, the blankets pulled around her neck. Ivy watched her sister, her heart overflowing with unconditional love.

She'd been ill-equipped to protect Sara from their father, but Ivy hoped she'd been spared the worst. Sara hadn't talked about what happened in any detail. She didn't have to.

Ivy had lived it.

Tomorrow. Tomorrow we will be free.

Marti had come through. Their IDs would be ready in the morning. It would take everything Ivy had stolen from Mrs. Neel, but Marti was even giving her a car to get to the border.

She retrieved a sleeping bag from the corner and unrolled it on the hardwood floor.

"Ivy?" Sara whispered.

"I'm sorry I woke you."

"You didn't. Sit with me."

Ivy climbed onto the twin bed and sat up, her back against the wall. Sara turned on the small lamp next to the bed and leaned against her. Ivy played with the ends of her hair like she used to do when Sara was little. "I like Father Paul."

"Me, too."

"Why can't we live here?"

"You know why. Other than the rules Father Paul is breaking just letting us stay here, eventually our father will find us. We need to disappear. I have some money, not a lot, but enough to get us into Canada."

Sara didn't say anything for so long, Ivy thought she'd fallen asleep. Ivy was drifting off herself when Sara whispered, "He started calling me Hannah."

Ivy was instantly awake, her eyes open, glancing around the room almost expecting to find him here.

But her father wasn't here. Not yet, anyway. He was in his fortress near the Pennsylvania border.

He would come, though. The FBI agent had talked to him, because that was the only way he could have known that Ivy had been diagnosed mentally ill.

Diagnosed by a quack doctor who lived on the mountain with her father and his followers. The same doctor who had given her drugs to make her compliant. So she couldn't fight her father when she turned fourteen and took her rightful place in his bed.

"I'm sorry I couldn't get you out sooner," Ivy said, her voice cracking.

"I knew you would come. You promised you would be back, and you came." She took Ivy's hand. "I didn't believe you until it happened. I'm sorry, Ivy. I'm so sorry."

"It's not your fault, Sara. You thought I was dead. I know what you were feeling, thinking. How could such a kind, wonderful man who picked wildflowers with me hurt me?" Ivy stopped before she made herself physically ill. Their father was a master at selling the act to the world both inside and outside the fortress. When she was a little girl, before their mother died, he made her believe they were special. That dreams could come true. That they lived in a fairy tale, in a castle, where God loved them best, where their daddy worked for God, saving people, helping them get to heaven. A dream where hope lived, all was good, and all good came from their daddy because he was specially blessed. And even after the car crash that killed her mother, she let herself believe him, because she desperately needed to.

She let him convince her that her mother tried to kill her and Sara when she crashed the truck. She didn't want to believe the truth, because she didn't understand it.

But maybe because of the seed her mother had planted in her mind that night, Ivy had doubts.

She had doubts because their older sister Naomi changed.

She had doubts when she found Naomi in his bed.

And she knew it was wrong when she read Naomi's hidden diary and found out what their father was underneath his pretty face. What disturbed her, even before she knew it was wrong, was that Naomi had convinced herself that she was anointed and special, that their mother died because she was ignorant of the truth and normal course of human nature. Through Naomi's diary, Ivy had learned what happened in their father's bed. She learned that Naomi was grooming Ivy to assist with this "important responsibility." All those sisterly words of wisdom about hair and clothing and perfumes and shaving were all because that's what their father wanted.

And she learned that once Ivy gave in to the will of their father, she would be responsible for grooming Sara.

So when she turned fourteen and he brought her to his bed, she knew it wasn't for a bedtime story.

But it wasn't until she gathered the courage to escape did she learn the truth about who betrayed her mother the night she died.

The night Marie Edmonds tried to save her daughters, she didn't know that her oldest daughter had gone straight to the devil himself. Naomi had told their father of her mother's plans to escape from the mountain, and that she expected Naomi to make sure the gate was open.

Ivy didn't know it either. Not until Naomi caught her trying to leave with then-eight-year-old Sara and told her the truth. Their mother didn't commit suicide, though Naomi was in denial.

"I put her medicine in her tea," Naomi told Ivy six years ago. *"I couldn't let her leave. I thought she'd pass out long enough to get Daddy. I didn't know she was going to get in the truck! I played along with her, told her I'd open the gate, but I went to the church instead."*

Naomi's eyes had been glazed, just like they always were. But even though she was on her happy pills, she was anxious. *"She took you and Sara. Put you in the truck. She wanted to kill all of us, because she was so sick. I saved your life, Hannah. Daddy and I saved you."*

Naomi believed it. Maybe she had to believe the lie in order to survive.

Marie Edmonds had been murdered when she found out she was married to a monster. And Ivy would never forget the promise she made to take care of Sara, forever.

CHAPTER THIRTY-THREE

Sean didn't talk to Paxton unless he had a specific question. He detested being in the same room with him. While poring over the schedules and lists he'd created, one part of his brain was working on how to take down the senator—as soon as the statute of limitations ran out in Massachusetts, which was months away.

Sean reviewed all the background checks he'd started on Paxton's employees, current and former, and nothing stood out. There were no spouses or boyfriends or girlfriends or exes or relatives that stood out as having a reason to take the locket and threaten Paxton.

"Why did Chris Taylor leave your office?"

"Because he deserved a chief of staff slot, and Dale Hartline is from my home state. I recommended him for the position."

"You wanted someone loyal to you in Hartline's office."

"Dale is a novice, and a good man. Too trusting. Chris wouldn't betray him."

"Or you."

Paxton slapped his palm on his desk. "I rearranged my night to meet you here. The locket went missing three weeks ago, the week *after* I gave the media the photos of Alan Crowley and the prostitute. I already reviewed the security tapes. No one came into my office outside of those meetings."

"Which reminds me—why did you keep it in your Senate office when your house is more secure?"

"More secure? You easily broke in."

"Not everyone is me."

"The locket has always stayed in the drawer in my Senate office, except when I travel home for break. I bring it with me."

Sean didn't think Paxton was being honest, but what did he expect? "Let's assume that whoever came into your office had a reason to be there," Sean said. "They had to have suspected you had something incriminating *in* your office."

"I thought of that. I went through the list of everyone I met with—there's no one who could have known about the locket or the note."

"But someone *did* know. If they *didn't*, then the locket and message mean nothing." Sean hunched over his laptop and re-sorted his lists. "Other than Mallory, who took credit for killing Morton, who knew the truth? Russo?"

Paxton nodded.

"And?"

"No one else. Dave Biggler, who's in prison after the WCF sting, wasn't there. It was just Mallory, Russo, and me." Paxton sighed. "I was not a good father," he said quietly.

"I don't care."

"I was a workaholic," he continued as if Sean hadn't spoken. "I didn't give Monique what she needed."

Sean ignored him. He didn't want to be drawn into a conversation with the senator about his daughter, because it would inevitably end up as a conversation about Lucy. His eyes wandered from the laptop to the shredding machine where Lucy's statement was in a million pieces.

"We're on the same team," Paxton pleaded.

"We don't even play in the same ballpark."

"You'd be surprised what you're capable of," Paxton said.

Though it was difficult to ignore that statement, Sean said, "I've divided the meetings into categories—those who had private meetings with you, and those who had group meetings. I can't discount group meetings because I can see any number of scenarios where someone in a group may have been left alone, or came back to the room because they forgot their papers or purse or briefcase."

Paxton didn't say anything. Sean could see he hadn't considered that possibility.

"The other thing: I strongly believe that the person responsible has been in your office more than once. They may have been looking for something incriminating without knowing what it was. They may have had an idea as to what to look for. Who knows you killed Roger Morton?"

Paxton reddened. "I've tolerated your disrespect all day. Do not push me."

"You put yourself in this position."

"I told you. Only Mick Mallory and Sergio were there," Paxton said quietly.

"Anyone else who might have suspected?"

"Fran Buckley talked to me about Mallory, but I never admitted to her that I was even there, let alone pulled the trigger."

"All someone needs is to *think* it's true. Someone who knows about the locket, that might think it has a secret that damages you—even if they don't know what the secret is."

Sean looked at his lists. He turned his monitor around and showed them to Paxton. "I ran the names of the individuals, every associate, common interests, some other factors, and came up with this short list of people who were in the office more than once since the beginning of the year."

"I wasn't the only one being blackmailed."

Why was Sean surprised that Paxton hadn't told him everything? "Who else?"

"I only know one for certain. Judge Robert Morgan."

Sean searched his memory—the name was familiar, but he didn't know why.

"Three months ago," Paxton said, "Bob killed himself in his chambers."

Now Sean remembered. "He called recess on a murder trial and blew his brains out, right?"

"He was a friend of mine."

"Sorry. And you think he was being blackmailed?"

Paxton didn't answer.

Sean closed his laptop and stood. "That's it, I'm done." He walked to the door.

"Wait."

"No. You need to tell me everything, or I'm walking out. I will tell Lucy what happened, and she'll deal with it like she's dealt with every shitty thing life has handed her. And you can feel like scum of the earth for putting a woman you ostensibly love like a daughter into the untenable position of losing her career and everything she holds dear because she was protecting *you*."

Paxton waged an internal battle, and Sean wasn't going to wait indefinitely.

He opened the door.

"Chris told me."

"Chris Taylor," Sean said flatly.

Paxton's jaw tightened.

"If I walk out, we're done. I will go to Noah. I'm willing to go to jail if that's what it takes. But I will tell him, and Lucy, everything you've said to me." Part of that was a bluff. Sean would leave the country before going to prison.

"Last year, Chris was upset about his wife's work. Really worried about her. I knew about MARC and the work they did, I wanted to help. If it was money, I'd pay it. If it was legal matters, I'd find them an attorney or draft legislation and get it fixed. That's what I do, Sean—I want to help people who no one else will."

"Save it for your fucking campaign."

Sean felt Paxton's hatred rolling off him.

Paxton said, "Sergio and I took him out for drinks. He's a lightweight. He told us Jocelyn was helping a young prostitute, and he thought she was too involved. It's all she was working on, a mission. I didn't know who it was at the time, but Sergio started following Jocelyn.

"Sergio took pictures and subsequently identified the

prostitutes Jocelyn was helping," Paxton continued. "Including Ivy. It was easy to put together that Ivy and her girls worked for Wendy James. I knew Wendy was having an affair with Bristow, a prick of a congressman from Colorado. But Bristow was single, so I didn't think anything about it. Then Sergio said he had evidence that Wendy wasn't a mistress, but a prostitute like Ivy and the others.

"Sergio got pictures of Ivy, Wendy, and the others with several prominent people—but nothing compromising. Then Bob—" He stopped.

Sean waited. He would wait all night, because this story just kept getting more and more interesting. And unbelievable. It was increasingly difficult to separate the truth from the lies.

"Sergio found out Bob was involved with Ivy. He was single, but I thought it odd that he would pay a call girl, considering he's a judge and older than I am. We'd been friends a long time, but I couldn't fathom being friendly with a man who was sleeping with a woman as young as Ivy.

"The day after Morgan's suicide, I had Sergio confront Ivy, and set up a meeting with me. At first she didn't want to talk, but I told her Bob was an old friend, that I wanted to know why he killed himself. She confessed that she'd been paid by Wendy James to make sex tapes with her clients. And then I realized, Wendy was blackmailing these people."

"A twenty-eight-year-old secretary blackmailing congressmen and judges? You think she could have pulled it off?"

"Ivy was truly upset by Bob's suicide. She said he'd been a client for three years and she regretted videotaping him, but she'd been paid twice what Wendy usually paid her. I offered her ten thousand to prove Wendy James was blackmailing anyone, preferably someone in a position of power. Something to use to avenge Bob's death, which had to have been connected. But she and Wendy had a falling-out over it. All she could get were pictures with Crowley. I used them, hoping that when they were exposed, the truth would come out. But Crowley and Wendy covered it up, called it an affair! It wasn't an affair. It was a paid relationship."

"And you reneged on your deal with Ivy Harris."

"Hell no! You know who she is. You did the research."

"I know she's the supposedly dead daughter of a wealthy televangelist."

"Her father is sick, and he's on my list."

"Stop." Sean closed his eyes and breathed deeply. He had already crossed the line, but he couldn't go any farther. "Do not tell me anything about crimes you plan to commit."

"What crimes?" Paxton answered with sincerity. Or fake sincerity.

"Who killed Wendy James?"

"I don't know!"

"You have to go to the FBI with this information. They have no idea about Judge Morgan, and they're just now figuring out the blackmail, but they don't have names or motive."

"I'm not going to the FBI. They need to figure it out themselves. And they're close. After talking to Noah and you, I think they're very close."

"How many innocent people are going to die because you're trying to protect your ass?"

"I didn't figure it out until Chris was killed this

morning." He looked at the clock. "Yesterday morning. I can't believe the feds haven't put it together!"

"Noah didn't tell you everything, but they don't have all your information. They don't know that Wendy was a prostitute, but they did find a room where recording equipment had been."

"Had been?"

"It was cleaned out."

Sean watched Paxton carefully. He was used to playing God. Sean wanted to take him down a peg.

"Five people are dead because you remained silent."

"That's *not* what happened!" He pounded his fist again. "I didn't have anything to take to the police! I haven't even really been blackmailed. I simply got the threat from this elusive *they* about Lucy's note and my locket. They're waiting to use it; I have to find them before they do."

"These meetings were three weeks ago."

"Correct."

"And no one has asked you to do anything specific."

"Correct."

Sean sat back down and opened his laptop.

"Do you remember the trial that Judge Morgan was running when he killed himself?"

"No—I think it was a homicide. He sat on a lot of capital cases."

Sean did a quick Internet search. "Commonwealth of Virginia versus Thomas Joseph Crandall. Ring a bell?"

Paxton shook his head.

Sean ran a program to pull out all the data he could find on Crandall.

"Anyone else?"

"Excuse me?"

"Anyone else you know about who Ivy or Wendy were blackmailing. We need a connection between those being blackmailed. And since they haven't asked you to do something yet, we don't have that—except we have a list of people who had access to your office that week. So think! Who else in the last year or so has voted in a way that had you suspicious?"

Paxton leaned back in his chair and closed his eyes. Sean thought he had fallen asleep. Maybe everyone was for sale and the list was too long to remember.

Sean read the report on Crandall. The thirty-three-year-old mechanic had been accused of killing a bank executive for no apparent reason. He refused to talk, had a history of misdemeanors and one felony hit-and-run when he was eighteen, which landed him three years in prison. It seemed like an open-and-shut case, though it was odd that even the prosecutor found no apparent motive.

There was a retrial, with a change of venue because Crandall's attorney argued that after the suicide of Judge Morgan the jury pool was tainted. Morgan was a known law-and-order judge with tough sentencing standards. The case was moved from Fairfax to Richmond, and a judge dismissed the case with prejudice because of prosecutorial misconduct. Crandall was a free man. He spoke to no one except his attorney during the entire yearlong process.

"There's Gene Carpenter."

Sean looked at the senator, who still had his eyes closed. "Who's he?"

"Senator Carpenter. This was over a year ago. He's a

friend, and I believed his excuse, but last week he told me he's not seeking reelection. One term in the Senate—it's rarely done."

"And he did what exactly?"

"The bill had something to do with a federal grant, but it was related to government unions. Gene was a big supporter of unions in general, but he opposed government unions on the grounds that no one represented the taxpayers in the negotiations. He wouldn't have had a complete change of heart on something like this, not without making a floor statement or publicizing it. I called him on it, and he said his wife had convinced him he needed to change his mind on the matter. It didn't sound right, because I had met her a few times and she seemed very uninterested in politics. But I let it slide because pillow talk always wins."

Paxton leaned forward and pulled up the legislation on his computer and printed Sean a copy.

"I don't know how this helps," he said.

Sean took the paper. "If you're right about Carpenter, it tells me that someone who benefited from the passing of this bill is involved. That, coupled with your list of appointments, will narrow it down. Wait—"

Sean stopped mid-sentence.

"Wendy James worked for a lobbyist, correct?"

"DSA."

"Does that stand for Devon Sullivan and Associates?"

"Yes." Paxton rose from his desk and leaned over to look at Sean's laptop.

"Bingo! DSA carried the bill your friend caved on. Devon Sullivan had a meeting with you the day you noticed the locket missing."

"Devon Sullivan."

"You know her?"

"Yes, but I know her husband better." Paxton sat back in his chair, his face surprisingly calm. "I will kill him," he said matter-of-factly.

"Who are we talking about?"

"Her second husband is Clark Jager."

The name was familiar. "A criminal defense lawyer, correct?"

"Yes. He—"

Sean interrupted. "He represented Crandall, the guy who was on trial when Morgan committed suicide."

"He also represented Fran Buckley."

"Lucy's former boss?"

"She's bitter and angry and hates me. She knows not to say anything against me because I know far more about her that never came out. But she knew I wanted Monique's locket. She might have thought it was for a reason other than nostalgia."

"I think she's right."

Paxton stared at Sean and shook his head, but his lips curled into a snarl, reminding Sean that they were enemies. "I think we have our blackmailer."

"We need to take this to the feds."

"It's two in the morning. I'll think of a plausible reason to talk to Noah Armstrong at nine about Devon Sullivan. I'll steer him in the right direction. You have seven hours to find the locket."

CHAPTER THIRTY-FOUR

Friday

"Thank you for agreeing to talk with us," Kate said over the speakerphone after introductions. Kate and Lucy were in their family room, the files spread around them. Hans was patched in on the conference call from his office at FBI Headquarters. Kerry, Mrs. Carson, and Agent Rachel Burrows were at the Carson house in Richmond.

Kate informed Kerry that they were recording the conversation.

The situation had become more volatile than they'd planned when Mrs. Carson wanted to wait until she could find a lawyer to represent Kerry's interests. The other missing girl, Bryn, was also staying at the Carson's. She was Kerry's fifteen-year-old sister. Hans convinced her that they had no intention of prosecuting Kerry, that they were trying to find Ivy before she ended up dead. Time was critical.

Kerry wanted to talk, and once Mrs. Carson reluctantly agreed, it was early Friday morning. Dawn had just broken by the time they had everyone on the phone.

Kate began asking the questions. They quickly recounted what Kerry had already told Rachel, then Kate said, "The arson investigator said that the cause of the fire was inconclusive. Meaning, he needs to investigate further as to whether the fire was arson or not."

"It was on purpose," Kerry said. "Ivy smelled alcohol and saw someone in the next yard, then woke everyone up."

"Alcohol?"

"The kind they use in hospitals."

"Did you smell it?"

"When I got downstairs. By that time, the smoke was coming up through the floor vents. Ivy said to run out the front because she saw someone in the back."

Kate asked, "Did anyone else see the intruder?"

"No, why do you care?"

"I'm just trying to get an understanding of what happened, maybe someone else could identify him."

"It was dark, and we've always been security conscious, but particularly now."

"Now? Why now?"

"That doesn't have anything to do with the fire."

"Is it because Ivy brought her sister to live in the house?" Lucy asked carefully.

"Partly."

"After the fire, what did you do?"

"We split up. We had to disappear. We didn't know if the intruder was hanging out or what."

Kate asked, "Did you have reason to believe someone was going to attack you?"

"No, but—" She hesitated.

Lucy asked, "Kerry, we understand that you want to protect Ivy. It sounds like you and Ivy were very close."

"You don't understand what we've been through. The last two weeks have been so hard on her—"

"Since Sara came to live with her."

Again, hesitation. "Do you know who their father is?"

"Yes."

"Ivy was terrified of him. And *nothing* scared her. Ever since I met her, when she finally trusted me enough to tell me her plans, it's been about saving enough money to rescue Sara and disappear. That's why she agreed to Wendy's proposition."

Kate and Lucy exchanged an optimistic look.

Kerry continued. "Wendy ran our group. I don't know how Ivy and Wendy hooked up, they knew each other before I met them. Wendy had a great system. We were making enough money for the house, and to save money for S-Day."

"What was S-Day?"

"February second. Sara's birthday. The day we planned to rescue her."

"That's still seven months from now—" Kate began.

"No, *last* February." Kerry took a deep breath before continuing. "Ivy didn't think it through. She wanted to get Sara away from her father before her fourteenth birthday. Because Ivy knew he would rape her on that day. It's what happened to her older sister, it's what happened to Ivy.

"But," Kerry continued, "she didn't factor in that for six years, Sara thought she was dead. Then all of the sudden, her sister is standing in her bedroom telling her that her father is an evil prick who's going to rape her.

What would you do if someone you loved had died, you went to the funeral, then they just walk in and want you to run away?"

Lucy could picture the scene vividly. "Were you there?" she asked Kerry.

"I was the driver, waiting in the woods." She laughed humorlessly. "I tried to warn Ivy, but she can be stubborn. And I guess I wanted to save Sara before she had to suffer through that."

"What did Sara do?" Kate asked.

"Started screaming. Ivy had to leave her or be caught. At that point? He would have really killed her, not just pretended she was dead."

"Pretended?" Hans asked. "Did Edmonds know Ivy faked her suicide?"

"Faked? She ran away. She tried to take her sister with her, but Sara was only eight and didn't want to go. She found out through his television show that he'd told everyone she'd killed herself. But that was before we hooked up."

Lucy understood now how Ivy had spiraled into such dangerous activities. While anyone can disappear into a big city, surviving cost money. If everyone thought you were dead, it was both freeing and soul-destroying. At fourteen, young Hannah Edmonds had no one to help her.

"Ivy was so depressed afterward," Kerry continued. "Wendy used that."

"You didn't like Wendy?"

"No," Kerry said without hesitation. "She was selfish and manipulative. She used Ivy. Ivy *knew* she was being used, but she was getting what she wanted, so she let Wendy get away with all this crap."

Lucy asked, "And that's when Ivy agreed to this proposition?"

"Wendy was videotaping her clients. These weren't just sex tapes; some of these guys are total pervs with all their weird-ass fetishes. Who cares anymore if two consenting adults have sex? And proving Wendy was a call girl would be next to impossible. But if you found out that your doctor liked to wear women's underwear and high heels while having sex? Or the guy you voted for could only get off if he were being paddled? I told Ivy it was risky, one of her clients would find out. And I was right."

Hans spoke up for the first time. "Do you think that one of Wendy or Ivy's clients is responsible for these murders?"

Kerry didn't say anything at first.

"Kerry," Lucy said, "Dr. Vigo wants to know if you have any evidence—no matter how small—that it is a client who is responsible?"

"I've been thinking about this since I heard about what happened to Wendy—I don't know. I don't have any reason to, I just assumed because who else would want them dead?"

Lucy kept her voice calm and soothing, less inter-rogative than Kate. "It's all right, Kerry. It was your first thought, and it would have been my first thought, knowing what you know."

"Do you know more?"

Kate said, "We're working on it. That's why this con-versation is critical—we have evidence that we can't connect up. For example, you said that Wendy was video-recording her clients. We found a hidden room in an executive apartment with wires that may have been connected to recording equipment, but the place was wiped down."

"Apartment seven-ten."

"Yes."

"We've all used it, but it was Wendy's place."

Kate said, "There were people who leased the space. How did Wendy know when it was available?"

"Betty Dare, the manager," Kerry said as if they were dense. "Betty scheduled the apartment. If she wanted information, she put people in that space. It wasn't just about sex—it was about secrets. That's what Ivy said. Ivy knew too much about what Wendy was doing, I think that's why someone is trying to kill her."

Kate sent Noah a message about Betty Dare. This could blow the case wide open.

Kate said, "We've gone through Wendy's finances and she's not getting any unusual payments that would indicate blackmail."

"It wasn't always money, not anything easily traceable. I don't know those details, and I don't think Ivy did, either. Ivy got paid in cash, though, for using the apartment to record specific clients. She had all that cash in the house when it was set on fire."

"How much?" Kate asked.

"It depended, between one and two thousand a pop. For an escort night, we made on the high end five hundred. Ivy had a list of clients Wendy wanted on tape, and she was working through them."

Kate said, "If Wendy wasn't getting paid in cash, how did she pay Ivy? It doesn't make sense."

"I don't know, but I saw the money, I swear to God."

"I believe you," Kate said, "I'm just trying to put conflicting information together. For example, was she being paid in jewelry? Property? Clothing? And if these guys were being blackmailed, why did they still pay her for sex?"

"After they were blackmailed, most stopped being clients. It's not like they were doing this every night. Maybe a couple times a month. And not everyone was a regular. Many were here in town for business. In our established escort service, we saw mostly out-of-town businessmen. Wendy took the calls, kept the schedule, kept the books, and took twenty percent."

There had been no record of any of that in her apartment, Lucy remembered. Where were these books? Most likely on a flash drive or something easily concealable. But the FBI had gone through both apartments three times and had found nothing.

It could be her killer already had it. But then why go after Ivy and the others?

"And Ivy helped her?" Kate asked.

"The money was good, and Ivy was desperate. Then—" She hesitated.

"Then?"

"Ivy stopped talking to me. Something was going down, it was like she was looking for a big score. Taking huge risks. It started when Sara called her. You gotta understand, Sara isn't allowed to use the phone. Ivy had hidden a disposable cell phone in the barn for Sara to call only when it was safe. Sara was crying, begging her to come back and get her. Ivy had already spent a small fortune to get her the first time, and she was hysterical about not having the money to go back. She started meeting with this guy I'd never seen before— not a client, at least she said he wasn't. And then two weeks ago, he came to the house with Sara in tow. I haven't seen him since."

"What did he look like?" Kate said.

"Older—forties. Nice-looking Italian guy, not short or tall. Buffed—he definitely worked out. I really don't think he was one of her clients—I can tell when men are pervs, and I didn't get that vibe from him. He treated Ivy like a sister or daughter or something."

"Did she hire him to kidnap her sister?" Kate asked.

"She did *not* kidnap Sara!" Kerry said. "She saved her from being repeatedly raped by her father. You can't possibly understand what they went through. Nobody understands what it's like to have the person you trust more than anyone turn into a monster. My stepfather was so fucking drunk the first time he raped me that he didn't know I wasn't my mother. And then my mother, so desperate to keep a man, told me *I* was the whore."

Lucy understood far more than Kerry thought, but she wasn't going to say a word, especially when this conversation was being recorded. Her heart broke for what they had suffered.

Kerry said, "You got to let them go. Let them escape. If Reverend Edmonds gets his hands on Sara, you'll never get her back."

"The FBI isn't going to send Sara back to a bad situation," Kate said. "All she has to do is tell us she was raped and we'll keep her in custody, give her a full medical exam."

"And what if he gets to her first?" Kerry said. "What if he takes her home? Are you going to break down his door and take her away? I'm telling you, if he takes Sara back to the mountain, no one will see her again."

Lucy said, "Kerry, I give you my word, when we find Sara, we will protect her." She ignored Kate's look of concern. There were promises agents couldn't always keep. But Lucy would do everything possible to keep this promise. "You have to understand there is a killer searching for Sara and Ivy and Mina. And you, for that matter. We have to find the girls first. Do you have any idea where they might be?"

Kerry sounded distraught, and Lucy could hear Mrs. Carson consoling her in the background. "Ivy called Jocelyn, because Jocelyn always promised to help. And now Jocelyn is dead. Would you go to someone you care about if you thought they might get killed for it?"

"No, I wouldn't," Lucy said. "Not for me. But if I was protecting someone, if someone else counted on me to keep them safe, I would do anything to guarantee their safety."

Hans said, "Kerry? We know that Ivy stole five thousand dollars. What would she do with it?"

"Buy two passports so they could go to Canada," Kerry said without hesitation. "That was her plan all along, and she had the passports, but they were destroyed in the fire."

"Where did she get the first two?"

Kerry didn't speak. Then she hedged, "I thought of someone she might go to. She was really close to the black lady who had a little church and school on Thirty-first Street."

"Marti North," Kate said.

"She's not dead too, is she?"

"No. We spoke to her and she claimed not to have seen Ivy."

Lucy frowned. There had to be another place.

"How did you and Ivy communicate?"

"We all had disposable phones," Kerry said. "But I've been trying to reach Ivy and her phone isn't working."

Lucy pictured the two phones underwater in the sink of the Hotel Potomac.

Lucy pulled out the rental agreement that the owner of the Hawthorne Street house had faxed over. She asked, "Do you know Paul Harris? Ivy listed him as her father, but we know that's not true. Was it a false name?"

"Father Paul," Kerry said. "She hasn't talked about him in years. He helped her when she first came to DC, and once or twice she'd mention something in passing about Father Paul. I don't know where he lives, I've never met him."

"Father Paul?" Lucy asked. "Is he a priest?"

"I don't know, I guess he could be."

Lucy typed the address from the rental agreement into her mapping program on her laptop. She smiled and said, "St. Anne's Catholic Church." She stood, antsy.

Kate held up her finger. "Kerry, thank you for your help. We'll find Ivy and Sara, and it'll be because you helped."

They disconnected and Kate said, "We need backup, Lucy, we're not going in blind. I'll set it up."

The phone rang again and it was Hans. Kate answered. "I'm sorry I hung up on you. I need to put a team together for this op."

"We just got a search warrant for Betty Dare and Noah and Stein are already on their way. I'll have a SWAT team meet you two blocks east of St. Anne's—you don't want to tip your hand. I don't think Ivy is violent, but I do think she'll kill to protect her sister."

Lucy concurred, but didn't comment.

"And Lucy?" Hans said.

"I'm here."

"Good job."

While Kate put the team together, Lucy went upstairs to change. She was still sore, but the ibuprofen she'd taken earlier had finally kicked in. She opened her bedroom door and jumped back, an involuntary yelp escaping before she recognized the back she was staring at belonged to Sean.

He turned around. "I'm sorry—I heard you and Kate on the conference call and came up here to write a note."

"You could have come into the family room."

He crumpled up the paper he'd been writing on and tossed it in the garbage gan. "Now I can tell you in person that I love you." He smiled and hugged her, not tightly. "You're still sore," he said.

"A bit. We have a lead on Ivy Harris. She's friends with a priest at St. Anne's, a small Catholic church. Kate and I are going to talk to him now."

"I hope you find her."

Sean wasn't quite himself, but Lucy couldn't figure out what it was in his demeanor that was off. If roles were reversed, Sean would know exactly what was bothering her. His insight into her personality and moods could be annoying, but she also found it comforting at times. And right now, she suspected Sean needed something from her.

"Sean, what's wrong?"

He smiled and kissed her. "I'm sorry I didn't come back last night. I wanted to, but got wrapped up in a project."

"That's okay. You'll make it up to me, I'm sure," she teased. But that wasn't the only thing on his mind. Lucy pushed. "Is it a difficult case?"

"Nothing I can't handle." He played with her hair. "I don't want to keep you, I know you have work."

"I have a few minutes." She sat down at the foot of her bed, and patted the space next to her. "Sit."

"Yes, ma'am." He did, then pushed her gently back onto the bed. "You, me, bed—want to play hooky?" He kissed her neck, then her jawline, all the way to her lips.

He was avoiding her question. She recognized his ruse to sidetrack her.

"We both have work to do," she whispered.

"I missed you, Princess." He sounded like they'd been apart for a week, not one night.

"Tell me what's wrong." She sat up. Sean still lay on his back. "You always listen to me, I want to know what is bothering you about this project."

He didn't say anything for a minute, but that was okay with Lucy. She let him think about it while she changed. He sat up to watch her. Though being watched by strangers still made her extremely uncomfortable, Sean didn't. He was one of the few she felt so relaxed with that she almost felt normal. He'd healed wounds so deep she hadn't even known they were there until he exposed them to light, and to love.

When she was done dressing, she sat back on the bed and kissed him.

Sean said, "It's a complicated case."

She didn't say anything, but let him continue at his own pace. Sean was rarely reticent—he shared everything, his thoughts and emotions, both good and bad. His sharp wit and biting criticism of law enforcement had often gotten him in trouble with Noah and others, but one of the many things Lucy loved about Sean was that he didn't keep everything bottled inside, like she did. He believed in addressing problems head-on.

"A college kid, from my alma mater MIT, did something stupid." He hesitated again.

"I'm not going to turn him in to the feds, if that's what you're worried about."

"I'm not." But he relaxed, just a bit, and Lucy wondered if that's what his fear really was—that he couldn't share something because of her position with the FBI.

"Sean, you know you can trust me. I'm not so naïve to think that RCK doesn't handle some less-than-squeaky-clean cases. Two of my brothers work there. Don't let my job make you think you have to keep secrets."

"I trust you, Luce, more than anyone." He took both her hands, kissed them, then held tightly. "It's just complex. He's nearly twenty-one, he should have known better. He decided to play Robin Hood."

"Steal from the rich and give to the poor?"

"You make it sound like a crime."

"It is a crime."

"What if he stole from a thief?"

"It sounds like you have a complicated case."

"I'm trying to help him fix things so he doesn't do any jail time."

Sean had such a soft spot for young people. The teenager in the Adirondacks who nearly burned down the lodge they were staying at, who nearly killed Sean, had been only the most recent in a long line of desperate kids who felt they had nowhere to turn for help. She knew part of his drive was because of his own troubled childhood, losing both of his parents in a plane crash when he was fourteen, and his subsequent rebellion against a brother who was himself too young to know what to do with a grieving genius.

"I know whatever you do, you'll fix it and everyone will get what they need." She smiled and kissed him. "That kid is lucky to have you on his side."

There was a loud knock on Lucy's door. "Get your butt downstairs, Lucy," Kate said, "and tell Sean he wasn't so smart that I didn't know he broke into my house *again*."

"You need a better security system," Sean called back.

"Ass," Kate said. "Two minutes, Lucy."

Sean grinned. He really liked Kate. "She loves me," he said.

"That doesn't mean she won't get back at you," Lucy teased.

"That'll be fun." Sean wished he had more time with Lucy. He needed her. But she had a job to do. And so did he. He probably shouldn't have even stopped by this morning, but it was early and he'd just wanted to see her.

"I have to go—set the alarm on your way out, or Kate really will have your hide."

Lucy kissed him one last time and left. Sean wondered if she would have been as understanding if she knew the kid from MIT he'd told her about was himself, nine and a half years ago.

He heard Kate and Lucy drive off. He retrieved the note from the trash can, glad he had changed his mind. Lucy didn't need any additional pressure, and he shouldn't leave it in writing. He blamed lack of sleep for his near-slip.

Luce—
  You were right about Paxton. Do not trust him. Do not believe anything he says. He's not your friend.

He tore it into quarters, then went downstairs to Kate's office. He pushed each piece through the shredder, glad that there was already paper in the can beneath. To be safe, he mixed up the small squares, then left.

He had another house to break into.

SSA Josh Stein acted like a kid on a sugar rush, he was so excited by the new intel, coupled with the financial statements of all the businesses and individuals who had rented executive suite 710 in the last six months. Noah almost began to like him.

"Look—they all connect somehow to DSA. Enviro Solutions hired them as their lobbyist. They get the suite, and then their retainer doubled. Mrs. Erica Craig is in the suite and wham, she makes a big donation to a non-profit client of DSA."

"It'll still be difficult to prove there was illegal activity. Unless someone comes forward as a blackmail victim, Devon Sullivan can claim she's just a good saleswoman."

"I'm going to prove that she's corrupt. Because she is. It's all here—I feel it. And when I get little old Betty Dare in interrogation, she's going to sing. She gives us one word that Devon Sullivan bribed or attempted to bribe, blackmailed or attempted to blackmail, even one person, the AUSA has a judge on standby. This is the biggest case of my career. Of your career!"

Noah didn't agree. It would probably be the most high-profile case of Noah's career, but he would much prefer to stick to the relative anonymity of violent crimes, putting killers behind bars rather than gunning for con artists and corrupt politicians. But he realized while working with Josh that they needed agents with passion for what they did, because criminals, violent or not, needed to be stopped.

"Devon Sullivan didn't kill five people," Noah said. "Betty Dare has only been implicated as part of the blackmail scheme."

Josh waved his hand in dismissal. "You know what they say—we get them any way we can. Al Capone was a killer, but we nailed him on tax evasion. So if we can't get her on conspiracy of murder, then we get her with this." He tapped his files.

"I want the killer. There are three young women in grave danger, Josh," Noah said. When he saw that Josh wasn't paying attention, Noah barked out, "Stein!"

Josh looked at him, startled.

"Did you hear me?" Noah said.

"Yeah, you want to find the killer." He was already turning his head away to look at his columns of numbers. "I'm with you on that."

Noah grabbed his wrist and squeezed.

"Shit, Armstrong! Let go!"

Noah held on. "If you blow this, if you and your pet AUSA offer any immunity without talking to me, I will make your life Hell. Devon Sullivan did not kill Wendy James. She did not slit the throat of Nicole Bellows, or stab a social worker to death. I want to know who did it, and if she hired the killer, I want her, too. For first-degree, premeditated, special circumstances, *homicide*."

Josh's eyes darted to the SWAT driver as if looking for rescue, but the other cop didn't acknowledge him. Noah dropped his wrist. He'd made his point.

The small SWAT team that was helping Noah and Josh execute the warrant reported that they had arrived, were in position, and were awaiting instructions.

Noah took the command headset from Josh. "On my call," he said.

They got out and entered the lobby two minutes after seven that morning.

Noah took the stairs up to Betty Dare's second-floor apartment. He pounded on the door. "FBI! We have a warrant! Open up!"

No answer.

He pounded again, shouted, "FBI! Search warrant! We're coming in!" He waited a beat, then commanded SWAT to prepare to ram the door. Two men held the heavy steel battering ram.

"FBI! Stand back! We're entering the premises!"

He nodded to the team, who rammed the door, breaching in one swift movement. Everyone stood aside, while two more agents held assault rifles on the room, visually searching for any threat.

The smell in the apartment was horrendous.

Noah walked down the hall, away from the apartment. Josh Stein looked confused. "What happened? Why aren't you going in?"

Noah didn't respond. He waited for the SWAT team leader to issue the all-clear report.

"Agent Armstrong?"

"Here."

"We've cleared the apartment. One deceased, female."

"How?"

"Appears to be a gunshot to the back of the head."

"Silencer?"

"Poor man's silencer. The pillow is still in place."

Noah walked carefully through the apartment. Betty Dare had been murdered in her bedroom. On the bed was a half-packed suitcase. Had she been scared of prosecution? Or more terrified of who she worked for?

She'd used the extra bedroom as her own private office. Stacks of video-recording equipment were in the closet. The hard drive had been pulled from her computer. She had an industrial-strength paper shredder, filled.

"Call forensics," he said to Josh. "This place is all yours."

He left the apartment building on Park Way and called Kate. "I'm on my way, where are you?"

"We just arrived at St. Anne's. Lucy and I are going to talk to the priest, I'll let you know."

"Be alert. Betty Dare, our potential witness, is dead."

CHAPTER THIRTY-FIVE

Devon Sullivan and her husband, defense attorney Clark Jager, lived on a sprawling country estate in Chantilly, Virginia, about forty minutes southwest of DC.

Sean stopped far from the property line, uncertain of the security layout. He downloaded all public satellite data of the spread as well as property records. There was only one way to get to the main house, down a quarter-mile-long driveway.

With all that land, Sean figured there would be security cameras at any potential breach point. A seasonal creek ran along the western edge of the property. The southern edge backed up to their neighbor's horse stables. Twelve properties were listed on the long, narrow dead-end street.

The benefit for surveillance was that Sean could park out of sight on the main road because everyone in the Sullivan/Jager neighborhood had to drive to the main road to leave. To the right was the small town of Chantilly. To the left, two miles away, freeway access.

Sean parked his Mustang at a closed business on the main road where he could watch the cars leaving. He had pulled the vehicle ownership records for both Sullivan and Jager. She drove either a gold E-class Mercedes or a white Lexus SUV. Jager had a small black Mercedes C300. Sean would love to drive the C300 someday. All three vehicles were pricey. The spread had been bought when they first married nine years ago, for nearly three million dollars. Now, even with the market slump, it was worth over four million.

Sean had run basic financial profiles on the couple. Jager was a partner in his law firm and specialized in criminal defense. Sullivan had opened her lobbying firm nearly twenty years ago, after she divorced her first husband, with whom she had two sons. Both of them lived in the greater DC area.

Even with two successful careers, this was an expensive piece of land filled with expensive toys. A place that would have hired staff.

Normally, a breach like this required intelligence gathering and extensive planning, but Sean didn't have time for anything like that. Winging it was his MO, and if he was feeling nervous, he had to trust his instincts.

He considered what little he knew of Sullivan and Jager. They blackmailed people either for money or out of the thrill of the game, or both. Information was power. They would be extremely private people. Have staff, but probably not live-in. If they did have live-in help, they would have a separate residence on the property, not in the main house. Security would be tight, but primarily they would rely on surveillance equipment with a direct line to the police rather than more involved options. Response times would be quick, considering Jager's line of work. Though many cops probably didn't care for him, no one would want a defense attorney dead on their watch.

Sean needed a partner. He was loath to call Sergio Russo, but he didn't have a choice. He needed backup.

Paxton must have already given Russo a heads-up, because he told Sean he was less than ten minutes away. Sean wouldn't let his guard down—the senator had been furious with Sean when he'd left this morning. He might be thinking he could get the locket and simultaneously take out Sean.

Sean scanned additional information about Jager on his laptop while he waited and came across an article dated more than twenty years ago, showing a young, suave attorney. He'd just won his first case, an acquittal for a suspected killer.

Harper Acquitted!
Prosecution "Stunned"; Defense "Pleased"

Falls Church, VA
Reginald Douglas Harper was acquitted this morning of all charges in the rape and torture of coed Amanda Jane Morris. Morris died of her injuries four days after she was found, without regaining consciousness.

Harper, who didn't take the stand in his defense, sat stone-faced during the reading of the jury's verdict, which came after six hours of deliberation. Harper's attorney, Clark Jager of Acuna & Bigelow Law Offices, took Harper's case pro bono because he said the defendant wasn't getting a fair trial.

At a press conference immediately following the reading of the verdict, Jager said, "Justice has been served. For too long, prosecutors in our state have been violating the constitutional liberties guaranteed to all citizens, both victims and criminals. When one innocent man goes to jail, the entire system is corrupt. Reginald Harper is innocent of the charges he faced; a corrupt system extracted a confession under extreme duress. As we proved to the jury, Mr. Harper was tortured through the denial of water, bathroom breaks, and sleep. Six detectives questioned him for twenty-nine hours straight until he broke down and confessed to a crime he didn't commit."

Jager, who has a degree in criminal justice from Boston College and a law degree from Columbia Law School, practiced in the public defender's office in New York City for three years before joining the established law firm of Acuna & Bigelow late last year. His biography says, in part, "I became a defense lawyer because my brother was convicted of a crime he did not commit, and died in a prison brawl five years later. After his death, a court overturned his conviction when DNA evidence proved him innocent."

Sean suspected that "Hang 'em High" Senator Jonathon Paxton wasn't Jager's favorite person. Yet Jager had represented Fran Buckley, charged with conspiracy in the murders of several paroled felons. Was it for information? Jager and his wife thrived on information, and who better to share than Paxton's bitter fall guy.

Sean looked up to see a car stopped at the end of the private road. Jager. He turned left toward the highway. It was 7:10 A.M.

A few minutes later, Sergio Russo pulled up. He slid into Sean's passenger seat. "I'm glad you called."

"I'm not," Sean said. "I need backup, and you're the only one who can do it."

" 'Thanks' doesn't seem quite right for the comment."

"I don't trust you, but I trust you more than Paxton. That's not saying much."

Brian figured out where the girls were hiding based on the unmarked federal car on the street out front.

He was tired and punchy, but finding the little church had been divine providence. He'd have laughed at the thought if he weren't so weary and depressed.

Brian hadn't thought twice about killing the others. Except the social worker. She had stared at him, eyes wide like a deer, and said, "Please, don't."

He lost it with her. She made him *think* about what he'd been doing, made him feel bad about it when it was just a damn job. He shouldn't feel bad about cleaning up this mess.

He'd gotten over it, because once she was dead it didn't matter anymore. The choice had been made. But last night at Betty's . . .

He couldn't stop thinking about her.

Betty had been nicer to him than his own mother, admired his intelligence, and done her job well. He'd wanted to give her enough money to leave the country. He'd have joined her. And if Betty hadn't been so demanding, he could have gotten his mother to agree.

But she asked for a million dollars. His mother said a hundred thou. And Betty laughed at her. Big mistake.

Once again, Brian was sent to fix the problem. No second chances.

He didn't want to scare her, he didn't want her to know that he was going to kill her. So he went over to see her and lied that he had a deposit on the million Betty wanted. That he would take her to a cabin in West Virginia that he owned, until everything settled down.

While Betty was packing, he came up from behind her, pushed her down. Heard a bone break and she cried out. As he grabbed a pillow from her bed, she began to crawl away.

"Brian, please don't do this."

Please, don't

Please don't do this

He held the pillow on the back of her head and fired two bullets into her brain before he could change his mind. He destroyed all the records he found and left.

That's how Betty ended up dead and Brian ended up with a guilty conscience. He couldn't stop picturing Betty on the ground, scared, crawling away from him. Why couldn't she have been like the others?

He told Ned, "I'm parking around the corner. You go sit at the bus stop across the street, got it? Let me know immediately if anyone goes inside."

"I still think we should burn it down," Ned said.

"Because that worked so well for us last time?" Brian wanted to throttle him. "Do what I tell you."

He must have looked more serious than usual because Ned said nothing.

He let Ned get settled at the bench before he left the car and walked around the block. There was no alleyway, which would have made it easier, but there was a four-story apartment building that backed up to the school.

The apartment building's security was minimal, and he entered easily. He headed up the stairs to the roof.

The door had a busted lock—people probably came up here to smoke or get fresh air. God knew he couldn't live like this. The longer he was in DC, the more he wanted to return to the islands. Frankly, *any* island.

He didn't care about the other girls, not anymore. Poison Ivy was the only one who knew anything, she was the only one he was going to kill. Then he was leaving Ned on that damn bus bench, driving to the train station, and saying adios to DC for good.

His duty to his family was over.

From the roof, he was blocked from the cops' view by the surrounding buildings. That gave Brian the opportunity to use the fire escape. He looked at the metal—didn't look like it would hold him. He didn't trust these rickety pieces of crap city fire escapes. More than the weight of one person and it looked like the bolts would tear away from the building.

Carefully, he put his weight on the first landing. Surprisingly, it held him. As quietly as possible, he lowered the ladders to get to the second floor. The ladders didn't cooperate. They made such a racket that a woman popped her head out of a window two over and yelled at him. He glared at her, and she went back inside.

On the second-floor landing, he inspected the cinderblock fence that surrounded the church. Barbed wire was embedded along the top of the fence, but if he jumped over it and landed with a roll, he should avoid the sharp barbs. It was only twelve feet.

He jumped before anyone else popped a head out of a window and made enough noise to alert the feds. He landed on his feet and immediately fell into a roll. But he rolled over a sprinkler head and felt the sharp edges cut into his back.

The pain made him angry.

Dammit, that he should have to go through this shit just to find one little whore who tried to play with the big girls. Maybe he would just kill them all before he left, just on general principle. He jumped up, trying to shake off the pain.

The back of the church was completely shielded from the front. Half the building had no windows, the other half had high windows. He went to the nearest door, turned the knob.

Locked.

He searched for an easier entrance, but there was none—the only other door in the back was also locked. But the second door was better concealed, so he had more time to break in. It took him several minutes. He became frustrated, especially since he could feel his shirt sticking to the blood on his back. Finally the lock popped.

When he stepped in, the first thing he heard were children singing.

Children.

He was not going to kill children.

This day could not have gotten worse.

He pulled out his gun and stepped into the room. Six pairs of pint-sized eyes stared at him. The teacher, a tall black woman, jumped up.

"Hold it," Brian said. "I don't want to hurt any of you, but I will if I have to. I want Ivy, I want her now. Or I will start shooting."

He looked the teacher in the eye, could practically see her little mind running through all her options. "Don't," he warned, adrenaline combating his fatigue. "I've had a real shitty couple days and frankly, I'm not in the mood for heroes."

CHAPTER THIRTY-SIX

Lucy had always admired her sister-in-law, but she'd never seen Kate in action. The only time she'd watched her at work was in her home office. In the field, Kate was all business.

Kate approached the four agents who were their backup.

"Monitor exits and entrances, you know who we're looking for and why. But also be careful—someone is stalking her, we have no idea what he looks like, so keep your eyes and ears open."

Lucy remembered Ivy's comment about "Dumb and Dumber." She said, "There may be two male suspects, working together or separately."

"They already killed six people," Kate said. "And one of them shot a cop. We want them alive, if possible, but preservation of innocent life is our number-one goal." She motioned for Lucy to follow her into the church. "Ready?"

Lucy nodded. She was calm and focused, her eyesight sharp and vivid.

St. Anne's was a small, gothic church with dark pews and tall, elaborate stained-glass windows. An organ that appeared to be far too big for the church dominated one corner. Several parishioners were dotted around the room, kneeling in prayer.

Lucy followed Kate to the front of the church. The sacristy was behind the altar. Father Harris was coming out as they approached, startled when he saw them.

"May I help you?"

"We're looking for Ivy Harris," Kate said after identifying herself.

"Why?"

"She used you as a reference on her rental application. She said you were her father."

"You mean her priest."

"No, her flesh-and-blood daddy."

"I'm sure there's a mistake."

"Do you know her?"

"I'm not sure." Father Harris looked at his watch. "I have an appointment, then I can look at my records—"

"Father," Lucy said, "Ivy is in grave danger. We know about her sister, Sara, and we know about their father. We want to give them both a chance to tell the truth and find peace. But someone has killed six people this week, and he is looking for Ivy. We have agents outside, but if she's not here, we need to put them out looking for her."

She could tell the priest was undecided about whether to speak.

"Please, Father, we need your help," Lucy implored.

"I can contact her. Wait here."

Kate stepped forward. "I can't do that. I can't give you the opportunity to help her disappear."

"I give you my word."

"Sorry. You make the call, but I want to talk to her."

"Very well. There's a phone in the rectory."

The rectory was across a small courtyard adjacent to the church. As they walked across, Lucy saw movement along the back wall, to her left.

"There," she said, gesturing to a small toolshed. Someone was trying to climb the fence.

Ivy.

Kate ran over and grabbed her, pulling her down and pushing her prone to the ground. She searched her and came up with a gun. She was about to cuff her when Father Harris ran over. "Please, don't treat her as a criminal. She's been through so much."

"It's protocol, Father," Lucy said.

Ivy shook her head and pleaded, "You have to let me go. I'm going to be late."

"Late for what?" Lucy asked.

"He's going to kill Mina."

"Who?" Kate asked, handcuffs dangling.

"I don't know his name! Wendy called them Dumb and Dumber."

"There are two?"

"They're brothers. I saw one of them when he ran us off the road. I'm sorry I left, I had no choice. Please. Mina needs me. He's going to kill her."

"Where is he?"

"If he sees any of you, he's going to kill everyone."

Kate repeated, "Where is he?"

Father Harris squatted beside the distraught Ivy. "Child, you need to let them help."

Ivy's cell phone rang and she stifled a scream.

"Is that him?" Kate asked.

She nodded.

"Answer it. I'm going to listen in."

Ivy answered the phone. "I told you I'm coming!"

"Tick tock, Poison Ivy. Your ten minutes is now eight minutes."

"Don't touch her, you bastard!"

He cut off the call before she finished her sentence.

"How do you know she's alive?" Lucy asked. "Have you talked to her?"

"He called right when you walked into the church. Gave me ten minutes. He let Mina tell me she was alive. There are kids inside!"

"Children?" Lucy blanched. "Is he at His Grace?"

"Yes. I tried Marti, but no one's answering. Oh, God, why is this happening?" She looked at her watch.

Kate got on her phone. "Hostage situation, His Grace Church, Thirty-first Street—"

"No!" Ivy screamed and lunged for Kate's phone. Kate got her into an arm lock so quickly Lucy almost missed it. "If he sees the police, he'll kill them. Don't you people listen?"

Kate looked at her sternly. "Sit down or I'll cuff you." Into her phone she said, "Code S, I repeat, Code Silent."

"He'll still know!"

"FBI SWAT is good. He won't know," Lucy said.

Ivy started crying. "I have to save her. She trusted me to protect her and I've let her down every time."

Kate said to Lucy, "Get her in the car. We'll drive there and figure out where this guy is holed up." She looked at her phone. "Slater," she answered. "Kate Donovan here, we got a hot call."

They walked Ivy out of the church and to the car.

While making an illegal U-turn, Kate said to Slater, "We have a hostage situation, unknown suspect, extremely volatile, children are involved. He said he'll start shooting the kids if he sees a uniform." She turned to Ivy. "How many?"

"Um, I don't know, I haven't been there in a long time."

"Guess."

"No more than twelve. And it's early, maybe only a couple."

"Adults?"

"Just Marti and Remus, the custodian."

"Church secretary?"

She shook her head. "I don't know. Maybe."

Kate told Slater, "Up to twelve minors, preschool; up to three adults. One teenage hostage who's the target."

Kate made a wide turn, far out of sight of the church, and parked. "What's your ETA, Slater?" Then to Lucy, she said, "Ten minutes."

"That's too late," Ivy cried.

"Call him."

"I can't."

"Will he call you?"

"To taunt me."

"We'll buy time." Kate assessed the area, put the SWAT leader on speaker so she could pull out a map. "Slater, you still there?"

"Yes, we're on our way. Do you have more intel?"

"No. I'm assessing possible breach points where the suspect can't see us. Come around parallel to Thirty-first, park at the V. No line of sight from any part of the church property."

"Roger that. Stay hot, but I need to switch channels."

Lucy sat in the backseat with Ivy. "We spoke to Kerry this morning."

"Is she okay?"

"Yes. She and her sister are with Amy in Richmond."

Ivy stared at Lucy then closed her eyes, smiling widely. "Thank God. Thank God. They're safe."

"Ivy," Lucy said, "you need to trust us. We're here to help you and your sister, Sara."

Ivy stifled a cry. "I'm not telling you where she is."

"Kerry told us about your father. We're not turning Sara over to him."

"You're right, because she's safe, and she's going to stay that way."

"Your father has accused you of kidnapping. Without Sara's statement, we can't arrest him."

"You won't arrest him anyway! He's too powerful."

"I don't care if he's the president of the United States, if he raped a fourteen-year-old girl, he will be prosecuted," Lucy said.

"I'd love to believe it, but I know how the system works. My father has hundreds of people who think he walks on water. I did go to someone after he r-raped me." Her voice cracked for the first time. "I was so stupid. Growing up, I'd been told over and over that if there was any trouble at *all*, that the police would help. That I could trust them. So I went to the police chief. I knew him, he went to my father's church. He was so nice . . . and then he brought me home and told my father what

I'd said. Then do you know what my father did? Took me to a doctor, told him I was showing the same signs of mental illness as my mother. They put me on drugs. I was so out of it for months. And then I realized that's how my older sister coped all these years. She has no emotions left, they've been drugged out of her."

Kate said, "I'm going to check this building. I have an idea. Stay put." She got out and ran across the street.

"I'm really sorry about yesterday," Ivy said. "Is that detective going to be okay?"

"Yes. She was shot in the arm, had surgery, gets released tomorrow morning. Genie's a tough woman." Lucy hesitated, then said, "The next few days are going to be difficult, but it'll be worth it."

"I just want Mina safe." She looked at her watch. "Less than two minutes." She implored, "Please let me go."

"He wants you dead, Ivy. You understand that? *He wants to kill you.* There's no reason for him to leave Mina alive. Or any of them. As soon as you show up, he'll kill you. And then what will happen to your sister?"

"I've made arrangements."

But she was worried, because she wouldn't look Lucy in the eye.

"We've pieced together some things, which you can help confirm, but we don't why Wendy was killed."

"I don't know either. Except—" She hesitated, then said, "I think it was because of me."

"You? Why?"

"I'm the one who took the pictures of Wendy and that congressman."

"You gave it to the press?"

"I sold it. I needed the money to rescue Sara."

"Who did you sell it to?"

"I never knew his name."

Even though Ivy looked her in the eye, Lucy knew she was lying. It was the calm certainty while highly agitated that gave Lucy the clue.

She was protecting someone. Why?

"That person could be responsible for all this."

"He's not. I would recognize him if I saw him, and he's neither Dumb nor Dumber."

Kate jumped back in the car. "I told Slater we have a valid entry point via the southwest corner, kitty-corner to the church. We can get to the roof without being seen. But we need floor plans."

"I know the place," Ivy said.

"You're staying here."

"They want *me*."

Kate handed her a notepad and pencil. "Draw what you know."

Ivy's cell phone rang.

Kate said, "Tell him you're almost here. Five minutes."

"He won't wait any longer!"

"Give him a location five or six blocks away. Indicate you're on foot. Lucy, listen in."

Ivy answered; Lucy put her ear to the phone and Ivy held it so they could both hear. "I'm on my way!"

"It's been twelve minutes. By now, I should have killed two of the kids."

"Don't! I'm coming as fast as I can. I want to talk to Mina."

Kate nodded her approval.

"I already let you talk to her."

"How do I know you didn't shoot her after you hung up?"

"You don't. Start running. I'm giving you two more minutes. That's it. Come through the chain gate; I left it propped open for you."

He hung up.

Ivy screamed out her frustration.

Kate said over her headset, "Slater?"

"I heard. Get me some intel I can use. Do you think he'll really start shooting? What do you know about this guy?"

Kate looked at Lucy, and Lucy said, "He's smart, but impulsive. His entire mission—and he considers it a mission—is to kill Ivy. If she walks in, he'll shoot her immediately. He doesn't want to hear excuses or explanations. I don't know if he'll kill anyone else, but he's capable. He will not hesitate. He's already made the decision."

Ivy tried to open the door, but it was locked. She hit the handle. "I don't want anyone else to die because of me."

"No one's going to die," Kate said, but Lucy saw concern in her rigid expression.

Slater and his SWAT team drove up. Slater gave them orders, and a pair went into the building Kate had identified as having visual of the church grounds.

He approached Kate's car. "Armstrong's ETA is four minutes," he said.

"We don't have time to wait," Kate said.

Slater looked at Lucy. "We need to buy time."

"How?"

Slater glanced at Lucy. "Kincaid, you and Ivy are

roughly the same height and build. You don't have to do this, but—"

"Yes," she said before he finished.

"Luce—" Kate stopped. "Shit, shit, shit. Okay, you two go to the van and swap clothes. You're wearing a vest, Lucy. Don't argue. Hat, glasses, don't go in. This is for *show,* to expose the shooter."

"There's no time," Ivy said. "He's calling again."

Lucy grabbed the phone from Ivy as she started taking off her clothes, motioning for Ivy to do the same.

"I'm here," she said, panting to mask the difference in their voices. "I'm coming. Around the corner. I ran. Whole way. Please, please. Let me talk to Mina."

"Finally, some fear. It's about fucking time, Poison Ivy. Mina, say hi to your girlfriend."

"Ivy, don't, he'll kill—"

The suspect came back on the line. "But you already knew that, right?"

"I'm not coming in until Mina is safe."

He laughed. "You're in no position to negotiate. Tick, tock. I don't see you."

Slater helped Lucy with the bulletproof vest. It wouldn't stop a headshot, and they both knew it. But unless the guy was a trained sniper, he would most likely go for the widest target, her chest.

"I want to see Mina before I come in."

"She'll come to the fence. That's it. You come in, then we'll talk. Ten. Nine. Eight." He hung up.

Lucy pulled on a torn, greasy sweatshirt to hide the vest. The SWAT guys had been using it as a rag and it reeked of oil. She messed up her hair, then put it in a loose ponytail and grabbed a baseball cap that Slater had in the back. He hooked up her earpiece.

"Count to ten," Slater said. "My men aren't in place yet."

"What's the plan?" she said.

"First clear shot."

Noah drove up as Lucy was finished. He ran over to Slater and Kate. "I told you not to put her in!"

"I outrank you, Armstrong," Slater said. "There are children inside. We have two men on that roof," he pointed, "and two more in position across the street."

Lucy squeezed Noah's hand. "I'm going to be fine."

She crossed the street so she'd be opposite the church. It would buy her both time and cover since the east side of the street was shaded in the morning.

She looked all around the small church. She couldn't see the snipers, but she didn't expect to—they were good. She trusted Slater and the SWAT team.

No one was coming out of the church. Something looked off. The windows. They were clouded.

She ran across the street, but stayed as best she could behind a tree to avoid the line of fire.

Slater said in her earpiece, "We have full coverage once he steps out of the building, either entrance."

She nodded, not wanting to talk.

The gate leading into the courtyard and play area had been propped open with a rake.

"Mina!" she called, then said quietly for Slater, "Something's wrong."

She stepped away from the tree and toward the gate. "Mina!"

"Get back," Slater said in her earpiece.

"Dammit, you promised to let her go, you fucking bastard!" Lucy shouted. The heat of the morning plus her adrenaline had her sweating and red-faced, so she really did look like she had been running. She had listened to Ivy long enough to mimic her well.

Then she smelled smoke.

At the same time, Lucy had the overwhelming sensation of being watched. Ever since her attack seven years ago, she was acutely aware of eyes on her. It was mostly a curse, but times like this it was a gift.

"He's on the street," she whispered and turned to the right, the tree only half obscuring her.

A dark-haired man had a gun on her. "Hey, Poison Ivy—You really are stupid." He frowned. "Who the fuck are you?"

He made a move for her, and over the bullhorn came, "FBI! Put down your weapon and put your hands on the back of your head."

The man looked around, then made a move to grab Lucy. She sidestepped him. He crumpled to the sidewalk at the same time Lucy heard the report of a high-powered rifle.

She went over and kicked his gun away, then ran into the courtyard. "Fire in the church!" she shouted.

Smoke was billowing out from cracks in the windows and doors. She ran to the main entrance and pulled; the doors were locked. She ran through the security gate and tried the side door; locked. She pounded on it. "Open the door!"

Noah was at her side a moment later. "The fire department is already on their way."

"There are kids in there!" she shouted.

Matt Slater came up with a battering ram. He and Noah rammed into the side door, splintering the wood. Smoke poured out; now Lucy could hear the flames.

"Stay low!" Noah ordered.

There was no fire in the church proper, just a lot of smoke. Noah motioned that the school was in the back.

Slater grabbed a fire extinguisher from one of his men and entered the building. Three more of the SWAT team entered, all with guns. They didn't know if the second man was in the building or not, but assumed there was still a hostage situation.

Lucy followed Noah into the smoke-filled room and stifled a cry.

Six children and two adults had been duct-taped to their chairs.

Noah picked up two kids, with their chairs strapped to them, and carried them out as quickly as he could. Lucy followed his lead, grabbed the closest child, and followed Noah out.

Visibility was nonexistent. Her eyes burned, her throat was raw, she couldn't stop coughing.

The little boy in her arms was unconscious.

She made it outside, collapsed in the playground, and pulled at the tape.

Each SWAT member ran in and brought out the remaining children and adults, one by one.

Lucy began to give mouth-to-mouth resuscitation to the little boy.

"Come on," she willed him, listening for breathing, but the sound of the fire drowned it out.

Not these kids. God, please, haven't enough people died?

She repeated the cycle and waited a beat.

He began to cough.

She cried tearlessly.

Matt Slater ran out the back carrying a teenage girl.

"She's alive, but she's been shot in the back. We can't find anyone else in the building. We're pulling out." He said into his headset, "Ambulance?"

"Three minutes," one of his men said. He shook his head and carried her to the street just as the fire trucks pulled up.

"We need a medic STAT!" Slater called. "Female victim, shot twice in the back. Difficulty breathing. In and out of consciousness."

The scene was organized chaos. Lucy watched as everyone did their job quickly and efficiently. Kate escorted Ivy to see Mina. A SWAT medic was applying pressure to her wounds. Ivy cried and held her hand. Kate stood there, stoic, watching the scene around her, both participant and observer.

Lucy sat with the little boy, who clung to her like a life vest. She hugged him back.

"God saved us," the four-year-old said.

"Yes He did," Lucy said. "With a little help from SWAT."

He looked up at her with his dark face and darker eyes. "I want to be a SWAT."

She smiled through her tears. "You will be."

She saw Noah through the crowd. He came to her, knelt in front of her. He was coughing, filthy, and his hands had first-degree burns. He hugged her spontaneously, the child cradled between them.

"You okay?" He inspected her for injury, though Lucy assured him she was fine.

"How did you know where he was? No one had the visual until he approached you," Noah asked.

"I felt him watching me."

He hugged her again. "Good job, Lucy."

A tall black woman was sitting nearby and consoling the children. "Where is he? Did you find him?"

Noah said, "He didn't survive."

"What about his partner?"

Noah tensed. "There were two?"

"One inside and one outside."

Noah got Slater on the phone. "We have another suspect, and he's on foot."

CHAPTER THIRTY-SEVEN

Devon Sullivan didn't leave until after eight that morning. As soon as her Mercedes drove out of sight, Sean pulled out of the parking lot and turned down the private street.

He monitored the end of every driveway without slowing below twenty-five miles per hour, to avoid drawing attention from residents or any household staff. Not every owner had security along their fence, but the Jager/Sullivan house did. A quick assessment told Sean there were cameras at the end of the driveway and each corner of the property. He recognized the manufacturer and smiled.

"They're all digital. But the system has a glitch," Sean explained to Sergio. "It won't take me more than a minute to freeze all the cameras. If someone is monitoring them, they'll see a picture, but unless they're looking carefully—or if someone gets captured on the film and is shown motionless—no one should notice anything different."

He parked his Mustang in the camera's blind spot and took out his backup laptop. He opened it up and found the signal from the security feed. "This is even better. I can get into the main system and access every camera in the house to see if there is staff. Once we're inside we'll be blind, though—the cameras will be frozen."

"Won't they know someone was here?"

"They will if we find the locket. But the security system is designed to photograph as well as provide a video feed. It's full of problems. What I'm forcing it to do is take a picture throughout the system and freeze— even the security company that installed it will say it's just a glitch."

"Why would they put in an inferior system?"

"Ninety percent of security systems can be neutralized in less than three minutes." Sean grabbed the main feed and scrolled through each camera. "Three here in the front, over each entrance, inside the pool house, seven in the back—they think they're vulnerable from the rear. Or they don't trust their neighbors," Sean joked.

"You enjoy this."

"I like my job." He glanced at Sergio. "I don't like who I'm working for."

"Jonathon saved my life."

"Save it. I know the story. And I am sorry about your daughter. Truly. But Paxton thinks he's God, and he's playing with the lives of people I care about. And he's lying to me, I just haven't figured out what, or why."

Sergio didn't say anything, which was good because Sean was growing irritated remembering his conversation with Paxton the night before. Remembering that Paxton had a copy of Lucy's confidential FBI file. Who had given it to him?

"No internal cameras. I'm searching the grounds and I don't see vehicles that aren't registered to the house. Okay, I'm going to freeze the cameras, then I'm going in. Alone. Take my car and go back to where we parked before. I want to know if anyone turns down this street—make and model of their car. If they are feds. *Anything.* Text me. When I'm ready," he pulled out the satellite map of the property, "go down this parallel street. These horse lovers that the Jagers don't trust have no security cameras. Park at the end of their drive-way."

He handed Sergio his keys. "And be careful with my car."

When the ambulance arrived, Lucy handed the little boy off to one of the DC cops who'd arrived on scene. She joined Kate and Ivy, who were with Mina as she was being strapped onto the gurney. Only seven minutes had passed since Slater carried her from the church.

Ivy wiped away her tears. Soot covered her face from the smoke, though the fire was under control.

"You're going to be okay, Mina," Ivy said. "I promise. I need you, Mina. I need you just like I need Sara."

Mina lifted her hand off the gurney and Ivy grabbed it. "Mina! It's me, Ivy. I'm sorry. I'm sorry I left you."

Mina squeezed her hand, then dropped it.

"Blood pressure's falling," one of the medics said and finished putting her in the ambulance. They closed the doors and drove off.

Lucy watched the scene with Kate. As soon as Mina was gone, Kate walked over to Marti North, who was keeping the kids settled while they were checked out by the medics. Lucy and Ivy followed. "What happened?"

"He came in through the back. I should have canceled school, but I didn't think we were in danger. He had a gun and forced me to tie up the children. I tried to make a game out of it, but they knew I was scared. Dammit, I spent three years in the Army and that bastard terrified me!"

"And then?"

"He used my phone to call Ivy, and of course she picked up." Ivy clasped Marti's hand.

Kate said, "You knew that the FBI was looking for Ivy, yet you kept her location a secret?"

"I didn't trust the system. She doesn't know who's after her."

"But she knows why," Lucy said. She looked at Ivy.

"I didn't know any of this would happen. All I wanted was to save my sister."

"And you did," Lucy said. "You made a decision and you're willing to stand by it. I respect that. But you have to live with it and make it right. We need all the information you have." She glanced at Marti. "And anything you can remember about the suspect."

"He was shorter than me, not quite six feet tall, brown hair, blue eyes. He was wearing a blue polo shirt and his back was bleeding. He was really angry about it, I could tell he was in pain. He kept saying he wasn't going to kill the kids, he just wanted Ivy. Like he was explaining and justifying his actions.

"He was getting antsy, worried about being caught," Marti continued. "I had no idea there were two of them, until he started talking on his phone to another guy he called Ned. Mina wasn't tied up—he wanted to be able to move her around, I think. As a hostage. He told Ned to shoot Ivy as soon as she approached the front. When

Mina heard that, she screamed and tried to get his gun. He pushed her down—she practically flew across the room. She couldn't get up, but he just shot her. Twice."

"Why didn't the stakeout team hear it?" Lucy said.

"We were in the back. It was a twenty-two. The kids started crying, and he seemed almost stunned that he'd done it. I thought she was dead. That's when he set the fire. I think he was trying to make a smoke screen to escape, but it was too hot and the artwork caught on fire. He waited until the smoke was thick and went out the back and along the north side. It's narrow, but the fence is wooden and easier to climb. He has to be cut up, though, from the barbed wire."

"We're looking for him. We need a full description, have you look at some mug sheets," Kate said.

"I can do you one better."

She reached into her pocket and pulled out her phone. "I took his picture right after he shot Mina. It's crooked because my hands were bound."

Lucy and Kate looked at it. It only showed his profile, but it was certainly clear enough to distribute widely.

"Marti, you're brilliant." Kate sent the picture to everyone on the internal FBI distribution list, and a copy to her assistant at Quantico to resize, sharpen, and run through facial recognition.

Noah came up to the group. "The suspect out front is Theodore Abernathy. He has a record, served time. His known associates include his brother, Brian." He pulled up a DMV photo. "Is this the man who shot Mina?"

Marti nodded. "That's him."

"Thanks. I'm getting this photo out to all hospitals and transportation hubs. How much time did he have?"

"He left about two minutes before you came in."

Noah looked at his watch. "That gives him a twenty-minute head start." He stepped away to call in the information.

Kate turned to Ivy. "Where's your sister?"

Ivy hedged.

Kate snapped, "He could be going after her. Where is she?"

"I'll tell you, but I have to come. She won't trust anyone. She's terrified, and last night she said if our father takes her, she's going to kill herself. She's still jittery from the drugs he was feeding her to keep her compliant. I'll tell her it's okay. She has to hear it from me."

Matt Slater was listening to Ivy's explanation. Before he said anything, Noah stepped back into the group. "Theodore and Brian Abernathy are the sons of Devon Sullivan from her first marriage."

"Wendy James's boss?"

"Josh Stein just got the search warrant for DSA based on the information we obtained about Park Way apartments and Betty Dare. Stein's already on his way to her office, wants me to lead the team to search her house." He looked at Slater. "Okay, boss?"

Slater nodded. "Go. Donovan, you're point on this situation."

Noah motioned for Lucy to talk to him in private. "Lucy, I'm sorry for being hard on you. It's been a difficult week and I didn't handle the pressure well. I have no excuse."

"Noah, you stood up for me time and time again, knowing that if I screwed up you would be taking the heat. This case taught me more about FBI bureaucracy and personalities and conflicts that I could ever have learned in the Academy. And I did overstep my bounds, and it wasn't the first time. It was just the first time you called me on it."

Noah took both her hands and squeezed. "Good job. Go get Ivy's sister and get her statement so we can keep her father away from her. Without it, legally he can take her back to his home." He looked at his watch. "Our Baltimore agent said she was meeting him at headquarters at eight, but he was late."

"I'll call her and fill her in." It was nearly nine.

Noah left and Lucy turned to Ivy. "Let's get your sister."

Kate said, "Matt, we need a pair of agents—can you spare two?"

"I'll join you and pull Spencer with me. My guys have this contained. Ms. North, we'll need you to make an official statement, if you'll talk to that agent over there who's with your custodian. We've also contacted the parents; you'll probably have your hands full."

Sara sat in the small room above the rectory, reading. Reading was her escape. At home, she read a book a day. She loved historical fiction, rich with beautiful words and dashing knights and fair maidens. She particularly loved Merlin and King Arthur and had read every variation of the stories she could find. She'd read *The Crystal Cave* by Mary Stewart a dozen times and never grew tired of it. Father Harris didn't have a copy, and all the books Ivy had bought for her had burned with the house. But Father Harris had given her four books by J.R.R. Tolkien, and she was already done with *The Hobbit* and halfway finished with *Lord of the Rings*.

Books had enabled her to survive during these dark

months. She realized that reading while her sister was meeting with the man who wanted to kill her was not a sane thing to do. But if she didn't read, she'd panic out of fear for the one person who had done everything to save her. So she read more, faster, drowning out the doubts and anxiety that crept in.

She jumped when she heard sirens. Lots of sirens. They weren't coming here, but His Grace Church was only a few blocks away.

She ran down the stairs, searching for Father Paul. He wasn't in the rectory. She ran across the courtyard, stumbling over a bench. She fell hard on her knees, the book skittering from her hand.

Sara jumped up and retrieved the book, brushing dirt from its pages.

"Hello, Sara."

She froze.

Slowly, she turned her gaze until she met the cold blue eyes of the monster himself.

"Daddy."

CHAPTER THIRTY-EIGHT

For people who were security conscious, the Jagers were very predictable.

Sean didn't think they were very good criminals. He disabled the security cameras and used a standard lock-pick on the back door since the front was bolted and getting in that way would have required visible force. He didn't want them to know anyone had been here until they checked on the locket.

Sean quickly assessed that the house was empty. There were two dogs—small Pomeranians who yapped up a storm when they saw him, but they were locked behind a child safety gate in the family room, where a dog door led to a small dog run. As soon as Sean disappeared from sight, they forgot about him and the house became silent again.

The Jagers had adjoining libraries, both bigger than most New York apartments. They, and the master suite, filled the east wing of the sprawling ranch-style home.

Devon's library had pictures of her with, it seemed,

everyone she'd ever met. In fact, there were more photos than books on the shelves. They filled the walls and all the surfaces. Her desk was glass and had no storage. She had a locked file cabinet built into the wall.

Sean pulled out his pocket computer and ran a program to detect hidden wires or trips in the room. There were none.

The file cabinet opened easily enough with the right tool, and Sean searched the contents. He smiled.

Devon Sullivan had files on every person she'd blackmailed. What she knew, how she knew it, how she used it or if she had plans to use the intel. There were hundreds of files in alphabetical order by last name. This was an FBI wet dream.

He immediately went to P for Paxton. There was a file.

Could it be this easy?

He pulled it out and opened it.

It was empty.

But judging from the permanent bulge in the folder, there had been a thick stack of paper in here at one point. Why had Sullivan removed it? Had the locket been in here?

Shit.

He skimmed the other names. He recognized a few—judges, politicians, law enforcement, business owners, union leaders, nonprofits—Devon Sullivan was one busy, busy lady. Sean would have loved to have photographed every file, but he needed to find the locket, so he only looked for specific names. Like his.

He had no file in the drawer, nor did any other Rogan. There was nothing on Wendy James or Hannah Edmonds/Ivy Harris, which was smart if Sullivan was the one who ordered them dead. He found Judge Robert Morgan and pulled the file. It wasn't thick.

He opened it, took one look, and closed it.

Inside was an explicit photograph of the naked Morgan with Ivy Harris. Morgan was a hermaphrodite.

He put the file back.

If Sullivan blackmailed him for some reason—such as to rule on the side of the killer her husband was defending—with this photo, Sean could see how a distinguished judge might be driven to suicide. He didn't want his condition revealed to the public, but he couldn't let a killer walk free.

Sean went from disliking Sullivan to hating her.

It was close to nine and if Paxton was true to his word, he'd be calling Noah at nine. Even if they raided the place immediately, it would take them at least forty minutes to get here, realistically closer to an hour. Sean didn't want to be here that long. He was about to close the drawer when he saw a very familiar name.

KINCAID, LUCY

Sean pulled the file and shut the drawer.

Inside was a complete copy of Lucy's FBI file, more complete than the one Paxton had. There was also a disk labeled with a date seven years ago.

Sean's pulse sped up. His hands clutched the file so tight he left marks. He put the entire file in his satchel. No way was he leaving it behind.

Lucy's file was marked high clearance. Someone had copied the file for Sullivan. Who wanted to destroy Lucy? Who was in a position to do so? Why?

Sean needed to find the locket and get out. Devon Sullivan didn't have it in her drawer of secrets, so he went to Clark Jager's adjoining office. The space was darker and cooler, there were very few photographs, and the bookshelves were filled with books—90 percent law and nonfiction.

Trying to think like Jager, Sean quickly went through the room looking for a safe. Jager wasn't the type of man to leave incriminating evidence in an easy-to-open cabinet.

Sean was right. He found the safe behind a picture of Jager and Sullivan on their wedding day.

It had the best security in the house.

"Damn."

He took out his tools and got to work cracking the safe. It was going to take him at least ten minutes.

CHAPTER THIRTY-NINE

As soon as Slater pulled up in front of St. Anne's church, Ivy began to panic. "He's here."

"Your father?" Lucy asked, surprised.

"That car—that's his car! The driver—that's Foster. I don't know if that's his first or last name, but he's been my father's right hand since before I ran away."

She opened the door and Kate pulled it closed again. "Ivy, listen to me. We're not going to let him take her. Got it? You have to let us do our job."

But Ivy was becoming hysterical. Kate slapped handcuffs on her and attached them to the handle. "I'm really sorry, but we can't worry about protecting you while dealing with this situation."

Slater said, "Spence, detain the driver."

"Yes, sir." He got out of the vehicle.

"Donovan, what are we looking at in there?"

"Any number of people. The priest. Sara—" she turned to Ivy. "Where was Sara this morning?"

"In the rectory. There's a small room in the attic where we've been staying. I told her not to leave it under any circumstances. The only way to the rectory is through the church and the courtyard."

Slater called in another team then said, "Let's do this. Donovan, based on this guy's track record, he probably isn't going to listen to a woman. I'll do the talking. You keep your sights on him. If he shows a weapon and makes any threatening moves, you have clearance to drop him. Lucy, you focus on the minor. First opportunity, bring her out."

"Yes, sir."

"How did he know we were here?" Ivy said. "No one knew. No one until you showed up this morning. Did you tell him? Dammit, I knew I shouldn't trust you!"

"It didn't come from my office," Slater said emphatically. "We'll find out exactly where the breach occurred and, believe me, if anyone turned that little girl over to a man who abused her, I will destroy their career." He caught Ivy's eye. "Do you believe me?"

She blinked away tears and nodded.

"Lucy," Ivy said as Lucy was getting out of the car. "Take my necklace. Sara gave it to me so that when I sent someone for her, she would know that she could trust them. It was our mother's."

Lucy unclasped the necklace. The pendant was a sapphire drop with three tiny rubies at the top. Small, but exquisite. She understood how hard it was for Ivy to trust anyone. The guilt when someone else got hurt because of the unintended consequences of your own choices. But without trust, without hope that grievous wrongs could be made right, there was only darkness and despair. Lucy had been there. Sometimes it was easier to let the regret and hopelessness take over, than it was to trust a stranger, or a friend, or a lover.

She put the pendant around her own neck. "I'll take care of it."

Lucy got out with Kate and Slater. Slater motioned for Kate to open the doors while he guarded them. She pulled. They were locked.

Kate motioned toward the stone wall that blocked the courtyard from the street. There was a gate in the wall, but it too was locked. Slater stood on a low ledge and peered over the top with a spyglass. He jumped down.

"No one's in the courtyard. Donovan, you go first."

Kate stepped into Slater's cupped hands and then pulled herself up to the top of the fence and quickly scaled down the other side.

"Clear," she called quietly.

Lucy and Slater followed. The courtyard was clear. Lucy found an abandoned book on the bricks.

The side door was ajar, and the tall, gothic structure made voices in the church softly echo.

"I'm sorry, Reverend, I can't let you leave with Sara. She has sanctuary here," a man said.

"She is my daughter. I am taking her home." The minister's voice was calm and even.

Kate opened the door and Slater stepped in, Lucy behind him. Kate took the rear, gun out, trained on Kirk Edmonds, who appeared unarmed. Father Harris was standing by the front doors, preventing Edmonds from leaving. Sara sat alone in a pew, a few feet from her father, not looking at anyone.

Slater said, "Reverend Edmonds, correct?"

Edmonds was fifty with dark blond hair shot with silver, a tall, lean body, and cool, intelligent blue eyes.

"You bring a weapon into the Lord's house?" Edmonds said.

Kate didn't budge. Slater said, "Let's defuse the situation and talk about this, all right? Sara, are you okay?"

She didn't answer. She stared at her hands, unmoving.

"She doesn't talk to strangers," Edmonds said. "I raised her right. Hasn't she suffered enough? Have you found that devil who kidnapped her?"

Lucy kept her eyes on Sara. She was shaking, but would not make eye contact with anyone. She jumped when Edmonds called Ivy a devil.

"I agree, she has suffered more than enough. That's why we're going to take her to a doctor, have her checked out, get her a clean bill of health. You want that for her? Make sure she's healthy."

"She has a doctor at home."

"I'm sure he's great, but that's a long drive. We have some of the finest hospitals on the East Coast, right here in DC," Slater said.

"Tell that man he needs to let us out," Edmonds said, his voice still calm and reasonable. "He's held my daughter, and me, against our will."

"And my office will definitely discuss the situation with Father Harris and explain he can't lock people in the church." Slater looked pointedly at Harris. At first Lucy didn't understand, then she saw that Father Harris stepped to the side, blocking the lock. Slater wanted him to unlock the doors, but quietly.

"I'm curious, Reverend, how did you find Sara? We've had our best people on it for nearly forty-eight hours, ever since we identified her, and we just figured it out this morning."

"She called me. She wants to come home." Edmonds looked at his daughter, almost beaming. "She missed me like I missed her."

Slater looked at Sara. "Sara, I'm Matt Slater," he said with a lighter voice. I'm with the FBI. Did you call your father? Do you want to go home with him?"

She nodded rapidly, but still didn't make eye contact.

"I told you," Edmonds said. "Please tell the priest to move aside."

Lucy understood what Ivy meant about her father. His voice was wonderfully soothing, almost a pleasure just to listen to. She'd said five minutes alone with Kirk Edmonds and Sara would go with him. Even though there were four adults in the church, all willing to protect Sara, Lucy had no doubt if they didn't make a move to stop Edmonds, Sara would walk out with him on her own accord.

"We need to talk to Sara about a crime she witnessed," Slater said. "It won't take long. Then she's free to go home, if that's what she wants."

"She just said it was!" Edmonds raised his voice for the first time. She then noticed sweat under his arms and beads forming on his forehead. Lucy recognized the signs of extreme stress. He'd thought he could come in here and walk out with Sara and no one would stop him. He wasn't used to anyone contradicting him.

Edmonds continued. "Did you find Hannah? I'm pressing charges. She terrorized my family. Faking her death. Kidnapping Sara. Lying to my little girl about me. I want that girl in a psychiatric ward. She's crazy, just like her mother."

A small squeak came from Sara.

Edmonds didn't seem to notice.

Lucy started moving slowly to the left, away from Slater, while Slater kept the attention focused on him. She willed Sara to look up, but the girl didn't move.

"Sara," Lucy said quietly, "it's okay. I promise. My name is Lucy, I can help you."

Edmonds suddenly raged. "Do not talk to my daughter!"

Sara jumped. Lucy continued. "Ivy is safe. She gave me something that belongs to you. She wants to give it back before you leave."

Edmonds wrestled with his anger, tried to keep his voice calm, but his words came out as an order he expected to be promptly obeyed. "Agent Slater, take control over your staff. Order her to remain silent."

Lucy forced herself to ignore Edmonds. She had her hand on the sapphire pendant. Sara was trying to look at her without letting her father see, by hanging her hair down to shield her eyes. Lucy continued moving closer, slowly, to draw Sara's attention.

Sara is eyes widened as soon as she saw the necklace, and she met Lucy's gaze. Lucy nodded.

"I've had enough!" Edmonds bellowed and Edmonds started to move toward Sara.

"Stop!" Slater commanded. "Do not approach the girl."

"She's my daughter!" Edmonds took two long strides and stood at one end of the pew Sara was sitting in. Lucy was on the opposite side.

"We're leaving. We're going home. Everything Hannah told you is a lie. She let you think she was dead for six years."

"I—I want to see her before we go," Sara whispered.

Edmonds looked at his daughter. Mixed emotions clouded his expression. In a soft, loving voice, he said, "Sweetheart, you are the princess of my castle. I have been so scared for you while you were gone. The world out here is dangerous. It's not safe for a sweet, beautiful girl like you. I've always protected you, I always will."

Tears rolled down her face. "You did," she said. Sara stood up and faced him. Lucy held her breath. Slater was about to intervene, but Lucy signalled him to stop.

Some things had to be stated in order for a person to begin healing.

"Daddy," Sara said, "I loved you so much. I remember when I was eight we went to the field behind the barn. You told me about God's creation. How a tiny seed planted in dirt, with sun and rain and God's love, grows into the food we eat or into a beautiful flower. You said I was a flower, a little bud that would grow into a beautiful rose. I laughed, because my middle name was Rose, and I loved the idea. I'd think of me as a flower. Do you remember when I drew roses all the time? I'd put faces on them."

Edmonds nodded. His face was frozen, as if seeing his daughter for the first time.

"That was because you called me your rosebud.

"Then on my fourteenth birthday, you destroyed the image I loved when you told me that I had grown into the beautiful rose you knew I'd be. And you raped me."

No one spoke. Even Lucy, who had suspected Sara needed to accuse her father or be forever troubled by pain and doubt, was surprised at the speech.

"That's. Not. True."

Sara turned away from her father and toward Lucy. "Please take me to my sister."

Lucy held out her hand. Sara took it.

Edmonds screamed in pain and rage. He fell to his knees.

Slater sprinted around the front of the church, toward Edmonds. Edmonds's hand came up with a gun. He aimed it at Sara's back.

Lucy pulled Sara into her, spun her around and out of the line of fire. She heard a gunshot, followed by three more in rapid succession. She fell on top of Sara, a sharp pain in her back. She couldn't catch her breath.

I can't breathe.

CHAPTER FORTY

Sean's phone vibrated. He ignored it, because he was at the most sensitive part of cracking this particular safe. If he screwed up, the digital password would reset and he would have to start all over again. He didn't have the time.

The lights flashed green and the door *swooshed* open. He grinned and glanced at his watch. Twelve minutes, thirty-two seconds. His safecracking skills had gone out of use and he wasn't as connected with the latest technologies. He'd have to rectify that, or how could he convince future clients that they should trust him to find the flaws in their security?

His phone vibrated again and he pulled it out of his pocket.

He'd missed three calls from Sergio. A message read urgent.

THREE FBI SUVs plus SWAT. Get out.

Sean looked in the safe and flipped through the documents, not taking the time to read anything. In the far back there was a small box.

The Pomeranians' yapping echoed through the house. Sean grabbed the box, put it in his pocket, closed the safe. It locked automatically, and he put the picture back up. It hung crooked, but he didn't have time to fix it.

He heard the SUVs on the driveway, but he also knew that the FBI would come around back to cover any exits.

He glanced out Jager's window. The first SUV pulled to a stop. Out jumped Noah Armstrong.

By-the-book. That bought Sean a minute.

He grabbed his satchel and quietly left the office. The master bedroom had French doors that led to the backyard. He could see the horse stalls of the neighbors a hundred yards away, up against the Jagers' back fence.

Between that and him was open space.

To the right was a line of trees, but that was also visible from the driveway. To the left was the patio and he'd have to cross in front of a wall full of windows. If the FBI entered they would see him run. But once he passed the house, a gentleman's vineyard had been planted. The leaves were full and green, he could easily disappear down the rows.

He took the risk.

Sean sprinted across the patio. He heard voices in the front, but he didn't stop to listen. He focused on getting to the grapevines.

He made it. He still didn't stop, but slowed down so he wouldn't trip over the rough ground.

At the edge of the vineyard, he turned left again into a grove of trees. By the time he got to the fence, his adrenaline was pumping so fast he could hear his blood rush in his ears.

He hopped the fence and slipped into the first horse stall. The old mare looked at him with disinterest.

Sean reached into his pocket and removed the box. He breathed deeply to slow his heart rate and opened the lid.

Inside was a locket. Simple. On the back the initials *MEP.*

There was also a note. He opened it and his stomach clenched.

It was Lucy's handwriting.

This belongs to you.

That was it. Paxton had lied to him, embellished what Lucy had written to force him to help.

Sean looked carefully at the locket. There was nothing remarkable about it. Pretty, for a teenage girl.

He opened it. Inside was a picture of Monique and the senator.

All this cloak-and-dagger crap for *this?*

He spied a narrow crack on the inside of the locket. He pulled his lock-pick set from his satchel and used the narrowest metal pick to pop off the false back.

Behind the thin backing was a microchip.

Sergio expected to take the locket to the senator, but Sean told him he wanted to deliver it personally. At first, Sean expected Sergio to fight him for it, and Sean was primed to go a round. He was sick and tired of being jerked around by Paxton and his games. But then Sergio nodded, and got into his car.

"Watch your back," Sergio told him.

"Are you threatening me?"

"I'm not a threat." He gave Sean a half-smile. "You're good, I have to admire that." Then he became serious. "I don't think Senator Paxton is who you really need to be concerned about. You Rogans seem to have loyal friends, but vicious enemies."

"What are you talking about?" Sean demanded. But Sergio rolled up his window and sped off.

Sean put the conversation aside and drove to Alexandria, where the senator was waiting.

Without preamble, Paxton said, "Can I see it?"

He handed Paxton the box. He pulled out the locket. Relief flooded his face. Then he noticed the note was gone. "The note?"

"I'm keeping it."

"I guess I understand. Thank you, Rogan. Truly, thank you."

"Your daughter was beautiful. I'm sorry about what happened to her."

Paxton froze. "You opened my locket?"

"Had to make sure it was the right one."

Paxton fumbled with the delicate clasp. The locket popped open. He pressed firmly on the clasp, and the false back popped off.

"It's gone!"

Sean pulled out the small microchip from his pocket. "You're looking for this?"

"Give it to me."

"No. This is now my security chip. When the statute of limitations runs out, I might give it to you. But if anyone mentions Massachusetts to me before March? I'll either destroy it, or turn it over to whichever law enforcement agency can nail your ass to the wall."

"You don't know what you have!"

"I'll find out."

"You're making an enemy here, Rogan!"

"Funny, I thought I already had one."

Sean quickly exited Paxton's house. He wasn't a hundred percent certain the senator wouldn't shoot him. Driving toward DC, he called Lucy. He needed to see her. Just . . . to see her.

No answer.

Lucy was probably still working on finding Ivy Harris and the other girls. He was worried, but only because it was a dangerous job. He had complete confidence that she'd find them.

He called Kate, just to check in and make sure everything *was* okay. When Kate's phone went to voice mail, that's when he became concerned.

He called Noah.

"Armstrong."

"It's Sean. I can't reach Lucy or Kate. What's going on?"

"There's a hostage situation. There's been a shooting. I don't have the status, but I'm on my way now."

Sean sped up. "Where?"

"St. Anne's."

Sean hung up and added more speed.

Sean had to park down the street from St. Anne's because of all the cop cars, ambulances, and FBI vehicles.

He strode purposefully to the police barrier, flashed his P.I. identification hoping the cop wouldn't notice, but he did.

"Hold it."

"I'm expected."

The doors of the church were open and a gurney

with a body bag was wheeled out. His stomach heaved. He looked around for Lucy, but didn't see her.

He continued forward and the cop got in his face. "Stand back or I'll have you arrested."

He wanted to hit the cop. And maybe he would have, if Kate hadn't see him.

She ran over. "Officer, he's with me."

Sean brushed past the cop. "Where is she?"

Kate followed his eyes to the body bag.

"Lucy is fine. That's Kirk Edmonds."

He glanced at her belt. Her gun was gone.

She said, "They always take the weapon pending official investigation into any discharge of a firearm in the line of duty."

"You okay?"

She nodded. "Dillon's coming home tonight. I'll be better when I see him. Lucy's in the courtyard of the church—it's private, quiet, and she needed to talk to Ivy and Sara about what's going to happen next. Ivy has a lot of talking to do, but if she cooperates fully, I think she'll avoid prison time."

Kate added, "Lucy was a hero today."

"I'm not surprised."

"No, truly, a hero. We faced two serious situations and she was calm and quick thinking. She's really grown up."

Sean said, "She's been grown up for quite a while."

Kate walked with him to the church and cleared him through the security. Sean found the courtyard. Ivy and Sara were sitting on a bench holding each other. Lucy was sitting on the bricks being treated by a paramedic. He didn't see any blood.

She saw him and smiled so brightly all anxiety fell away.

He sat next to her. "Hey, Princess. I heard you had an adventure."

"Did Kate tell you?"

"Some of it. I hear you're a hero."

"Sara's the hero. She stood up to her father. She's going to be okay. I'm more worried about Ivy, but with time . . ." She breathed deeply, then winced.

"What happened?"

The paramedic handed Sean a bulletproof vest, then finished cleaning up his supplies. "Those things are amazing," the paramedic said. "Need anything else, Ms. Kincaid?"

"I'm fine, thank you."

Sean held the vest in his hands. The bullet was still embedded in the vest.

"Don't touch it, it's evidence," Lucy said.

"This is the back. He shot you in the back?" He lifted Lucy's shirt up from the back. A large round bruise had already formed. He kissed it, though containing his anger was becoming difficult. Between Paxton and no sleep and what happened to Lucy—he needed to decompress.

Lucy sensed his tension and hugged him. "I really am fine."

Sean held on to Lucy as tightly as he could. He feared he would lose her. To her job, to violence, to his own mistakes. He'd told her before that he needed her more than she needed him, and she'd never truly believed it. He didn't care, because he knew the truth. Lucy gave him hope. Lucy made him realize he needed love in his life—love, trust, commitment. That there were things greater than him worth fighting for.

His past was a danger zone. He had to protect Lucy

from it. While he knew that she could handle anything life threw at her, deep down he feared she'd turn her back on him when he needed her the most.

"I love you, Luce."

"Sean—" She kissed him warmly, with a deep passion he craved from her. Needed from her. She pulled back and smiled. "I love you, too."

They sat like that for a long minute, then Sean asked, "How did he find her? Did he have someone in the FBI on payroll?"

Lucy shook her head. "He told Sara he put a GPS chip under her skin. At the base of her neck. Like she was a pet. After Ivy ran away, he didn't want to lose her. But proximity mattered—it didn't work beyond five miles. So when he learned she was in DC, he came here and just drove around."

Sean smiled, then burst into laughter.

"It's not funny. It's rather scary."

He hugged her. "I'm sorry. But I just came up with the name for your new cat. Chip." He grinned. "I know exactly what Wendy James did with her data."

CHAPTER FORTY-ONE

Saturday

Lucy and Kate were dressed in scrubs and stood sentry in the operating room. Chain of custody was critical, especially in a complex case like this. Kate had even set up a video camera in the corner in case the court had any questions about the procedure.

It wasn't every day that key evidence in a homicide investigation was hidden in a pet.

The veterinarian had put Chip under general anesthesia and the cat lay motionless on the table. Lucy frowned.

"What's your problem?" Kate said. "You worked at a morgue."

"Dead people don't bother me," Lucy said. "I really like this cat."

"He should be fine," the vet said. "Though whoever did this to him should have his license pulled. It's dangerous. The chips they put in pets for tracking are the size of a grain of rice. This one is much bigger."

He gestured to the X-ray that showed a square of metal on the back of Chip's neck.

"He's doing well," the vet purred. "Good kitty."

"I wish Mina's surgery had been this easy," Lucy said.

"She's healthy and the doctor is optimistic," Kate reminded her. "It's just a long road to recover."

"Are you doing okay with the shooting and everything?"

"It was justified. If I think too much about it, I remind myself that it was him or innocents." Kate glanced at her. "Him, or you. Thank God you didn't take off that vest."

Lucy rolled her sore shoulder and winced. It still hurt, probably would for days. "Sean said I was lucky not to have cracked a rib."

"Bingo," the vet said. He held up the chip with his tweezers. "It's coated in silicone."

"Plop it right in here." Kate held up an evidence bag. The vet dropped the chip in. Kate sealed the bag and signed the front. "Now to take this to the lab. This will be fun."

"When can we take Chip home?" Lucy asked the vet.

"Give him a couple hours. I want to make sure there are no side effects from the surgery or anesthesia. Come by after three."

Lucy and Kate left the vet hospital. "I'm going straight to the lab—do you want me to drop you home?"

"Can you take me to the hospital? I want to make sure Ivy's okay. Check on Mina and Genie."

Kate and Noah had worked a miracle to get Ivy on a tracking bracelet and into a halfway house in one day. She couldn't leave DC until the FBI was satisfied she'd shared all information she had.

"What's the word on Brian Abernathy?" Lucy asked. "I don't think he's just going to give up."

"Everyone is looking for him. His testimony could seal the indictment on his mother. But either he or his brother killed six people. We have plenty of evidence, so as soon as we get him in custody, we'll know for certain. He was smart on one level, but trace evidence is aplenty."

"Noah told me Devon Sullivan is not cooperating."

"She doesn't need to say a word—that's her right. But Josh Stein has her solid on major financial irregularities. And because of her wealth we were able to freeze her assets. She's sitting in jail all weekend."

"She doesn't deserve to walk free."

"We're working double-time to get hard evidence that she ordered the murder of Wendy James."

"What about the others?"

"If we can prove Wendy, it'll be much easier to connect the others. Without Wendy's case being solid, the others fall apart. At least to nail Sullivan with. Conspiracy is extremely difficult to prove. The search warrants were a huge bonus, but she has the entire Acuna and Bigelow law firm fighting every warrant, every piece of evidence. Now," Kate said, gesturing toward the chip in the evidence bag, "if that has anything of substance, we won't have to worry. The AUSA said the warrant on this extraction is air-tight."

Kate dropped Lucy off at the emergency room entrance. She went directly to ICU, where Mina was recovering from surgery. Ivy was there at her bedside; a DC uniformed officer was at her door. Lucy showed her identification to enter.

Lucy whispered, "How is she?"

"She woke up. That's good, the doctors say." Ivy glanced at Lucy. "I let her down. The night of the fire, I picked Sara over her and I can't forgive myself."

"You have to. It's hard, but you have to." Lucy paused, then said, "Seven years ago I was kidnapped and raped by a guy I met online. Long story—I thought he was someone else. But it was still stupid on my part. My brothers went looking for me, and one of them was nearly killed in an explosion. After surgery, he slipped into a coma and stayed that way for nearly two years. I've tried to forgive myself—and some days, I don't think about it. But other times, I feel hot and cold at the same time, and I picture Patrick lying in a hospital bed unresponsive. His brain working, but not working. And the guilt just washes over me. But, it's not every day. It's sometimes not every week."

Lucy knew remnants of that time would continue to haunt her. But she would survive and grow stronger because of her job, her family, and Sean. "The decision you made Tuesday morning, you made out of love. Love for your sister, love for the girls at Hawthorne Street. Mina knows that, in her heart."

The nurse came in. "Your ten minutes are up."

Ivy nodded and she and Lucy left.

"How's Sara?"

Ivy smiled. "I don't know what happened in the church, but she's doing amazing. Come see her."

Lucy pulled a box from her pocket. "This really helped. I know you want it back."

Ivy squeezed the box. "Thank you."

Sara was in the pediatric wing. She, too, had a guard on her door. Lucy was more concerned about Ivy—Brian Abernathy wanted to kill *her* more than anyone else. But no guard had been assigned to her. No one knew where Abernathy was—half the team thought he'd left DC. Lucy didn't believe it.

Sean walked down the hall toward them. He was carrying a large bouquet of daisies. Lucy smiled.

Sean shook his head. "These are for Sara. But I got you your own daisies, plus . . ." He took his hand out from behind his back. "A white mocha."

Lucy took the coffee drink from Sean happily and kissed him. "Thank you."

"You're very welcome."

They showed ID to the guard and went into Sara's room. She was sitting cross-legged on the bed and playing games on an iPad.

"Where'd you get that?" Ivy asked.

"The hospital delivered it. Look at the card."

Lucy read over Ivy's shoulder. The card was generic. Inside, there was no message, just initials.

S.R.

Lucy looked at Sean. "That's sweet."

"What is?"

"The gift."

Sean shook his head and took the card. He stared for a long time, so long that Lucy was worried. Then he grinned. "Hey, kid, can I see your toy? Can you believe I don't have one of these?"

Sara handed it to him and he handed her the flowers.

Lucy watched Sean check all the settings and apps. Then he downloaded an app. It took Lucy a minute to realize it was an anti-tracking app; it blocked GPS signals.

"*What?*" she mouthed.

"You can never be too safe."

"I agree," Ivy said. "I like your boyfriend, Lucy."

"Me, too." Lucy took Sean's hand. "I'll keep him around."

"How's Chip doing?" Sean asked.

"He's recovering. We can pick him up in a few hours."

"Good, I don't want him spending the night in the hospital. If he's anything like me, he'll hate it."

Lucy rolled her eyes, then laughed. "He's going to be a spoiled cat."

"I have to spoil someone while you're at Quantico." He kissed her forehead.

Ivy said, "Can I ask a favor?"

"Anything."

"I'd like to meet Detective Reid."

"We'd better do it now. I hear she's going home today."

"I'll keep Sara company," Sean said. "Any racing games on that thing?"

Sara giggled. Lucy and Ivy walked out. Lucy said, "She's amazing."

"I know."

"And you get the credit."

Ivy didn't say anything.

"You okay?"

"I'm getting there." She paused. "Is it wrong to not feel anything about him being dead?"

Lucy didn't have to ask who she was talking about.

"No."

She whispered, "Is it wrong to be glad?"

Lucy sighed. She shook her head. "You're going to feel a lot of different emotions over the next few weeks. None of them are wrong. Just don't linger in any one place, if you know what I mean."

"I do. Thank you."

Genie was in another building. They crossed the courtyard when Lucy saw a familiar figure walking briskly to catch up with them.

"Senator," Lucy said, stunned.

"It took me forever to track you down, but Noah thought you might be here." He smiled at Ivy. "Senator Jonathon Paxton."

Ivy shook his hand. "Pleased to meet you." She was skeptical, and looked to Lucy for direction.

"I interned for Senator Paxton years ago. He gave me a recommendation to get into the Bureau."

"I just came from meeting with AD Rick Stockton and he filled me in on the case. I also talked to Cathy Hummel at MARC. I wanted you to know, Ivy, that Cathy and I are establishing a foundation in the name of Chris and Jocelyn Taylor. And the first thing we're doing is rebuilding the house on Hawthorne Street. I've already talked to the owner, we're going to arrange a financially beneficial agreement for her, and I'll rebuild. It'll be a place for young women in transition. Cathy said the hardest age group to work with are eighteen to twenty-five—most programs are for minors."

"Why?" Ivy said. "Why do you want to help?" She sounded not only skeptical, but threatened. As if he were going to start making demands.

"Because I can. I've given a lot of money to MARC and similar groups over the years, and I think this cause is worthwhile."

He looked at Lucy, expecting her to vouch for him.

And on this, she could. Because even though she had some deep-seated problems with the senator, he did want to help others. He needed to help others. Maybe as penance for crimes he'd never admitted to.

She said, "I think it's a good thing. Is MARC running the house?"

"Yes, they're already set up, why create additional bureaucracy?"

"Thank you, Jonathon," Lucy said.

He smiled and took her hand. "It's always good to see you, Lucy. Please, don't be a stranger."

He turned to Ivy, shook her hand, then walked off.

"I have a hard time trusting people who give without wanting something in return," Ivy said.

"He's not doing this for you," Lucy muttered.

"What?"

She shook her head. "The senator is running from his own demons, I think. Philanthropy makes him feel better about himself."

Ivy said, *"Your money perish with you, because you thought that the gift of God could be purchased with money! . . . For I see that you are poisoned by bitterness and bound by iniquity."*

"Appropriate," Lucy said.

"I don't even believe anymore."

"It's okay," Lucy said. "I have a hard time when bad things happen to kids like Sara. But then I remember that the doctors never thought Patrick would wake from his coma."

They went up to Genie's room, which was filled with her family, including her grandson Isaiah. Genie seemed pleased to see Lucy, and relieved that the case was resolved.

"They're making me take two weeks off," Genie grumbled.

"I'll come visit."

"You'd better."

Lucy stepped aside so Ivy could talk to Genie. At first, Ivy didn't say anything. She looked around at the roomful of people, then stared at her feet, nervous.

Genie reached out and grabbed her hand. "Glad to finally meet you," she said to Ivy.

"I'm sorry," Ivy mumbled.

"About what? Protecting your family? You got nothing to apologize for, girl. I think *that*"—she gestured to the security bracelet around her ankle—"is punishment enough."

"Thank you for everything you did for my friends. Lucy said you're a great cop, and you cared about them, even when they were dead."

"Stop," Genie said, her eyes tearing. "Someone has to speak up for those who can't speak for themselves. I'm no saint."

"You are to me," Lucy said.

Sean was playing games with Sara on her iPad, while putting together the truth behind Senator Paxton's lies.

From the beginning he'd been the one playing with Sara's life. All the tidbits Sean had picked up from Lucy's investigation and from the senator himself found their proper places.

Sergio had kidnapped Sara and brought her to Ivy. He'd been the one who'd bought the virtual phone number so Ivy could reach him. Yet he'd allowed Paxton to play the game with Crowley, to release the photographs to the media that started this entire chain of events spiraling out of control.

That Sara was away from the bastard who'd raised her, and Ivy would probably get off with probation, were a small silver lining in a sea of blood—the blood of six people who'd been killed to cover up the crimes of Devon Sullivan and her cohorts.

Paxton was a danger not only to Sean but to others. He played the role of master chessman, sacrificing pawns and others in his quest to win whatever endgame he had in mind.

And it incensed Sean that he was getting away with it.

Not forever. He'd threatened Sean, but more egregious, he'd threatened Lucy. Sean didn't care how long it took, but he would destroy Jonathon Paxton.

The door opened and Noah stepped in. He looked worried. "Kate said Lucy was here with Ivy."

"They went to visit Detective Reid," Sean said.

"What's wrong?" Sara asked. She sat up. "Did something happen?"

"No," Noah said. "Everything's fine. You sit tight, I'm going to talk to Sean for a minute outside."

She didn't believe him, and neither did Sean. He followed Noah out.

"What?" he demanded.

"We thought Abernathy took a train to New York, but when it arrived at the station, he wasn't on it. It's just a precaution, but we should let Lucy know—"

Sean didn't let him finish. "Reid's room is across the courtyard," he said as he bolted for the staircase.

Lucy and Ivy left Genie a few minutes later and went back across the courtyard to the pediatric wing.

They were just passing the fountain in the middle of the garden when the hair rose on the back of Lucy's neck and she felt eyes on her.

"Ivy!" she said sharply, pulling her to her side. They were being watched.

A man in a hoodie walked briskly toward them. Lucy saw a flash of metal up his left sleeve.

"Brian," Lucy said.

He stopped, whether startled because she knew his name or because she'd spotted him.

"Stay behind me," Lucy told Ivy.

"I just want her," Brian said. His voice was garbled and he sounded sick.

"No you don't," Lucy said. "You don't want to kill anyone."

"Get out of the way."

He stepped toward her.

"Ivy, run," Lucy said.

She didn't, but took two steps away. "Stop!" Brian commanded and showed the knife. "I will kill your friend, Poison Ivy."

"You won't," Lucy said. Her mind ran through Psycho 101, as her favorite professor called it. Then she remembered Brian wasn't a psychopath. He had no remorse, but he got no pleasure from murder. It was a means to an end.

"I just want to leave," Brian said. "I hate this city. These people. I never wanted to come back. She made me."

Lucy took a gamble.

"Your mother."

"To keep Ned out of trouble." He barked out a laugh. "Ned! Dumb-ass brother of mine. And she thought he walked on water."

"I'm sorry about your brother."

"Yeah. Well." He sniffed. "I loved him, you know? Really. He was so stupid sometimes, but we were buds."

He was grieving, she realized. And he probably had never felt real grief before.

"My nephew was killed," Lucy said, working on building a rapport. She didn't dare look, but she sensed movement in her peripheral vision.

"Nephew?" he said with a sneer.

"We were the same age. My oldest sister and my mom were pregnant at the same time. And it was like losing my brother. Justin and I did everything together."

"Yeah." He paused, used the back of his hand to wipe his nose. "I always looked out for Ned."

"This can all stop, right now. Put the knife down, Brian."

"I can't. I have to finish this."

"Look around you. They're not going to let you leave."

He did, and Lucy hoped she was right. That there were cops along with the spectators.

"I just want to go home."

"Where's home?"

"Hawaii."

Lucy gambled. "They're not going to let you go, and if you throw that knife, you might kill me, but you'll be dead when a dozen bullets hit you. And Ivy will still be alive because she's behind me. I'm not moving. You don't want to kill me because I'm not the problem, am I. It's your mother who started this game."

If one of those cops got an itchy finger, they'd lose their only witness to Devon Sullivan's culpability in Wendy James's death. Lucy had to talk Brian down.

"Dear God, I hate that woman."

"I'm not a big fan myself."

He coughed, then winced.

"Are you hurt?" Lucy asked, showing genuine concern. "I heard you fell on a sprinkler head."

"It's bad. Still bleeding a bit. Hurts like hell."

"We're at the hospital. There are a hundred doctors here who can take care of that. Give you something for the pain."

He didn't say anything.

Lucy sensed movement to her right. She put her hands up and to the side, hoping the security guards knew to stand down. Behind Brian she saw Noah and Sean approaching slowly. Noah was using hand signals to direct Sean, who nodded. They were splitting up, Noah going right, Sean to the left. Both outside of Brian's peripheral vision.

She briefly caught Sean's eye. His expression was focused. He gave her a half-smile while his attention was on Brian's knife.

"Brian, let me help you."

"Can you just step aside so I can finish this?" he said without heart.

"I can't. But I can make you an offer I think you'll like."

"There's nothing."

He was in pain, sick, and depressed. Worse, he'd lost hope. He knew he wouldn't leave the courtyard alive if he tried to kill Ivy. Suicide cocktail right there.

"Lower the knife."

He dropped his hand an inch.

"Good. Your mother is going to prison on a multitude of crimes, but she's telling us she had nothing to do with killing Wendy James and the others. She says that's all you."

He grimaced. "Bitch."

Lucy knew he wasn't talking about her, he was talking about his mother.

"If you help us prove her wrong, help us prove that she ordered the hit on Wendy, then I will do everything in my power to get you back to Hawaii."

"You're not going to let me go free. I'm not stupid. Not after what I've done."

"No, you won't be free, but there's a federal penitentiary in Honolulu."

Brian's face brightened. His hand dropped another inch. "You can do that?"

"I know a lot of people high up in the FBI. And I will tell them, I swear to God, I will tell them that you voluntarily dropped that knife, that you showed remorse to me for your crimes. That you will help fill in the blanks in their case against Devon Sullivan."

He looked at her quizzically. "What about Clark?"

Her heart raced. "Clark Jager?"

"Yeah. Can't I testify against him? Do you know what he's done?"

"No, I don't."

Brian laughed, and it ended in a cough. "This whole thing was his fucking idea." He dropped the knife. "I'll tell you everything, but please, I really need a doctor." He fell to his knees.

Both Sean and Noah ran to Brian. Sean kicked away the knife while Noah cuffed him. "He needs a doctor, Noah."

"I'll get a guard on him and take him to the emergency room."

Lucy turned to Ivy. "You're okay, right?"

She said, "He killed them?"

"Yes. We think so."

"And shot Mina?"

"Are you okay?"

"He's so . . . pathetic."

"Some of us get handed great parents, and life still turns bad. Others get bad parents, and they either overcome it—like you—or they become what they hate. Remember you are better than your father."

"My mother tried to save us. That's why she died."

"Then remember her sacrifice and rise above what's happened. I know you can do it, Ivy."

"Can I go to Sara?"

"Of course."

Lucy watched her leave.

"Lucy." Sean came up behind her.

Without a word, Lucy wrapped her arms around him and closed her eyes. She didn't realize until that moment that she was shaking.

Sean ran his hands up and down her back until her adrenaline dropped. "Let's get Chip and go home. I have a hot tub that's begging for us to enjoy it."

Lucy tilted her head up and kissed him. "I need it. Please don't let me out until I'm shriveled like a prune."

"That's an attractive vision." Sean frowned. He kissed her. "Stop scaring me, Princess."

"It's been one of those weeks. I'm sure you'll have your chance to make me worry."

"We have two weeks until you go to Quantico. Think I can get you to take a couple days off? Two? Can I hope for three?"

Noah came up to them. "How about four?"

"We'll take it," Sean said.

"You've earned it, Lucy," Noah said. "Not just here,

but yesterday. Matt Slater told me what he said to you the other day."

"I wish he hadn't—"

Noah put up his hand. "I didn't go out on a limb bringing you in as an analyst. You're an asset, and I trust your judgment. Matt shouldn't have put those doubts in your head. He feels shitty about it."

"He should," Sean said.

"It's over and forgotten. I just hope Matt will forgive me. I kind of promised Abernathy that he might be able to serve his sentence in Hawaii."

"I heard. And if he can put Clark Jager *and* Devon Sullivan in prison for the rest of their lives, I'll make certain he serves his time in Honolulu."

They walked toward the parking lot.

"Why are you here?" Lucy asked Noah.

"Kate called. The chip you pulled out of the cat?"

"She could read it?"

"It has everything we need to put Devon Sullivan away, and she only pulled ten percent of the data off. Audio recordings, some video, JPEGs that appear to be snapshots of financial documents. Kate's planning on spending all weekend categorizing the information. I told Josh Stein and you'd think he'd won the lottery."

"A great ending to a really miserable case," Lucy said.

"I need to check on my prisoner. See you on Monday."

Sean frowned. "I thought you gave her four days off."

"The four days before she reports to the Academy. We need all hands next week going through the mountains of evidence and paperwork."

"I'll be there," Lucy said.

Noah went into the hospital, and Sean put his arm

around Lucy. "*Now* can we go get our cat and sit in the hot tub?"

He steered her toward his car and grandly opened the passenger door for her. She slid into the leather seat and closed her eyes.

A week of paperwork followed by four days alone with Sean. She finally admitted to herself that she needed the time away.

Sean got into the driver's seat and Lucy asked, "Where do you want to go on our vacation?"

"I hesitate to call it that, considering how our last vacation turned out." He turned the ignition. "How about a cottage up in Cape Cod?"

"Massachusetts? That's kind of far."

"Not by plane. I got word this morning that my Cessna is ready. I'm picking her up on Monday. While you'll be neck deep in paperwork, I'll be flying over the Adirondacks."

"You know what? After being shot down in that plane, I'll take the paperwork instead."